"If you enjoy a political thriller dripping with black humor delivered by a protagonist who never calls a spade a manual front hoe, trust me (the author), you'll like this." —DAVID ROLLINS

But don't just take the author's word. Read what the critics are saying about David Rollins and

A KNIFE EDGE

"With intelligence and wry humor, David Rollins crafts an all-too-believable story about power, corruption and cover-up that has shocking international consequences. . . . Strong characters, nonstop action, and superb suspense . . . Vin Cooper has a powerful, true voice that never wavers." —NELSON DEMILLE

"Two elements are essential for a successful thriller, and David Rollins has both in spades in *A Knife Edge*. . . . You need a protagonist readers will care about, and you need dialogue that is true to life. . . . When you add in the **top-notch story** at the heart of *A Knife Edge*, you've got **one of the best thrillers** of the past few years." —*North County Times*

Also by David Rollins

The Death Trust

*And ask your favorite bookseller about the new
David Rollins thriller:*

HARD RAIN

A
KNIFE
EDGE

A THRILLER

DAVID
ROLLINS

BANTAM BOOKS
NEW YORK

2010 Bantam Books Mass Market Edition

Copyright © 2006 by David Rollins

All rights reserved.

Published in the United States by Bantam Books,
an imprint of The Random House Publishing Group,
a division of Random House, Inc., New York.

BANTAM BOOKS and the rooster colophon are registered trademarks
of Random House, Inc.

Originally published in hardcover in Australia
by Pan Macmillan, Sydney, in 2006.

978-0-553-59001-2

Cover design: Carlos Beltran

Printed in the United States of America

www.bantamdell.com

2 4 6 8 9 7 5 3 1

Those who know how to win are much more numerous than those who know how to make use of their victories.

—Polybius (200–118 B.C.)

Acknowledgments

I'd like to thank a number of people who helped me out on this book with their time, expertise, and encouragement. First and foremost, there's Lieutenant Colonel Keith, U.S. Army. The colonel came on board for *The Death Trust*, and stayed around for *A Knife Edge*. He's out of the military now, editing a music magazine. I wish him all the best of luck with it. It's a wonderful thing to be doing what you love.

Then there's Richard "Woody" Woodward, a man who knows a thing or two about the USAF because he used to be in it. Woody's another longtime helper whose e-mail and phone lines never close.

I'd like to thank Lieutenant Colonel Mike "Panda" Pandolfo. He has both an amazing eye for detail, and infinite patience to go with it. I met Panda when I toured Elgin AFB in 2007. He has given a lifetime of service to his country and I admire him enormously.

Elizabeth Richards, a special agent with the AFOSI, has also been enormously helpful and generous with her time.

I'd like to thank Dave Millward and Manly Fight Gym for teaching me some moves that I've passed onto Special Agent Cooper. Hopefully they'll help keep the guy alive for a few books to come.

Thanks also to my friend and fellow author Tony Park, who read the proofs and gave me some great tips on Afghanistan, where he served with the Australian Army.

I'd also like to thank Dr. Malcolm Parmenter, Tricia and Michael Rollins (my parents), Andrew Sargant, and Kelli Anderson, who all read early proofs. And Craig "Moose" Moore for a few NFL tips.

Saving the best till last, I'd like to thank Sam, my wife, for continuing to believe in my promises, even though she has heard them all before.

A KNIFE EDGE

Prologue

The shark's back was the width of a boardroom table and crosshatched with countless battle scars. It cruised a foot and a half beneath the surface, dorsal fin knifing the oily blue swell above. There was little apparent caution in the way it meandered back and forth alongside the *Natusima*. If the cook didn't know better, he'd have said it seemed to be waiting for something. The inevitable theme music from the movie *Jaws* playing in his head, he took a final drag on his cigarette, then flicked the butt into the water. He glanced left and right and, satisfied the coast was clear, motioned at the kitchenhand to tip the pot containing what was left of last night's stew over the railing. The pot was heavy and the young man grunted with the effort required. The cook knew he was risking his job. The damn tree-huggers aboard ship would have his balls if they found out about this. "Don't feed the animals," one of them had said when someone had suggested throwing scraps to the shark. All the other guy wanted was to bring it in close to get some cool snapshots for the wife and kids.

"Now, that there's a goddamn fish," the cook said

to the kitchenhand as he lit another Chesterfield and watched the shark glide past with its mouth open.

"Fuckin' A," agreed the young man.

The massive shark broached as it turned back toward the splash made by the stew hitting the water, displaying multiple rows of white teeth set in red, pulpy gums. But then the fish appeared to change its mind, resuming its original course. It circled back for a pass beyond the stern, trailing a wake like a boat with an outboard motor. The cook experienced the cold realization that the brute seemed more interested in the meat moving around up behind the railing and beyond its reach—namely *him*—than it was in the chuck steak sinking slowly into the depths. Confirming this, the shark appeared to fix him with its ancient and fathomless black eye.

The kitchenhand muttered, "Fuckin' thing gives me the creeps. Why the hell are we feeding it, anyway?"

"So we can tame it. Maybe we can teach it to roll over," the cook said.

The kitchenhand gave his boss a look that said, *Are you serious?* He found his boss's preoccupation with the thing freaky. He tugged the zipper on his jacket up to his chin and clapped his gloved hands together. It was getting cold, or perhaps it was the company that gave him a chill.

The cook found himself wondering what it would be like to be down there in the water alone with that fish, helpless. The skin on his arms prickled with goose bumps. What would it be like watching a man being mauled by it—how long could you last? *Now, that would be some entertainment,* he thought.

The shark had appeared two days earlier, trailing the ship. A veteran seaman claimed the animal had been following them for far longer as they motored up the Japan Trench.

The man-eater's presence had excited much interest at first—it was the biggest shark anyone had ever seen—but that had waned as the scientists and submersible specialists readied and then launched the *Shinkai.* There was some concern about what the beast would do when the deep-diving craft entered the water, but in fact the meeting between the two was a nonevent. The sub was over thirty feet long, barely ten feet longer than the great white, and it bristled with many delicate sensors and remote-operated arms, any and all of which could easily be damaged by the shark if it became inquisitive. It did indeed approach the sub, but then turned away with a flick of the tail, snubbing the vessel, much to the relief of the scientists.

*   *   *

The recovery ship, *Natusima,* was "anchored" in a relatively shallow part of the 29,500-foot-deep trench, thrusters linked to its navigation systems keeping the ship stationary above a point on the seafloor. The *Shinkai* had been down for over six hours already, diving on hydrothermal vents at the very extremity of its 21,000-foot performance envelope.

At a depth of 20,374 feet, the world outside was

solid black, so utterly black it seemed almost to suck the very illumination from the *Shinkai*'s spotlights. Weird and delicate creatures in all their phosphorescent glory curled, snaked, drifted, or darted past the submersible's portholes, indicating that this blackness was in fact teeming with life, and was liquid rather than solid.

"Back us up a tad," said Professor Sean Boyle.

Dr. Hideo Tanaka's thumb shifted a toggle on the hand controller. There was the slightest vibration accompanied by an electrical hum and the *Shinkai*'s twenty-six tons eased away several feet from the volcanic rock face. Darkness rushed in to fill the widening gap.

"That's it," said the professor. He watched one of the video screens, leaning toward it with intense concentration.

"You OK about going down again?" asked Tanaka, a little concerned about his research partner's well-being.

The professor nodded. Perspiration dripped from his forehead onto his sweat-soaked T-shirt.

The technician handling the buoyancy controls made the adjustments and the sub slid horizontally into the depths. The hull popped a couple of times. Outside, the pressure was close to 630 atmospheres. If a seal gave out now, even a thin stream of water under such pressure would slice through the three men inside like a wire through soft cheese. Professor Boyle was aware of the danger and it weighed heavily on his mind. Dr. Tanaka had spent a lot of time in deep-sea submersibles over many years and experience had taught him this fear—a kind of claustrophobia—was irrational. These submersibles were overengineered and the *Shinkai*'s real limit, before the weight of the sea above the hull crushed it to the thickness of a slice of bread, was probably closer to 23,000 feet.

"Let's get below the smoker," said the professor reluctantly.

Tanaka agreed. The American-born Japanese nodded at the technician and together they completed the maneuver.

Beads of sweat dribbled into Professor Boyle's eyes while he watched the monitor. The screen displayed what was visible on the volcanic plate just beyond the bow of the *Shinkai*, as well as providing real-time data for sea depth, current direction and speed, sea temperature, and hull pressure. The temperature, barely 37°F sixty-six feet away, was climbing rapidly as the sub neared the hydrothermal vent.

What had seemed to be bare rock gradually became a meadow of enormous pale yellow tube worms captured in the *Shinkai*'s lights. The tube worms, each over a yard in length, swayed in the gentle convection current. A movement at the corner of the screen caught the scientists' attention. Dr. Tanaka toggled the external camera so that the view in the monitor swept left. A huge white spider crab crawled into view, reminding Tanaka of something from a horror movie. It was gobbling something, long and slender poles ending in claws feeding torn strips of worm into its mouth. "Christ, what a monster," muttered Boyle.

An angelfish drifted into view as the submersible continued its descent. "Now there's a face only its mother would love," said the technician. The small fish dangled its glowing lantern in front of a grotesque, lethal-looking underbite, the brutal fangs in its wide mouth poised for the strike. Alarmed by the sound of the sub's motors, the spider crab darted away.

The temperature climbed further as they descended. "Anyone for a hot tub?" inquired the technician.

"Pass," Boyle muttered, eyes glued to the screen in front of him. The sea temperature had soared to 86°F as the smoker came into view. They were several yards up-current from the volcano that was spewing a plume of black, superheated seawater, hydrogen sulphide, and iron monosulphide into the surrounding sea. By rights, this area should have been devoid of life. There was no oxygen down here, and no light, only boiling liquids capable of stripping the paint off a ship's hull. And yet around the base of the smoker's funnel was a thriving community of life, life that would, perversely, find existence in a more conventional environment lethal.

"Jesus," Boyle said under his breath.

As far as Boyle and Tanaka knew, this was the deepest anyone had ever dived on a smoker, and here laid out before them was an improbable Garden of Eden. The bed of worms had become denser and the creatures themselves were as big as anacondas. Shrimp the size of house cats darted between the tubes waving in the current. There were more giant spider crabs, and clams so big they looked like footballs. The tube worms and the mollusks had been well-documented phenomena present at other hydrothermal vents at shallower depths, but those were nowhere near as big as the ones here. Strange fish neither scientist had ever seen before hunted over the tube worm beds, chasing smaller fish and shrimp. None of the life bore the usual hallmarks of fish found at this depth—the huge eyes and teeth and the lights swinging from various protuberances. There was so much life down here it was literally bumping into itself.

"Amazing," Boyle said, awestruck by the information provided by the monitor. It'd been years of theoretical slogging to get to this point. There were moments when they'd been skeptical themselves about finding such a biologically diverse world at—he checked the gauge—nearly 21,000 feet. And yet here it was. This discovery alone would have made them famous, except that their research was classified. The people paying the bills, the U.S. Department of Defense, wouldn't have it any other way.

The technician sitting beside Tanaka tapped his watch. The *Shinkai* ran on battery power and the needles were leaning toward the red. They had an hour and a half at most before they had to start the climb to the *Natusima*. Tanaka nodded.

"Let's get to it," agreed Boyle.

The technician turned to another panel and readied the *Shinkai*'s arms. A thin appendage could be seen moving across the monitor, the clawlike hand flexing open and closed, ready to collect specimens. The motion reminded Boyle of the spider crab. And that thought reminded him there was a lot of work yet to be done.

* * *

The sea was flat; even the low swell of the past week had rolled onto the Japanese mainland beyond the western horizon. It was night and the *Natusima* could have been anchored on a lake of black glass. As he stumbled down the gunnel, Dr. Tanaka tripped on a part of the steel deck hidden in deep shadow. He swore under his breath and grabbed the railing to steady himself. He threw his head back to get some air and looked up into the cloudless night sky. The moon reminded him of a polished quarter, one that appeared glued to the Milky Way. The doctor managed to hum a couple of bars of "Moon River" before his stomach gave way, convulsing several times as a torrent of food and alcohol roared out of his mouth and spattered onto the sea below.

Vomiting made Tanaka feel better. He wasn't used to drinking alcohol—Red Bull was about as strong as his drinks got, and he never had more than three. But there was no Red Bull on board, so he'd been convinced to have an inch or two of Johnnie Walker. It was a celebration after all, and Boyle had been insistent. How many scientific quests end in failure? Tanaka didn't know the answer, but he reasoned the percentage would be high. And yet they'd struck gold on the very first day and bagged a huge variety of bizarre specimens. They'd had five days of uninterrupted diving and the hard work was largely done. Tomorrow, they would up anchor and leave, ahead of schedule. The ship's master informed them that the weather was going to turn nasty during the night—they were experiencing the proverbial calm before the storm—so they'd decided to end the expedition early and head for the port of Yokohama. With luck, the sulphide-oxidizing extremophiles they sought for further experimentation would be hiding among the specimens brought to the surface. No, damn the luck! "Luck's for schmucks," Tanaka slurred aloud, directing his comment at a winch. He and the professor had made their own good luck, and it had paid off in spades.

The celebration in the mess was still going strong, the music leaking through the metal and glass superstructure and up on to the stern deck. Eminem and 50 Cent were getting a rest. The Rolling Stones song "Sympathy for the Devil" played. One of the older members of the crew must be DJ-ing, Tanaka decided. There was a sudden short spike in the music volume, signifying that a hatch had opened and closed. Someone else had left the party to get some air. Tanaka peered drunkenly into the moonlight. The ship was illuminated by two large spotlights perched high on the crane's cross member, but the light was hard and stark and heavy black shadows thrown by a multitude of gear lay across the decks. "Hello," Tanaka called, but got no answer. He shrugged. Leaning on the railing, he looked out across the polished obsidian sea, his head spinning a little, his mouth sour.

Suddenly, he felt himself being lifted from the waist. Before he could struggle, he was thrown over the railing. The world spun and a cry escaped his throat before he hit the water and plunged below the surface. The shock of the cold seawater made him gag. He broke the surface spluttering, choking, instantly sober. "Hey, what the fuck?" he shouted, the saltwater searing his throat. "*Hey!*" The *Natusima*'s black hull reared up beside him, an unscaleable face. He slapped the steel slab with his open hand. "Hey!" There was no reply, although he thought he heard something. Was it a cough? There was a mechanical sound to it. "Hey! Someone there?" There was no repeat of the sound, just the distant beat of music coming from deep within the ship. He dashed the water's surface with his arms in frustration and anger, and kicked off his sneakers so that he could swim better. Phosphorescence swirled around him. "Who the fuck threw me in?" he screamed, the chill of the water like sandpaper rubbing against his skin. No answer. "Hey!" Tanaka's voice echoed back at him, bouncing off the cold steel hull. "Jesus . . ." he said in frustration, treading water. He peered up into the alternating dazzle and darkness of the ship and thought he saw the silhouette of a man's head and shoulders up behind the railing. "Hey, you!" he shouted. No response. Someone had thrown him in, right? Was it that shadow up there?

Tanaka's heart rate was up, mainly because of the shock of close-to-freezing water, but also because he realized getting back up onto the ship wasn't going to be easy if he couldn't attract someone's attention. He could be stuck out here, but not for long. The cold would soon cramp his muscles and then he'd drown. He knew he had around three minutes, max, before his muscles stopped working and he sank beneath the water. There was no convenient ladder anywhere on the hull—it wasn't that kind of dive vessel. His jeans and sweatshirt were weighing him down, making swimming difficult. He stripped down to his underwear, and noted that the phosphorescence illuminated his legs, accentuating their whiteness. He felt naked, exposed, freezing. His skin was already numb. The realization that there were nearly 30,000 feet of water beneath his feet added to his feeling of exposure. Nearby, he heard the vibration of a thruster automatically keeping the *Natusima* in position. The ship must be starting to drift, he thought. It turned slowly on its axis, as if moved by a giant and invisible hand, its stern swinging toward him. He swam away to prevent being struck by the hull.

"Hey!" he called out again. "Anybody...!"

The lights on top of the crane that launched and retrieved the *Shinkai* also lit the water behind the stern. Tanaka swam into the light. He'd be seen for sure now. He yelled out several more times and loaded on the expletives as his frustration grew.

Suddenly Dr. Tanaka felt the pressure wave behind him. And then he swirled into an eddy, which spun him around a couple of times. His mind froze, incapable of grappling with the nightmare finale to his forty-two years on the planet.

The impact of the shark's 2200 pounds drove the breath from his lungs. Its serrated teeth ripped through the flesh of his back, buttocks, and legs, and severed a number of major arteries and veins along with his spinal cord. He screamed and thrashed his upper body, fighting for a life that was already lost.

Bloody seawater streamed through the shark's gills. Its ancient brain had registered the torn, thrashing remains of the wounded animal above it, framed by a spreading pool of blood.

Tanaka felt no pain. In fact, he felt nothing. Everything had shut down, even consciousness. His eyes were open, but unseeing. His mouth was also open but no sound came out. Everything that was Dr. Tanaka was in hiding way down deep, 30,000 feet below the surface. For all he knew, his broken, crushed, and bleeding body was someone else's.

The shark was unintentionally merciful on the second pass. It hit hard and took nearly everything in a single bite, leaving only the doctor's head to roll, eyes hooded in death, bobbing in its wake.

Seconds later, up on the ship, a hatch opened and a shadow stepped inside. The music blared momentarily and then the hatchway clanged shut.

ONE

I'd been sent on a mission. Apparently I was the only man for the job. The going was tough, but I made it through. The cab driver was from Senegal or Swaziland, or maybe from somewhere else entirely. Whatever, he had absolutely no idea where he was going in D.C. Eventually, he did find the place, the address of which was written on the slip of paper I'd given him, now clamped between his lips: a shop in the 'burbs called Sea Breeze Aquarium that specialized in tropical fish. I bought the ones the Navy captain, my current commanding officer, had ordered for his tank, and composed an elegant resignation in my head on the return trip to the Pentagon.

"Your fish, Captain," I said, holding up the plastic bag with Nemo and an identical twin swimming round in crazed circles.

"Ahh, you're back." Captain Chip Schaeffer lifted his head and pulled his nose out of a file. He got up from behind his desk like he was starving and I was a delivery guy from Pizza Hut, and raced over to take the little orange fish into custody. "Good man," he said, relieving me of the plastic water-filled bag. "I trust you got receipts for these, and the cab fares. You don't want to get the Government Accounting Office ticked off."

"Sir, I quit," I said eloquently.

He poured the live cartoon characters into the tank, where they immediately and wisely sought the darkest place they could find: beneath a sunken plastic sub being strangled by a giant plastic octopus. His back to me, Schaeffer said, "There you go, fellers, your new home. Your orders are in the folder on the table. You leave this afternoon."

Who? Me, or the fish? I wasn't sure. Maybe the octopus was going somewhere. The captain couldn't have been speaking to me, could he? I'd done nothing for months except polish the vinyl of my chair with my butt. In between errands, that is. I was fed up with my "recovery." In darker moments I wondered whether it was just Uncle Sam paying me back for all the waves I caused during the investigation into the death of General Abraham Scott, my last case. Maybe they were making sure I played nice and predictable by keeping me on the sidelines indefinitely.

Arlen Wayne, my ex-drinking partner, and Anna Masters, my current love interest and coinvestigator on the Scott case, both agreed that the relaxed pace of my new assignment was for my own good and there was nothing sinister about it. My country was just going easy on me. After all, they said, the Scott case had nearly killed me several times. And had indeed killed Anna, at least according to the newspapers. But, as usual, they'd gotten it wrong. Instead, Anna was in a coma. Once she'd pulled through, her recovery had been fast. Her age and fitness had had a lot to do with that, the doctors claimed, though she later said that it was because she wanted to have sex with me. I preferred her theory to the doctors'.

I, on the other hand, recovered slow. The bullet wounds and the broken ribs took their own sweet time to heal. I only started to get better once I began helping Anna through her recovery a couple of times a day. Within a couple of months, I was ready to reassume active duty of the more military kind.

That, as I said, was quite a few months ago. Major Anna Masters had long since returned to Ramstein Air Base, Germany. I'd moved, too, out of the Air Force Office of Special Investigations, and across the Potomac to a suite at the Pentagon. My orders said I'd been transferred to the DoD's investigation arm, into the exclusive ranks of those supersecret sleuths who handle the cases too sensitive for ordinary mortals. I had, apparently, made The Team. Months later, what these people did was still a secret, at least to me.

Captain Chip Schaeffer, my boss these days, was Navy and getting near retirement. When I first heard that my new immediate superior was a captain, I thought maybe I'd been demoted, a captain being inferior to a major—my rank. But, in fact, a Navy captain is equal to an Air Force colonel. Confusing, I know, but the military likes it that way. It keeps the real enemy—civilians—guessing. Rumor had it that Schaeffer headed up some extra-special investigation arm. The Team within The Team. But, from what I could see, his job entailed reading volumes of DoD documents and picking out procedural errors. He told me that I was his backup, only I had no idea what correct DoD procedure was and so had absolutely no idea what I was backing up. The captain understood this, which was why he never gave me anything to check.

All this was running through my head, so I asked for clarification. "Me, Captain? Am I going someplace?"

"You think I'm talking to the fish, Cooper? I'm old, but I ain't that old." He sprinkled food flakes into the tank.

"No, sir. I don't think you're old, sir. So what's it about?" I asked.

"First things first, Cooper. Your resignation is *not* accepted. As for what it's about, and I take it you mean the case, we don't know. That's why we're sending you. Basically, what we have is an American scientist eaten by a fish."

Yuck? The picture of a man being attacked by a giant clown fish flashed into my mind. I was also a little puzzled. It sounded like this scientist had met his death through misadventure, and accidents—ones befalling American scientists or otherwise—usually fell within the jurisdiction of local law-enforcement agencies.

I was about to ask why the DoD was involving itself when Schaeffer said, "The scientist works—or I should say, worked—for a company doing some research for us."

That explained it. Research funded by the Department of Defense was usually highly sensitive, on account of it mostly having something to do with killing people—in the defense of our nation, of course, so that made it OK. "What was he doing for us?" I asked.

"Need-to-know basis, Cooper, and you don't. For that matter, neither do I, which is why I haven't been briefed on it either. There are, however, a few more details in the file, the one with your name on it, on my desk. Read it before you get on the plane."

I'm getting on a plane? I swallowed hard. I don't like flying, which I know is weird coming from an Air Force officer, but I had reasonable grounds for the problem: I'd been shot out of the sky a couple of times during my tour in Afghanistan as a combat air controller. Lately, I'd been doing some work on that issue with an Air Force shrink. It seemed I was about to give it a test.

Schaeffer cooed, "Out you come, fellas...chow time." One of the clown fish made a tentative break from the submarine, tempted by the flakes sinking through the water, but it turned and fled back to the safety of the sunken sub when something spooked it, most probably the vision magnified by the water of the captain's approaching lips formed into the shape of a cat's puckered anus. Or was it a kiss? I really needed to get the hell out of there.

TWO

I sat and stared at the floor and recalled our last phone conversation. It went something like this:

"Japan," I said.

"Where?" asked Anna.

"Japan. Yokohama, Japan."

"What's it about?" she asked, and then said, "Never mind." We both knew I wouldn't/couldn't elaborate. More of that need-to-know crap.

"What about you?" I said. "You missing me?"

"No," Anna said.

"Sure," I replied.

"Okay, maybe just a little."

"You're calling eight inches *a little*?"

She laughed. "Don't kid yourself, baby."

"How are you spending your spare time?"

"Bible study. I've joined a group."

"Yeah, right," I said. It sounded lighthearted and friendly enough, but the truth of it was our long-distance relationship was suffering. The conversation had become stilted, the gaps between the exchanges widening. We both knew where it would end, but neither of us wanted to admit it—not out loud, anyway.

"When am I going to see you?" she asked.

That was the question on both our minds. And we both knew the answer.

"You tell me," I replied.

The conversation's first bracket of silence followed.

"I saw a quote the other day," she said, abruptly. "Do you want to hear it?"

Whether I wanted to hear it or not, I knew I was about to. "A quote by who?" I said.

"John Steinbeck."

"Right, the piano people."

"No, you idiot. That's Stein*way*. Steinbeck was a writer."

"Oh, yeah, him."

If it's possible to hear someone roll their eyes, that's what I heard.

"Steinbeck said, 'There's nothing sadder than a relationship held together by the glue of postage stamps.' "

I paused. "You sure that wasn't Hallmark?"

"Yes."

"Just as well we communicate via e-mail."

"And why's that?"

"No stamps."

This time, she paused. "Do you ever take anything seriously, Cooper?"

"I'm serious about you."

"Are you?"

"What do you think?"

Another loud burst of silence followed.

"Then what are we going to do about it?" she asked.

"About seeing each other? I don't know," I said,

but I was thinking that we were going round and round the mulberry bush. There was one way to break the vicious circle—marriage. We'd discussed the M word before, but neither of us was ready for it. Not yet. Aside from the fact that we hadn't known each other all that long, and didn't even like each other when we first met, Special Agent Anna Masters wanted to concentrate on her career and I was still gunshy after my last attempt at unholy matrimony. And with good reason. Brenda, my ex, had married our relationship counselor, the guy she also happened to be having an affair with while I was paying him to sort out our marriage. I'd forgiven her, but I still wanted to smack the guy around some—I enjoyed it so much the first time. And in the back of my mind, I wondered whether I actually believed in the institution of marriage anymore. I had trust issues, apparently.

"Christmas is coming up. You could get leave," I suggested. "I'm sure Ramstein would get along fine without you."

"No, I can't. I had so much time off after I came out of the hospital. What about you coming here?"

"Possible, I guess. It depends on the case I'm working." We both knew me tripping over to Ramstein Air Base in Germany, would, in reality, be impossible. Like Anna, I'd had too much time off already, even if it was spent recovering.

"OK, then . . ." she said, with more than a touch of hopelessness. "So . . ."

"Hey," I said, attempting to change the subject, "I

haven't told you; I'm making real progress with the flying thing."

"That's good," she said.

I still needed to take a nervous dump before I got on a plane, and my palms sweated. But I could now travel drug-free, at last. "No more sleeping pills."

"That's really great, Vin. Congratulations. Pity you can't put it to good use and get on a plane to see me."

Silence. So much for changing the subject.

"Sorry," she said. "That was uncalled for."

More silence. The way we were going, I could see a point in the future where our phone calls would be mostly dead air.

Anna sighed impatiently. "Y'know, the trouble with men is that you're all spineless."

"A bit sweeping, don't you think?"

"It's true. You and I both know where this is going."

"And where's it going?" I said spinelessly.

"See what I mean? You and me, us, our relationship—it's going precisely nowhere, and you know it. But do you want to take charge? No. Oh, for Christ's sake, Vin . . . We had fun, when we weren't being shot at or involved in car crashes. We should have just left it at that."

And that was pretty much where we left it. There was a little discussion about us both being free agents, but nothing, thankfully, about us remaining friends— a surefire admission that we'd never speak to each other again.

The Boeing bumped around on some air currents and a light indicated that I should strap in. There being no lap restraints in the lavatory, I made the mental adjustment that it was time to take a seat without a hole in it.

I washed my hands, pushed open the concertina door and, leaning forward, climbed up the aisle toward my seat. The aircraft was still gaining height and the attendants were a little while from serving coffee and tea. The sessions I'd been doing to combat my fear of flying were working; I was almost getting on top of things. Actually, once airborne, it wasn't the fear of flying that chewed on me, it was fear of un-flying, like maybe the plane would suddenly realize it was doing something it shouldn't and drop out of the sky. Irrational, I know, but that's a phobia for you. I repeated the mantra: *The higher you are, the safer you are, the higher you are, the safer you are, the higher . . .*

We'd been airborne for ten minutes now, well out-side the forty-second danger zone where there wasn't enough altitude for the pilots to prevent a catastrophe if things went into the shitter and, say, a wing fell off. Actually, not even Chuck Yeager could do anything about a wing falling off—except to eject, of course—not an option, even for passengers traveling first class, last time I looked. My bowels were churning and my heart rate was up. Six months ago, the only way I could have done this would have been with a headful of barbiturates. Now what I wanted sleeping tablets for was so that I could maybe get some shut-eye and perhaps find myself in a dream with Anna, which was the only way I could see that I'd ever be able to spend any time with her.

THREE

The Tokyo city coroner, Dr. Samura Hashimura, wore a plastic sheath and clear plastic industrial glasses, and he breathed through an industrial face mask of the kind spray-painters use, while he worked over the corpse on the stainless-steel autopsy table. She stared with open milky eyes at the ceiling and appeared completely unconcerned that the coroner was digging around in her small intestines as if he was looking through his sock drawer trying to match a pair. My nose told me the woman had been dead about ten days, and hadn't been refrigerated for most of it. Once you experience the smell of death, you never forget it.

I was chaperoned by a uniformed officer from the local Tokyo police force who didn't know any words of English except for "Make my day," which he'd repeated enthusiastically several times already. An interpreter-slash-liaison officer provided by the U.S. embassy also accompanied me. Michelle Durban was around twenty-five, blond, petite, with pale blue eyes and a dimple in her chin. Think cheerleader. She'd look great in a schoolgirl-style tartan microminiskirt, the local male fantasy of choice if the advertising around town selling everything from motorcycles to seaweed snacks was anything to go by.

Needless to say, my interpreter-slash-liaison officer was not dressed in a microminiskirt. For one thing, it was too cold. The outside temperatures had taken a nosedive below freezing. Snow had begun to fall, sweeping off the mountains of Siberia and blanketing the island of Honshu. For another, Durban was CIA and microminis were not part of the dress code. Instead she wore slacks, boots, and a puffy parka that looked like a pink marshmallow with sleeves.

Dr. Hashimura set down a couple of instruments that looked disturbingly like chopsticks and mumbled a few words behind his mask. Ms. Durban replied in Japanese. The coroner grunted. His rubber nonslip shoes squeaked on the polished concrete floor as he made his way out the door and across to a bank of stainless-steel drawers. He detoured to a computer screen and consulted it before returning to open one of the drawers. He pulled out the tray within, which rattled lightly on its bearings as if it wasn't carrying any weight. On the tray sat a rectangular stainless-steel box covered by an opaque plastic sheet. The coroner nodded at the box. I didn't need to speak Japanese to know that here were the remains of Dr. Hideo Tanaka, U.S. citizen and former employee of Moreton Genetics, the DoD contractor.

The coroner peeled back the plastic and said something to Ms. Durban as we looked down on what was left of the late doctor. "What'd he say?" I asked.

"He said that they thought at first it was a coconut."

A coconut? The hairy ball in the tray could well have passed for one, especially if you weren't prepared to see it for what it was—a severed head. The coroner retrieved a large pair of forceps from a nearby tray and flipped the head over. The skin was greenish brown, the face swollen. The tongue was a livid purple. The eyes were missing, as were the eyelids. The stump of the neck was shredded. A single strip of muscle dangled from it, concealing a dirty white collarbone within.

Durban spoke to the coroner, who then scraped around in the ooze at the bottom of the tray with the forceps until he found what he was after. He pulled out something, then went over to a bench to wash it. He returned a moment later and gestured at me to hold out my hand. In my palm he deposited a white serrated triangle. Then he talked in an animated manner for several minutes. When he finished, Durban informed me, "There is no question that the doctor was attacked by a very large great white shark. The size of the tooth makes the animal over twenty feet in length. That's well over twenty-five hundred pounds of fish."

"So his head was like the pit?" I asked, motioning at the thing on the tray.

"What?"

"Like the pit in a piece of fruit—the bit you don't eat." Durban still didn't get it. "Did the shark spit the head out or something?" I asked.

Durban wasn't sure whether I was being serious. I was. Not knowing anything about shark attacks, I was interested to know why there was anything left of the man at all. She frowned, then put the question to the coroner. The man laughed like he'd just heard an extremely funny joke and then proceeded to play a little impromptu charade for my benefit. Durban interpreted as the coroner acted out. "He thinks the shark came up beneath the doctor and took his whole body in its mouth." Just as well Durban was on my team. I was still stuck on the coroner miming what appeared to be "*three words, first word rhymes with night.*" To assist my understanding, the Japanese man traced his hand across his own shoulder and neck. And then what he was acting out clicked: *bite.* Just as I caught on, Durban said, "He believes the shark bit clean through Tanaka's neck and shoulder. The tooth was found embedded in the collarbone."

I had an image of the shark using the doctor's collarbone as a toothpick and then licking its lips. "Have toxicology tests been done?" I asked.

Durban passed the question along and then handed back the translation. "Yeah. Seems he was smashed. Blood-alcohol content up over zero point one."

"How does he know that?" I asked. As far as I was aware, alcohol didn't hang around in the blood indefinitely, and I knew the head had been found almost a week after it had been parted from its body.

Durban asked Hashimura, and then said, "The human body processes around an ounce of alcohol every hour. But once you're dead, those processes stop. Also, the head's been kept chilled in near-freezing water a couple of days. That preserves the blood and tissue."

I nodded. The unusual circumstances surrounding the recovery of the doctor's head came to mind.

They'd been elaborated upon in my briefing notes. One of the engines on the *Natusima,* Tanaka's expedition ship, overheated and had to be shut down. A storm and dangerously high seas meant the ship, reduced to one engine, had to be towed to Yokohama. It was dry-docked and the problem was traced to a blocked seawater intake essential to the engine's cooling system. Inside the pipe, wedged there like a cork in a bottle they found Tanaka's head, which I now knew everyone thought at first was a coconut.

"Have the local police followed up?"

Durban repeated the question for the coroner, who nodded and then spoke.

"They have and they're satisfied," Durban translated. "Everyone's calling it accidental death."

"Yeah. I guess it'd be tricky murdering someone with a great white shark."

"I don't know . . . Several years ago, a guy dressed in a panda costume murdered a woman in a Tokyo park. He caught the train home afterward. True story," Durban added, just in case I was waiting for the punch line. I imagined a panda with bloodstained fur sitting cross-legged in the train, surrounded by Japanese workers heading home, everyone reading their newspapers. I said, "Do you think that's relevant to what we've got here?"

"No. What you said about someone using the shark as a murder weapon just reminded me."

Whether the shark had anyone inside it before it struck its victim, who knew? But it certainly had someone inside it now—Dr. Tanaka, or at least most of him.

FOUR

The Tokyo uniform gave us a lift to the Roppongi area in his patrol car. It was 1430 hours and already dark. The falling snow was light and dry. The wipers pushed the snowflakes around the windscreen like shredded paper and they swirled in bright spirals in our headlight beams. I looked into the swirls and felt like I was falling. It was hypnotic. I broke the spell by checking out the side window. There was enough neon bouncing around from all the signage to fry insects. "I'd like to talk to Tanaka's partner—the other scientist—and also to the ship's master," I said, picking up the thread where I'd left it.

"I'll arrange it." The look on Durban's face said, *You got suspicions?*

I elaborated. "It was at least twelve hours before anyone realized Tanaka was missing. I'd like to have that time accounted for." I didn't say that I'd come all this way and I needed to return home with something more substantial than a receipt for my minibar bill at the Hilton and a shark's tooth on a chain around my neck. Remembering the tooth, a present from the coroner, I pulled it from my jacket pocket. It was basically a blue-white equilateral triangle, each side over an inch in length. Serrations dimpled two of those sides and it came to a wicked point. I pictured a mouth full of these little steak knives attached to a fish that hit with the force of a runaway Cadillac. It wouldn't have been a very nice way for Dr. Tanaka to leave the party.

"You been to Tokyo before?" Durban asked.

"No," I said.

"What are your first impressions?" She took her hat off and tamed her straw-colored hair, running her fingers through it. I smelled lavender.

"It reminds me of a pinball machine I used to play, lit up for five times bonus and extra ball."

Durban smiled. "You want to grab something to eat?"

I didn't need to give the invitation too much thought. The alternative was heading back to the Hilton and reading the hotel's brochure on its extensive range of gym equipment. "Sure. What you got in mind?"

A short while later we were sitting on high stools eating raw fish, delivered by a stream of robots. A glorified cigarette machine with red lips and bumps on its chest area crafted to resemble breasts on a cold day delivered something to us that jiggled on the plate. The machine said something in Japanese in a breathy voice that sounded like it wanted to exchange brake fluids with me. Before I could say *"Domo arigato,"* the only words I'd managed to learn from the Lonely Planet phrase book, the machine did a one-eighty and rolled off into the crowd.

To kick the evening off, I said, "So, what do you call a woman with one leg?"

"What?"

"Eileen. What do you call a Japanese woman with one leg?"

Durban shrugged.

"Irene."

She laughed. "That's not funny."

"Hmm," I said. "Maybe I need to work on my delivery." An awful sound coming through the ceiling speakers distracted me. There was a karaoke stage. A businessman sweating sake was tonguing the microphone, his tie loosened and his belly hanging over his belt like he was six months pregnant. The song was vaguely familiar but at the same time not. And then I recognized it, The Beatles' "Hard Day's Night"—in Japanese. If I were one of the Fab Four, I'd be suing him for damages. Several women who were far too young and pretty to be accompanying him clapped excitedly, adoringly. This had to be the sort of behavior men paid for. Escorts, obviously.

"Those women—they're not what you think they are," said Durban, doing a little mind reading.

"No?" I said. "What do I think they are?"

"I saw the way you looked at them."

I wondered how I looked at them and decided not to respond with another question, in case Durban mistook me for a shrink.

"Japanese women handle things differently from Western women."

"Yeah?"

"Yeah, they missed the whole feminist thing here. In fact, this place is almost feudal in some of its attitudes toward women. The men believe they are superior beings. The women don't challenge that belief. Not directly, anyway."

"So, are you talking complete subservience to every male whim?" I found myself smiling at the two young Japanese women. Superior beings, eh? One of the women caught me looking at her and twittered to her friend. They both giggled at me from behind their hands.

Durban set me straight. "I meant, made to *feel* like superior beings."

"Thanks for ruining it," I said.

She shook her head. "Haven't you figured it out yet?" she said. "Yes, dear...No, dear...whatever. It's always an act. The women here work with what they've got. It's just a different angle."

"So, despite appearances, they're no different from the women back home?"

"And what are we like?"

"You want an example?"

Durban nodded. "I can take it."

"OK...A man goes to the doctor and brings his wife along. He has a checkup. Afterward, the doctor calls her into the office. He says, 'Your husband is extremely sick, and his fragile state is compounded by huge amounts of stress. If you don't follow my instructions explicitly, he'll die. In the morning, you have to let him sleep late. When he gets up, you have to fix him a good breakfast. Do not stress him out with chores. At lunch, make him something really delicious. Let him sleep in the afternoon. For dinner, cook something special again. Be nice, friendly, and for God's sake don't load him up with your own problems and concerns. The name of the game is to reduce his stress levels to zero. If you can do this for just one month, your husband will regain full health.'

"In the car going home, the husband asks his wife, 'So what did the doctor say?'

"She replies, 'You're gonna die.' "

Durban laughed. "Yep," she said. "That's us."

A tune from a well-known musical began playing in her jacket pocket. Durban pulled out her cell, then excused herself to answer it, turning toward a plate of raw salmon brought to us earlier by a fembot.

"This place one of your favorites?" I asked when she snapped her cell shut and put it in her pocket. I wasn't sure what I liked least, the food or the entertainment. I chewed on something cold and rubbery, which, come to think of it, was also a suitable metaphor for the music.

Durban nodded. "One of my regular haunts. It's cheap and it's authentic Tokyo. You ever eaten jellyfish before?"

"Never," I said.

"You have now."

It squeaked between my teeth like a piece of inner tube as I chewed. "Actually, it's not bad," I conceded. "Have some. Show me how it's done."

Durban shrugged and picked a few strands out of the bowl with disposable chopsticks. What I wanted more than anything was to spit my mouthful out and go find a hamburger. The sake was good, though, and it killed the taste of the cuisine. Maybe that's why they served it. I reached for the flask.

"No, no—you never pour your own sake. It's bad luck," said Durban. I switched cups and filled hers instead. She drank it down, perhaps a little too eagerly.

I said, "Don't think much of jellyfish either, eh?"

"Busted. More, please." She held out her cup. I topped it up again. "It's the one thing on the menu that makes me gag."

I picked up a napkin. "Do you mind?" I asked.

"Go right ahead," she said.

I spat the jellyfish into the napkin, then rolled it into a ball.

"Sorry," she said. "That was a bit of a test."

"How'd I do?"

"You passed."

A couple of businessmen beside us were tucking into a lobster pinned to a slab of wood. I saw its front legs move. They picked at it with their chopsticks while it tried in vain to escape. I lost whatever appetite I had left.

The guy doing over "Hard Day's Night" left the stage to wild applause—I guessed because he'd finally finished. "So, what about your boyfriend?" I asked Durban. "Is he going to be joining us?"

She studied me for a moment. "Boyfriend? A, how do you know I'm not married? And B, how do you know who I was talking to?"

"In answer to A, while you're wearing a ring on

your wedding finger that suggests you're married, the finger next to it bears the indentation of a ring recently removed. I'd say you've been asked by someone to baby-sit me and you've shifted the ring across to your wedding finger in case I turn out to be creepy and you need an excuse to hurry on home. As for B, and I admit this one's a stretch, that cell ringtone of yours, the tune 'The One That I Want' from the musical *Grease*? Just a guess, but, given the title of the song, I'd say that you've downloaded it especially and assigned it to a caller group of one. As I've just established you're not married, that one has to be your boyfriend. Also, it's the time of day when lovers call each other to see what's up." I'd just pulled the investigator's party trick, the equivalent of a clown twisting a balloon into the shape of a poodle. Nothing to get excited about, really, unless you were an impressionable girl with a few drinks in her, thrilled about being a long way from home. I was almost disappointed in myself.

"Hey, not bad. I'm impressed," she said, gazing at me with, if I wasn't mistaken, lust. "You're right on all counts—even about the baby-sitting gig. I've had to do it a couple of times in recent months and every time I've been hit on by a guy who thinks he can play because he's beyond his spouse's reach—you know, outside the five-hundred-mile zone."

"The what?"

Mischief curled a corner of her full and, I had to admit, sexy lips. "The chances of bumping into someone you know while you're out on the town, or ending up in bed with someone your partner went to school with, for example, reduce the further away you get from home. Five hundred miles, they say, is when your survival odds are greater than the risk of being caught."

"Nice to hear something useful is being taught at spy school these days," I said. Her knee brushed against mine under the table. Her cheeks were flushed with color brought on by the rice wine.

"As for the boyfriend, I've been dating my boss, the deputy assistant director, but it's not going anywhere," she informed me.

"Why's that?" I asked, not knowing what else to say.

"Because he's married."

"So much for the five-hundred-mile zone."

Durban wrangled those lips of hers into a pout. "Don't approve?" she asked.

I answered her question with a noncommittal shrug.

"What about you?" she asked. "Married?"

"Divorced," I said.

"Everybody's doing it," she opined. I considered telling her that I'd caught my wife having an affair—all four inches of it in her mouth, as I recall—if only to put a little distance between us, particularly between Durban's hand and my thigh, which she'd started kneading like she wanted to bake it. The truth was that while I was technically single, I still felt attached to Anna. And yet . . . there was a conflict of interest about this burgeoning between my legs. If I were going to avoid waking up tomorrow with Durban in my bed and a head full of regret, I had to leave, or get rescued. And fast. "So, is your boyfriend joining us?" I repeated with as much nonchalance as I could manage.

"No. I just told him I was working late." Her nails were now tracing figure eights on the fabric of my pants, the circles getting wider and coming dangerously close to The Wakening Serpent. "I told him we were going through the case . . . you know . . ."

There wasn't that much to go through that we hadn't already covered, but I said, "Good idea."

An ancient woman shuffled up to us and exchanged our empty sake flask for a full one. I protested, but she just waved at me and told me in Japanese not to be stupid. While I didn't speak Japanese, I'd been told not to be stupid enough times in a multitude of languages to know exactly what she said. Obviously, I was in the middle of some female plot to get me drunk, and it was working. "So, as I was saying, a recap of the case is a good idea."

"What's to go through?" Durban said. "The guy got drunk, fell off the boat, and became bait."

She picked up the flask and poured me another shot. Yeah, this girl had Trouble tattooed on her forehead. I felt a pang of sorrow for Mrs. Deputy Assistant Director—the woman was getting screwed, along with her husband. Time to refocus. "We don't know that as fact, do we?" I asked.

"Know what?"

"Exactly what happened to Tanaka?"

"So you don't think he got eaten by a shark?"

"Yeah, I'm sure he got eaten, but that's *all* we know."

"I guess." Durban sucked in her bottom lip and held it there.

"Tanaka was drunk," I said.

"I remember. So?"

"He didn't drink. Ever. Not according to the FBI, anyway."

Durban's eyes widened, like she'd just discovered a plot. "Really?"

"The Bureau could have been wrong. Or maybe Tanaka just chose that night to take a stroll with Johnnie Walker—either was more likely than any other reason."

"Like murder," said Durban.

"Yeah, like murder." The other minor outstanding issue was those twelve hours. Why had it taken so long for anyone to discover that Tanaka was missing?

Durban interrupted my thoughts. "So, what do you DoD people do, exactly? No specifics, of course, just in general. You guys are even more hush-hush than we are."

The CIA was "hush-hush"? That was a new one on me. Every now and then Durban said something that reminded me she was still really just a kid, albeit an oversexed one. First impressions aren't always right, but this was mine: The biggest struggle in her life had probably been with the occasional tight peanut butter jar lid. That, and she was way too pretty for her own good. Or anyone else's, for that matter.

"No, it's okay. I can give you specifics," I answered.

"For the past five months I've been waging war on apostrophes. You know, whether they go before or after the *s*? It's a huge problem. You'd be surprised how many people get that stuff wrong. Next month, I'm going after parentheses."

"You're kidding me."

"Honestly, all I've done since being transferred out of OSI is review paperwork—other people's. This is my first real case in six months."

"Six months?" She was surprised. Almost as much as I was. What was I still doing in the armed forces, anyway?

The fat business guy had muscled his way up to the microphone again and was launching into "Stairway to Heaven." Or hell, depending on your point of view. The female company at his table applauded. I wanted to throw tomatoes, or, this being Japan, star-knives.

"So that's your background, the Air Force's Office of Special Investigations?" Durban asked.

I nodded.

"OSI." Something flickered across her face. "Jesus! I recognize you now."

"Recognize me?"

"Yeah. The rank threw me. You were a lieutenant back then, right? Lieutenant Cooper. That's right, I remember reading about you. You busted up an arms-smuggling ring in Afghanistan. You were on that CH-47 that got shot out of the sky by the Taliban. Yeah, I read about you."

I ignored the wrath of the gods, poured myself

sake, and tossed it down. The whole Afghanistan thing was still giving me nightmares.

"You're a bit of a hero," she persisted, ignoring my body language. I was squirming. I've come to realize that there's not a lot of difference between a coward and a hero. The situation itself rather than a conscious decision often dictates a man's actions. I've seen heroes do cowardly things. And I once saw a man everyone thought was a coward rescue a dog chained to a booby-trapped 155-mm artillery shell. Both were killed when the device blew a swimming-pool-sized crater in the dirt. When I looked back on my service record, the moments recorded as glorious sparked only cold fear, loneliness, and a sense of pointlessness. And, of course, along with the cowards, many of the heroes I've known are also dead. Their heroism had done little or nothing to alter an outcome. Out of all this, one eternal truth has struck me—Death ain't real choosy.

"You okay?" I heard her voice as if from a distance. "Did I say something wrong?"

"What? No, nothing. What about you? Why the CIA?"

"My story's not nearly as exciting as yours, I'm afraid. I grew up in a Park Avenue apartment. Only child. Father was a banker, Mother a professional drinker—brandy with vodka chasers. Good schools. NYU, poli sci, psych, and languages."

So much for first impressions being wrong. "That's where you learned Japanese?"

"No. We had a Japanese doorman. I fucked him on

my thirteenth birthday when my mom was in bed with the bottle and my father was on some business trip. The doorman was the only one who remembered." She forgot about the gods and poured herself sake like she was trying to forget. The drink brought back her smile. "You know, the best way to learn a language is on your back?"

The hand was on my leg again. "As for why the CIA," she said, "I was recruited in college. My mother wasn't too happy about it but I think my father thought it was cool, something to brag about in the Hamptons." She paused to drink her sake and a thought struck her. "I think their attitudes changed after 9/11."

"Theirs and everyone else's," I said. I knew there was a reason why I was still doing this gig and I'd just been reminded of it. I glanced outside. The snowflakes were settling onto the vehicles out in the street like goose down after a pillow fight.

A man appeared to detach himself from the moving press of people shuffling along the sidewalk. He stepped into the sushi bar and launched a smile at me that could have come from a Tommy Hilfiger catalog. I was about to tell him he'd confused me with someone else when he said, "Hey, I knew I'd find you guys here!"

"Bradley!" exclaimed Durban. She spun around on her stool a little too quick when she heard his voice, like she'd been caught in the act. It didn't take Sherlock Holmes to figure out who Bradley was. I wondered why he'd turned up after Durban had given him the brush-off. Maybe he didn't trust her. Maybe he wasn't as vacuous as he looked. Bradley was impeccably dressed in a black Brooks Brothers coat with a bronze silk scarf tucked inside the lapels. He wore the arrogance of an Ivy League fraternity house like aftershave. I just knew we'd get along—not. He dusted the snowflakes off his shoulders and sleeves and JFK-style light brown hair, then unbuttoned his coat.

"Got a drink there for me, Shell?" he said, avoiding any overt display of affection for his mistress. I wondered how he'd behave if he knew *I* knew. "So, you must be Special Agent Vincent Cooper. Good to meet you. Bradley Chalmers. I'm with State."

Sure you are, Brad.

He held out his hand to shake. His white fingers were cold and wet, like pieces of sashimi.

"Call me Vin," I said, playing along.

"So, how do you like Japan, Vin? It'd be nice, only there's so many Japanese, right?" He smiled at his own banality.

"Yeah, it's nice," I agreed. It occurred to me that someone upstairs must have been listening, for a change. Here was my diversion. Whether I liked the guy or not, Durban's boyfriend and boss was my excuse to exit, stage left. "Well . . ." I said.

"Hey, where're you going?" Durban said with a frown.

"Yeah, c'mon," said Prince Chalmers with zero conviction, "you can't leave now."

"Appreciate the hospitality, folks," I said, "but I got

a report to write." The requirement to keep on top of the paperwork was something everyone working for Uncle Sam understood, paperwork being a monster with an insatiable appetite for the world's forests. I caught a look from Michelle while the karaoke racket distracted her lover boss. It was the slightest pursing of those lips, the raising of an eyebrow and the suggestion of a shrug. It said, *I'll shake this loser and then you and I can go wring some fun outta this town.* Although I could have gotten it wrong and it might have been just plain, *See you.* I stood and the blood rushed to my feet, leaving my brain bobbing in a high-water mark of sake. I swayed a little.

"You want me to get you a cab?" asked Durban.

"No, I can manage." I took a moment to center the bubble between the two black lines in my head before attempting further movement.

"I've arranged to have you picked up at your hotel at oh-six-thirty by a cruiser," she informed me.

"Got it," I said.

"You know where you want to go?"

I glanced outside. In the space of a few minutes, the snowfall had turned to blizzard. "Jamaica," I said. "Say sayonara to Brady for me."

"Bradley," she corrected me, her hand on my forearm.

"Him, too." I waved and headed for the sidewalk. I felt happy that something with Durban didn't get the chance to start . . . OK, maybe I'd feel happy about it in the morning.

FIVE

My body was still running on D.C. time, which explained why I didn't sleep much, and why at 0200 hours I felt like breaking for lunch. I watched a kung fu movie in my room and killed time till dawn reading over the briefing notes. Nothing stood out, and so my mind wandered to other more pressing topics such as replaying the last conversation I'd had with Anna. We were going nowhere, and so now we could go nowhere alone, without the inconvenience of having each other along for the ride.

I went to breakfast early. The buffet was deserted, a rare occurrence anywhere in Japan. I ate enough bacon to bring on colon cancer, plus two eggs, a couple of sausages, two hash browns, toast, and a whole cantaloupe. If I could go till dinner without having to face the local cuisine, the day's major mission was accomplished. I ate a cinnamon pastry as I rolled out into the foyer.

A police cruiser waited out beyond the end of a narrow strip of red carpet embossed with the Hilton's logo. Snow slush clumped across the vehicle's trunk, roof, and hood. The driver's window was opaque with water and mist. The window slid down and I got a wave. "Go ahead, make my day," the now familiar cop said with a smile. I could have slugged the greeting out of the park, but I let it go. All I'd get back would be a blank look anyway, and what would be the fun in that?

The rear door sprang open. I tossed in my jacket and climbed after it. I'd need the jacket. It was still only just a couple of degrees above freezing. The cold immediately found its way through the scar tissue I'd accumulated in recent years from all the bullet and shrapnel wounds.

"Morning," said Durban with the kind of singsong good cheer that makes me want to punch people, as she licked the froth off the underside of a lid of a cappuccino-to-go. "How'd you sleep?"

Alone. "Fine, thanks. You stay out late?"

"No. Bradley had to get home. One of his kids was having a birthday." She shrugged as if to say, *Shit happens.* It did and, no thanks to her, a good chunk of it was happening to Chalmers's family. And sooner or later it would blow back on Michelle Durban. Her situation vaguely reminded me of my own marital gumbo. In the sober light of day, the CIA woman had lost a lot of her gloss, but I wasn't here to moralize, let alone judge, so I put her private life out of my mind.

We meandered through the brown slurpee that the streets of Tokyo had become, pushing through the combination of snow-melt and grit, the tires throwing up a bow wave of slush. And then we were on the freeway between Tokyo and Yokohama, an impressive multilane strip of concrete seemingly held aloft by the roofs of the development that filled the space between the two cities. Whoever coined the phrase "Nature abhors a vacuum" must have seen this place.

Our cop chauffeur settled down to a cruise below the speed limit, I assumed to avoid any ice patches. Our speed must have annoyed the surrounding traffic, none of which passed us or honked. All super polite. Durban and I sat in silence. I watched the urban sprawl roll by when the opacity of the window cleared enough to allow it, and listened to the incomprehensible chatter coming over the comms. It occurred to me that there weren't many countries left in the world untouched by the English language, but this was one of them. The only words I recognized here were familiar brand names paraded on endless billboards. Like Durban, these signs didn't seem to hold the same attraction when they weren't all lit up for the night.

The port of Yokohama appeared suddenly when the curtain of mist parted in front of a sky of beaten lead. The water beneath it had the color of wet coal. Durban passed a yellow Post-it note through the steel mesh to the cop and the two exchanged a bunch of staccato words that sounded like the linguistic equivalent of carpet burn. I assumed the Post-it held our intended destination, because the driver checked it several times before punching buttons on the vehicle's navigation system. We turned off the main road and into the docks, reduced to a crawl because of ice. A car had fishtailed off the road and had somehow come to rest with the front end hanging out over the water. It teetered back and forth, balancing unsteadily. Emergency vehicles clustered around it, their strobe lights bouncing off the surrounding concrete like little electric shocks. Uniformed people waved their arms around, small white clouds in front of their mouths. Our driver ignored the scene and drove slowly on. We eventually pulled onto a pier and slid sideways down a small incline, the wheels losing traction on the ice, before pulling up next to a ship. It moved ever so slightly beside the pier like it was alive, breathing, the movement only perceptible against the stillness of a vast gray warehouse on the far side of the bay.

I stepped out of the vehicle and felt my scrotum contract, testicles beating a strategic withdrawal into the warmth of my guts. I reached for my jacket. I was right about needing it. The uniform stayed with the vehicle, stamping his feet and clapping his hands, making little bows while Durban and I walked carefully across the ice to the gangway. The tips of my ears and nose already burned with cold, and my breath steamed. I pulled a pair of leather gloves from a side pocket and put them on.

Durban took the gangway first, steadying herself on the incline with a gloved hand on the railing. Two black shapes met her as she stepped on deck. Introductions were well under way when I caught up.

"Professor Sean Boyle," said a man I knew from briefing notes to be fourteen years my senior. The cold burnished perfect pink circles on his shaved cheeks.

We shook gloves and I said, "Special Agent Vincent Cooper."

A second man said, "Moritzio Abrutto, ship's master." According to those briefing notes, he was American, as were most of the crew. The ship was leased to Moreton Genetics, the large U.S. firm which employed Professor Boyle and the late Doctor Tanaka. Abrutto was blond and fair-skinned. "Come inside," he said, leading the way through a hatch, warm yellow light beckoning from within.

The air inside the ship smelled of diesel and bacon. We followed the ship's master and Professor Boyle into a reasonably large area with bench seats on either side of a couple of tables. The mess. Photos on the walls showed various people, mostly men and mostly bare-chested, proudly holding various objects for the camera that could have been anything from offal to placenta. Life recovered from the deepest oceans, I assumed. Nearly all the photos were signed. I recognized the subjects in one as being Boyle and Tanaka. Boyle was bearded, and they stood together on the ship's rear deck in tropical sunlight. Both men had their hands on their hips, ready for action. I bent toward the photo to take a closer look.

"A great man," said Professor Boyle behind me. "I'm missing him already." He peeled out of his jacket. "That photo was taken a year and a half ago, cruising up the southern tip of the island of Honshu. We were heading for the Trench."

"The Japan Trench?" I asked.

"Yes," said the professor. "Our first expedition to these waters."

"The one just concluded was your second?"

"Third."

Three times. I hadn't known that. Perhaps the fact that Boyle and Tanaka had been on the *Natusima* several times before wasn't significant, but it reminded me that while the brief I'd been given was pretty good, there were still holes in it.

"Can I offer you people anything to eat or drink?" Boyle inquired.

"Not for me," I said, having eaten twice my body weight for breakfast.

"No thanks," said Durban.

"Take your coats off and have a seat. Get comfortable," said the master, taking his own advice. The rest of us followed his lead.

"So, Agent Cooper," said Boyle as he slid in behind the table, "how can we help you with your investigation?"

"I'm not really investigating," I replied. "I'm just prepping the DoD's files for closure."

The professor locked his fingers in front of him. "Well, then, what would you like to know?"

"Before you start, if you have no objection...?" I placed a digital recorder on the table and switched it on. Its red LED winked, letting me know it was recording.

"No, that's fine," said Boyle with a dismissive wave of his hand.

"I've already read your statement, Professor," I

said. "Is there anything you could add to it? Anything that has come to mind since you made it?"

The professor shook his head. "The truth is, Agent Cooper, I've tried my best to forget about the whole unpleasant episode. So, the answer to that is no, nothing."

"If you don't mind, would you go through events on that night again, anyway?"

The professor glanced at his watch. "If you think it'll help."

I nodded, fixing an expression of understanding on my face to put him at ease. Boyle didn't look much like a professor, but only because I believe all professors should look like Albert Einstein on a bad hair day. Boyle's, by the way, was thick and straight, and it was also unnaturally blue-black. Dyed. I guessed he was more self-conscious about gray hair than he was about appearing to wear a mixing bowl on his head. He had the appearance of a severe monk, the Spanish Inquisition kind, and I could easily imagine him lighting bonfires. But, as I said, first impressions can be misleading.

The written brief told me Professor Sean Boyle was forty-eight and that his parents had emigrated to the U.S. from Ireland when he was four. His face was intelligent and his dark eyes glittered with intensity beneath bushy black brows. His skin was pale all over, except for the glow on his cheeks induced by the cold. His lips were on the thin side, and there were vague acne scars on his neck. At a guess I'd have said he spent more time peering through microscopes than he did power-lifting and drinking protein shakes. He was also a valuable defense asset, according to Captain Schaeffer, and I had been ordered not to piss him off. I was to tread lightly, which I had every intention of doing.

Boyle glanced at his watch a second time. So, he had somewhere he'd rather be. Him and me both. "I'm sorry for asking you to be here today, Professor. I know you're anxious to get away and I won't keep you a moment longer than necessary."

"That's okay," he said. "I still had things to attend to on board. Dr. Tanaka and I collected a number of previously unrecorded specimens. I'm anxious to get them properly secured for the flight home."

"Well, thank you anyway, sir," I said, walking on tippy-toes as ordered.

The professor picked at a cigarette burn on the tabletop. "We'd been diving on the Trench for a week in the submersible."

"Who's *we*?" I asked.

"The doctor and I, and a technician."

"Is the technician still on board?"

"Yep," said Abrutto. "We'll catch up with him when you're done here."

"Okay," I said. "Sorry to interrupt, Professor. You were saying?"

"We had perfect weather, tides, and currents, and because of all that had managed to complete the dive phase ahead of schedule, which was fortunate because we had weather coming down on us."

The master agreed with a nod.

"We were having a bit of a celebration," continued Boyle. "Hideo was drinking, and I'd never seen him do that before—drink."

"What was he drinking?" I asked.

"Scotch. We only had that and sake on board."

"Do you know how much he drank?"

"Enough, obviously, though I didn't realize it at the time. I topped his glass up maybe twice, I think. As you may or may not know, Agent Cooper, many Asian people don't have the gene that allows them to metabolize alcohol effectively."

I nodded. Yeah, I was aware of the supposed Asian intolerance of booze. I wasn't aware it had become established fact. "So you had never seen Dr. Tanaka drunk before?"

"No, never."

"Did you see him leave the party?"

"No. I wish I had. Then perhaps he'd still be alive."

"Of course," I said. I then asked Abrutto whether he'd seen Tanaka leave. No, he hadn't. "Do either of you have any theories as to what might have happened that night?"

"As I wasn't there at the time, I can only guess," said Abrutto.

"Tanaka might have decided to get some air," Boyle said, "or he could have gone out to be sick over the side of the boat. He might even have gone down the stern to check on the *Shinkai*—the submersible—and fallen in. Once in the water, without someone to pull him out, the cold would have killed him in minutes. He was drunk, so maybe less."

I'd guessed the cold could have killed him, and I'd heard of cold having a bite to it, but nothing like what had latched hold of the doctor a couple of inches below his chin. "What can either of you tell me about the shark?"

The professor said, "*Carcharodon carcharias*—a great white shark. Top predator in this part of the world. They like the deep water and the cold—brings the seals, their favorite snacks. One decided to tail us as we cruised north to our dive zone. It was a magnificent animal. Very big, very powerful."

And quite partial to Japanese, I thought.

"We see them every now and then. More often these days, since they've become a protected species," said Abrutto.

"Did its presence concern you?" I asked.

"Only to the extent that it might damage some of the sensors on the sub, so no one did anything to encourage it to stay," replied the professor.

I glanced at Durban. If nothing else, at least we'd cleared up the question of whether the shark was just a guy in a costume. Someone like Boyle was sure to have spotted the difference.

"Dr. Tanaka wasn't discovered missing for some time—twelve hours, according to statements," I said. "Isn't that a long time to not notice somebody missing?"

Boyle shook his head again. "It might seem that way, but no, not really. The expedition was over. And everyone saw how drunk Tanaka was when he left. I guess everyone assumed, as I did, that he was in his room, sleeping it off. And, because we had no work to do, I was happy not to disturb him."

I doodled on the notebook like I was making an entry, because in fact I'd just found a problem in the professor's statement. He'd contradicted himself about *not* seeing Tanaka leave the party. "How about you, Professor Boyle? Were you drunk, too?"

"Yes. It was a celebration, and I was celebrating."

"How about you, Mr. Abrutto?" I asked.

"As I said, I wasn't there. I was on the bridge, on duty, on my third mug of coffee, I think—nothing stronger."

"And you heard and saw nothing unusual?"

"Afraid not. A storm was coming through and the weather updates were looking pretty ugly. As we weren't under way, I was concentrating on those."

"Do you mind if I have a look at the doctor's stateroom?" I asked.

"Sure, no problem," said Abrutto.

"Do you need me to come along, too?" inquired the professor.

"No, I don't think so," I said. "Not unless you want to."

He didn't.

"I'm sorry I can't be of more assistance, Agent Cooper," said Boyle, squeezing himself out from behind the table. "If you don't mind, I've still got a lot to do before I leave for the States this afternoon. If you need to ask me any more questions, here's my card." He pulled out a slim silver holder, slipped out a card, and put it on the table.

"Thanks for your help, Professor," I said. A logo for Moreton Genetics dominated the card, the *M* and the *G* twisted around each other in a double-helix pattern. I slipped the card into a back pocket and gave him one of mine. "In case anything comes to mind," I added. He nodded, and fed my card to his wallet.

Boyle grabbed his jacket and left. I moved out from behind the bench and picked up my coat.

"You won't need that yet, Agent Cooper. It's even warmer where we're going. You can get it on the way back." Abrutto stood and opened a hatch at the back of the mess, revealing a narrow hallway, and stepped through. Durban and I followed. The smell of diesel was stronger here. It was hard to breathe. A short walk down the hallway brought us to a door with police tape across it. Fingerprint dust powdered the door and a plastic bag was taped over the door handle. Tokyo P.D. had treated the room like a crime scene, not because a crime had necessarily been committed, but to preserve its integrity until someone like me absolved them of further responsibility.

I knew from the police report that only two sets of prints were found on the door handle: Tanaka's and those belonging to the man who checked his room, Master Abrutto. A deckhand had reported no sound from within when he had knocked, so he'd fetched his boss. I also noted in the report that nothing appeared to have been disturbed within the room. I peeled off the tape, opened the door, and took a look inside. The room was roughly the size of a large suitcase, but thoroughly unremarkable otherwise: steel walls, a porthole, a desk, and a few dirty clothes in a small pile on the neatly made bed. It was unslept in. On the desk sat Tanaka's computer, an Apple Power-Book, open, the screensaver parading snapshots of deep space. I knew that one—I used it myself.

The computer had been untouched by anyone other than Tanaka, according to forensics. His were the only fingerprints found on the keyboard, and a report from the hard drive showed the last use had been before the doctor disappeared. In short, there was nothing in the least out of order here.

We toured the ship and I talked to several other crew members, including the technician who helped Tanaka maneuver the submersible. No one had anything to add. The general consensus was that there'd been a party, there was music, there were no women. So how much partying could anyone do? No one particularly remembered seeing Tanaka, drunk or otherwise. The doctor was, apparently, the type who kept to himself, not unfriendly but no party animal either.

Next, we did a turn around the stern deck. I couldn't see how Tanaka could possibly fall in unless he'd climbed up on the gunnel and lost his balance. I did note that, iced up, the decks were slippery as hell. I shuffled along, keeping my feet in contact with the ice, and came around behind a large red drum leaking rust. It was a spool of greased cable, part of the mechanism that launched the submersible sitting under the crane that dominated the ship's stern. I took a look over the ship's side. The black water was a long way down, flecked with light snow that melted moments after settling. Once over the side, getting back up on deck unaided would be tricky, if not impossible.

A cone of cigarette smoke suddenly appeared from behind the spool. Being an investigator, I investigated. I maneuvered carefully around the drum and found a large, bearded man in a red, oil-stained jacket, sucking hard on a cigarette. The man looked at me, swung his eyes back to the dock, and acknowledged my presence by taking another drag.

"You part of the crew?" I said.

"Who's asking?" he replied, blowing a mixture of condensation and tobacco smoke over the machinery.

"Santa Claus," I responded.

"Don't think much of your sleigh," he said with a nod to the police cruiser now blanketed in snow, parked on the wharf.

"So then you know who's asking," I said. "Why don't you smoke inside? Gotta be more pleasant than standing out here in the cold."

" 'Gainst the rules," he said. "Damn peckerheads on this cruise won't allow it." He coughed, a sound like a car changing gears without a clutch. Something came into his mouth, which he chewed once or twice. I was thinking lung. He spat overboard and a globule arced through the falling snow, plopped onto the water and spread. Something came up from beneath and pecked at it, just in case it was edible. It wasn't.

I noticed that tobacco butts collected over a considerable time had stained brown the ice and snow under his feet. "Anyone else on board smoke?"

"Nope."

"I'm looking into the death of Dr. Tanaka for the U.S. government," I said, officially clarifying my presence on board.

"Good for you," he replied.

"Did you know the doctor?"

"Nope."

"Were you at the party the night the doctor went missing?"

"Nope."

"What were you doing at that time?"

"What I always do after dinner's done. I secured the kitchen."

"So . . . you're the cook?"

"Yep." The man drew on his cigarette so hard I thought he was going to turn the thing inside out. He took a pack of Chesterfields from his jacket pocket, shook one out, and lit it from the butt. Then he flicked the butt into the water and blew a vast cloud into the air.

"You got a name?" I asked.

"Cooke. That's with an *e* on the end."

"Your name's Cooke and you're the cook?"

"That's right. Al Cooke. He got eat."

"He got eat?"

"By the shark. It was waiting."

"Did you see the doctor fall in?"

"Nope," Cooke said, clapping his hands together. A wave of cooled tobacco smoke and old sweat rolled over me.

If he hadn't seen the doctor fall, then he wouldn't have seen him get mauled by the shark either. I looked at the man. I was familiar with the type, the type that saw nothing and heard nothing, even if he did. "Thanks for your time," I said. I handed him a card with my D.C. number on it, just as I had with every other crew member I'd talked to. "If anything occurs to you, give me a call."

"Yeah," he replied, stamping to warm his feet. I did the same and realized mine had gone numb. I could see Durban and Abrutto waiting for me over at the gangplank, breathing funnels of steam. I moved off to join them.

It was obvious that there was nothing else for me to do here. The defense of the U.S. had lost an important asset, eaten by a fish that could care less.

As Durban and I walked toward the police cruiser, I was thinking of Sean Boyle. The professor didn't seem terribly upset about losing a friend and colleague. I could see that the guy was utterly consumed by his work. Had it even dawned on him that Tanaka was gone forever? "What do you call an Irishman who bounces off walls?" I asked.

"Ric O'Shea," Durban replied promptly. "Everyone knows that one."

She was right—they do. I was off my game, distracted. Just around the corner was the plane trip home, and my stomach was already grappling with a cold, sour knot because of it.

SIX

It was after 2030 hours by the time the taxi pulled up outside my apartment in D.C. I'd moved back to the city after being released from the hospital. My new residence was a one-bedroom apartment in a four-story block over a couple of restaurants duking it out for survival—a Korean barbecue joint on one side, vegan on the other. After three months' residency, I was on a first-name basis with Kim, the proprietor of The 38th Parallel, but was barely on nodding terms with the people in Summer Love, Kim's tie-dyed competitors next door, which says a lot about my dietary preferences.

"Vin. Good to see you." Kim looked up from his cash register as I walked in lopsided, struggling with my suitcase. "Where you been?"

"Disneyland."

"Hah, Disneyland, always Disneyland. You wan' the usual?"

"You got jellyfish on the menu?"

He shook his head after a moment of consideration. "No, no, sorry..."

And to think I could have learned to hate it months ago. "Never mind," I said. "I'll stick with the usual."

"Yes, sure, sure. Good choice, good choice. One large serve of *bulgogi* coming up. You wan' rice?"

I nodded. The exchange with Kim was all very cheery. And, in fact, I was cheered to be home, even though there was nothing and nobody waiting upstairs for me, not even a potted plant.

Kim's toothy good humor changed to a scowl as he barked the order to his wife like he was a vicious dog going at an intruder. His old lady seemed impervious to it and simply trudged off into the back room to rustle up my order. Mr. Kim attended to several other take-out customers over the phone while I flicked through a couple of old *People* magazines on the counter. The covers featured the usual parade of Hollywood fuckups, people who had every reason to believe they'd won the lottery of life, but were instead hooked on a brand of narcissism that ensured they were unable to love anyone as much as their own manufactured self-image. Divorces, tantrums, dishonest trysts, clinics, bizarre surgery, drunken traffic accidents, affairs. If it wasn't pathetic, it'd be hilarious.

I sifted through the pile. On the bottom lay a three-day-old copy of the *Post*. According to the front page, since I'd been away, Pakistan had had a change of government. A couple of soldiers in the previous president's bodyguard had decided they didn't like his policy of being friendly toward the U.S. and so they'd peeled open his vehicle like an orange with a dozen or so pounds of Composition B while he was still inside it. Fundamentalist gangs were roaming through Karachi and Islamabad beating up anyone who looked like they were living in the twenty-first century. India was jumpy. America was nervous. After years of relative quiet, shots had already been exchanged over the long-disputed territory of Kashmir. Everyone's nightmare was no longer just a bad dream: we now had a bunch of religious dimwits sitting on top of an unknown number of fission-boosted atomic warheads and the missiles capable of delivering them. Another pressure cooker—just what the world needed.

"Here you go, Mr. Vincent, sir. You enjoy."

"Thanks." I dropped the newspaper back on the counter and exchanged the plastic bag he was holding toward me for the handful of shrapnel jangling in my pocket. "Keep it," I said, knowing the tip was around five bucks. As Mr. Kim was also the building's unofficial security guard, I figured he'd earned it.

I avoided the elevator, my usual practice, and took the fire stairs to the second floor. The stairwell was poorly lit, with a little halfhearted graffiti here and there as if the artists could barely be bothered. I knew how they felt. The place was around forty years old and going through a kind of architectural midlife crisis. The ceilings were a little low, the rooms just a bit too tight for comfort, like wearing a sweater that shouldn't have been thrown in the dryer. The place was in need of a new coat of paint, or maybe a wrecking ball, I couldn't decide which. But the rent was cheap, and Mr. Kim's *bulgogi*—beef in soy sauce—was a real winner.

I arrived at my apartment, put down my suitcase, and fed the key into the lock. Problem. The door was already unlocked. It was only then I noticed a faint strip of light outlining the door's bottom edge. Did I leave the place that way, unlocked with the lights on, before heading off to Japan? No, I did not. There wasn't much inside worth stealing, but that didn't mean I wanted some stranger looting it. What I did have was a small safe bolted to the floor, where I kept various articles that were valuable to me—passport, birth certificate, favorite lucky rabbit's foot, my M9 Beretta service pistol as well as a worn U.S. Army-issue Vietnam War–era Colt .45 an uncle of mine confiscated from a dead VC. I put my ear to the door panel but heard nothing within. Was the intruder still inside, or long gone? I turned the knob and pushed. The catch scraped against the plate. The hinges squealed. *Shhh, goddamn it!* I hunched, ready to charge. And then the doorknob was wrenched out of my hand.

"How long does it take you to ride an elevator to the second floor?" said Major Anna Masters, standing in front of me, hand on hip, wearing one of my shirts and a smile.

"I took the stairs," I said. Anna was the last person I expected to see. She was in Germany, at Ramstein Air Base, wasn't she? "What are you—" Our bodies slammed together. Our lips found each other, tongues searching. I was instantly erect, like any good soldier should be.

"Get your clothes off, for Christ's sake. I'm hungry," she said, breaking from the clinch.

I fumbled with my belt. "I usually dress for dinner."

"Not tonight," Anna replied, breathless, like she'd just run a race.

I kicked off my shoes and left a trail of socks, pants, and other items on the floor. I ripped my shirt off, the one Anna was wearing, and lifted her as I walked. Her back was hard and lean and her legs wrapped around me. I wasn't going to make it to the bedroom.

"There," Anna commanded, gesturing at the table, which was set for dinner. I lowered her onto a place mat. She swept the cutlery away, sending it clattering among my clothes on the floor. Then she wound a hand around my neck, grabbed the edge of the table for leverage and ground her pubic bone into me. Neither of us wanted to bother with the entree. We went straight for the main course.

*   *   *

We had a second helping in the bedroom. Afterward, we lay in each other's arms in bed and watched the reflected neon from The 38th Parallel's sign below my window change color on the ceiling. It brought back Tokyo and, for the barest instant, the image of Dr. Tanaka rolling around in a stainless-steel tub. Professor Boyle's little inconsistency about seeing his partner leaving the party swam about in my mind. If Anna and I were working the case together, that would have been something we'd discuss. Perhaps later I could play back the recording I'd made of Boyle's statement to see if it also struck her as odd. And then the memory of Michelle Durban and our dinner in the sushi bar sprang up, along with a pang of guilt even though nothing had happened. But, if it had, I'd been outside the five-hundred-mile zone, which would have absolved me, wouldn't it?

Anna's weight shifted on me and her perfume flooded my brain. "I forgot I mailed you a key when I took this place," I said. "When I saw the door open and the light on, I thought you were a burglar."

Kim could have warned me. He knew Anna, and I'd have put money on him knowing she was upstairs, but he'd chosen to keep the secret. I might have to ask him for that five dollars back.

"So...haven't given a key to anyone else?" she asked.

"Handed out about a dozen. You're just lucky my harem's out of town." I thought of Durban again.

"What?" Anna had caught the slightest twitch, or perhaps it was the slimmest surge of electricity beneath my skin. Whatever, she read it like a polygraph.

"Nothing," I said, wondering how it was that women could do that—read a man's conscience.

"You're looking fit," she said, tracing the definition of my stomach muscles with a fingernail.

"I've discovered Jane Fonda's home-workout video. How about you? Over the headaches?"

"Hope so. Haven't had one for a few weeks." She sipped coffee, holding the mug between two hands like she was praying. Those headaches were bad ones, so maybe that's exactly what she was doing, praying they'd gone for the duration.

I'd been shot twice on my last case, once in the flesh under my upper right arm, the slug passing clean through the skin and missing the triceps muscle. Not such a big deal—a few stitches and purple, puckered scarring to remember it by. The other bullet, however, had shattered the humerus in my left arm—the big bone between shoulder and elbow—drilled a hole through the shoulder muscles, clipped a rib, executed a backflip with pike, and found its way into the subclavian vein, where it was then flushed through my heart. They located the slug in the bottom of my lungs. The good news, the doctors told me, was that I would live. The bad news was, so they believed, it would not be very well. I responded as I usually do to professional opinion and ignored it, in this instance the advice being to sit in a recliner rocker for the next forty years and watch sitcom reruns. Instead, I chose to do the opposite and put myself through eight hours of daily torture. Once I could crawl, I forced myself to walk. When I could walk, I tried to run. Now, most mornings, I was running twelve miles. After the run, I was doing push-ups—a hundred or so. I'd more or less given up the booze and was working on my halo. In truth, I was probably in the best physical shape of my life, and I had the doctors to thank for it. Had they said I'd recover fully, I'd probably still be a pinup boy for Jack Daniel's.

Anna also had permanent injuries by which to remember our case together. In fact, she lost the big toe off her left foot due to the car accident, or should I say car crash—it had been no accident—that put her into a coma for a week. There appeared to be no physical impairment resulting from her head injury, although she was now suffering from regular and terrible migraines.

"Aren't you going to ask me what I'm doing here?" Anna inquired.

"I know exactly what you're doing here, and who you're doing it to."

She punched me in the arm. "No, I mean in D.C."

"So tell me."

"I volunteered to escort a prisoner Stateside."

"How'd you manage that?"

"Like I said—volunteered. You know, took one step forward. The opportunity just came along."

Anna moved her head and I felt her hair slide across my chest. I pictured her standing in the doorway when I first arrived home, the hair that reminded me of melted dark chocolate flowing over her shoulders. I lingered on the image, the light from the kitchen behind highlighting her curves beneath my borrowed shirt. Anna's breasts were larger than I remembered. Back in the here and now, I cupped one in my hand. It was warm and heavy and it filled my palm, the nipple still hard with excitement from the recent sex fizzing through her cells.

"I've missed you," I said.

"I can tell," she whispered, reaching for the erection that refused to go away, stroking it softly, apparently happy that it wasn't going anywhere.

"How's the Bible study going?" I whispered back, getting short of breath.

"Coming along nicely," she answered. I felt the heat in the caress of her lips as she kissed me on the way down. She bit me several times, in case I forgot who was boss, and then, beneath the sheet, I felt her mouth close around me. I clamped my eyes shut. The pleasure was almost unbearable. Almost.

* * *

"So what was Japan like?" she asked, sitting at the table in Class As, eating a little reheated *bulgogi* and rice for breakfast. She had bought something from the vegetarian restaurant before coming up to the apartment, but after a night in my fridge, it looked far less appealing than Mr. Kim's finest, and there was nothing else in the fridge that was edible unless you were a mold.

I poured Anna a cup of coffee. "What was Japan like? Well, they have vending machines there so that if you feel the need you can get a pair of girl's underwear—used—packaged up with a picture of the young woman herself wearing them."

"That's sick."

"I know. You'd think they'd at least wash them."

"You're sick, too."

"Actually, I haven't felt this good in a long while," I said honestly.

"Yeah, me, too." Anna smiled. Her eyes caught the morning sun streaming through the window and flashed blue-green like they'd received a jolt of electric current. We looked at each other in silence, neither wanting to speak and break the moment, perhaps because we both knew that a particular set of difficult questions and answers was hovering too close for real comfort.

I broke first. "So, when are you heading back?" There it was. I'd said it.

Anna took a breath and slowly let it out. I knew I wasn't going to like what was coming. "This afternoon."

"You're kidding."

She shook her head. "Got a court-martial at Ramstein starting midday tomorrow."

I said nothing, which pretty much said it all.

"That'll teach me to volunteer." Anna was suddenly finding eye contact difficult.

A loud burst of silence followed. It reminded me of our telephone calls.

I said, "Y'know, after our last conversation, just before I went to Japan, I was pretty sure things between us were done." What had Anna said on the phone? *You and me, us, our relationship—it's going precisely nowhere... We had fun... we should have just left it at that.*

Her turn not to say anything.

"Why'd you come?" I asked. Our mood hadn't so much shifted as completed a one-eighty.

"Well, you know... a girl has needs," she said, trying to lighten it up. The attempt flew like the Hindenburg, and she knew it. She glanced down at her coffee again. "Perhaps I shouldn't have come."

Yeah, perhaps you damn well shouldn't have, I thought. I was just getting used to the idea of being apart. But one night and I was hooked on her again.

"I don't know when I'm going to be back," Anna said.

I nodded. "Uh-huh."

"I was going to suggest you take the day off and spend it with me, but I think I know what you'd say to that."

Perhaps the heat in my face had given her a clue.

Anna's chin trembled and there was a film of tears in her eyes. "I'm sorry," she said.

"Me, too." I stood and took my coffee cup to the sink and poured the remains down the drain. "Anna, I have to go," I said. I wasn't being a martyr. Captain Clownfish was expecting me at 0930.

"The defense of our great land waits for no one." She forced a smile.

"Stay as long as you like," I replied. If she wanted me to be big and tough, I could be that guy. "Just leave the key downstairs with Kim when you go."

"OK . . ." she said. The privilege of surprising me in one of my shirts had been rescinded.

I drove my old Pontiac Parisienne to the Pentagon. It was snowing lightly, the early morning sun having been swallowed by a sudden cold snap. I didn't have an accident, but I probably caused a few.

SEVEN

I was on time, 0930 as requested, but Captain Schaeffer wasn't. Fine by me. I told myself to snap out of the Anna thing and get busy. I started with the e-mails. The box was crammed with unread CC'ed crap. None of it was specifically sent to me, except for one with the inviting subject: "The proper completion of a DD Form 1351–2." CC'ed e-mails are a waste of time, although the one about the 1351–2 reminded me to put in for my Japan expenses. I selected All and consigned the lot to the trash. I pulled my wallet and extracted the wad of receipts from my recent overseas junket and began filling out the form online. It was tedious going, but I don't earn enough that I can fund investigations for the government out of my own pocket. The online paperwork completed, I dispatched it and then forwarded the hard receipts to Accounts Payable through the internal mail.

Checking my wallet for any hidden receipts, the great white's tooth given to me by Dr. Samura Hashimura, the coroner in Tokyo, dropped out onto the desk. I examined it, holding it between thumb and forefinger. It was white and hard and made for cutting and tearing. With so many of these teeth ripping simultaneously into Dr. Tanaka, the unfortunate guy probably wouldn't have felt a thing. I taped the tooth to the frame of the computer monitor. Thus were fifty-nine minutes of my working day accounted for. It was going to be one of those days.

Next I pulled out my notebook and the voice recorder. There was a report to be written. An hour and a half later I was two thirds of the way through it and getting to the point where I felt I needed to rehash the interviews conducted on board the *Natusima*. I listened to them all, then tabbed to the time code marked in the device's memory.

My voice: *"What was he drinking?"*

Boyle's voice: *"Scotch. We only had that and sake on board."*

"Do you know how much he drank?"

"Enough, obviously, though I didn't realize it at the time. I topped his glass up maybe twice, I think. As you may or may not know, Special Agent, many Asian people don't have the gene that allows them to metabolize alcohol effectively."

"So you had never seen Dr. Tanaka drunk before?"

"No, never."

"Did you see him leave the party?"

"No. I wish I had. Then perhaps he'd still be alive."

Yeah, maybe. Boyle was one condescending asshole: *"As you may or may not know, Agent Cooper, many Asian people don't have the gene that allows them to metabolize alcohol effectively."* I tabbed the memory button again.

"Dr. Tanaka wasn't discovered missing for some time— twelve hours, according to statements. Isn't that a long time to not notice somebody missing?"

"It might seem that way, but no, not really. The expedition was over and everyone saw how drunk Tanaka was when he left. I guess everyone assumed, as I did, that he was in his room, sleeping it off."

Did you see him leave the party? I'd asked. Boyle had replied, *no.* A few minutes later, under a bit of stress, suddenly everyone including Boyle is watching Tanaka reeling out of the joint legless. Did this mean something? Or nothing? Very few statements contain no contradictions. The ones that don't more often than not tend to indicate coaching. And yet—

"Ah, Cooper, you're back," said Captain Schaeffer, interrupting my thoughts, his head peering around the edge of the door. "What are you doing?"

"Sir," I replied. "The report on the death of Dr. Tanaka. I'll send it over in about half an hour."

"Forget about it for the moment. I'm afraid you have some visitors. I did warn you . . ."

Warned me? What about?

The two men swept into the room like a couple of big cats released from their cage, circling the space in front of my desk, ready to eat. One was Caucasian; his buddy, Asian. Both were in plainclothes. Actually, there was nothing plain about their clothes. Their suits were possibly Italian and improbably expensive, and they carried themselves a little like spooks, but far more like stockbrokers with a pitbull cross. I recognized their manner immediately. I was getting a visit from the most feared government department in D.C.: the General Accounting Office.

Schaeffer closed the door. I pictured a steel bolt

slamming home. Escape was futile. "What can I do for you gentlemen?" I asked.

They flipped their credentials at me and then glanced around for something to sit on. The room was empty except for my desk and a faded color photo of our last President stuck with tape to the wall behind me. If they wanted to sit, they had the choice of the floor or my desk. Both chose to hang a cheek off the latter. I leaned back in my chair to get out of their personal space, or rather to get them out of mine.

"Don't think much of your decorator," said the white guy.

"I'm living in it for a while before I renovate," I said. "You guys got names?"

"De Silver," said one.

"Wu," his partner said. "We've had our eye on you, Cooper." They were playing Good Accountant Bad Accountant.

"Really? Which one are you sharing?" I asked.

"Watch your mouth, Special Agent. We can make this pleasant or we can spoil your day. Your choice."

"You're too late," I said. "It's already curdled."

Wu slapped down a piece of paper on the desk in front of my keyboard. I leaned forward to get a closer look. It was DD Form 1351–2. Receipts were attached.

"That yours, Cooper?"

"Looks like." I glanced over the figures. "Problem? Didn't I carry the one?"

"We sent you a priority e-mail about this and the system told us you never opened it."

"Right, the e-mail. I filed it." It was a half-truth. I still hadn't emptied the trash.

De Silver took a notebook out of his inside jacket pocket and opened it. "You went to a Sea Breeze Aquarium three weeks ago?"

"Correct," I said.

"You got a receipt for a cab ride there that cost thirty-five bucks. Seems the return journey cost just ten."

"And?"

"Why the discrepancy?"

"So this is about twenty-five bucks?"

"It's not just the twenty-five dollars, Cooper," said De Silver.

"No, then what is it about?" Actually, I was anxious to know because, among the three of us, we'd already blown more than that in lost productivity.

"It's about procedure, systems, accountability," Wu informed me. "You haven't answered the question."

"Which one? There've been a few."

"Were you on DoD business the entire time you were in that cab?"

I was about to answer when Wu said, "We've red-flagged you, Cooper. We're going to go over every receipt you've entered for the last six months. And the paperwork had better be in proper order."

"So, you want to tell us about the cab ride?" De Silver again.

I can only take so much bureaucracy in one hit and I was starting to overdose. "There's nothing to tell. Stevie Wonder drove me out. A homing pigeon brought me back."

One of them snorted.

"Your expenses will get reimbursed this time, Major. But know you're on our watch list." So that's what this was all about. They just wanted to let the new kid on the block—me—know who was boss.

"Sure. Thanks," I said with my best have-a-nice-day smile as they snatched back the 1351–2 and moved toward the door. "And, guys—no matter what everyone else around here says, you're doing a great job. Keep it up."

Wu and De Silver turned and glared. They weren't used to receiving a "fuck you," no matter how it was couched. The GAO had a problem. They were worried that there was another of those Defense-procured $7600 coffeepots out there, or a $9000 wrench worth a buck fifty, ready to be thrown into their works.

Schaeffer's head appeared around the door again seconds after they left. I wondered whether he'd had a glass to the wall. "You want to fill me in on Japan?" he said. "Now's a good time."

He disappeared. I gathered I was to follow.

"I warned you about the GAO, Cooper," he said over his shoulder.

"Yes, sir, you did."

"What's the upshot?" he asked.

"Don't hurry back, I think is the lesson, sir."

"Good advice," he said.

I have no idea if he knew what I was talking about. In the six months I'd been in Chip Schaeffer's section, I'd learned that you could say just about anything as long as you said it nice. We walked past a number of offices, all occupied with personnel hunched over paperwork. I wondered if they were working on cases or sentence construction, and if, like me, they were on probation. I noticed they all glanced up when we walked past—not much happens around here. I also noticed they all sat facing their doors. They reminded me of moray eels in their holes. The area was gloomy, the dour atmosphere accentuated by the extensive use of overhead fluorescent tubes, most of them dusty. We were in D-ring, the hall that, colonlike, runs right through the center of the complex. This meant we had zero natural light. In fact, our offices had very little of anything in the way of staff-friendly amenities, an indication, I believed, of the department's true place in the pecking order. By comparison, I'd heard the GAO had a wet bar and sauna in theirs.

Captain Schaeffer's box was twice the size of mine, though also windowless. I finally understood why he was so keen on the fish tank. It bubbled away happily in one corner, lit up like a Tokyo shopping center. I counted two clown fish plus a couple of arrivals that had been added since my trip to the Sea Breeze, and saw that the octopus was still throttling the boat. I didn't see any sharks.

Schaeffer's desk was littered with paperwork. The wall behind his chair was a shrine to the heavyweights of D.C. There was a picture of the current President, flanked by a snap of the Secretary of Defense. Between and below the two men hung a photo of the Chief of Naval Operations, a woman. She smiled like she had something going with the other two.

"So, this scientist. What happened? Give me the bottom line."

"Sir, Tanaka had been drinking. He went out on deck, presumably to get some air. Somehow, for reasons that may never be established on account of there being no witnesses, he ended up in the near-freezing water where he was eaten by a shark." I neglected to add that this was one of the rare instances where the sashimi actually got even.

"Just as the preliminary from the Tokyo Police had it figured." Schaeffer nodded. "So you're done with the case?"

"Pretty much, Captain. Got a few procedural aspects to clear up." This was me playing for time. It would hardly do for the department supposedly overseeing matters of procedure to be seen bucking it. What I wanted was time to check up on Professor Boyle and his employer, Moreton Genetics, before being redeployed in the war on grammar. Something about the guy troubled me, besides the odd Tupperware haircut.

As expected, Schaeffer said, "Better get on with it then. Dismissed."

I went back to my office. I shut down all the internal software on my PC and opened a Web browser. A window came up reminding me of the U.S. government's policy about downloading files with viruses, cookies, and pornography. The advice: Don't. I brought up Google and behaved like a normal, everyday nosy citizen. I tapped "Sean Boyle, Ph.D." into the search bar and pressed return. There were plenty of hits, approximately 78,000 of them. There were only five for a

Professor Sean Boyle. One was a professor of English, the other a Ph.D. in automotive technology. I found references for the guy I was after on page two. He had three entries: two related to academic papers he'd written, the other an invitation to download the PDF file of a speech he'd given to the science faculty of Berkeley. I took up the invitation and double-clicked.

While I waited for it to download, I Googled the late Dr. Tanaka. There were nearly a thousand hits on the name, but I found my Dr. Tanaka on the first page. There was already a link to an obituary on him in the British newspaper *The Observer*. According to the article, Tanaka had headed numerous deep-sea diving expeditions on hydrothermal vents from the Arctic to the Azores. A marine biologist, he was apparently the leading authority on the unusual life forms found in these hazardous environments. The article included a picture of the guy with his head attached to his body. I barely recognized him.

I went back to the PDF of Boyle's speech. On the first page were the words "Playing God." Interesting title. I hit the print button, sat back, and considered my next move. Moreton Genetics employed these two guys, and they were both working together on a top-secret project for the U.S. Department of Defense. One was a geneticist, the other a marine biologist. I was intrigued.

I tapped moretongenetics.com into the search bar to see where it took me. Almost immediately an animated double helix appeared, the *M* and *G* that I remembered seeing on Boyle's business card, revolving slowly, while the rest of the site loaded. The main image on the home page was of the Moreton Genetics offices and research complex, an architectural representation of the double helix constructed of steel and glass, nestled among ponds of reeds and birds, and set, the accompanying text told me, within five acres of land on the edge of Silicon Valley, California. The place radiated high technology. And money. I surfed the site. Apparently, Moreton Genetics had been one of the links in the chain that had helped unravel the human genome. The company had also isolated a gene responsible for switching off the production of insulin, resulting in new therapies worth millions. Most recently it had produced a sterile strain of the varroa mite, the creature that had single-handedly almost wiped out California's entire population of honeybees and, with it, virtually all flowering plants and crops in the state. Something like that— saving California's agriculture—would have earned Moreton Genetics a lot of money, not to mention kudos.

I checked the price of the stock, information also available on the site. MG was looking good. Their stock had increased its capital value by eighteen percent in the last year alone. If I had money, it would be a terrific investment, but then so would a decent pair of running shoes, I told myself, which was a fair indication of just how much spare cash I had lying about. I kept trolling around the site, but for what I had not the slightest idea. I saw that the MG complex was environmentally simpatico. It produced its own electricity supply through a combination of wind generators and solar panels, and had become a net contributor to California's power grid.

Across its lush acreage, it was also providing habitat for various flora and fauna, those birds that featured on its home page, as well as a couple of endangered species of frogs and a rare variety of pond slime. To summarize, MG was an extremely successful company with a social conscience, except that it was sponsoring programs paid for by the Pentagon—to be fair, an organization not known for loving its fellow man of the non-American variety. I also noted that this fact was nowhere to be found on MG's site. Didn't fit with its caring-and-sharing corporate image, no doubt.

I wondered what MG was doing for the DoD. I wondered whether I wondered about it bad enough to get into trouble finding out. The phone rang. I recognized the caller ID. "Arlen?"

He said, "I just spoke to Anna."

"She stayed at my place last night."

"I know."

"She's going back to Germany this afternoon," I said.

"I know."

"It's over."

"I know."

"If you say 'I know' one more time, I'll drive over and punch you."

"So, what's next? What are you going to do?"

"What any red-blooded American would do. Go to a sports bar, get drunk, watch old NBA repeats, visit a hooker."

"You hate the NBA," he reminded me.

I shouldn't have been surprised that Arlen had found out so quick. When Anna had been hospitalized, he'd kept her room stocked with flowers on my behalf. When she'd been released, he'd kept her company while I spent hour after hour in physical therapy. During that time, they'd become close friends. And he was right; I probably wouldn't meet anyone like Anna Masters again, but then she wouldn't meet anyone like me again, either.

"How was Japan?" he said.

"Different. You'd love the food. Has a certain bite to it." The memory of it gave me an idea. "Arlen, could you do me a favor?"

"No."

"Why not?"

"Because it'll get me into trouble."

"No, it won't," I said.

"Yes, it will, Vin. Your little favors always lead to trouble. What's it about?"

"I can't say."

"Then definitely no."

I could tell he was weakening. "You don't want to know because then you won't have deniability."

"Will I need deniability?"

"It's the best defense."

"Will I need a defense?"

"Could you stop repeating everything I say?"

"Sorry."

"Look, I need you to find out something for me. I can't dig around because I've been told specifically I don't have need-to-know. But *you* haven't had the official NTK bullshit on this one."

"OK, before I say absolutely, categorically no, you

want to at least give me something so that I have some idea what I'm saying no to?"

Arlen knows how to ask a question. I said, "A company called Moreton Genetics is doing some work for the Pentagon. I want to find out, even if just in general terms, what they're doing."

"Is this related to what you were doing in Japan?"

"That's something I can neither confirm nor deny," I said, slipping into jargon for absofuckinglutely.

Even though I couldn't see them, I knew Arlen's lips were clamped into a thin line.

"You'll need a code," I continued. It would be easy to find the information I was after, but not without a thing called a case code. Whenever any classified information was required, or petty cash claimed, or resources allocated, a case code had to be cited so that an investigation could be traced, tracked, and costed as it wound its way through the system. With the proper code, Arlen could go straight to the DoD's archives and pull the paperwork. The problem was that his interest in Moreton Genetics would be on file if things did end up in the crapper.

"I'm doing a little general digging at the moment for a federal oversight committee. The job has a general access code. All areas. Maybe I can do it discreetly. Might be suitable."

Damn right. "I owe you, Arlen."

"Indeed you do, Vin. What are we up to now?"

"Convert the favors into dollars, I'd say around a million or so."

"You ever going to cough up?"

"Next payday," I vowed.

"I'll see you in half an hour in the Pentagon cafeteria," he said.

I hung up and almost immediately the phone rang again. I didn't recognize the caller ID on this one. It did, though, have an unfamiliar international area code. I picked up.

I heard a cough echo down the line. I knew that cough from somewhere.

"Hello? North Pole?" said a male voice.

"Sorry?" I replied.

"Is this Santa Claus?"

"What?"

"You remember? You gave me your card."

That wasn't a big help. I handed around my card like flu virus got handed around on public transport.

"I met you on the *Natusima*. The name's Cooke." He coughed again, a rasping metallic sound.

My memory kicked in. "Cooke with an *e*, right? You're the cook."

"You got it."

"What can I do for you, Mr. Cooke?"

"You said I should call if anything came to mind."

"That's right." The line wasn't great. There was a couple of seconds of delay every time he answered a question. I wondered where he was calling from.

"You asked me whether I saw the guy who got eat fall in the water. I told you no."

"I remember."

"Well, y'see, I said no 'cause I didn't see him fall. That's because he didn't *fall*—the Jap guy was thrown."

EIGHT

T hrown? So you saw this happen?"

"I was having a smoke on the deck, in my spot—the place where I met you," he said. "There wasn't much light from the moon. It was real calm, but cold. A storm was comin' in. I saw the doctor come out the hatch. He was drunk. I watched him lean up against the gunnel and I heard him puke over the side. I turned to flick my smoke into the water. Next thing I hear is a shout and a splash. I look back and the doctor ain't there no more."

"You said he was thrown. How do you know he didn't slip?"

"You've been on the boat. The gunnel—where he was standing—comes up around your chest. If he'd slipped, the only place he'd have landed would've been his ass. Going over the side there wasn't possible, not without help. And he wouldn't have been able to jump it. He weren't no athlete. And anyway, like I said, he was drunk, swaying about like the ground was movin' under his feet, only it wasn't."

"What about you, Mr. Cooke; were you also drunk at the time?"

"I'd had a drink or two, but I wasn't fallin' down."

"If you saw a man in the freezing water, why didn't you raise the alarm? Or throw in a life preserver?"

"He went under right away. I couldn't see him."

This didn't feel right. Cooke saw, or rather heard, a man go overboard, yet he'd done absolutely nothing about it. So what if he couldn't see him? With a little fast action, the doctor could have been saved. And then it hit me. "You wanted to see what would happen."

"What?"

"You said you saw him . . . I think the words you used were 'he got eat.' "

"Did I say that?"

"Yes, you did." I sensed a shrug coming down the line like I'd accused him of accidentally burning a hole in my parka with a cigarette. "You watched the shark eat a man for the hell of it—for entertainment." I had the image of Dr. Tanaka in the water, screaming for help, choking with white cold fear. No one would have heard his cries—everyone was at the party. Everyone except for Cooke, and according to him one other person—the killer.

"I didn't do no crime," Cooke said.

There's nothing in the rule book that makes it a crime to stand around eating popcorn while you watch someone else commit murder. There's also nothing in the rule book that said I couldn't make him squirm. "In a certain light, you could be portrayed as an accessory to murder. You witnessed a crime take place. You were right there, and you did nothing to stop it."

Cooke came back fighting. "Accessory? I don't think so. Like I said, it was a dark night, and the doctor was in shadow. It might be that I could change my mind about what I saw. And anyway, you know and I know, there ain't no crime in minding your own damn business."

I'd met plenty of people like this guy over the years, the type that enjoyed watching others take the heat and, in this particular instance, get eaten alive. "So what you saw was hidden in shadow, and you were also drunk," I told him. "That makes anything you might tell me worthless." Even a half-wit prosecutor could chew holes in this guy's so-called eyewitness account.

"There's a killer walking around who should be locked up. I'm just a concerned citizen, doing my duty."

"Yeah, right."

"Do you want to know who threw the doctor overboard, or don't you?" he said.

At this point, I had no investigation. That was because, according to the Tokyo Police and indeed to my own report, the one I was about to submit, no crime had been committed. So of course I was anxious to know if Dr. Tanaka had been murdered, only I didn't want to give this asshole the satisfaction of knowing he was the one about to wind me up and set me loose. Sometimes, though, Justice has to take whatever she can damn well get. "Just tell me what you *saw*," I said, making my voice sound bored.

"After the shark had had its fill, I saw another person on deck."

"You keep going on about how dark it was. So how come you can all of a sudden see someone's face out there?"

"I got a good look at him when he opened the hatch to go back inside. He stepped into the light."

This asshole was drawing it out like a wood splinter.

"I saw the professor," he said.

"Professor Boyle?" I asked, making sure.

"There weren't any other professors on board," he replied, enjoying the moment.

Why would Boyle murder his associate? The question reminded me of Durban and her story about the panda. Perhaps there was another shark there that night cruising the *Natusima*'s stern, a shark in a man's skin. "Where are you calling from, Mr. Cooke?" I asked.

"So now you're interested, right?"

I let the delay in the line answer for me.

"I'm on the *Natusima*," he said after a lengthy pause that ended with a cough.

"You still tied up in Yokohama Bay?"

"No. In the Philippine Sea, heading toward the Marianas. I'm using one of them satellite phones."

There was the delay accounted for. Wonderful. "Why didn't you tell me any of this when I was on your ship?"

"I wasn't sure about what I saw."

"And you are now?" I wondered if Cooke had waited to see if there were any angles worth playing. Had he perhaps unsuccessfully tried to blackmail Boyle before this attack of civic-mindedness had overcome him?

"Yeah—couldn't get it out of my head."

Sure.

"I also thought maybe you'd think I done it. And if

the professor fingers me, it's my word against his. Who're you going to believe—a guy who peels spuds for a living or a doofus with letters after his name?"

He had a point. But something about Professor Boyle didn't jell. And now I had a witness to the crime, albeit one whose story was as flimsy as a bride's negligé. The question now: What to do about it?

"When are you back in port, Mr. Cooke?" I could see myself being winched out of a helo onto the deck of the *Natusima* to take Cooke's statement in person. Like hell I could.

"Just over a week. We'll be pulling into Guam."

Guam: Andersen Air Force Base. I could get OSI there to take Cooke's statement or, failing that, someone from JAG. "Mr. Cooke, I want you to write down everything you've told me, date it, sign it, and have it witnessed by the ship's master. Then I want you to fax it to me." I gave him the number. "When you arrive at Guam, you'll get a visit from someone who'll ask you a bunch of questions."

"One of Santa's little helpers?"

"You got anything else you want to tell me?" I asked.

"Just Merry Christmas to you and Mrs. Claus."

The line went dead. He'd hung up. Mrs. Claus— Anna. "Thanks for reminding me, asshole," I said to the handset before putting it back on the cradle. I glanced again at the title page of Boyle's speech: "Playing God." I recalled my last meeting with Dr. Tanaka in the coroner's refrigerator. If Cooke wasn't lying, the professor sure was pretty good at smiting. The phone rang again.

"Hello, Arlen," I said.

"Who've you been talking to?"

"Don't I get a hello?"

"We've already done all that. I've been down here twenty minutes already."

"Where's down here?"

"The cafeteria."

I realized why he was angry: He was probably drinking the coffee. "Have I been on the phone all that time?" I looked at my watch. A good half an hour had passed since we'd last spoken.

"I don't know—you tell me. You've got seven minutes to get down here."

"You got anything for me?" I asked.

"That's six minutes, fifty-five seconds."

Seven minutes. Arlen was referring to the often-quoted brag that, despite occupying close to four million square feet and having three times the floor space of the Empire State Building, no point in the Pentagon was further than seven minutes away from any other point in the Pentagon. It's probably true, but only if you're Jesse Owens in spikes. I made it in eight minutes thirty.

The smell of the cafeteria always spoke to me well before I arrived there. What it was telling me was to turn around and run in the opposite direction. If I could have dissected that smell, it would have been a combination of sugar, deep-fried dough, grease, and the aforementioned coffee.

Despite this, however, the cafeteria was always reasonably full, as was the case this time, the gentle roar of hundreds of conversations rising toward the ceiling. It was a sea of uniforms. Every military service was represented here, mixed in with politicians, clerks, public servants, contractors, spooks—the individual cogs that made up the inner workings of the greatest fighting machine the world has ever known. The place had to be bugged.

I scanned the floor and saw Arlen standing, waving his arm above his head. On the small, round table in front of him were two cups of coffee, one half empty, and two sugar doughnuts, one with a bite out of it.

"Stale?" I said, gesturing at the spread.

"Yeah," he replied. "And so are the doughnuts. What took you?"

He wasn't expecting an excuse so I didn't offer one.

At the nearest table a couple of tanned, gray-haired marine gunnery sergeants stared angrily at a third man, also a marine, who wore the insignia of the JAG corps—a lawyer. He was speaking to them in hushed tones, underlining the point he was making with hand movements. Whatever he was saying, it wasn't giving the two older men a whole lot of joy. I wanted to tell the sergeants my current favorite lawyer joke to cheer them up, but I could sense that they were well beyond being humored, so, to get things rolling, I said to Arlen, "Hey . . . a couple of lawyers are in a bank when a gang of robbers bursts in and begins taking the money from the tellers. Another gang member lines the customers up and starts stripping them of their wallets, cash, and jewelry. While this is happening, Lawyer One feels something being jammed into his hand by his associate, Lawyer Two. Lawyer Number One whispers to Lawyer Two, 'What's this for?' To which Lawyer Number Two answers, 'It's all that money I owe you.' "

"They're not getting any better, are they?" said Arlen.

"Seemed appropriate," I said, gesturing at the JAG guy in a huddle with the marine sergeants.

"Where do you want to start?" Arlen asked, but he already had his own thoughts on how to get things under way because he said, almost immediately, "Vin, I'm sorry things worked out the way they did between you and Anna."

I gave him what I hoped would pass for a smile and said, "So how'd you make out with Moreton Genetics?" After a moment's hesitation, Arlen reached down to a briefcase at his feet and pulled out a plain manila folder, placing it on the table. I made a bet with myself that a hidden surveillance camera had picked up that action and captured it on tape.

"I think you should wait till you get out of here before you go through this," Arlen advised. His eyes held not the slightest flicker of emotion. Sometimes nothing can say everything.

"So," I said, placing the folder on my lap. "How's everything across the river?"

But something had distracted Arlen. The expression on his face had changed. In fact, he now had one. He was also looking past my shoulder. Somewhere close by, I heard a cup smash on the tiled floor. I was about to say, "Another happy customer..." when Arlen got to his feet. I glanced around and saw that several people were following suit. One of the Air Force lieutenants had her hand up against her mouth, her eyes wide with shock, and I realized that the entire cafeteria had fallen silent, like it was holding its breath. I'd experienced group shock like this only once before, one day in the month of September that was both a long time ago and just yesterday. I turned and saw all eyes focused on the television monitors scattered about the place. The channel was tuned to CNN. Then the cells and beepers began to ring, a chorus of two hundred assorted ringtones— Beethoven's Fifth, dogs barking, bells tolling, rock songs, rap, blues, applause, a door slamming, the growl of a NASCAR V8 revving up... My own cell was vibrating against my leg. On the television screen was a view being filmed from a network news chopper. The caption read, *Live*. Smoke, fire, and torrential rain made it difficult to see what was going on below the aircraft. The helo flew into relatively clear air revealing a familiar skyscraper with many of its upper-story windows smashed and its lower floors shrouded in smoke. The helo continued on past a building that had collapsed in on itself and was burning fiercely. A second title appeared on the screen.

It read, *San Francisco Attacked*.

NINE

When I arrived in San Francisco, the air was still heavy with dust that stank of burnt concrete, scorched paper, and cooked sewage. The smell took me back to Baghdad and Afghanistan and Kosovo, the three war zones I've been unlucky enough to experience firsthand. The smell would hang around for some time—it was the type that sticks to the back of the nostrils and puts down roots. San Franciscans wouldn't forget that smell for years to come, nor would any town downwind.

The Transamerica Pyramid building in downtown San Francisco was built to withstand significant earthquakes and so its structural integrity had not been compromised by the blast, despite numerous assertions by so-called experts on television that it would come down like a World Trade Center tower at any moment. Several other buildings in the immediate vicinity, in particular an upmarket apartment block, had fared far worse. That had been utterly consumed, along with the majority of its residents, by a gas explosion and subsequent fire. Broken glass had fallen away from buildings three blocks from the epicenters of the twin blasts, causing a frightful array of injuries.

A command center had been established two blocks from America's newest ground zero, within the closest building to have kept its windows. The place was a nightmare of shouting people, sirens, phones, and heartbreak. Homeland Security had assumed control, unless you talked to the FBI, who begged to differ. The San Francisco Police Department maintained the crime scene and so believed it was the lead agency, except that the San Francisco Fire Department was concerned about secondary cave-ins and gas leaks, which meant you couldn't get near the Transamerica Pyramid building without their consent and escort. The National Guard was securing the wider area, telling everyone where they could and couldn't go. CIA was there, covering its butt in the event that the culprits turned out to be on its watch list. And, of course, there was little ol' me, representing the DoD's interests. The situation reminded me of the one about the various parts of the body arguing over which was more important, the head because it did all the thinking, the heart because it pumped all the blood, the stomach because it processed all the food, the legs because they provided the locomotion, and so on. The joke went that eventually all the contenders agreed on the most important part of the body being the asshole, which won the argument. It did so by refusing to do its thing and clamping up solid. Within a couple of days, the brain could no longer think, the stomach could no longer deal with food, the legs couldn't move, and the heart threatened to stop pumping altogether. I wondered which agency would turn out to be the asshole here, a question quickly answered when the representatives from my fellow crime-fighting agencies were introduced to the CIA's SAC—the special agent in charge.

"Ah, Special Agent Cooper. So nice to see you again," the man said with a smile as genuine as his fluorescent teeth.

"You're a long way from Japan, Brady."

The smile never wavered. "I have always had a roving brief. And it's Bradley, Bradley Chalmers."

We shook on it. If I was not mistaken, he actually tried to roll my knuckles.

"So, what's the DoD's interest here?" he asked.

"Same as yours—to get in the way of the people doing the real work. How's the wife, by the way?"

I could tell Chalmers wanted to move on, but he also didn't want to desert the field of battle. "She's well. I wasn't aware you'd met her."

"I hadn't. Your girlfriend Michelle told me all about her."

"Ms. Durban? Girlfriend? Administrative assistant, more like, and not a very good one. I'm in the process of having her transferred."

Yeah, I was right about the asshole question being resolved. Before I could punch him in the nose, Chalmers was evacuated to a separate briefing by a harried captain of the SFFD.

The rest of us made our way to an area that had formerly housed a telemarketing operation. Rows of chairs faced a large whiteboard displaying unintelligible scribbles, plus a lectern displaying the crest of a well-known investment bank. A short, thickset man, dressed in a cheap suit, with a bald head so round and white it reminded me of the ball on a bottle of roll-on deodorant, made his way through the crowd and took up the position behind the lectern. His name was Captain Eugene Metzler. He was the lead detective from the SFPD heading up the crime-scene investigation. I'd already met Metzler briefly and I liked him— a tough, no-nonsense cop with the kind of halitosis that smacked of a serious garlic habit. Uniformed and plainclothes police flanked him. Metzler waved his arms over his head and said "Hello" a couple of times into the lectern's microphone in the hope of generating some quiet in the room. After a few unsuccessful attempts at this, he gave up. He nodded to a fellow cop, who brought his fingers to his lips and whistled loud enough to make me wince.

"Hello, can I have your attention!" Metzler's voice boomed through the speakers into the sudden silence.

He cleared his throat, then continued. "OK. So we got a lot of people here working for different masters, but last I heard we're all on the one payroll so we thought it appropriate to share with you our initial findings and thoughts. I don't need to remind you that everything said in this room must remain confidential, at least until further notice. We have a team liaising with the press so no one needs to talk to the media. I hope everyone's clear on that..." Metzler referred to a sheet of paper in his hand. "Working in conjunction with the Federal Bureau of Investigation, as well as the various departments within the SFPD, we can now confirm that a vehicle loaded with explosives—ammonium nitrate and diesel fuel, we think—parked out front of the Transamerica building, was the cause of the initial explosion." He had the room's full attention.

"Surveillance cameras picked up this vehicle in front of the building shortly before the explosion. I can confirm that it belonged to a courier company and that it had been stolen from a location in south central Los Angeles a week before the bombing."

There was a general nod from the audience. Progress.

"We also believe that the secondary gas explosion was deliberate. It originated beneath the Four Winds apartment complex, in its basement parking lot, which accounts for the high levels of loss of life and damage at that location. Forensics has yet to conclude how the gas leak was engineered or how the explosion was touched off. They're telling us we should know within the next twenty-four hours.

"All this would seem to indicate a highly organized, systematic attack, though no organization has so far claimed responsibility for the bombing. That is all we have at present. I don't have to remind you all that if you come across information important to this case, share it.

"Another progress report will be given in ten hours' time at four this afternoon. That is all, thank you."

A firestorm of questions followed, which I didn't hang around for. Metzler had given up everything his team had found and, I noted on the issue of solid leads to go on with, that was a fat zero.

I made my way to the office Metzler was using. I badged the guardsmen covering the door. "I have an appointment," I said to the young sergeant. She looked at me like I was a ghost, then let me pass. I'd received that same look before. DoD investigators are mythical creatures, up there with yetis and unicorns. That uniqueness has its uses, one of them being the ability to open doors others found locked.

Inside, I scoped Metzler's seconded office. Nice digs. According to the various Kodak moments scattered around, the usual occupant was a young guy who earned far too much money. His girlfriend—it could have been his wife—was too good looking. He drove a Dodge Viper, water-skied, went parachuting, and liked to go deep-sea fishing with his buddies. A vacation snap showing him standing beside a large shark caught my attention. The fish was hanging by its tail over some wharf down in the Florida Keys, with its guts spilling out its mouth. Maybe sharks had a case for revenge, after all.

Metzler arrived ten minutes late, peeling his collar undone and loosening his tie as he made his way to the desk. The desk phone was ringing. He picked it up, his back to me. He listened for half a dozen seconds and then said, "Aw, shit, I don't know! *You* work it out!" before slamming down the receiver.

He turned and gave a small jump when he finally saw me. "Christ, how did you get in?" he demanded.

"Actually, the name's Cooper. Through the front door, and I can come back," I replied.

"No, sorry. It's all right. I remember. Special Agent Cooper, right? DoD?"

I nodded, impressed by the guy's memory. He'd met at least a hundred new faces in the last couple of hours.

He gestured at the phone. "We've got six hundred wounded—crush injuries, cuts, broken bones—and nowhere to take them. Not my problem."

Something about Metzler's manner told me he'd make it his problem. I'd heard about this guy. San Francisco was his town, and he cared about it.

"So," he said, "you want to tell me what the DoD's interest is in this event?"

"We're concerned about one of the residents of the Four Winds apartment block."

"You and fifty thousand others."

I hoped all those thousands weren't interested in the same person I was.

Metzler elaborated. "Seems everyone living there had a dozen relatives apiece."

"How many you got missing?"

"Plenty. A lot of people are buried under a hundred thousand tons of rubble. Not many managed to get out of the Four Winds alive. It went up at nine A.M. Most everyone home at that time were mothers with small children under school age, old folk, retirees— slow movers."

Captain Metzler was obviously affected by the things he'd seen down at what was left of the Four Winds. His chin quivered and he had to take a moment. "Could have been worse," he continued. "If it had been hit early in the morning, we'd have had double the casualties."

I nodded.

"At last count, we had a hundred and sixty-five unaccounted for. But we were missing over two hundred and fifty yesterday, so we are finding people. You been down there?"

I shook my head. I hadn't. I've seen enough destroyed buildings with people trapped inside to know what they looked like. "What about the Transamerica building?"

"Superficial damage, and surprisingly few casualties. They had antiblast traffic barriers in place on the street, as well as bombproof glass on the lower floors installed recently as part of a general security upgrade."

"Who're you looking at? Any clues?" I asked. There were rumors and guesses. Media commentators suggested the usual suspects who get fingered every time a bomb goes off in the Western world.

"Some seriously fucked-up nutcases. I'll let you know when we narrow it down further."

Something about this didn't feel right. Terrorist bombings were usually meticulously planned and executed so as to cause maximum damage to life and/or property. Sure, the Transamerica had taken a hit, but it was more of a jab than a knockout punch. A few doors down the road at the Four Winds, however, it was a different story. The place was completely destroyed, and intentionally, according to forensics and bomb squad people. If I didn't know better, I'd have said the bombing on the Transamerica was no more than a diversionary tactic and that the real target was the apartment building. Only, why would a terrorist organization light the blue touch paper under an apartment building? I glanced at Metzler. He was watching me think, or maybe he was listening to the cogs whirring. Whatever, I had the feeling he was holding out on me. "You want to tell me what you really think happened here?" I asked.

Metzler's arms were so tightly wrapped around himself that he looked like he was wearing a straitjacket. He unfolded his arms, picked up a pencil, and drummed it on the edge of the table beside his leg. "OK, we have got a theory," he said. "Actually, we're hoping it's more like a coincidence." He continued drumming on the desk, but didn't speak. Whatever this coincidence was, it appeared to be causing him some anxiety. I gave him a little push. "Didn't someone out there," I said, gesturing at the door, "say it was important to share?"

He gave me a half smile. "First I want to know why the DoD is sniffing around—and who is this person you're interested in? Or perhaps I should say *was*—because if he or she was in the Four Winds, there won't be much left to have any interest in."

"A guy doing some work for us lived in that building. I was just following up," I said.

"What kind of guy? A bad guy?"

"Jury's still out on that point."

"Right about now I'm just lovin' this spirit of cooperation."

"Sorry. National security issues." I'd given him nothing, which was basically all I was authorized to offer.

The captain picked up another pencil from the desk and tapped out a beat with it. "I'd appreciate it if you'd keep a lid on what I'm about to tell you, at least until this afternoon when we're releasing it as a possible motive—unless something else comes up."

"Cross my heart," I said.

"OK . . ." Metzler fiddled with the pencil some more as if he hadn't convinced himself of the wisdom of letting me in on the latest. "We lost a team of good cops in the Four Winds. Eight men and women. We had a wise guy under observation there, in one of the Four Winds' serviced apartments. A big fish—the biggest. We'd turned him. He was supposed to be meeting a bunch of other wise guys for breakfast half an hour *after* the gas leak exploded."

One of the phones on the desk began to ring. Metzler ignored it.

"You think his breakfast associates found out about it?"

Metzler nodded. "There's that chance. The timing was impeccable."

"You're saying the real target was not the Transamerica?"

"Yeah. It looks to us like the bomb in front of the Transamerica building was—is—a diversion. The perpetrators wanted us to think it was a terrorist job."

I felt hollow inside. So, nearly a thousand men, women, and children killed a couple of days before

Christmas to keep a godfather from spilling the beans? "And keeping the wise guy bottled up in the safe house was your operation?" I asked.

"Uh-huh."

That was tough. Along with everything else, Metzler had to be swimming in an ocean of guilt. I reached into my pocket, pulled out the photocopies of various documents, as well as a photo, and spread them on the desk. "This is the guy we're missing."

Metzler took a look. "Is that a bowl on his head?" he asked.

It wasn't a great photo of Professor Sean Boyle, but then I didn't think the guy was particularly photogenic. "No," I said.

"Has he got any relatives?"

"Only Uncle Sam," I said. "That's why I'm here."

By now, both phones on Metzler's desk were ringing. So was his cell. Someone was also knocking on the door. I'd taken up too much of the captain's time.

TEN

Before I'd left, Metzler had promised to do what he could, circulating the documents among the emergency services crews without giving a specific reason for the fuss, but he warned that things were still a mess. There were plenty of victims of the bombing suffering severe shock with no clue who they were, and plenty of corpses burned beyond recognition. It could take weeks to sort through the identity issues. He said it was likely that some people might never be found or accounted for. He also advised me to keep an eye on the Web site where the names of the newly positively identified were being posted every minute. More than that, he warned, he couldn't do.

I made my way through the confusion of the command center and headed for the exit. Outside, I took shelter under an awning. It was raining heavily, the weather aligning with the city's mood. Low gray clouds scudded across a backdrop of a deeper gray and dumped buckets of the Pacific Ocean on the frantic rescue attempts still going on down in Clay and Montgomery streets. Sirens, seemingly hundreds of them, wailed and screamed through the dark city canyons.

Somewhere close by, there were helicopters in the sky, hovering, braving the nil visibility.

I ran to my vehicle, an old beige Ford Crown Vic, with my jacket bunched up over my head. The car had been left for me to pick up at the airport. The thing sagged to the left when I sat in it. Inside, it reeked of sweat, cigarettes, and stale sex.

The financial district had been evacuated and sealed off by the National Guard. The streets not in use by the emergency crews were eerily deserted. I drove to the checkpoint and stopped beside a huddle of Humvees and a cluster of armed guardsmen wearing black ponchos slick with rain. I hit the switch and the window came down.

"Sir?" said a kid with a high voice and an M16 who barely filled out his uniform. "Can I help you?"

"I'm heading to Palo Alto. What's the best route through the city?"

"It's all gone to crap beyond here, I'm afraid, sir." He put his head in the window and pointed down the street. I smelled beer and ham sandwiches. "You're on Grant. Continue straight ahead till you get to Market. Then turn right and go all the way till you get to Van Ness. You'll know you're going the right way when you see signs for Highway 101."

I repeated the instructions to make sure I had them straight. The kid nodded and his helmet nearly fell off, sliding forward over his eyes.

The directions turned out to be meaningless. With the financial district closed to public access, a major part of the city's road system had been effectively amputated. Beyond the guard's control point, the traffic became a snarling tangle of flashing lights, patrol cars, detours, and gridlock.

The detours funneled the traffic through the retail part of town, where Santa Claus reigned like a South American dictator. Posters and plastic models of the fat guy were everywhere, along with tinsel, lights, and the usual Christmas paraphernalia.

Santa Claus. Seeing him reminded me of Al Cooke, the cook aboard the *Natusima,* the man who accused Sean Boyle of throwing his research partner, Dr. Tanaka, into the waiting mouth of a hungry great white shark. I reminded myself not to be so dramatic. The shark wasn't exactly waiting. And weren't the damn things *always* hungry?

I crawled past a group of people taking down the display of a sleigh pulled by reindeer. The bombing had stripped everyone of their Christmas cheer.

It took three hours to reach the 101, where things began to move quicker. The highway wound its way in a southeasterly direction through passing showers and tendrils of shredded cloud. Off to the left, San Francisco Bay hid behind a wall of solid rain. Meanwhile, the highway ran through a sea of fast-food joints, tire stores, and car dealerships.

An overhead sign said the turnoff I was looking for was coming up in two miles. Boyle was a geneticist. His "Playing God" speech had discussed the science involved in creating what he termed "designer life"—life created by genetically reengineering existing life forms to do specific tasks. I hadn't understood his speech completely, but the gist was easy to follow. Basically, according to Boyle, it was now possible to genetically engineer organisms and then patent them. Companies could own a new life form and demand royalty payments for its use year after year. There were examples of drugs being produced in this way, as well as various seeds used in agriculture. Theoretically, it was even possible to produce human-animal hybrids that, despite looking and acting the same as human beings, had a slightly different genome that was patented, meaning these human beings weren't technically human at all and therefore had no constitutional protection, no rights. They could thus be owned, a euphemism for enslaved. Nice.

In his speech, Boyle said that while this sounded like science fiction, a lot of it was technically feasible right now, with the balance theoretically possible in the not-too-distant future. For example, tomatoes could be reengineered with a gene from sole—the fish—that resisted freezing, allowing the fruit to be kept in freezers so that it could be stored longer. It was now possible to reengineer salmon to grow to forty times their normal size. The speech gave numerous examples of how this technology was pervading all our lives.

Boyle's specific area of interest was in the genetic reengineering of bacteria to produce new medicines.

It all sounded scary, and yet, in the way Boyle couched it, noble. This research was being done not for corporate profits, but for the betterment of humankind. Except that, according to the information obtained by Arlen, Boyle was in fact working on a new type of organism that was so secret there was no documented outline of exactly what it was. But there were clues. Boyle's partnership with Tanaka was unique. Both men were renowned experts in their respective, seemingly unrelated, fields. Tanaka was a marine biologist specializing in deep-sea life, specifically the search for previously undiscovered organisms that lived in the ultrahostile environments provided by hydrothermal vents. So Tanaka came up with new life, the genes of which Boyle manipulated to produce...what? Something the DoD was prepared to pay big money for.

I reached the turnoff. The road brought me out at the gates of an area of light industrial compounds. Signs pointed the way to Moreton Genetics. I followed them until I saw the distinctive double-helix building raised above the plain on its man-made hill. A high electrified fence surrounded the complex. There were plenty of surveillance cameras. I took a left turn into the security checkpoint, a brick bunker with a heavy steel gate across the access road. More cameras. A fit young woman accompanied by a bodybuilder type complete with roid acne came out to check on my reasons for being here.

"Good morning, sir," said the woman in a perky way, taking the lead, all teeth and blond hair, leaning into my open window. She wore a short-sleeved white shirt stretched across a lean, athletic torso. The double-helix symbol was embroidered on a breast pocket. The name tag pinned below it informed me her name was *"Jacki."* Jacki and partner—I immediately named him Jill—wore the ubiquitous security earpiece. A Taser stun gun was clipped to her belt. Jill, similarly dressed and blond, the sleeves of his short-sleeved shirt looking like tourniquets around his pumped upper arms, was likewise packing. Were they expecting trouble here at MG?

"Morning," I replied to Jacki.

"So, how can I help you today, sir?" she asked, beaming bright enough to give me a tan.

"Special Agent Vin Cooper, Department of Defense. I have an appointment with Dr. Freddie Spears." I gave her a good look at my DoD credentials. So far, so good. I rarely called ahead when I wanted to interview someone, particularly when that someone might not want to be interviewed. Still, I had made sure Dr. Spears would be out at MG by making an appointment and using the name of a *TIME* journalist lifted from the magazine's editorial credits. Dr. Spears would be crazy not to stick around for an interview with the respected magazine read by thousands of potential MG stock buyers, wouldn't he? So I could assume the guy was in; I just had to get to him, and that meant getting past Jacki and Jill.

Jill extracted a personalized digital assistant from a pocket and began stabbing at it with a pencil-like implement. After a few moments, he shook his head and showed Jacki the screen.

"That's Cooper with a *C*," I said helpfully.

The guy shook his head again.

Jacki's smile switched to a look of concern. "I'm sorry, sir, but you're not on our list of today's visitors."

"Gee," I said, matching her concern with some of my own. "Freddie's expecting me. We're old friends. He'll be real disappointed if I don't show up."

I must have said something wrong because Jacki's expression became instantly suspicious. "Can I ask what this is in regard to, sir?"

Time to come out swinging. "Sure, you can ask, but it's none of your business, so I probably wouldn't tell you," I said, confusing her with my sweetest smile. "But what you can do is tell Freddie that Special Agent Vin Cooper from the DoD is here to see him. You can also tell him I'm filling in for Steve Liu from *TIME*, and that I don't seem to appreciate being kept waiting. And then let's just see if my name doesn't miraculously appear on that PDA of yours."

I wasn't sure what it was about these two that stuck in my craw. It could have been the fact that they looked like a couple of dummies in a gym-equipment store window. But it could also have been the Tasers, those nasty little antipersonnel devices on their hips, that set me off. I'd trained with this so-called non-lethal weapon. It fired a pair of probes attached to the "gun" by small wires. An electric current designed to disable the human nervous system surged down those wires and through the probes, curling the target into a helpless quivering ball on the ground. Trouble was, far too often those electrical impulses had the same effect on the heart, stopping it permanently.

"There is no need to be rude, sir," she replied.

"Jacki, this is not me being rude. This is me being obstinate and determined. But I can do rude if it would make you feel more comfortable. Although, trust me, it wouldn't."

Her mouth opened and closed a couple of times, and her partner was speaking into a handset while giving me his best glare. Jacki touched a finger to her ear and then disappeared briefly inside the bunker. Maybe she was feeling the cold, after all. Or perhaps it was to activate the gate, which swung outward.

"Have a nice day," I called to them as I drove through. One of the cameras followed me—like the eyes in those paintings, the ones in old horror movies. I'd been to sensitive military establishments with less security. Again I wondered why a nice, friendly company like MG would need to arm its gate guards with Tasers.

The access road meandered through the reeds, birds, and, no doubt, the rare endangered species of frogs and pond slime featured on the Web site. The drive gave me time to think about how I was going to play this interview. Chip Schaeffer had given me the green light to pay MG a visit. His tone had shifted from the earlier stay-the-hell-away mode to the maybe-go-have-a-snoop-around one. Frankly, his change of heart made me nervous. Something was going on at the DoD, and I'd had enough experience with this feeling to be wary of it.

As I drew nearer, I glanced up at the MG complex crowning the top of the man-made hill. The structure was a lot bigger than it appeared to be on the Web. It was also an extraordinary feat of both architecture and engineering. A movement out to the right caught my attention. It was a golf buggy, a couple of security personnel on board. I was either being shadowed or we all happened to be heading to the next tee.

A heavy rain shower crashed down, reminding me of a descending curtain. I hit the button to wind up the window, but the electric motor chose that moment to expire with the window stuck two thirds of the way up. The smell of burnt wires filled my nostrils. I swore as the rain began to slant in through the opening, soaking my sleeve and pants. I turned in toward the complex and pulled into a covered foyer. Through the condensation covering the windscreen, I saw I had a reception committee waiting.

I climbed out of the Crown Vic, a suspicious-looking wet patch stretching from groin to knee. "Shit," I said, pulling the soaked, freezing fabric away from my skin.

"Special Agent Cooper," said a woman's voice. "I'm Dr. Spears."

I looked up. What? Freddie was a woman? *Freddie's expecting me. We're old friends.* He'll *be real disappointed if I don't show up.* No wonder Jacki and Jill at the front gate had lost their happy faces. When I'd surfed the Moreton Genetics Web site, Dr. Spears's picture hadn't been posted. And when I'd called to see if the doc was in, I hadn't thought to check the male/female angle. I'd just put "Doctor," "CEO," and "Freddie" together and come up with a bald guy in his mid-fifties wearing thick glasses and a lab coat. "Frederique?" I asked.

Dr. Spears nodded and even added a smile. "You're not the first to make the mistake and I'm sure you won't be the last. And I gather, along with being Special Agent Cooper, you're also Steve Liu, *TIME* journalist?"

"Yeah, sorry about that," I said.

She shrugged and gave me her public-relations smile, not overly perturbed by the ruse. "It worked, didn't it? Got you in. But I assume you do have the appropriate credentials—this is a high-security facility."

"I noticed."

"Do you mind?" She held out her hand and I gave her my badge. She examined it in detail for several seconds before returning it.

Satisfied, she said, "So, Special Agent Cooper. Pleased to meet you." She held out her hand to shake. I obliged. The grip was firm but still womanly, businesslike. I figured she'd had plenty of opportunities to get the pressure just right. "Come inside. I'll get you a towel."

She gave the MG security personnel—both carrying Tasers—a nod. They drifted away.

I guessed Dr. Freddie Spears was in her late forties, though she looked a little younger. She was a naturally large-boned woman who, I surmised, had an eternal struggle with weight. Currently, she was winning the battle. Rightly or wrongly, I had the impression that this close to Hollywood you had to look younger than your age if you had any hope of trampling over your contemporaries on the way up the corporate ladder. She wore a gray silk skirt with a hemline below her knees, and matching jacket. Her hair was black, dyed, worn in a bob, and her earlobes featured diamonds that were too big to be real, only I guessed I was wrong on that score. There was a matching diamond on a thin gold chain at the base of her throat. Her wedding finger was bare. Including her shoes I guessed she was wearing about a hundred grand. If Mattel ever got around to making an executive power doll for the daughters of corporate-conscious parents to play with, I could see it modeled on Doc Spears.

I walked beside her across the black slate floor. A vast glass wall slid soundlessly to one side as we approached. Inside was a cavern of glass and triangulated steel that formed intricate patterns high overhead. A big LCD screen monitor, tuned to the mess going on in the city, held a large group of people enthralled. "Are you involved with the tragic business down at the Four Winds?" Spears asked.

"No. Not directly."

"It's terrible about Professor Boyle being caught up in that."

"Terrible," I agreed, although if he'd done what I thought he'd done to Dr. Tanaka, dying quickly over a bowl of breakfast cereal like so many of his fellow residents at the Four Winds was probably not terrible enough. "Moreton Genetics has had a bit of bad luck lately."

"You mean with what happened to Dr. Tanaka too? Yes, awful."

Awful, terrible, tragic. If we kept going along this
line too much longer, we'd be reaching for the the-
saurus. A young male sat behind a glass desk, a slim
stainless-steel laptop the only object on it, answering
phone inquiries through a headset while his eyes
were locked on the news report. Dr. Spears had a
quick word with him. I scoped the place while I
waited. The waiting room for corporate visitors was
up a set of stairs like thin steel blades leading to a Per-
spex floor suspended from the roof on cables. Visitors
could sit there on blocks covered in dark chocolate-
colored leather. The hard, impersonal nature was
softened only by a collection of very large and brightly
colored beanbags on the main floor.

"Just organized a towel for you."

"Thanks."

"They're supposed to represent living cells," said
Spears, anticipating my question about the beanbags.
"Can't see it myself."

I couldn't, either.

"Do you get the symbolism of this place?" she
asked as she entered a glass box I suddenly realized
was an elevator, holding open the door for me.

"The double helix? The molecule of life?"

"Very good. Two right-handed polynucleotide
chains coiled around the same axis. The colored steel
arms you can see represent the proteins adenine,
thymine, cytosine, and guanine. The white bars are
the hydrogen bonds."

If my answer was "very good," then why did I

suddenly feel like a thumb-sucking three-year-old talking to a grown-up?

"The double helix—we sometimes call it a Slinky," she added.

"Thanks," I mumbled. "You'd lost me there for a second."

"The truth is, a lot of it is still beyond us. For example, we can see why each tiny change in the combination of those proteins leads to a radical change in the organism, but we just don't get how this bunch of chemicals . . . well, comes alive."

"And then sits down to watch a game of football with a six-pack of Budweiser on its belly?"

Dr. Spears laughed. "Actually, yes. Exactly. The team that consulted with the architects who designed this building played an expensive joke on our stockholders. Like I said, small changes in the protein sequences lead to radical changes in the organism. So we thought we were getting a representation of a mouse, the animal that has been used so extensively by science to uncover the mysteries of life. But when we actually checked, we discovered we were working within the gene for the plague."

The elevator stopped, the doors slid open, and Dr. Spears led the way into a glass-walled room suspended in space by lattices of color-coded steel bars. I saw that the entire level was made up of a number of glass-walled rooms secured to the main structure and suspended eighty or so feet above the ground. All the people I could see were wearing business suits.

"So where do all the people in white coats work?"
I asked Spears.

The doctor handed me a towel that had been placed
on the boardroom table. "All this is just admin, accounting, sales, marketing. Below us—underground—
is where most of our research is done. Please have a
seat," she said. "Water?"

I declined. I'd had enough of the stuff already. I
took the digital voice recorder from my pocket and
placed it on the table. "Hope you don't mind, Doc.
I've been known to forget my own mother's name."

"No problem." Spears wore an executive smile that
packed as much warmth as a cardboard box in No-
vember. "How can I help you today?"

"Doc, I spent last week in Japan, investigating the
possible murder of Dr. Tanaka—"

She blinked and leaned forward in her seat.
"Murder?"

"I said *possible* murder."

"But I thought...Hideo had been attacked by a
shark."

"A witness has come forward."

"Oh, my god...who—"

"What sort of relationship did Dr. Tanaka and Professor Boyle have?"

The doctor frowned. "You believe Professor Boyle
could have had something to do with Hideo's murder?"

Spears was no dummy. "Don't infer too much from
my questions, Doc. I'm just following lines of inquiry."

"I knew Hideo better than I know Sean. He was
vocal about his passion—a real fanatic. The deep sea

was his life and he was determined to imbue everyone with a sense of wonder about what a special world it was down there. Sean is more reserved—keeps pretty much to himself. They were both great scientists, at the very top of their respective fields. I believe they got along, but more because they were opposites attracting than because they were best friends."

"So they were buddies."

"They weren't enemies," she corrected.

"What were they working on?" I asked, knowing exactly what the answer would be.

"Can't tell you that, Special Agent. You'll have to find out through channels at your end. All I can say is that they were working on something for you, or rather, your employer. But as a DoD investigator, you know that, otherwise you wouldn't be here, right?"

Doc Spears might have been surprised to hear how little I actually did know. As for the secrecy issue, there was always the chance she might forget about all the agreements she'd signed to keep her mouth shut. Yeah, about as much chance as I'd have of waking up married to Penelope Cruz. Next question. "How long had Tanaka and Boyle been working together?"

"Their research program had been running around two and a half years."

"Is it unusual for two specialists from completely different branches of science to work together?"

"Not so long ago, I'd have said yes, because until recently there was very little collaboration between the branches of science. But that's changing these days. There's a growing realization that intuitive leaps in one field can sometimes come from another entirely different one. The newer branches of science, like genetics, are helping this along. Here at MG we have geneticists working with medical doctors, agriculturalists, infectious disease specialists, and so on."

I threw a curve ball. "Why's it necessary to arm your security personnel?"

"What's that got to do with Dr. Tanaka's death?"

"At the moment, Doc, as to what's relevant, I don't know what is and what isn't."

She gave a barely perceptible shrug. "There are a large number of people who don't agree with what MG does. We gained a public profile from the work we did eradicating the varroa mite. You know about that?"

"Yes."

"Well, not all the attention was helpful or positive. We've had our fair share of threats and demonstrations. Some from religious fanatics—the sort of people who are convinced Galileo should have been burned at the stake. Others from environmental extremist groups. And then there are always the animal rights activists. Finally, there's the possibility—remote though it may seem in these days of wireless information transfer—of industrial spies sneaking around. The weapon you're referring to is the Taser, I assume?"

"Uh-huh."

"Which is purely defensive and nonlethal. We have

a duty of care to the people we employ to protect us. They require their own protection." She tilted her head and put a finger to her lips as if she was considering both her answer and the question. "You might not know what's relevant or not to your investigation, Special Agent, but would you mind telling me at least *why* you're asking?"

"Arming your security with NLWs like Tasers seems a little at odds with your public profile—the friendly, socially aware, politically correct one you push so hard. I checked out your Web site, Doc, and you're greener than green, with a halo Mother Teresa would have envied."

"Welcome to business in the new millennium." She said it defensively.

"I'd like to talk to some of the people who worked with Tanaka and Boyle."

"I'm sorry, Special Agent, but that's impossible. Unless I get the proper security clearances. Provide them, and you can talk to whomever you choose."

I doubted that I would get those clearances without a ton of forms signed in triplicate, by which time everyone would have lost interest—at least on the subject of who did what to whom, especially when "who" was now, in all probability, every bit as dead as "whom." But my gut told me people at the Pentagon were worrying about something going on here at Moreton Genetics, only no one wanted to turn on the lights and give me a good look at whatever it was. "So tell me, Dr. Spears, what happens with the Tanaka/Boyle research program? Do you shut it down, file it away? Or does someone else take it over?"

"Much of their research program was backed up. We've got their hard disks but unfortunately we've lost their genius. Professor Boyle and Dr. Tanaka were unique, Agent Cooper. They are irreplaceable. Nevertheless, we're hopeful of being able to pick up the threads."

The doctor might have been hopeful, but she didn't seem all that certain. Maybe without Tanaka and Boyle on the job, the program was dead in the water. No pun intended. I waited for more information but none came. Spears glanced at her watch, and then at the door of another glass box across the void, impatient to be someplace else. "Special Agent, I'm sorry, but I have another appointment. If you have no other questions . . . ?"

"Just one more, Doc, for the moment. Can you think of any reason why Professor Boyle would want to murder Dr. Tanaka?"

"Oh, my god . . . so you really think that's what happened?" Spears leaned forward and wrung her hands. "You think Sean threw Hideo into the jaws of a shark? Is that what your witness saw?"

"As I said, I'm just checking lines of inquiry." I ignored her questions and reiterated mine. "So—any reason?"

The doctor shook her head slowly. "No . . . no . . ." But the way she said it, the fright in her face as she stared back at me, I wasn't so sure.

ELEVEN

At the MG security gate, I gave Jacki and Jill a parting wave and earned scowls and folded arms in return. The drive back to town was slow going. Twenty minutes out on the 101, the traffic ground to a halt in a snarl that trapped me between two exits. Also, either the fuel gauge was broken or the engine was running on fumes. It didn't look like I was going anywhere for a while, so I killed the ignition. The motor kept going, though, rumbling and coughing until it finally made up its mind to stop with a knocking sound that also violently shook the vehicle.

There was nothing to do but sit and think. I had a dead Dr. Tanaka, murdered, according to an unreliable witness, by a now-dead Professor Boyle, who was himself killed by an apparent attack of either karma or bad luck—I could take my pick. I had the company they were working for, Moreton Genetics, saying nothing, as mute as the people back in Washington who were paying all the bills. I also had ice-rain slanting in through the broken window like a shower of little razor blades. I needed something to stuff in the gap. There was plenty of rubbish on the floor of the passenger side—disposable cups and burger wrappers—but nothing that wouldn't get turned to instant mush by the deluge, so I shook the pages out of the manila folder Arlen had given me and used the folder. Then, with nothing better to do than watch the steady stream of emergency vehicles making their way up and down the lanes closed to all other traffic, I flipped through the material itself. I'd already skimmed most of it, except for an addendum about the latest in NLWs—nonlethal weapons.

That was intriguing in itself. Arlen had included it for a reason. Did it confirm, in an oblique way, that what Tanaka, Boyle, and Moreton Genetics were developing was some sort of biological nonlethal weapon? Or was it included because MG had developed NLWs for the military in the past? As for NLWs, generally speaking, the "nonlethal" part was a misnomer. It implied some caring for the target on the part of the targeter. From my knowledge, however, no one had ever been disabled by a nonlethal weapon that carefully placed them in a comfy chair with a hot dog. More often than not, NLWs were used to set up the target for a sucker punch, which was, in most instances, lethal in the extreme.

Arlen's notes confirmed this. There was a description of the Taser, which I already knew about. There was also a page about the missile that fried all electronic circuitry within a three-hundred-yard range so that an air base could be approached and stealthily overwhelmed by an attacking force and, theoretically, wiped out without one of our people breaking so much as a fingernail. I had no ethical problem with this—if someone was going to get killed in a battle, I was all for it being the other guy. But, being in the language police, the term "nonlethal" made me want to reach for my handcuffs and call for backup.

I checked the traffic situation. No one in front or behind was moving. It occurred to me that it was the night before Christmas and nothing was stirring except for San Francisco's entire fleet of emergency services vehicles. I went back to reading.

Here was something I didn't know: stuff called "Liquid Ball-Bearings" containing hollow smart particles that released an ultraslippery agent in response to heat. The idea was that you could spray it on a doorknob, making it impossible to twist open by anyone not wearing special gloves. It could also be sprayed on floors, saving a fortune on banana skins. It was totally nontoxic and water-soluble. I could see it being placed in kids' Christmas stockings sooner or later, along with the next item, called "Spray 'n' Stay." Cute. Again nontoxic and biodegradable, this was a substance created by the genetic modification of a protein used by the orb-weaving spider in the production of its web. The spray, which came out of the nozzle as a kind of string, quick-dried as strong and fine as fishing line. Who came up with this shit? Silly question. I knew that already and two of them were dead.

The car behind me honked. I hadn't noticed that the traffic had started to move. I turned the key. The starter motor ground out a dirge. I gave it another try.

Same result. First it didn't want to stop and now it didn't want to start. I tried again and it rumbled into reluctant life.

I turned on the headlights. The tourist blurb I'd found in my hotel room said night didn't fall around here till five o'clock at this time of year, but it was only four-thirty and it was already dark.

As the section of traffic jam I was in nudged toward the city, I could see the smoking Transamerica building, helicopters circling it, spotlights on full flood. I rang the cell number Eugene Metzler had given me. After half a dozen rings, he answered it with a snarled, "Yeah?"

"Eugene, Vin Cooper."

"Yeah, Cooper, what can I do for you? Haven't seen you around here."

"Wanted to keep out of your hair."

"Please, no hair jokes. What can I do you for?"

"Just checking in. You still thinking it was a hit on a wise guy made to look like something else?"

"Yeah. Be honest with you, Cooper. Some things don't fit but it's still the only theory that makes any sense to my people. We got no one sticking their hand up to take credit, except for the usual bunch of crackpots. But no one did for 9/11, right? Also, we've got a preliminary report in from the FBI forensics teams. The gas leak at the Four Winds was intentional. The gas main was tampered with and they've found the ignition system—an electric spark unit straight off a barbecue, wired to a pager."

"Would you know if my guy has turned up yet?" I asked.

"Remind me. Who's your guy again?"

"One of the residents at the Four Winds. Sean Boyle."

"No, he hasn't turned up. What floor was he on?"

"The third." I gave him the apartment number.

"OK, well, I'm just gonna tell you again what I might have told you already. Where the gas explosion originated meant those bottom floors were the worst hit. Unless your professor happened to be out splitting the atom someplace else, you can cross him off your Christmas list, because only Jesus and the angels are gonna be on his."

Or maybe the other guy would be on his list, I thought, the one downstairs with horns and a pitchfork.

"Take down this number," Metzler said. "It's for one of my people, Detective Sergeant Ed Rudenko. Tell Ed I told you to call. He's coordinating the missing-persons angle. It might take a bit of persistence to get through as he's kinda busy right at the moment."

I jammed my knees under the steering wheel while I dug a pen out of my jacket and wrote the number down on the back of Arlen's notes. "Listen, Captain," I said, feeling a little guilty about the prospect of having a lazy tumbler of Glen Keith by the fire back at the hotel bar, "you need a hand with anything? Happy to help—"

"I appreciate the offer, Cooper, but we got enough

cooks spoiling the broth down here already. Hey, maybe there is something you could do," he said. "You being a fed an' all . . . could you come up with a strategy to get this CIA guy off my back?"

"Is this CIA guy like a dose of stomach flu dressed up as a Brooks Brothers model?"

"I get the clothing reference, but stomach flu?"

"He gets up your nose and then gives you the shits," I replied.

"Yeah. That about nails him."

"So, Bradley Chalmers . . . what's he up to?" I asked.

"Making life difficult. He's looking for someone or something, but won't tell us who or what. We got a crime scene down here and the guy's jumping all over it like it's a trampoline while he orders people around in the name of national security."

I had no jurisdiction over Chalmers. If anything, the jerk outranked me, the CIA being a lead agency at the scene.

"Sorry, can't help you, Captain. All I can tell you is that the guy's a known asshole wanted in Japan for crimes against his spouse."

"Hey, stop right there. You're speaking to a happily divorced man—three times. I'm liable to break out in sympathy for the guy. Look, gotta go, Cooper. Good luck."

I thanked him and let him get on with his day, which would probably keep stretching through the evening and into the following weeks. I wondered why I was so down on Chalmers. The man was a philanderer, but then, as a famous guy once said, go ahead and throw a stone if you reckon you're any better. Maybe I was still hurting over the way my own marriage ended.

I steered with my knees again while I thumbed the number for Detective Rudenko into the cell's keypad. I got through to his answering service. I did what the recorded message said and left a name and number.

Finally off the freeway and into town, I went against the signs and took the long way round to the San Francisco Hilton, figuring that with the traffic situation in the crapper, it'd probably end up being the short way. Maybe it was, maybe it wasn't. All I knew was that a drive I thought would take ten minutes soaked up two full hours. I reminded myself that it was only an inconvenience. There were plenty of people who were far more inconvenienced than I was, folks who'd be spending their Christmas Eve at various city morgues identifying loved ones who wouldn't be coming home to hang up their stockings.

My cell rang. I recognized the number. Rudenko. The man had a big, slow voice. I pictured Johnny Appleseed. I told him what I wanted and he said he'd have to call me back. I was OK with that. I was pulling into the Hilton parking lot and the drink I'd been thinking about was only two floors away, calling.

The bar wasn't full by any stretch but the people there, including the barkeep, all had their eyeballs glued to wall-mounted television sets where the events downtown were playing out. Having seen enough devastation firsthand, I decided to pass on the bar and headed for my room.

Fifteen minutes later I was showered and feeling human again. My cell rang. "Special Agent Cooper? Rudenko. Good news. I could have your guy down here, but it could also be a very large sausage someone left on the grill about a month too long."

* * *

There were several makeshift morgues. The one I wanted was in the foyer of a building owned by a large insurance company, taking over the space usually occupied by an expensive restaurant, which possibly accounted for the slant of Detective Rudenko's humor. Rudenko, the man, was about five suit sizes smaller than his voice. His Adam's apple bulged like he'd swallowed one whole. "So, you want fries with that?" he said when he pulled back the plastic sheeting.

I had to admit, the body—if it could be called that—appeared less than human. The heat generated by the explosion and subsequent fire had been so intense that this person, whoever it was, had had their arms and lower legs scorched clean away. The detective handed me a plastic bag. Inside was what appeared to be a toasted sandwich. Only it wasn't.

"It's your guy's wallet," he said. "It was found under the body."

The documents inside the wallet appeared to be remarkably well preserved, singed a little at the corners but otherwise unscathed. I peered at the photo ID. I'd recognize that haircut anywhere. Boyle's photo was only slightly fire damaged.

"We got eight others like this guy so far, and we're gonna find more. When they're toasted like this, you can forget about dental records. According to the coroner, we'll be lucky if there's any DNA material worth harvesting for matching purposes, either. The wallet...finding some identification...that was a break and a half." He shook his head, considering the stark reality. "If it wasn't for this wallet, we wouldn't even know if this was a John or a Jane Doe. Human is about as close as we could get. So, what do you wanna do, Special Agent?" Rudenko stood with his hands on his hips on the other side of the gurney, impatient. I handed the evidence bag back to him.

Something didn't add up here.

"Well, hello," said a familiar voice behind me.

I glanced over my shoulder. It was that walking stomach flu—Chalmers.

"As you know, I'm the SAC on this case," said Chalmers.

"So?" I said.

"So, back off."

I shrugged and did as he asked. Chalmers leaned over the charred remains on the gurney. He looked like a Hamptons country club member, a sweater around his neck, the cuffs on the sleeves rolled into a little ball. It reminded me of a superhero's cape that had shrunk badly. "Did I hear someone say this was Sean Boyle?" He nodded at the lump of charcoal between us. "Thank you, Officer." He relieved Rudenko of the plastic bag containing Boyle's wallet. "National security."

"Hey," the detective said, ramping up to a protest.

Chalmers slapped a folded sheaf of forms against Rudenko's chest, hard enough to swat a fly, and said, "The paperwork, Officer. Makes it official."

"Where are you going with that? Why are you interested in Boyle? And who dressed you this morning?" I said, annoyed.

"To answer your questions: none of your goddamn business, none of your goddamn business, and fuck you, Cooper," Chalmers replied. As he sauntered past, he gave me the kind of smile he might have given someone he didn't like very much who was having his fingernails pulled out with pliers. The prick was obviously enjoying himself, mostly because he was denying me what was potentially valuable evidence. There was nothing I could do to prevent his claim on the wallet, and he knew it. "You should get your wife to do something about your fashion sense, Chalmers," I said. "What would work with that thing tied around your neck? I know . . . try wearing your underpants on the outside." This succeeded in wiping the smile off his face, though only because he had not the slightest idea what I was talking about. But I did, and that was all that mattered.

As Chalmers stalked out, I asked Rudenko, "Did you call the CIA?"

"Yeah. Metzler told me to give you both a call."

I got on the phone immediately to Metzler. Busy. I kept hitting the redial button until I got through.

"Metzler," said the harried voice down the line.

"Cooper," I said.

"Oh, yeah, thought I'd get a call from you."

"So you know why I'm calling?"

"Finally discovered what your flu virus wanted. Let me guess: He was in the vicinity when you found it?"

"Uh-huh. What gives?" I asked.

"Can't give you details, Cooper. But only 'cause I don't have any. Orders came down the pipe. I was told if your guy turned up to let the CIA—and only the CIA—in on it. Rudenko called me when the wallet belonging to this Boyle fellow was found. I told him to call Chalmers *and* you."

"Even though you were ordered not to."

"You got it."

"Thanks," I said, digging deep to swallow my frustration.

"So now I've done you a favor, you can pay it back. Tell me why everyone's so interested in this professor?"

"I can't tell you that."

"You gonna claim national security on me, too?"

"Depends on what your next question is." I heard a sound on the phone like the detective was sucking air through his front teeth. He was thinking about it.

"Has Boyle got anything to do with the hit on these buildings?"

"That I don't know, Detective. He lived in the Four Winds. He was a scientist, doing some work for the government. That's all I can tell you."

He gave me that sound again, the air-whistling-between-his-teeth one. "I guess that's better than nothing."

"You still hot on the mob-hit theory?"

"Unless you got a better one."

I said that I didn't and then I thanked him for his cooperation.

"Don't mention it," said Metzler. "One more thing. Can you tell me why the hell the CIA is sticking its pecker into a domestic case?"

"Yeah, well, good question. I'll ask Chalmers next time I see him," I replied.

"I'm sure you will, Cooper. Gotta go." Metzler rang off.

Rudenko fired off a shrug at me when I caught his eye. He was embarrassed. "Sorry," he said. "I thought the CIA was just coming to have a look."

"That's OK," I said. Different rules applied during a terrorist act on home soil. The local police didn't stand a chance against federal agencies that got boners at the mere mention of the word "terror." And that certainly seemed to be what we had in downtown San Francisco, even if no one knew who was doing the terrorizing. "If anything more turns up, you've got my number, right?" I pulled a DoD business card from my pocket.

Rudenko gave me a nod as he took it and walked out.

I asked myself again why the CIA would be interested in Boyle and came up with nothing except for the fact that they were specifically interested in the guy. Was Boyle the reason the Company was on the scene? Was he the only reason? There was something strange going on here, besides Chalmers's fashion sense. I thought about the wallet. If I still had it, I'd be handing it over to forensics immediately to have its authenticity verified. But I didn't have it. All I had were the remains of someone I could, if I wanted to, claim was formerly Sean Boyle, Ph.D., murder suspect. The trouble would come when I decided I didn't believe it was Boyle here on the bench, which was right about now.

TWELVE

I sat on the bed and flicked through a pamphlet left on the pillow, something about a low-fat breakfast special for Christmas Day—tomorrow. The pamphlet informed me that if I ticked the box I could enjoy it upon waking in my room. I gave some thought to calling Anna in Germany to give her season's greetings, but it would be 5 A.M. where she was based and I didn't want to shoot any remaining goodwill between us in the foot. So I called Chip Schaeffer in D.C. instead.

Ordinarily, I'd have said the chances of finding Chip at his desk at eleven P.M. on Christmas Eve were somewhere between zero and none, but the events in San Francisco made the times unusual. So I wasn't entirely surprised when he picked up.

"Captain Schaeffer," he said.

"Sir, Special Agent Cooper."

"Cooper. How's it going?"

Chip sounded tired. I knew from past experience that the military would have moved to a higher state of readiness and nerves would be frayed.

"Pretty grim, sir," I said.

"Yeah, Washington has broken out in hives. Word is it was a hit-on-a-wise-guy thing?"

"Yes, sir."

"What do you think?" he asked.

I told him what I thought, which was that I didn't buy it. Mainly because if it proved to be true it would turn every federal and state law-enforcement agency into an instrument focused almost solely on dismantling organized crime. Carrying out a terrorist act such as the one here—no matter what kind of beans the informant was likely to spill—was just plain bad for business, and my reading of organized crime was that anything compromising the bottom line was to be avoided at all costs. Chip agreed. I told him I believed Metzler was sticking to it as a theory only because he had nothing else to offer, and that the world was on his back to *do something*.

"You got any theories of your own, Cooper?" Schaeffer asked.

"Not yet, sir." That wasn't accurate. I did have a theory, only I wasn't ready to share.

"But you feel one coming on?"

I gave him a clue. "Professor Boyle's wallet was found beneath burned human remains."

"Those remains been positively identified?"

"I don't know, sir."

"Why not?"

"Because the CIA has taken over on the ground here."

Schaeffer grunted. "Yeah, I know. That's the way the wind's blowing."

I could still see the smug satisfaction on Chalmers's face as he carried away the evidence bag containing Boyle's wallet, prancing out of the morgue, his middle fuck-you finger raised high and proud. War had been declared.

Chip asked me other questions relating to the written case report I had yet to submit on the death of Dr. Tanaka. Unlike the last time he asked me these questions, I told him what I really thought had happened to the man, rather than what the hard evidence outlined. I told him I believed Boyle had a hand in his partner's death. I decided on this course because of a couple of factors that had come to light since my last debrief on the inquiry, most notably the verbal account given to me by Al Cooke, the *Natusima*'s cook. There was also the uneasy feeling I had after the interview with Dr. Spears at Moreton Genetics. I thought my conclusions would take Schaeffer by surprise, but I got nothing back from the captain other than the tone and direction of his questions, which, the more I thought about it, only added to my suspicions that the case was less about a straightforward investigation into an accidental death and more about something I still hadn't been briefed on. There was just too much official and specific interest in Tanaka's demise coming at me, and now in Boyle's. But I could hardly tell Schaeffer that *his* interest in the case was one of the reasons I suspected there might be more to the business than an accidental death.

"Well," said Schaeffer after a little small talk, "with the Company taking over, there's no point in you hanging around. In fact, I want you back here as soon as you can get on a plane. Your orders have come through. You're being transferred back to your old unit—OSI at Andrews. Something has come up and they're short-handed."

I was stunned. Off the case, ordered back to D.C., and transferred, almost all in the one sentence. Was I being rapped over the knuckles for something?

Schaeffer wished me Merry Christmas and a pleasant flight home. I stared at the handset for a few moments before I hung up, and tried to persuade myself that I'd had enough experience with command decisions over the years to know that reason didn't always follow rhyme in the military. The problem was, I was slightly more able to convince myself that flying reindeer could deliver presents to millions of children all over the world in a single night.

Then I surprised myself by having a long, uninterrupted sleep, waking at just after seven A.M. with the thought of a plate of low-fat Christmas bacon and pancakes on the brain.

I lay in bed thinking about what to do next. There wouldn't be a next—at least, not on progressing this case. As I was officially removed from the investigation, standard operating procedure said that all my case notes, reports, phone logs, and evidence would have to be turned over. That meant that as the SAC, Bradley Chalmers would be the recipient. Galling was the first word that came to mind. Fuck was the second.

I peeled back the covers and headed for the shower. The firm water pressure meant I had to stay

in there at least twenty minutes. The bacon and pancakes would wait. I got out and toweled off. The light
spilled from the bathroom directly onto the door to
the hotel room. A large white envelope lay on the
chocolate brown carpet. This being Christmas morning, it could only be two things: evidence of a visit
from the fat guy in a red suit, or the express checkout
bill.

I turned on the lights, dressed, and threw back the
curtains to let in the natural light. There wasn't much
of it—the windows were streaked with heavy rain
falling from a gray sky as solid and heavy as armor
plate. I got down on all fours and examined the envelope. It wasn't the bill. Grabbing a hotel laundry bag
and a couple of forks to use as tongs, I turned it over.
Nothing obvious on the flip side. Not even "Attn Vin
Cooper" written on it. I carried it across to the dinner-
table-for-one and placed it on the laundry bag. The
weight of it and the way it bent indicated the envelope carried something more substantial than a letter.
Keeping my fingers off it, I slit the envelope open
with a bread knife and tipped it up. Out slid a disk. I
picked it up using the plastic laundry bag as a glove.
The top side was blank; the underside was green,
which meant it was a DVD. Both sides appeared to be
free of scratches or prints. I checked the inside of the
envelope. Empty. There was a player on the bedside
table. I turned it on, placed the disk in the machine,
and pressed "play."

THIRTEEN

I had to watch it several times but even then I didn't understand it—not the bigger picture, anyway. The starring role was played by Sean Boyle before his conversion to carbon. I'd recognize that haircut in my sleep. The cinematographer was a security camera—actually several of them. A display indicated the time and date: nine-thirty P.M. on the second of August—nearly five months ago. I guessed that the location was most likely Moreton Genetics. I played with the sound, but there wasn't any.

In that sketchy way security cameras operate, I saw a white room full of electronic apparatus I didn't recognize, plus a few scrolling computer screens. Boyle was leaning over something. He walked to a different bench to check on something else, then headed to yet another white box closer to the camera that featured a bunch of dials as well as a little screen. He could have been baking a cake for all I knew. Then one of the computer screens went blank, followed by two more. A desk light went out, and I noticed the streamers on the air-conditioning duct beside the camera grow less excited and then hang limp.

Boyle stood up straight. He was smiling a private,

self-satisfied smile. Then a line went through the screen, freezing the picture for an instant, before the screen went blank. Nothing happened for a few moments and I was wondering whether the show had finished, and then the picture returned. I was looking down on two people standing in a stainless-steel box. I assumed the location was an elevator. The time-and-date display had returned. One of the people, a male Caucasian in a uniform with a hand truck carrying bottles for the water cooler, was in a panic and pounding the doors, while a woman, also Caucasian, just stood there like a store dummy. I couldn't see her face—her head was tilted down away from the camera until the very last split second. Was she calm, or frozen in panic like the guy in there with her? It was impossible to tell. And then she turned and, as she did so, the picture again went blank—no signal again. I fast-forwarded but there was nothing else on the disk.

The time display told me only a couple of seconds had passed from the footage of Boyle fiddling with equipment to the pair in the lift. The familiar double-helix logo in the elevator confirmed I was seeing something that had happened at Moreton Genetics, some kind of power surge or power failure. But wouldn't a high-tech place like that, with all its delicate and important ongoing research, have some kind of emergency backup power source—generators—that would kick in? I was intrigued by what was on the disk because someone thought it important enough to slip under my door and because whoever did so wanted their identity kept secret.

I went to my laptop and called up the home page for the *San Francisco Chronicle*. I became a member and surfed around the site's archive, but I couldn't find any reference to power failures in any part of San Francisco in or around last August. If the power was cut, wouldn't everything at MG go out at the same time, rather than in a staggered fashion? I set up the news service to forward any articles containing the keywords "Moreton Genetics" to my Hotmail address.

I took the disk from the player and put it into my laptop's CD drive. I made an MPEG copy and e-mailed it on to Arlen at OSI with a note explaining what I wanted him to do about it. Then I called Moreton Genetics and received a recorded message letting me know that MG would be closed until the fourth of January. Ten days. I turned to the online phone directories next. If I could get hold of Freddie Spears, perhaps she'd be able to tell me what I was seeing on the disk. But there was no Dr. Freddie Spears listed, nor was there any Frederique Spears in the data base, although there were twenty-three "F. Spears" in the San Francisco area. For a moment, I thought about cold-calling complete strangers on Christmas Day. I decided against it.

I carefully removed the disk from the slot in the laptop and returned it to its envelope. Then I placed the envelope in the laundry bag and put it with the rest of my stuff. What to do next? A rumble in my stomach told me it was getting impatient for those low-fat yuletide bacon-and-pancake stacks. Problem solved.

FOURTEEN

Cooper! So you made it back in one piece," Schaeffer said, looking up and then leaning back in his chair.

"Yes, sir," I replied.

"Take a seat." The fish tank's air filter thrummed away in the background. "How was it out there?"

"They seem to be getting on top of things, sir," I said. Schaeffer made a "humph" sound and raised a skeptical eyebrow at me. "You're best out of it, son."

"Yes, sir," I said, not believing him but not having much choice anyway.

"You'll make available all materials on the Tanaka case."

"Yes, sir," I said. "Would you know whether the CIA intends to share any forensics with us from the Four Winds site?"

Schaeffer ignored my question. "Anything turned up on the Tanaka thing I don't know about?"

As much as I didn't like being excluded from the loop, there wasn't a lot I could do about it. I gave up what I didn't tell him when I called in from San Francisco. "Sir, I have a statement from a witness claiming he saw Boyle on deck moments after Tanaka was thrown overboard."

"Then why didn't this witness do something to help the guy in the drink?" he asked.

"I don't know, sir, but it's a good question." A couple of better ones would be to ask whether Boyle pushed Tanaka overboard and why. And whether the Transamerica bombing was somehow linked to Boyle and therefore related to Tanaka's death.

"Some people . . ." he said, shaking his head.

"I strongly recommend that this witness be interviewed by the SAC," I said. I strongly recommended it because the Marianas was a long way to go for nothing, the witness, as far as witnesses went, being a waste of time.

"I'll be sure and pass that on to CIA," said Chip.

"I also received this." I set the envelope containing the disk, still wrapped in the laundry bag, on his desk.

"What is it?"

"Possible evidence, sir." I told him about the disk, gave a précis of what was on it, and explained how it came into my possession.

"I trust you haven't made copies."

My fingers were crossed where he couldn't see them. "Can you tell me why the CIA has taken over the case, sir?"

"No, I can't," he said, cracking his knuckles one by one. "Look, you've done a good job on this, Cooper. You've performed some fine work here and I've enjoyed having you on my team. That's going on your Officer Performance Report, by the way."

"Yes sir," I said, but I was thinking, *what fine work, exactly?* Sure, I could buy tropical fish with the best of them. I already knew the Tanaka case was no longer mine, so I was a little surprised. Was Chip attempting to soften me up for something, even if it was just for me to move on quietly? Or was he feeling bad that a difficult case I was making headway on had been handed to a jerk like Bradley Chalmers? I wasn't going to get any answers to these questions, so I let them slide.

* * *

Twenty minutes later, I was at OSI HQ, Andrews AFB. An agent I'd never met was sitting in the office that had my name on the door, so I walked down the hall to Arlen's. He was on the phone. He gave me a nod and shifted in his seat, half turning his back to me. He cut the call short and said, "Vin! Here already? That was quick. We haven't really had time to prepare for your triumphant return."

"I wondered where my parade was. Merry Christmas, by the way."

"And a big ho-ho-ho to you, Vin. So, back in OSI's clutches now."

"This week. Did you get the MPEG I sent you?" I asked.

"Yep."

"You done anything about it?"

"You want to get some air?" he asked. "I can also brief you on the case you're gonna be working."

"Okay, but give me ten," I replied. "I'd better clock in with my new boss first."

From the commanding officer, Brigadier General James Wynngate, who was drowning in mucus from a bad head cold, I received a lecture about the new OSI. After sneezing what appeared to be around a cup and a half of concentrated rhinovirus over my service record spread out in front of him, the general eventually got around to telling me that Arlen would brief me on the case I'd been assigned to.

And so, another twenty minutes later, I was back where I started. It had begun sleeting outside so Arlen and I detoured around the corridors of the HQ block and arrived at the cafeteria. It was much smaller than the Pentagon's and nowhere near as crowded. Arlen led the way to a table in a corner.

"You want coffee?" he asked.

"That depends. Is it any better than the mystery fluid they serve at the Pentagon?"

"No."

"Then I'll just watch you have one," I said.

"Suit yourself," he replied. "Can you fire this up while I go get it?"

He pulled a laptop out of the briefcase tucked under an arm and set it on the table before making his way to the counter. He returned with a Styrofoam cup containing what looked like muddy rainwater just in time to have his thumbprint scanned by the computer's inbuilt security program.

"So what are we doing?" I inquired.

"This case we're getting you to work, the investigating special agent came down with acute appendicitis and was hospitalized. With the stuff going on on the West Coast, we had no one available to take the guy's place, so I put in a special request for you."

"Really. *You* did that?" I asked. "Had me pulled off the Tanaka case?"

"Whoa, buddy! I just put in a request. I didn't think it'd be acted on."

I wouldn't have believed so either, unless it fitted in with someone else's plans. "And here I was, wondering whether there might have been darker forces at work. Why me? I'm sure I'm not the only special agent on this planet, although it is true that I'd have to be one of the best."

"If not *the* best," said Arlen.

"Well, you know, modesty forbids . . ."

"Since when?" he asked.

I cracked a smile, the first in a while.

"Vin, you've been moaning for months what a drag it is at the DoD filling in forms."

"Correction," I said. "Correcting forms *other* people had incorrectly filled in."

"Whatever. I just thought I could do you a favor, you know? And I also had a case but no one to work it, so there was that, too."

I could have been angry. I didn't like being manipulated, even if the intentions were honorable, but the reality was that the Tanaka/Boyle case was out of my hands anyway, removed by powers far above Arlen's head.

"So where do you want to start?" he asked.

"With the MPEG I sent you."

FIFTEEN

Arlen ran through it a couple of times. "So what do you think's going on here?" he asked as the air-con in the security footage shut down.

"Beats me. I thought it might have been a power failure."

"Yeah, I ran down that angle, too. There were no cuts and no blackouts reported in the Palo Alto area on the day in question. And, also, a company like this would have its own generators, wouldn't it?"

"You'd think," I said.

"I haven't had much time to do anything too interesting with the clip, given everyone has an Orange up their butt," he said, referring to the fact that the Homeland Security Advisory level had been raised to High, orange, lower only than Severe, which was red. "And I'm not so sure you want this thing passed around, right?"

I nodded. "Right." No one specifically asked me not to make copies. Chip Schaeffer said he hoped I hadn't made copies, not whether I *had*. After six months in the DoD, I was a master of fine print.

"But I have had time to sort out the back end, as you requested."

Arlen replayed the disk. We watched Boyle baking his cake, the computers shutting down, followed by the desk lights and the air-con. The picture went black and then came back to life in the elevator. Arlen stopped the show. "I've had this last scene separated into individual frames, and the last dozen or so computer-enhanced." He ran the frames one at a time. I studied the way the passengers' bodies jerked in the elevator, indicating that it had come to an abrupt stop. The lights flickered and the water-cooler guy became agitated, pounding the doors. The woman stood rooted to the spot for quite a few frames before suddenly turning toward the camera. Now, because of the computer-enhancement work, I could make out who it was.

"You know this woman?" Arlen asked.

"Yeah."

"Who is she?"

"The CEO of Moreton Genetics—Dr. Freddie Spears."

"You want to clue me in here?" asked Arlen.

"Are you sure you want to know?"

Arlen examined my face. "Probably best I don't, right?"

"Probably," I said. "But thanks for helping out."

Arlen sipped his coffee. I knew him well enough to know that he wanted to ask me a question, and I could guess what it was. "I'm not going to pursue this," I told him. "I'm off the case."

"Yeah, right," he said.

"Really. I'm done."

"So you're not at all interested in knowing what this footage is all about?"

"OK, I would like to know that."

"So you're not done with it?"

"I can't help my curiosity, but I'm off it now, out of the loop. I'm not going to get any more clues coming my way. A Tommy Hilfiger model freelancing for the CIA is handling it from here on."

Arlen frowned. "Who?"

"Never mind—not important. So what's the new case about?"

Arlen looked at me dubiously. He knew me too well. He gave up trying to extract any further assurances and said, "Another accident." He used his fingers to indicate I could put quote marks around the word *accident.* "The coroner down there is not convinced."

"Down where?"

"How do you feel about Florida?"

"Can I take a train?"

*   *   *

I went back to my apartment to pack the essentials, such as my one and only Hawaiian shirt. I knew the victim, the one the coroner wasn't convinced about. (He was convinced the victim was dead, just not how he came to be that way.) We'd served together in Afghanistan when I was in the CCTs—the Air Force's elite combat controllers squadron. His name was Ruben Wright, or Wrong Way or Dubya-Dubya, as we called him, and he was a master sergeant, which, being pretty high in the echelons of the noncom positions, meant the guy knew what he was doing.

Last I heard, Wrong Way had been offered an officer's commission to keep him interested in hanging around. I also heard he'd declined, because the only thing that interested him was combat, and officers, he figured, didn't like to get their hands dirty.

Wrong Way, despite his nickname, never did anything wrong. He was the perfect combat airman—committed, brave, sometimes foolhardy, but with nerves of steel and a resolve that was unshakable. After serving with him, I was real pleased he was on my team and not the enemy's. In hand-to-hand combat, I'd once seen him break a man in two over his knee like he was making a length of wood more manageable for the campfire. The enemy deserved it, though—the guy had made the mistake of firing a pistol at Wrong Way, not that that was the problem. The issue, as far as I could tell, was not that the bullet had dragged through the muscle in Wright's thigh, missing his testicles by less than an inch, but that basically the raghead had failed to kill him. "Well, he ain't never gonna make that mistake again, is he?" I remembered him saying as he staunched the blood flow with a compression bandage.

So I was pretty surprised to hear that Master Sergeant Ruben Wright was dead. I thought the guy was invincible. But then I'd learned the specifics of how he'd died: His parachute harness had malfunctioned and he'd hit the State of Florida at around a hundred and twenty miles per hour. Wright was tough, but not that tough.

Both The 38th Parallel and Summer Love, the vegan joint, were closed till the New Year. I grabbed my mail and edited the pile into things to read and things to send to landfill. I was amazed at how much my box had accumulated in just a few days. Mostly, I'd been bombarded by leaflets from other fast-food joints in the vicinity eager to muscle in on Kim's territory while the guy's back was turned. There were a few love letters from the phone and electricity companies, as well as three Christmas cards. My popularity never ceased to amaze me.

I dropped the cards and bills on a table and went to the fridge. The shelves revealed that I was on an air, mold, and beer diet. I extracted a Bud and went back to the living room. The window on the answering machine was glowing with one call. I stabbed the play button and went into the bedroom to pack.

"Vin. Just calling to wish you Merry Christmas . . ."

It was Anna. A deep pit opened up inside.

". . . But you're not in . . . well, call you later."

"Bah, humbug," I said to the four pairs of socks as I pulled them from the top drawer and dropped them into my bag.

I gave the Bud another tilt and walked out of the bedroom. And then the phone rang. I changed course and answered it. "Hello?"

"Vin?"

Yeah, last time I looked. "Hello," I said. The call had a hollow, faraway sound and it took a moment to register the voice.

"Hey, you're home. How you doing?" It was Anna

again, only this time we were going live. "I called earlier," she said.

"I know. Just got home ten minutes ago and
switched on the machine. I see you've sent me a
card—haven't had a chance to open it." The envelope
was pink. I picked it up off the table, turned it over,
and tore off a corner.

"It's just a dumb card," she said.

I wasn't sure what to say. I hadn't sent Anna anything, unless waves of disappointment dispatched
through the ether counted for anything. I looked at
the card. It was a cartoon of a man and a woman in
bed. On the floor was a trail of red clothes, boots, and
so on. One of Santa's large-breasted helpers was on
top of the man, naked. The guy's wife was lying beside them and she was pissed, saying, *"But I've been*
better *than he has . . . !"* Inside, the printed caption read,
"Have a Merry Christmas—share it with a friend." Beneath this was hand-written, *"Have a Merry Christmas,
Vin. Love, Anna."* There was a photo of Anna wearing
red felt reindeer antlers and blowing me a kiss.

"Nice," I said. "You must have sent this almost the
day you arrived back in Germany."

"Yeah. You have no idea how hard it is finding a
decent Christmas card in this country," she said.
"Where's mine?"

"Coming," I said.

"Should I hold my breath?"

"Best not."

"I thought so."

One of our pauses followed.

"Hey, thanks for the card," I said, breaking in on it. "I'll put it on the mantelpiece."

"You don't have a mantelpiece."

"Okay, then, beside the toaster."

"I just spoke to Arlen, Vin. He told me you were out at the Transamerica mess."

"Yeah."

"How was it?"

"A mess."

"Do they know who or what or why?"

"If they do, they're not telling me."

"Are you seeing anyone?" she said, jumping around like she was walking on hot beach sand. Was this the question she really wanted an answer to?

"Don't let's do this, Anna. I might get the wrong idea."

"What idea is that?"

"The one you don't want me to get—that you might actually give a shit."

"That's unfair, Vin."

"Look, Anna, we're either together or we're not. And it seems to me we're not."

"Can't we be—"

"I have to go," I said.

"Vin, I—"

"Unless you're gonna say I'll see you at arrivals at Dulles tomorrow, save it. Thanks again for the card, and the calls."

"Okay, Vin . . . I'll see you." The line went dead.

Gee, that went well, I told myself. I sat on a chair and chugged down the rest of the Bud.

SIXTEEN

The temperature at the bus terminal at Panama City was barely sixty-five degrees—tropical compared with D.C. I changed into my Hawaiian shirt in the terminal's bathroom. I liked the pattern—a woman in a bright green grass skirt with long black hair and a flower lei that covered her ample bosom. She was smiling as she played a ukulele against a backdrop of yellow and orange hibiscuses. If I couldn't have a vacation, at least I could look like I was having one.

There were buses from Panama City to Hurlburt Field, but I'd had enough of buses. I took a cab.

The road from Panama City to Fort Walton Beach, my destination, more or less followed the curve of the Gulf of Mexico. Although they got a lot of sun down here, even in winter, today the clouds moving toward the beach from out over the Gulf were heavily pregnant, and any moment their waters threatened to break. I had the windows down anyway, the wind-blast ruffling the women on my Hawaiian shirt so that they danced the hula. I kept my eyes on the scenery, though it passed without me really taking it in.

The cab pulled off the highway into Hurlburt Field,

which was the home of the Air Force Special Operations Command as well my old squadron, the CCTs—the Combat Air Controllers.

I paid the driver and got out, hoisting my bag off the backseat. A civilian security guy accompanied by a couple of armed airmen approached and motioned to see my credentials. I handed them over and they passed the black leather folder back and forth between them, examining the fine print while one of the airmen scowled at me and massaged the butt of his M16. Maybe it was my shirt that bothered them. The civilian guard eventually handed back my shield and waved me on.

I walked the block to the OSI building, the wheels on my suitcase squealing as I pulled it along.

Like a bedroom kept for a child long since grown to adulthood and departed, nothing had changed since I'd left here eight years ago. Hurlburt Field was no different from any other U.S. military base on the planet in that it was pretty much indistinguishable from all other U.S. bases. The buildings were the same, the uniforms the same, the attitude the same, and even many of the on-base street names were the same. U.S. bases reminded me of McDonald's or Burger King. You could go to just about any one on the globe and feel pretty much like you never left home. The only real difference was the people you shot at when you stepped outside the gates.

Hurlburt Field was part of the sprawling Eglin Air Force Base, the largest military base in the Western world, covering over seven hundred miles of swamp, hill, forest, and sea. It was so big, they live-tested missiles here—fired 'em off at one end and collected 'em at the other. You could get lost here, and people did. You could also get killed here, like my old pal Ruben Wright.

I walked around the back of the OSI building, through the parking lot. A bunch of airmen were swimming in the pool, horsing around. I hated that pool. It was where I'd done my water survival training; where I'd learned to drink gallons through my nose.

I opened the door and went into the waiting room. There was no bell to ring so I did what the room suggested and waited. Eventually, an OSI agent came in, asked who I was. Apparently I was expected. He punched the combination into the cipher lock so that I could access the OSI offices, and then left the way he came in, talking into his cell phone.

It was like a morgue inside, only without that smell. The CO was away on an extended training mission, and just about everyone else was apparently out in San Francisco. The only person in was the duty officer, a captain. I tapped on his door just as a pile of folders stacked high on his desk toppled and splashed onto the floor, sending paper to the four corners of the room.

"Should I come back in five?" I said. The man's name, Lyne, was stitched to his breast pocket. Lyne had a hare lip and the flustered manner of an overworked man.

"Shee-it," he said, with a Texan accent, surveying

the mess. "Goddamn it, I don't know...tell me who you are and then let me decide."

"Special Agent Vin Cooper."

"Cooper...Cooper..."

"I'm down from Andrews," I said, "taking over on the Ruben Wright inquiry."

"Cooper...yeah, Cooper. I remember now. Hey, sorry. Woke up slow this morning."

Having a natural affinity with underachievers, I took an instant liking to Lyne.

"Take a seat and watch me clean up this crap, or you could give me a hand. Take your pick."

I helped.

"What do you know about the case?" Agent Lyne asked while we collected paper.

"I know the dead CCT was working with a bunch of Limeys. I also know somewhere between walking out the back of the C-130 and hitting the ground he came to be separated from his parachute."

"Well, there you go. You know more than me, Special Agent." He pulled a folder caught under the leg of a desk, checked the title on the front, then passed it to me. "That's pretty much everything the previous investigator had—the coroner's report, forensics. No interviews with suspects yet."

I skimmed the contents. "Got all this already," I informed him.

"Like I said, you know more than me."

Lyne divided the single precarious mountain of paperwork on his desk into two smaller, more manageable foothills. "I bet the company that invented the laser printer owns the entire Amazon basin. Look at this shit." He glared at his desk, hands on his hips. "So, where was I? Um . . . That's right—I've got accommodation for you on the base. And a vehicle—you'll probably need one. I don't know how long you'll be staying, and probably neither do you, right?"

"I'm hoping not to get comfortable," I said.

"Trust me, you won't. The place I've secured for you ain't exactly the Ritz. The housing for officers and transients is all full, and there's a waiting list a mile long. You're lucky. One became available unexpectedly. I reckon I can hold back the tide for ten days, max." The captain handed me a key with a tag on it. "Tell anyone I let you jump the line and you're a dead man."

I nodded. "Thanks." I didn't think he'd end up having to evict me. The case involving the death of Master Sergeant Ruben "Wrong Way" Wright was a touchy one involving our allies the British. According to the previous investigator's notes, Wright's final jump had been in the company of a small team of their Special Air Service, the SAS, here to learn our methods and tactics. Nothing unusual in that. The SAS often trained with our people. Reading between the lines of the report, it was likely one of this particular unit of SAS guys—probably a staff sergeant by the name of Chris Butler—was going to see the inside of a U.S. military correctional facility. And that was unusual. I knew from my own experience that visiting forces from other countries were usually on their very best behavior when they were on our turf. From what Arlen told me, I had the impression everyone wanted this case to just go away.

"So, you know where to go?" the captain asked.

"Yeah, I was stationed here during the first Afghanistan deployment."

"With the OSI?"

"No, back then I was a special tactics officer in the CCTs."

Special tactics officer? "You were one of those lunatics?"

"I grew out of it," I said.

"Woke up one day and realized you were mortal, eh?"

"Something like that." In fact, it was exactly like that. The CCTs were part of the Air Force's Special Forces. They parachuted into enemy territory with Navy Seals, Army Rangers, and, occasionally, Special Forces from other countries. Their motto was "First in," because they always were. It was the CCTs' duty to open airstrips for assault forces or reinforcements, or to lay navigation beacons on hilltops—often in hostile terrain—that would guide the bombers on their final run in on the target. Sometimes CCTs acted as forward air controllers, directing and separating the traffic in the sky, "boogying on the mic," as one guy I knew described it. Like all Special Forces, CCTs did the impossible, and thrived on it. I'd been one of them until the CH-47 I was in got blown out of the sky, and I found myself on a hill in Afghanistan with a bunch of guys who either got shot or had their heads removed from their necks by Taliban fighters. A second CH-47 helo was sent in to evacuate the survivor, me, only it was also shot down. Somehow, I survived the crash, but my nervous system wouldn't let me fly again. And my reputation for being a Jonah—a bad-luck charm—was spreading. As I saw it, I had two choices: get discharged or transferred.

"Take this, anyway." Lyne handed over a laser-printed sheet showing a small section of the base. The OSI building was circled. "The memory's not always infallible, right?"

"Thanks," I said, accepting the map. Lyne had insight. There'd been a little serious drinking done in the intervening period and it was highly possible many of the brain cells charged with remembering the details of this place just plain didn't exist anymore.

"No, thank *you*," he said in exaggerated fashion. "In case you haven't noticed, we're a bit light in the resources department around here. Glad to have you around. The name's Lloyd, by the way. You need anything, give me a shout and I'll do my best to ignore it." He smiled.

I'd been sent to Florida because the people down here were all in San Francisco, exactly where I'd just been. The Air Force could have kept me there and left these people here, but that would have been too easy. "Got that vehicle handy?"

"Oh, right. I forgot. Take your pick. At least with everyone gone, transport's something we have plenty of. You can have anything you want, as long as it's dark blue." There were several sets of keys hanging off hooks on the wall behind a low filing cabinet.

"I saw you've got a few SUVs out front. I'll take one of them."

"Uh-huh," he said, unhitching a set of keys and tossing them to me. "The registration's on the tag. Just sign here." He slapped a form on the desk.

Outside, the rain was coming down like shotgun pellets. The air smelled of rotting seaweed. It reminded me of Japanese food. I ran for the vehicle as a small knot of airmen hunched over in sodden battle-dress uniforms jogged past, gray water splashing up on each other with every footfall, their full packs doing their best to tip them over backward. Once upon a time I was one of these guys. There was no wistful nostalgia in the memory.

The base looked and felt like it was on alert. No one walked; everyone seemed in a rush. There was a war on and the business in San Francisco was yet another reminder of it. The place was on a leash fraying with the strain.

I got in the SUV and followed the map. Finding the accommodation was easy enough. It was in a small block, not unlike my home in D.C., though perhaps more utilitarian. I wasn't sure how a family could be expected to live in it comfortably, unless you happened to be a family of spiders, of which there were several nestled in the corners of the ceiling. I dumped my gear on the bedroom floor and plugged in the laptop, making myself at home. Some thoughtful soul had piled folded sheets and a towel on the bed.

It was dark inside the house, probably because night was falling outside, though not as heavily as the rain, which was making a roaring sound, the clouds having flicked the switch from downpour to fusillade. Thinking that maybe time had managed to get away from me, I checked the clock on the oven: 5 P.M. I was probably too late, but I rang base information anyway and got a phone number for the investigator who I knew from the report was based here at Hurlburt Field. I called. Lucky me, the DI was in.

* * *

White lettering on the thin, black plastic plate screwed onto the bare wood-veneer door announced that this was the office of Lieutenant Colonel Clare Selwyn, DI. I knocked and stood in the doorway. The colonel was leaning over something on a bench that ran along one side of her office. She glanced up and frowned. I watched her eyes flick from the Hawaiian shirt to my face. Being out of uniform, I was an unknown quantity, either a temporary interruption or a more long-term pain in the ass.

"Special Agent Vin Cooper," I said, narrowing it down to the latter.

"Come on in," she said.

Lieutenant Colonel Selwyn had attended Master Sergeant Ruben Wright after he splashed down. Selwyn was at least thirty-six years of age—had to be, given her rank—though she appeared much younger. Having met quite a few death inspectors over the years and knowing what they did in their regular nine-to-five, her youthfulness was surprising. Death had a way of leaving his imprint on your face, but not on hers. Her eyes were soft, brown, and intelligent, and her dark eyebrows contrasted with hair that was almost white blond. If she let it loose from her pony-tail and gave it a flick, I'd be thinking Swedish sham-poo commercial. A thick strand of that hair had managed to escape the elastic and hung in front of her face. The colonel tucked it behind an ear with a finger and then spread the photos out on the table. All fea-tured Ruben Wright, and the poses weren't flattering.

"He looked a lot different the last time I saw him," I said. For one thing, the guy in these photos didn't have a beer in his hand or a grin on his face. For an-other, in these he resembled a puddle wearing clothes. One photo showed a close-up of a distinguishing mark, a Superman symbol tattooed on his shoulder. There was a tear in the *S* where the skin had split. On the other shoulder, Wright had sergeant's chevrons tattooed in khaki. I recalled the day and the place where he'd had both tattoos done. We were in Bangkok, with a bunch of Navy Seals, looking for ac-tion. As I remember, we found it. The morning after, Ruben visited a tattoo artist in a back alley. When the job was done, he bought a bottle of whiskey, drank half, and poured the rest of it over his newly acquired artworks. We then went on to find some more action, again successfully, I believe. Bangkok was that kind of town. I've been told it still is.

"You knew the deceased?" Selwyn asked, standing up straight. She was tall, around five ten.

"In a different life I was in the CCTs. I served with Sergeant Wright in Afghanistan and other places."

"Oh."

"So, would you mind taking me through your problems on this thing?" I asked.

"Sure. This is my problem." Selwyn slid back a door beneath the bench and pulled out a large, clear plastic evidence bag.

I recognized the item as a parachute harness and chute bag. The chute appeared to have been removed. I must have made some kind of face because the colonel said, "I've also got the parachute."

I nodded.

"It was one of those ram-air chutes the Special Forces guys use, and there was nothing wrong with it. The problem was with the harness itself." The colonel dug around through the plastic until she found what she was after. "Take a close look at the thigh strap."

"Appears to have been cut," I said, aware of the problem with the harness, and now also of her perfume.

"Go to the head of the class."

"Had the chute been deployed?"

"Yeah. We found it a mile from your friend's point of impact."

With that thigh strap cut, the considerable unbalanced forces coming into play when the chute popped open would have flicked Wright out the bottom of the harness like a stone from a slingshot. The reserve chute would have also gone with it. Ruben was freefalling with no chute and with possibly around twenty seconds to think about what would happen next. Pinpricks of perspiration erupted on my top lip.

The guy had lived my own personal nightmare, and then it had killed him.

"You OK?" Selwyn asked. "You've gone kinda green."

"Bus lag," I said. "So, one theory is that Sergeant Wright cut the thigh strap himself and then deployed the chute. He would have known exactly what would happen. The chute and harness went one way, he went the other."

"Suicide?" said Selwyn with a snort. "Sure. Then I could've signed the autopsy and gone to lunch."

"So why didn't you?"

"Because that's not what happened."

"Then what did?"

"Let's run with the suicide angle a minute. If Wright intended to kill himself, why not just forget to pull the rip cord? Why the hell would he go to all the trouble of cutting himself out of his own harness?"

I couldn't think of a single reason, except that people who do commit suicide are rarely what you'd call reasonable.

Selwyn fetched another evidence bag from the cupboard. "He had two of these—one's missing from its scabbard, probably the one that did the cutting. Only, where is it?" In the bag was a distinctive knife, a British Fairbairn-Sykes commando dagger. I remembered it being Ruben Wright's preferred close-in weapon. He'd had this one modified, honed to a razor's edge on both sides. Inscribed along the slender blade were the words "*Truth. Justice.*"

"If he did cut his own harness and then dropped

the knife, you'd think the dagger's trajectory would have been vertical like his own. You should have found it close to his body," I said.

"Yep."

Thinking aloud, I continued, "There's no way the knife could have somehow got caught up in the suspension lines, or the wing itself, and come down somewhere between where you found Wright and where you found the chute?"

She shook her head. "The deceased and the knife would have been on a divergent course to the chute, pretty much the instant it was deployed."

"OK, so let's look at the accidental-death angle. I understand this was a night-training jump."

"Yep."

"What if he became disoriented for some reason when he came out of the plane, found himself tumbling, and the chute didn't come out of the bag clean? What if he needed to cut himself out of the main chute before he could open the reserve, and accidentally sliced through his thigh strap instead?"

"And maybe leprechauns live in my underwear drawer," she said.

Lucky leprechauns. I glanced at Selwyn. She wasn't smiling. OK, so this theory was dumb, every bit as dumb as the suicide angle.

"You and I both know there's a far more likely scenario that fits the facts," she said. "I examined the suspension lines and the chute. Everything was in A-one condition. If Wright got in a knife fight with his chute, you'd expect pretty extensive damage to it, right?"

I nodded. "You would. Did you ascertain whether Wright had his second knife on him when he went up? If you can't find it, is there a chance he left it in his locker?"

"You know these people . . . sorry, what did you say your name was?"

"Special Agent Cooper." I took a card from a back pocket and placed it on her desk.

She picked it up and checked it over. "Special Agent, as an ex-CCT yourself, you'd know that guys like this are pro airmen with a capital *F* for fanatic. They do it right. Having all their gear present and accounted for is a given."

I took a stroll around the room. What Selwyn said was generally true, but professionals did get sloppy, even careless. I once knew a guy in 82nd Airborne who'd done over three thousand jumps—spent his whole life stepping out of planes. And then one day he did a demonstration jump with some buddies. The idea was to land on a pontoon moored in San Francisco Bay. For some reason, he decided not to wear a helmet. There was a wind shift. He made the pontoon OK, only he landed a little hard and hit his head on a bollard. This knocked him out cold and he toppled quietly into the bay. His buddies all high-fived each other while he drowned under their noses.

"Let's say Wright did leave one of his knives behind, and did commit suicide," said Selwyn. "Do you really think he'd have cut through the harness with the knife in your hand there, and then have the presence of mind to replace it in its scabbard?"

No, I didn't.

"So, what's the terrain like where Wright came down?" I asked.

"Open, but scrubby with a few trees. The chute drifted and landed in a stand of slash pines half a mile from where the body was found."

A thought occurred to me. "Those knives are balanced for throwing. It would've come down point first, traveling fast. If the ground's soft, it would have come to a stop four feet under."

"I know. I personally combed every inch of ground in the vicinity of the deceased for exactly that reason. I found nothing."

"And I suppose you also scanned with metal detectors?"

Selwyn leaned back against the bench, hands in her pockets, lips pursed. "Turns out the area was a former dump. All sorts of old World War Two scrap was bulldozed into the ground thereabouts, much of it metal. The screen on the scanner lit up like stage lights." She tilted her head, studying me. "So, are we going to get around to discussing the only theory that fits the facts, or what?"

"You mean the one where the men he jumped with—possibly the leader of the stick—attacked him in midair, used one of Ruben's own knives to cut him out of his harness, and then pulled his rip cord for him?" I said.

"Yeah," she answered with a crooked smile. "And here I was thinking I was going to have trouble with you."

Wright was the kind of guy who'd embrace death only if he could take maybe a dozen bad guys with him. He wasn't the suicide type. So that left murder. That meant I was looking for a murderer. I was also looking for a drink. The clock on the wall said so, it being almost 2100 hours.

"You want to join me for a whiskey?" I asked Selwyn. The invitation was purely business, of course.

"Love to, but my man will kill me," she said, reaching to switch off the laser printer.

"You married?" I asked. She glanced up at me. Maybe I was getting a little personal.

"Was." She picked up a framed photo from her desk and handed it to me. "My man," she said. The photo was a family shot—Colonel Selwyn, her husband or partner, and a three- or four-year-old boy. They were standing together on a sandy beach, the water lapping at their toes. All three seemed happy to be there. "My husband, Manny's father, was killed soon after this was taken, in an aircraft accident—a light plane, engine failure. He was a passenger. Manny knows his father, but only through photos and home videos."

"I'm sorry," I said. Truly, gravity sucked. Change-the-subject time. "Listen, I'm not sure what your schedule's like tomorrow, but I'd like to go and have a look at where Wrong Way came down."

"Who?"

"Wrong Way—the deceased. That's what we called Ruben Wright. If you could walk me around the area, it'd save me some time."

Colonel Selwyn picked up a briefcase and motioned me toward the door. "OK, but it'll have to be first thing in the morning. I'm taking a half day—being a mom, you know."

"Oh-nine-thirty good for you?" I asked.

"Yep. You'll need a four-wheel drive." Selwyn flicked off the interior lights after we stepped outside. Motion-sensitive lights took over, pushing back the twilight. Insects began strafing runs on the bulbs.

"Is the officers' club still worth a stopover?" I asked.

"Sure—if you like testosterone over ice. Otherwise, head on over to Destin. Plenty of good places there. Try The Funkster. The beer's cold, the music's good—if you like blues. Can't miss it. On the left as you come into town."

Destin. I'd had some wild nights in that town, but that was in another life. We exchanged thanks, and I stood by my vehicle and watched the DI drive off until the lights on the building behind me switched off.

SEVENTEEN

Four black guys on steel guitars, a snare set, and an accordion were cooking up some zydeco music that brought gators and marsh gas to mind. The bar was weathered, smelled of beer sweat, and was bathed in neon from Miller Lite and Budweiser signs on the walls. The place was full, though perhaps not compared with when the summer-vacation crowds got thirsty. I ordered a Glen Keith on the rocks and found a spot among the wallflowers, watching the talent with one eye and the band with the other.

I'd barely settled in when I heard someone with a broad English accent yell behind me. "That was a fuckin' wanker's shot, mate."

I glanced over my shoulder. Three men were playing pool.

"And you're a fuckin' tosser," roared one of them over the music.

I heard the guy beside me grumble to his drinking buddy, "Those goddamn SAS assholes get away with murder."

So the loudmouths were British Special Air Service—SAS. That accounted for the accents. I didn't need to be a cop to sense a situation brewing. They were drinking shots of something bright green. Maybe it wasn't the alcohol they were reacting to but the artificial coloring. Lined up on a windowsill behind them was a collection of over twenty shot glasses. That was a lot of artificial coloring. The apparent ringleader, and the oldest of the three, had light-colored hair dyed blond at the tips and brushed forward like he'd stepped out of Julius Caesar's Rome. He had narrow brown eyes and pale skin strewn with freckles, and was slightly taller and thicker set than his comrades. The Brits were showing off to a couple of attractive local twenty-somethings occupying the other pool table, both of whom were doing their best to ignore the attention.

"Eh, 'ave you ladies ever sampled the delights of an English lad?" I heard the guy with the Roman haircut inquire.

Again, no response from the women. They were being polite, but standoffish. It seemed to me they just wanted to play their game in peace.

"Basically, luv, what 'e was sayin' was, 'ave you ever gobbled an English knob?" said another.

His buddies thought this comment uproariously funny. One of the men had to steady himself with his cue stick, using it as a crutch to stop himself from sinking to his knees.

I glanced beside me. Knuckles were bunching.

"Limey assholes," I heard another guy say beneath his breath. He took a step forward, into my line of sight. He looked like a Special Ops guy, one of ours, pumped muscle with a bony skull shining beneath hair cut as short as pig bristle.

The guy with the blonded tips sauntered on vaguely wobbly legs over to the objects of their attention. He put out his hand toward the woman's butt as she leaned over the cushion to play a shot. I took a couple of steps toward them. It was a nice butt, so I knew where he was coming from. I also knew where he was going if it landed—into a Dumpster out back, especially if she objected. I took another step and, before my left hand knew what was going on, my right had reached out and caught his by the wrist.

The Englishman turned. "'Ere . . . wot's your fuckin' problem, mate . . . ?"

"OSI," I said. I held my shield in his face. I could tell his eyes were having trouble focusing. My mind went blank at this point. Where to from here? My reflexes were aware, even if my brain wasn't, that someone had to do something before two teams of trained killers quite possibly put that training into practice on each other.

"Yeah . . . and . . . ?" One of his buddies pushed forward into my space as I let his friend's wrist go.

"We've been looking for some tourists—civilians—who took a Humvee for a joyride," I improvised. "Couldn't help but catch your accents."

"Yeah? And just where were these tourists from?"

"New Zealand," I said.

"New-fuckin'-Zealand? Can't you tell a fuckin' Englishman when you hear one, Mr. Plod?"

"Watch your language, buddy," I said. "Ladies

present." In fact, the two ladies had vacated the area. I also noticed that the band had stopped and that several SOC neanderthals were now standing behind me, shoulders interlocked, in case I called for backup.

"This is bullshit, boss," said one of the three Brits, a short guy with no lips and a busted-up nose, the only one of the trio aware that the attention of the whole bar was fixed on our little show. "The music's fucked and the buggers don't even have football up on the telly. More fuckin' hockey. C'mon. It's time to fuck off out of here anyway..."

I glanced over my shoulder at one of the aforementioned "tellys." Ice hockey was playing. Ice hockey. *Canadian* ice hockey. What was wrong with the NFL? Hell, I'd even settle for croquet over Canadian ice hockey. Maybe the guy had a point. Maybe I should leave, too.

The three Englishmen pushed past with a drunken swagger. I could ignore attitude much easier than a swinging pool cue. I kept an eye on the door to make sure no one else followed them out. No one did.

"Hey, nicely done," said one of the SOC guys who'd backed me up.

There was something familiar about the guy's face. I knew him from somewhere. As I was trying to sort through the Identi-Kit pictures in my head, he said, "Hey—it's Vin. Vin Cooper, right?"

I still couldn't make the connection.

"Drew McNaught," he said. "Remember?"

The dime dropped. "Yeah, Drew...Didn't recognize you there for a second...How ya doin', buddy!"

"It *is* you!" McNaught and I shook hands. "God-damn it. Long time, Vin. What you doin' round these parts, brother?"

I told him about OSI. He told me he was instructing static line parachute jumps.

We got past the small talk and current affairs—the events in San Francisco—and moved on to old times. McNaught and I had been in combat together back when I did completely stupid things. As part of Operation Allied Force, we'd jumped onto a hill in Kosovo to plant an aircraft navigation beacon so that our airmen would be able to pin the tail on the donkey. Trouble began the moment we landed. The weather unexpectedly closed in and our extraction was canceled. Also, a platoon-sized band of Serb militiamen saw us put down and tried to outflank us. From the way they moved, we guessed they were farm boys and were most probably out to settle old scores with their neighbors, but that didn't make their bullets any less lethal. They outnumbered us seven to one, and took potshots at us as we retreated toward UN ground, severely wounding one of our guys. McNaught was the ranking noncom on that mission, a hard and fearless man. On the second night of our retreat, he crept into their bivouac and killed five of them, taking their heads, without being discovered. The Serbs broke off the engagement that morning. Perhaps they no longer liked the odds.

On a more personal level, McNaught was also the father of twins and cried in movies, if my memory served me correctly. But that was a long time ago and maybe he'd toughened up. He introduced his buddy Marco. I shook the guy's hand, which was calloused and felt like a brick in my palm.

The band hung around till about eleven P.M. and so did McNaught, Marco, and I. A couple of interesting facts emerged by about my sixth or seventh single malt. The first of which—and perhaps the most surprising—was that McNaught had divorced and come out of the closet, and that he and Marco were on a date. The other interesting thing I learned was that one of the Limeys I'd shown the front door to earlier was Staff Sergeant Chris Butler, the same man who'd possibly helped Master Sergeant Ruben Wright on his one-way ride to the refrigerator.

EIGHTEEN

Early the following morning, I found myself beside an area the size of a basketball court outlined with yellow crime-scene tape. Colonel Selwyn didn't end up making the trip. Her son had come down with something, and so company was limited to a map and a handheld GPS. It was reasonably open ground peppered here and there with scrub and low trees, surrounded on three sides with thick pine forest and a cleared hill on the fourth. The air was thick with the smell of pine sap, wet grass, and decaying peat. It might once have been a dump but nature was doing a reasonable job of reclaiming it. I put on the sterile over-boots so that I could walk around the scene without introducing anything new to it, though my caution was probably unnecessary; in the open air, new material was being brought into the site and taken away constantly by the wind and insects. Proving my point, a couple of squirrels scampered about, picking up bits of foliage.

I ducked under the tape. I had no idea what I was looking for. Maybe the missing knife. Or maybe it was just to let Ruben's ghost know that I was on the case. This was not a Road Runner cartoon and so there was no depression in the ground where my former squadron buddy had come to rest, although there was a white spray-painted outline on the grass around a small bush that had been flattened, its thin green trunk snapped off at ground level. Presumably it had done its best to break Wrong Way's fall. Its best hadn't been near good enough.

Two hours later, I'd found nothing inside the tape, but I did firm up my theory that if the knife *had* come down here, it wouldn't have been just lying around waiting to be picked up. The earth was soft and loamy. The knife would certainly have kept going, burying itself well over the hilt and pulling the dirt in behind it. The sun was out, but the air was cool and still smelled of rain. I had no pressing engagements so I began to walk the area outside the tape. I needed the exercise. I hadn't been able to do my usual morning run for over a week. And also, the walk gave me time to think. Colonel Selwyn was right, there really was only one possible theory that fit the facts we had: Wright had been cut out of his chute. It couldn't have happened in the plane on the climb to the drop zone. It would have happened on the way down. Special Forces, especially SAS and CCTs, do a lot of aerial work—they are highly adept parachutists. The sort of maneuver required in midair of the assailant would have been difficult, but not impossible. The unanswered question was whether it was murder or an unfortunate accident. Perhaps there'd been a collision. It had been a night jump. Maybe Wrong Way had just been plain unlucky. But if that's what had happened, why would the men who jumped with him hide the truth?

More than a hundred and fifty feet from the taped area, I scuffed my shoe over a tuft of grass and something caught my attention. It caught my attention on account of it was red where everything else around it was green. I pulled an evidence bag from my pocket and used it as a glove to remove the object. It was a sliver of plastic. If this was a supermarket parking lot, I'd have said it was possibly part of the remains of some housewife's brake light. Maybe it was nothing, but, this close to a crime scene, maybe it was something. A tearing sound, far overhead, distracted me. I knew that sound.

I stood and used my hand as a glare visor, squinting upward. The source of the noise took a moment or two to locate. And then I saw them. They were dropping fast, small black fleas against the blue. I counted five. At a height of perhaps fifteen hundred feet, black parachutes opened. A second or two followed before I heard the distant, familiar cracks, like the sound of a baseball bat smacking into a heavy punching bag. I watched the parachutes fly in a descending corkscrew pattern. The way they came down reminded me of the double helix. That prompted me to wonder how Bradley Chalmers was getting along with the *Natusima*'s cook in Guam. I sure hoped he was getting absolutely nothing from the trip besides a tan. Actually, I hoped it was overcast.

The fleas landed on the far side of the open, marshy ground that separated us. Watching them flare their chutes and touch down safely, gently, made me wonder how Wrong Way had come down. Had he panicked or had he resigned himself to his fate? What thoughts had gone through his mind just before his boots did? A Humvee pickup appeared from the scrub between the parachutists and the crime scene. It splashed across the marsh, heading toward the soldiers as they gathered their chutes under their arms.

After making the collection, the vehicle headed back to the point where it had appeared. But then it did a sudden ninety-degree detour in my direction. I stood my ground and it stopped. Its rear door swung open. Two guys hopped out as three others jumped down from the rear. They were all wearing Disruptive Pattern Material camouflage—different from our "woodland pattern" battle-dress uniforms, or BDUs. In other words, they were visitors. I gave them a quick once-over. They appeared to be fully kitted up with ammunition pouches and various stores attached to webbing points. They were minus their chute bags, Kevlar helmets, and weapons, all of which were piled in the back of the Humvee. The driver stayed behind the wheel, keeping the motor running.

The men facing me had their faces painted with camouflage. I was wondering what they wanted, when the guy in front said, "Well, if it isn't Mr. Plod . . ."

And then I saw the blond tips and it clicked. "What did you say?" I asked.

He shrugged, hands on hips. "You're a copper. Back home, Mr. Plod is what we call coppers. Term of endearment, an' all."

"You're a long way from home, Mack. And here you can call me Special Agent Cooper." Once I'd established that he wasn't endearing himself to me, I said, "And you are . . . ?" I already knew, of course, but I didn't want the guy knowing that I'd already attached his name and face to the death of Sergeant Wright.

"Staff Sergeant Chris Butler, Her Britannic Majesty's Special Air Service Regiment. I heard a rumor there was going to be a new investigator appointed. If that's you, then you'd know I was with Sergeant Wright when he bought the farm. And please accept my humble apology, *Special Agent*. No disrespect intended."

"What are you doing here?" I asked.

"So, *are* you? Taking over the investigation?"

Asking questions was my job, not his. "What are you doing here, Staff?" I repeated.

"That's our drop zone," he said, indicating back over his shoulder. "We were in the vicinity, so the lads and I thought we'd come over and pay our respects to the late sergeant's ghost."

I didn't buy that. Most probably on his way down Butler had seen the beacon that was my Hawaiian shirt loitering around the taped-off area and was just being nosy.

"Are you and your men around later today?" I inquired.

"I've got nothing planned. Lads?" He turned to get a consensus from his men. They gave a collective shrug.

I gathered they'd be around, too.

"You know where we're staying?" Butler asked.

"I'll find you. Expect me at sixteen hundred hours."

"We'll put on a brew," he said.

Something irregular caught my attention. "You've lost your flashlight, Staff." A flashlight was part of a para's inventory, just like a knife, and, as Clare Selwyn had said, Special Forces soldiers were fanatical about their gear. It was usually attached to the webbing on the chest.

"Oh, hadn't noticed. Must have left it back at the hacienda," he said, padding down the front of his webbing.

In my pocket was, I believed, a fragment from a low-light red lens, the type commonly found on a typical military flashlight. Maybe the fragment had come from Butler's. If so, what was it doing here? How had it come to be smashed? And if it had come from his flashlight, why lie about it? Maybe I'd found a genuine clue here. Or maybe the fragment belonged to one of those squirrels.

"Anything else we can help you with?" Butler asked.

"Not just at the moment," I replied.

"Well, we'll catch you later, then, eh?" Butler climbed back into the Humvee, all smiles. The others climbed up after him, all except one. Unlike the rest, this guy wasn't smiling. He also had an anxious look on his face like he'd just passed a monkey wrench. I wanted to know why.

NINETEEN

It was just after 1400 hours by the time I made it back to my quarters. I fixed myself a sandwich with supplies bought from the Hurlburt Field BX, and stoked up the coffee machine. I phoned Agent Lyne and obtained an address for Butler and his team. According to Lyne's information, the men were all renting an apartment in Destin together, which made sense. It was quite near The Funkster, where I'd come across the Brits the previous evening. Lyne was interested in knowing how it was all going. I assured him that it was going quite well, although, unbeknown to him, I was referring to the pastrami and cheese on rye I was halfway through.

I bumped my laptop, which woke it from its slumber, and I saw the e-mail icon jumping. I put the sandwich down and checked my Hotmail mailbox. I had a long list of unread messages—bonus deals on bulk purchases of Viagra and e-mails dripping with virus. I trashed all but one, an electronic notice from the *San Francisco Chronicle*.

The subject of the e-mail caused a double take. It read, "*CEO leaves Moreton Genetics.*" I clicked through and skimmed the article that originated in the newspaper's business pages. Basically, in a move that had surprised the market, Dr. Frederique Spears had resigned after less than two years in MG's top job. Her stated reasons for doing so were personal. The article said Spears had thrown in the towel late on the day after Christmas. The stock market had since reacted negatively to the news and MG's stocks were trading sharply down. Yadda yadda. Spears had resigned barely a day and a half after my interview with her. Had the interview been the cause of her resignation? The timing sure was fascinating. I recalled the look on her face when I'd told her that I believed Boyle had murdered Tanaka.

I finished off the sandwich while I contemplated this. Down here in Florida, working a new case, I'd been living in a bit of a news vacuum the past couple of days. I went to the *Chronicle*'s home page to check on the latest events there. Security-camera footage taken in the area of the Transamerica building showed the van packed with explosives several seconds before it blew. It turned out the van had been rented by two Americans "who looked like a couple of Arabs," according to a woman at the rental company. The story said the ethnic heritage of these "Arabs" was unknown. I was skeptical about that. More than likely, the police knew everything there was to know about the perpetrators by now, only the information was being selectively released to the media. The bombers apparently had no prior record or known contact with terrorists. Hadn't even collected so much as a parking ticket between them. As far as their friends and neighbors were concerned, they were Americans. Had to be—they wore Nike sweatshirts and baseball caps.

To reduce suspicion, the "Arabs" had not used ammonium nitrate, the oxidizing agent of choice in most truck bombs. Instead, they'd purchased potassium nitrate for use in glassmaking—glassmaking being their stated business and occupation. Basically, the bomb makers knew exactly what they were doing. Potassium nitrate is every bit as potent as ammonium nitrate, especially when combined with diesel oil, rubber, and sand in what the FBI's forensics team determined to have been "ideal proportions." Meanwhile, over at the Four Winds, the gas had burned so fiercely that no items of forensic interest had been recovered from that scene.

The body count at the scene had risen since I was there. Far too many of the critically injured had failed to respond to treatment. I noted that the numbers of people missing as a result of the bombing had shrunk to twelve.

I put in a call to Arlen on his cell. "Hey," I said when he picked up.

"Vin. How's it going down there?" He was instantly suspicious. "You *are* still down in Florida, aren't you?"

"Of course."

He relaxed a little. "So how's the tan coming along?"

"Coming along great. Haven't left the hotel pool since I got here."

"Really? I looked at the weather channel this morning and I saw it'd been raining."

"Raining sunshine, buddy."

"Well, whatever, you're lucky you're down there and not in D.C. Round here, sleep is a dirty word at the moment."

"It's pretty frantic here, too, you know. You have to remember to flip over on the hour to avoid sunburn."

"Yeah, yeah. Something I can do for you, Vin?"

"As a matter of fact, no."

"That's a nice change."

"Just rang to say hello and ask if the tests on Boyle's wallet have come through, and whether he's still on the missing list."

"I class that as something—and you're not in the loop on that one anymore, Vin," Arlen said, after a pause.

"C'mon, Arlen."

"I'm not in it, either."

"I know, but you're like the girl in reception. You know everything going on."

"You really know how to stroke my ego, Vin."

"I read Freddie Spears resigned shortly after I spoke to her."

"Really? What did you say to her?"

"To make her resign? I told her I believed Boyle got Tanaka drunk and then threw him to that shark. She liked Tanaka and, from what I could tell, didn't think much of Boyle. Anything on that DVD, by the way?"

"Vin, c'mon. You promised to let this one go, to concentrate on the case you're working down there..."

"I know, and I haven't broken that promise. I just

got an automated e-mail from the *Chronicle* about Spears's resignation. Got me thinking, is all."

Arlen let this sink in before answering. "I know you're not going to believe me, but I don't know anything. I've heard nothing further about either the DVD or the wallet recovered there, or the case in general. And I'm not asking questions, either."

He was right; I didn't believe him. "Can you just find out one small thing for me?"

"No."

"I just want to know whether Boyle's body has been positively identified."

"No."

"It hasn't been IDed?"

I heard Arlen sigh. "So how *is* it going down there?" he asked again.

"You know what Florida's like?"

"Actually, I've never been there."

"Lots of women in bikinis," I said.

"Lucky you."

"Who're mostly pushing seventy."

"Thanks for that image," he said. "So, you going to answer my question?"

"You going to answer mine?"

"Vin, Jesus . . ."

"OK, OK," I said. "So far, from what I can see, it looks like a homicide."

"Seems there's a lot of that going around at the moment. I gotta go, Vin. Got a world to save here. Keep fighting the good fight, buddy."

"Talk later," I said.

"Yeah, later..."

I heard dial tone. He was right about one thing. The Boyle/Tanaka case was no longer mine, and I was completely out of the loop, but I had my own theory about Boyle and I had my doubts about Chalmers being able to successfully muddle his way to the truth.

I made a supreme effort to do as Arlen requested and put that case out of my head. I opened the refrigerator door and noticed a small triangle of paper poking out from under the appliance. I bent and picked it up. It was a photograph. I flipped it over and saw a picture of Ruben Wright smiling back at me. It had been taken at night. He had a beer in one hand and barbecue tongs in the other, which was draped around the shoulders of a redhead, a real looker. A Chicago Bulls cap was on his head. The guy was happy. This was the Wrong Way I remembered, only why was there a photo of the guy under the fridge in this place, and who was the redhead with eyes as green as an Irish meadow? I bent again and checked under the fridge in case there was a whole family album hiding there, but I couldn't get my eye down close enough to floor level to see. I found a broom, pushed the fridge so it tilted back against the rear wall, and raked under the machine with it. The harvest amounted to the lid from a jar of pickled cocktail onions, a bottle top, six giant balls of greasy dust, three dead cockroaches, and a pale blue pill.

I looked at the dusty collection on the floor, glanced at the picture, and tried to figure this out. There was only one possible answer. The area under the fridge is the home's equivalent of the belly button. I made another call.

"Agent Lyne."

"Lloyd, Vin Cooper."

"Hey. How you doin'?"

"Great. This place you've put me in. It was Ruben Wright's, wasn't it?"

Silence.

"Hello?" I said.

"Well, um, yeah, briefly."

"So that's why it had become so available all of a sudden? The tenant died?"

"Um . . . yeah, I guess."

"You guess? Why didn't you mention it?"

"I thought you might get a little . . . I don't know . . . maybe get a little squeamish."

"Where's the rest of his stuff?" I asked.

"We boxed it."

"Was he married?"

"No."

"Then where's it going?"

"Hang on . . ."

He put the phone down and I heard him wrestle with a filing cabinet drawer. After a few moments, he came back on the line. "He didn't have much in the way of family. He had an uncle. Lives over in Gainesville. Left the guy a few things—pictures of his folks, not much else. Pretty much willed everything to one Amy McDonough."

The name didn't mean anything to me. As Lyne had already pointed out that I knew as much as he did, I didn't ask him what her relationship was to Wright. I'd ask her. "You got an address? Contact details?"

"Address only. Lives in Pensacola."

Now that I thought about it, I vaguely recalled something about Ruben's old man running off when he was a kid. His mom died when we were in the CCTs together—cancer, if I remembered correctly. There'd been a little money left to him, along with a farm somewhere, which Ruben had sold. The service had become his mom, dad, sisters, and brothers, precisely because he didn't have any, except for that uncle, whom he never mentioned, at least not to me. "You said his effects were being sent."

"Yeah."

"So they're still here on the base?"

"Yep. You want to see them?"

"If you're taking requests," I said.

"I'll arrange it."

"So, put me ahead of the game here. You got an inventory handy?"

"Says here . . . a little furniture—sofa, table and chairs, gym equipment, home entertainment system . . ." He rattled off a number of items. "Hey, the guy had some nice stuff!"

Last I heard, consumerism wasn't a crime in this country. And Ruben was unmarried—had to spend his money on something. Why not himself?

"There are a few books, clothes, photos . . ."

"Any records?"

"As in The Beatles, Elvis . . . ?"

"As in tax, phone company..." I wondered how long Lyne had been in OSI, so I asked.

"Three months. Does it show that bad?"

"No," I said, both of us knowing it did. But the guy was doing his best. "I'd like to see a copy of Ruben's will, along with those records."

"No problem. I'll get them brought in, along with a couple of tables so you can spread it all out."

"I also want the service records of Staff Sergeant Butler and his men."

"Easy," said Lyne.

"Can you get them to my quarters now?"

"Done."

"What about medicines? Did he have anything prescription listed among his personal effects?" I picked the pill off the floor between thumb and forefinger. I cupped it in my hand. It was pale blue and pitted—nibbled? None of the roach carcasses appeared to be dried-out husks. They hadn't been dead long. A week maybe. Perhaps they'd all keeled over at roughly the same time. Maybe it was something they ate.

"Let me check." I heard paper being flicked over. "No...no, nothing special. The list here says... Tylenols, floss, condoms, antiseptic cream, hemorrhoid cream—the usual. I thought you had all this."

I told him I didn't. I only had the coroner's report along with Selwyn's and the previous investigator's notes, all of which suggested that if Butler didn't do it then one of his helpers did. So far, I hadn't seen anything that might have led me to disagree with this broader view. But I had a few things to check on and I wanted to keep an open mind.

*   *   *

I followed Highway 98 as it tracked the shoreline, in one side of Destin and out the other. I checked the number on the white stucco wall to make sure it matched the address I'd written down in my notebook. SAS Staff Sergeant Butler, Corporal William Dortmund, Lance Corporal Brian Wignall, and Troopers Damian Mortensen and Brent Norris were shacked up nice and cozy and convenient—for me—in a detached mock-Spanish–style house on the cheap side of the highway, the landward side.

The clouds had rolled away and the sky down toward Cuba was the color of polished copper. The molten sun sat a couple of inches off the horizon as I pulled into the driveway.

One of Butler's men answered the doorbell—I recognized him from the photo attached to his file. Trooper Norris was the shortest of the Brits, stocky, with powerful arms and legs like Christmas hams. He had dirty blond hair and skin flushed a bright red. It was the type of skin that was always that color, like it was reacting badly to something. Maybe it was something in the air, like America. Whatever, he invited me to come in and so I followed him into the small living room, which had been converted into sleeping quarters for three of the men.

Sleeping bags were rolled up out of the way. Gear was stacked neatly everywhere. Their mothers would have been proud. Two of the men were cleaning and servicing various items. The place smelled of male body odor, spray deodorant, and old pizza, boxes for which were piled neatly on the kitchen table. The door opened to what I guessed was a bathroom because Butler walked out with a towel around his waist and another around his shoulders. "Oh, just a sec," he said, ducking behind another door and appearing a moment later dressed in shorts and a T-shirt that stuck to his skin where it was still wet.

"Sorry, guv'nor," he said. "Didn't realize the time."

Butler smelled like he'd bathed in cologne, and his hair was gelled up like a cockscomb. I handed him five of my cards, each with a time written on the flip side.

"What are these for, then?" he asked.

"I want to interview you and your men separately tomorrow morning. I've checked your training schedule and you've got a rest day. The appearance order's up to you, Staff Sergeant, except that I want to see you last," I said. Butler and his men had been together long enough after the death of Sergeant Wright to have put their stories in order. I figured another twelve hours wouldn't make any difference. And, in fact, there was really only one of the men I wanted to talk to. I just didn't want Butler to know that. "In the meantime, do you know who this is?" I showed Butler the photo I'd found under the fridge.

"Yeah, that's Sergeant Wright."

"Thanks. The woman. Who's the woman?"

"The light's not good. I think that's Amy. What do you think, Norris? Is that Amy?"

He showed the picture to Norris, who nodded tentatively. "Yeah," he said. "Could be."

The light in the photo wasn't great, but the woman's face was clearly visible. "That would be Amy McDonough?" I asked. Poor light or not, there couldn't have been many women around who looked like Amy, let alone women who looked like Amy and who also had the same name.

Norris mumbled something. He glanced at Butler. Butler took over. "Yeah, Amy McDonough. I think Amy and Sergeant Wright were friends."

"What sort of friends?"

"The sort that's more than friends. Or were."

"You care to speak American for me, Staff Sergeant?"

"They were shagging, but I believe they split up," said Butler.

All but one of the men seemed relaxed about making eye contact. The guy who wouldn't look me in the face was the same man I remembered seeming uncomfortable at the crime scene. "Do you know where she works?" I asked.

Butler shook his head. His men played "Sergeant says," copying him. It was easy to see who was boss, and it wasn't me. They were cautious, like I might be the kind of animal that could turn around and bite them. Butler, on the other hand, was a known quantity to these guys. He *would* maul them. I'd met guys like Butler before. They made life hell for the people around them and beneath them, while they buried their noses between the ass cheeks of their superiors. They were not good leaders. In battle, they got good people killed. In peacetime, they got good people in trouble.

"Well, if you guys run into Amy, tell her to give me a call. You've all got my number." It wasn't the only reason I handed out my card to each. I wanted Butler's men to have someone they could contact if anything was preying on their minds. "I'll see one of you tomorrow at OSI, Hurlburt Field, oh-nine-hundred. Sharp." I walked out without waiting for acknowledgment.

*   *   *

Later that evening, I was beginning to think that maybe I was slipping. It could be that Butler always dolled himself up before hitting the sack, but I doubted it. The Explorer I was sitting in was backed into the shadows provided by a building a little down the road from the house Butler and his men had rented. The local radio station was rotating through the hit parade, just filler for a barrage of inane advertising for local restaurants, tire stores, and the casinos in Biloxi selling cheap rooms to suckers. Three hours of this and my brain was turning to mush.

But then, at just after 2130, a cab arrived. Butler ducked out his front door and jumped in.

I followed the cab for thirty miles down Highway 98 to Laguna Beach. There, it pulled up to a bar with a flashing neon palm tree over the entrance. More flashing neon informed me this was Miss Palm's. It was the sort of out-of-the-way place where Butler was unlikely to run into anyone he knew, unless the meeting was of the arranged variety. Butler got out and went inside. I pulled the SUV under the fronds of a stand of real palm trees and told myself to give it ten minutes. I only had to wait five. A red Chevy Cavalier in need of a wash pulled into the lot. The brake lights went out, and the interior light came on. I watched a woman touch up her lipstick in the rearview mirror. She got out of the vehicle—a looker in jeans, heels, and leather jacket. The light wasn't so good, but Amy's red hair shone. And she was tall, maybe five eleven. Striking, was the word that came instantly to mind. I made a note of her license plate.

There were plenty of cars in Miss Palm's parking lot, indicating a crowd. I took a calculated risk and walked in. The decor was designed to resemble a tropical beach shack—the sort created by expensive architects following local building codes to the letter. The air smelled of barbecue, sautéed garlic, perfume, and wine. U2's "Beautiful Day" was playing through hidden speakers. Amy McDonough and Butler were at the bar, sitting behind a couple of super-sized margaritas. Amy seemed angry. Butler was doing the talking, attempting to mollify her. I couldn't get close enough to hear what the problem was, not without revealing my presence. But whatever he was trying to sell her, McDonough wasn't buying it. They weren't exactly making a scene. Her anger was more the smoldering kind, the sort generated between people who'd shared bodily fluids and were maybe starting to regret it.

I hadn't been there more than ten minutes before I realized the crowd in the place was thinning. I didn't want to be seen. I left as Amy stomped off to the ladies' room while Butler stared at the floor, shaking his head. Maybe he, too, was thinking about the drive back to Hurlburt Field with nothing but the local radio station for company.

TWENTY

I woke in darkness, ran five miles in the dark, and had enough time left over to boil a couple of eggs before the sun finally rose, revealing a sky so blue and cloudless it could have been a dome of spray-painted metal.

The run had done me good. I'd missed doing regular exercise. Going for an extended jog around the place also gave me the chance to refamiliarize myself with the layout of Hurlburt Field while I thought about Sergeant Wright, Amy, Butler, and those dead cockroaches. I also thought about the DVD, about who might have put it under the hotel room door, and about what the pictures on it meant. Moreton Genetics was a high-security facility, as Dr. Spears had pointed out. Cameras were everywhere, inside and out. While I ran, I also ran these thoughts around my brain until they all started to run together like the colors in a four-year-old's painting, making even less sense than when I started.

After breakfast, I called Colonel Selwyn on her cell. She was already in. I met her at her office ten minutes later. She was at her desk, head obscured by a computer screen, filling in forms, keeping on top of the triplicate beast. "Morning. How's your man?" I asked.

She glanced up. "Hi—he'll live. But I don't know about his mother. I've had about three hours' sleep in the last twenty-four."

She looked pretty good, I decided. Sleep deprivation agreed with her.

"You ever going to change out of that Hawaiian shirt? First thing in the morning, it kinda hurts the eyes, you know what I'm saying?"

"Just keeping that Christmas feeling," I said. "A few things have come up," I added.

"Like what?"

"I'm not sure yet. You did toxicology tests on Wright?"

"SOP. Screened for cocaine, barbs, alcohol, meth— that sort of thing. You know from my report he was clean. Why? What are you thinking?"

"Could be nothing, could be something. Can you test this for me?" I pulled the small plastic bag out of my pocket.

"What is it?"

"I'm hoping you'll tell me."

Selwyn squeezed the pill into a corner of the bag and held it up to the light for closer inspection. "Looks prescription. Where'd you find it?"

"Under the refrigerator at Wright's house. They missed it when they cleaned the place out." It wasn't necessary to tell her that I'd been billeted in his last place of residence.

"Was he there short term or long term?"

"Short term."

"Whatever this is, it might not have been his. Could have been a previous tenant's."

"I guess."

"Like you said—could be something, could be nothing. I'll get it tested."

"I found a photograph under there, too. Can you have a look at it?" I handed her the bag.

"Who's the woman?" asked Selwyn.

"Her name's Amy McDonough. I think she was Ruben's girlfriend. There's also this." I pulled another evidence bag from my pocket. "Could be a piece of flashlight lens. Can you check it for me?"

"You found this under the fridge, too?"

"No. Out near the crime scene. In the general vicinity thereof."

"What do you term 'the general vicinity'?"

"Within a hundred yards of it."

Selwyn shook her head, angry with herself. "I walked every square inch of that damn patch of swamp."

I said nothing.

"What are you hoping for?" She was examining the piece of red plastic, frowning at it.

"A blinding flash of clarity wouldn't hurt."

"Oh, right, one of them." Selwyn held up the bag containing the pill. "I'll have to send this off. Might take a couple of days."

The clock on the wall said I had to get my ass across to OSI. I was late. I had interviews to conduct.

*   *   *

I'd been getting the same answers for two hours. Butler's men repeated identical stories and even repeated
a lot of the same phrases. And then it was Lance Corporal Brian Wignall's turn under the blowtorch,
which, in this instance, was a bank of overhead fluorescent tubes, one of which buzzed. If I was an epilep-
tic, it would be grand mal time.

Wignall had a broad Liverpool accent, sandy hair,
and sandy skin. The muscles in his jaws worked when
he talked, like they were chewing steel.

I went through the questions and he went through
the responses—no deviation from the details related
by his buddies. But, unlike his buddies, Wignall was
uneasy. I asked about Wright's relationship with the
squad generally, and with Butler in particular. I asked
about Amy. I asked about the High Altitude Low
Opening drop—Wright's last. What I got was that
Ruben Wright was well liked by the men and by Butler. I got nowhere further on Amy. I got a mirror-
image account of the drop. I got a bunch of half-truths
and semi-lies.

The interview concluded, Wignall stood and took
half a step. Then he stopped and turned, as if he was
reluctant to leave. His fellow squad members had almost sprinted to get out the door.

"You're not going to get another chance like this,
Wignall," I said. "If there's something eating away at
you, now's the time to tell me what that something is."

Wignall took another halfhearted step toward the door.

"Y'know, I can always do it different—I could detain you. Start the interview later today, or even tomorrow," I told him. "Maybe get your military attaché involved."

Wignall's palms were sweating. He wiped one on the front of his pants.

"If you know something, sooner or later you'll spill it. Like I said, we can do it now when no one need know, or I can single you out for something long and drawn-out. That'll send a message to your buddies on the other side of that door—choice is yours."

Wignall bit into the skin beside his thumbnail and peeled it away. "Staff Sergeant Butler is a very fit man." He said it slow and steady, like he'd rehearsed it in his head.

"And...?" I said, motioning at the chair.

Before he sat, Wignall pulled something from behind his back and placed it on the desk between us. It was a flashlight, a military flashlight, the sort of flashlight paras use. Its low-light red lens was smashed. Part of that broken lens came loose and fell out onto the desk, making a tinkling sound.

"I liked Sergeant Wright," Wignall said, going another round with his thumb, his front teeth sliding back and forth over a shred of skin. "He was a good man. A good soldier. I don't know what happened when he died—not exactly—but I can guess."

"I can do my own guessing. Just tell me what you know."

Wignall glanced at his watch, and then at the door again, weighing odds. His interview had been the shortest of the bunch. The question was written into the lines that appeared across his forehead and the glances at the door: *How much time do I have before the others get suspicious?*

"I'm not good at games, Lance Corporal," I said. "If you have information that could help this inquiry along, you're obligated to provide it. I can guarantee you that you will not be named as an informant."

After what seemed like an age of eye contact, he responded. "OK."

The digital recorder was on the table between us. I pressed record.

"Is that necessary?" he asked, glancing back at the door, nervous.

"Don't worry about it. It's just more reliable than my notebook. Mostly, I can't even read my own handwriting."

Wignall took a deep breath. "In for a penny..." he murmured. He hunched forward, hands clasped between his knees. The overhead fluorescent tube blinked on irregularly like a metronome with a busted spring.

"It was a night drop," he began. "The skies were clear—a little high cloud above us at twenty thousand feet. Visibility was clear, as good as it gets. Between us and the DIP"—the desired impact point—"it was clean air. We were doing a High Altitude Low Opening jump."

"Was this your first HALO with Sergeant Wright?"

"No. We'd done six or seven by then. We were in the groove."

"What was the purpose of the jumps?"

"Training. Nothing special. We're doing more and more work with Special Forces from other countries these days, especially the U.S., of course. We do stuff with Delta, Seals, the CCTs...It's about making sure we do the same things and that we do them right."

I knew that speech. I'd heard it enough times over the years—even given it myself on a couple of occasions. Without the accent, Wignall sounded like typical Special Forces—full of confidence for "The Mission." With that Liverpool accent, though, I kept thinking he was going to break into "A Hard Day's Night."

"Tell me about the last jumps," I said.

"We were in a C-130, climbing. There was no talk, but only 'cause you can't hear yourself think in a C-130, let alone hear what anyone's saying, right? The atmos in the plane between the lads was relaxed. It wasn't like what we were doing was anything out of the ordinary, though there was the tension between Sergeant Wright and Staff Sergeant Butler before we took off."

"What was it about—the tension?"

"The Staff's not the easiest person to get along with. It's his way or the highway."

That brought back a memory—we used to say it was the Wright way or the highway. But, in this instance, I believed there was more to it than professional ribbing.

And she had red hair. "What about Amy McDonough?" I asked.

"Yeah, she was part of it. A big part of it, at least as far as Sergeant Wright was concerned. None of us was sure what sort of relationship he had with her—whether it was on or off between them. But we knew what Butler was up to, 'cause he likes us all to know how successful he is with the birds. The Staff fancies himself as a bit of a ladies' man, if you know what I mean. He's the type who likes to get the business done quick so he can get down to the pub and brag to his friends about it. He was bonking Amy sideways, and everything else he could get his hands on. It's a thing with Butler, sir. He'd shag the bristles on a hairbrush."

"You sound a little like you were offended by all this."

"I'm a Christian. I don't agree with sex before marriage. It's against my religion."

The words "you're kidding" nearly slipped out. Displays of Christian fervor from anyone other than a priest or a movie star collecting an Oscar always took me by surprise. I cleared my throat. "Do you know whether Sergeant Wright knew about Butler and McDonough?"

"No, but, you know . . ."

"No. I don't," I said.

"Staff or Amy might not have told him they were together. Not in as many words, but the vibe was easy to pick up . . ."

Hmm. Interesting. I said, "So you're in the plane and nearly everyone's having a great time..."

"We jacked out of the aircraft's oxygen system three minutes from the jump, when the red jump lights came on, and switched to our own bottled oxy. The idea was for the stick to come out in a packet—all of us hanging onto each other as we exited the C-130. So we could keep a tight formation on the way down and all land together."

I knew the routine. I'd done exactly this kind of thing myself before the issue between gravity and me got personal.

"We got ourselves set on the ramp. I remember looking out the back, into the night. It was pitch-black. No moon. We grabbed a handful of each other—a sleeve, webbing—and half walked, half shuffled down to the edge of the ramp. That's where the problem started. As half the packet fell out, Butler tripped and his stumble broke us up. We came out of the plane in dribs and drabs. No big deal, I thought, and it wasn't—not at first. We re-formed in the air, the lads getting themselves into position, making a V as we descended. Below me, I could see the green reflective strips on the back of the guys' helmets and chute bags. The way we rehearsed it, Staff was to be the point of the arrow, the lowest. Above and to his left was supposed to be Mortensen. Over his right shoulder, Billy Dortmund. Above Dortmund, Norris. Above Mortensen, me. Over all of us, in the center of the formation, was Sergeant Wright's station, observing. That's when I knew there was a problem. Below me, I should have been able to see three reflective strips—Mortensen's, Dortmund's, and Butler's. But I could only see two. One of the fluorescent strips was missing. It wasn't because we were dropping through cloud. The night was cloudless. I didn't know who was out of formation until I landed—it could have been Mortensen, Dortmund, or Butler."

This was a departure from the events relayed by the other guys, and an important one. "So you're on the way down and you can see someone's not in the formation. Are you concerned at this point?" I asked.

"No, not really. I saw Butler stumble. It bugged me because I like these things done proper. But being able to iron out the kinks is why we train. Anyway, I deployed my chute at three thousand feet, and I hit the DIP light as a feather—a perfect drop, except for the fuckup at the beginning. At this stage, I knew it was Butler who was out of formation because I watched him land. If he'd been in formation, he'd have been first on the ground. Also, there was no Sergeant Wright anywhere to be seen. We waited around for a few minutes, but he didn't show. Any minute, I expected him to walk out of the bushes with his chute tucked under his arm, with an offer to buy us all a pint or three, but there was just silence. Something was wrong—we could all sense it, feel it in the air. I pulled my flashlight and started to sweep the area. Perhaps he was down and injured. There were trees on the edge of the DIP; he might have been hung up on one of them, I thought. The rest of the lads did the same, searching with their flashlights. The only one of us who didn't was Butler. He was having difficulty bundling up his chute. The way he was moving I thought he might have hurt his back or a shoulder. I didn't know at the time that his flashlight—the one you got there—was unserviceable, that the lens was broken."

"Did anything set off any alarm bells at the time?"

"Honestly? No, sir. And not when we found Sergeant Wright's body, either. Accidents aren't unheard of—equipment fails. I could see he'd become separated from his chute harness."

"Is that when you became suspicious?"

"More confused than suspicious, sir. I wondered how he got separated from his harness and then the concern began when the investigation started. The questions, Butler's evasion, especially then when you asked him about his flashlight. I went looking for it. I found it in our garbage can back at the house. Also, I've noticed that Butler's injuries haven't improved. I reckon he's broken a couple of ribs, though he's trying to hide it. Made me wonder why. And then we heard Sergeant Wright was cut out of his harness on the way down." He paused and scrutinized me. "Is that what happened, sir?"

I didn't answer.

There was a little more back-and-forth with Wignall—a reiteration of questions and answers—but none of it of consequence. I stopped the recorder as I watched Wignall open the door. Butler was standing behind it, waiting. Or was he listening?

TWENTY-ONE

I drove through the town of Fort Walton Beach. In my head I went over the next interview, the one with SAS Staff Sergeant Chris Butler. Unfortunately I'd had barely fifteen minutes with the guy before Dortmund cut it short with the unit's movement orders. Butler and his men were required at Fort Bragg immediately. Butler politely excused himself, got up and left, and there wasn't a damn thing I could do about it. I'd been in this game long enough not to disagree with a document bearing a lieutenant general's signature.

An hour later, I drove to the flight line. The wind whipping in from the beach was peppered with grit and raindrops. I watched the SAS unit ferry their gear from a couple of Humvees onto the tail ramp of a C-130. I couldn't help but notice that Butler didn't lift, he supervised. Protecting those ribs?

I stayed until all the gear was stowed and only the ground crew remained. As one of the aircraft's props began to rotate and I restarted the SUV's engine, a man walked back down the ramp and out from the deep shadow thrown by the transport plane's tail assembly. It was Butler. He waved at me.

It didn't feel like good-bye. It felt more like fuck you.

Heading back to OSI, I was pissed enough to consider an eleven-hour drive straight to Bragg. I could be a sore loser, especially when the players just up and leave the board before the game's over. Then I thought about it some more and decided chasing Butler was a bad idea. The Brit might only be spending a short time at Bragg—it might merely be the staging place for a mission elsewhere. I might get there and find them gone, jumped off to another destination. If that happened, I might feel like a moron.

My problem was that, in all probability, I had a murder case on my hands, only I had no real evidence and only hearsay to hand over to JAG. Evidentiary facts and maybe the odd reliable eyewitness or two— the only things that counted in a court-martial—were thin on the ground.

I picked up the recorder and hit play.

My voice: *Take a seat.*

Butler: *Ta.*

If I had a moment when Butler would be caught off guard, it was this. Last to be interviewed, he'd have asked his men where my line of questioning had gone, but he wouldn't know for certain whether one or none of his men had departed from the party line. My intention was to come out swinging.

My voice: *So . . . why did you kill Sergeant Wright?*

Butler: *Wright killed himself.* I thought I'd get angry denials, maybe a little outrage. Butler, though, was cool and self-assured. It was the reaction you'd expect from a man used to high-pressure situations.

My voice: *Maybe it was an accident. You didn't mean to kill him.*

Butler: *Guv, I was just as shocked as any of the lads to find Wright dead.*

My voice: *What happened to your flashlight?*

It got broken.

How?

Gear gets broken. A knock here, a bump there.

Take off your shirt.

I'd seen Butler without his shirt on back at the hacienda, but there had been a towel draped around his shoulders at the time that masked any injuries. Now he knew for certain someone had talked.

Through the small speaker, I heard the sound I knew to be that of his chair creaking as he stood, the slap of his webbing slipping its buckle, the faint rustle of fabric as he opened his buttons and removed his shirt. I'd seen bodies in a similar condition to Butler's, but mostly they were in a morgue. His torso carried numerous ugly scars, two of which I recognized as the entry scars made by bullets. He'd also been badly burned at some point. The skin at the base of his neck and around across his left shoulder was red and purple like boiled rhubarb. His left nipple had been completely sliced off by shrapnel—an old wound. Beneath the skin under his right arm was the yellow, purple, and black puddle of a deep bruise on the mend—the specific injury I was hoping to find.

My voice: *How many ribs you got broken, Staff?*

Butler: *Two.*

I was impressed. Butler moved easily, each movement economical and fluid, like he was in peak condition. This was one tough hombre.

My voice: *Been to the hospital for an X ray?*

Butler: *What, and get sidelined?*

You want to tell me about how you got it?

I know what you're thinking.

What am I thinking?

You reckon I plowed into Wright intentionally, and cut through his harness.

Is that what happened?

I'm not sure I know what happened. We all jumped together, but we all didn't walk away together. I didn't kill Wright. I reckon he knocked himself off.

Take me through the jump.

Will it help?

That depends.

On what?

On whether you're convincing.

The recorder picked up the sound of Butler putting his shirt back on. *A night HALO drop. We were high—twenty thousand feet. A clear night, free of cloud, but black as a black cat's crotch. We planned to make the drop in close formation, which meant coming out the back of the C-130 in a packet. The formation was to be arrowhead, with myself at the lowest point and Wright at the highest so he could keep our reflective strips in sight and check that the formation was tight and right. Anyway, that was the plan. Coming out of the plane, Wright tripped. Looking back, he might have done it on purpose. In regaining his footing, he pushed a couple of the guys off the ramp. No big deal—we're all wearing parachutes. The rest of us tumbled out to try to make*

*something of the drop anyway. When I looked down, I could
only see two of the reflective strips. The formation was a lost
cause—I had no idea where the other guys were. Then all of
a sudden, out of nowhere, I got rammed in midair. I'd been
hit by one of my own people—and hard, hard enough to
break ribs. And then I saw it was Wright. I recognized him
right away—he was a lot bigger than any of the lads. I also
saw he had his knife in his hand. As we dropped side by side,
I watched him hack through his own thigh strap, saw him
pull his rip cord. I was watching when he went one way and
his chute bag and harness went the other. There was nothing
I could do.*

So it was Wright who rammed you?

That's right, mate.

Do you think this was intentional, or an accident?

Dunno.

I remembered wondering as Butler told me this
whether Wright really had rammed into him intentionally, whether he wanted the SAS sergeant to see
him cut his own thigh strap. This thought was
strengthened as I listened to Butler again. But what
would Wright's motive be for doing that? What would
he hope to gain? Did he want Butler to witness his
suicide, if that's what really happened? And, if so,
why would he want Butler to watch?

Wright had made thousands of jumps under extreme conditions. This was a calm night, a training
jump, a low-stress walk in the park for a man with
Wright's experience. I found it hard to believe that he
would just fly into Butler. Unless he had a damn good
reason for doing so. And, of course, Butler could be

making all this up to hide the truth that he killed Wright.

My voice: *So what are you thinking as you land?*

Butler: *Well, I know Wright's dead. Cutting his harness like that? He might as well have sucked off his Beretta. I counted the lads as I flared. All present except one. At this stage they had no idea what had happened.*

You didn't raise the alarm. Why not?

I knew Wright had bought the farm and I knew how. I also knew I had broken ribs. Put these things together and it looked bad for me.

Yeah, it did then. And, as far as I was concerned, it still did.

When Wright didn't show, the lads got nervous. They started checking around with their flashlights, looking for him. I was going to do the same, only I discovered my flashlight was broken.

Were you and Wright's girlfriend, Amy, having an affair?

An affair? Who told you that?

Is that a yes?

That's a definite no. Again, Butler had been cool and calm, his face giving away no clues as to what he might be thinking.

The recorder picked up the knock on the door—Mortensen's untimely entrance. I clicked off the recorder, took a left turn, and slotted the SUV between a pair of white lines painted on the blacktop outside the OSI building. I killed the ignition and listened to the engine ticking. The thing with Amy McDonough was more than a little interesting. Wignall said Butler was having an affair, Butler said he wasn't.

Wignall said Butler tripped into the stick on the C-130's ramp the moment before the jump, but Butler said it was Wright who'd done the stumbling. Either Wright or Butler broke up the formation, but which one?

There was no doubt, however, that a midair collision between Butler and Wright had occurred. Whether intentional or not, the impact of them crashing into each other as they dropped through the thin, high-altitude air at over a hundred miles per hour was substantial enough to crack Butler's ribs and shatter his flashlight, a piece of which dropped out and tumbled to earth.

*   *   *

"Here's the details of that vehicle registration you asked for." Lyne wandered in with a large Post-it note hanging off the tip of his forefinger. "The phone company said they'd fax through the details of those calls."

I said thanks and stuck the Post-it in my notebook.

The paperwork of Ruben Wright's recent life was spread out on the table and across the linoleum floor, a little like the way the man himself ended up. Wright had been reasonably good with record keeping, saving receipts for things he bought—mostly for warranty purposes. There were quarterly reports from his bank, and he'd also made some pretty good investments in a couple of funds over the years. I was envious. The only thing I'd made over the last few years were bets—most of them bad. He had a couple hundred thousand dollars sloshing around in various accounts. The money was unusual—there weren't a lot of rich sergeants in the armed forces. If I hadn't known about the inheritance, I might have wondered where the zeros had come from.

I rubbed my chin and then scratched my head. Wrong Way had turned into a gadget man, and, according to the dates on the receipts, the conversion had been a reasonably recent event. Over the past two months, he'd acquired a new sound system, a new iPod and cell phone, a new digital camera, home gym equipment, a massage chair, a Harley-Davidson, new cutlery and dinner set, a new iron, new furniture, new clothes, and so on.

"You need anything else?" Lyne asked.

"Yeah. I don't see a copy of his will anywhere here. I also want access to his effects." I stretched, arching, pushing my hands into the small of my back. A couple of vertebrae gave way with a crack.

"Here's the will." A thick envelope landed on the desk beside my elbow with a heavy slap. "And no problem getting his effects. Which ones do you want? As you can see, there's a truckload of stuff."

"I'll make a list," I said, opening the envelope. It contained documents for various investment funds and life insurance. The will itself was straightforward. To start with, the date made it a couple of years old. I was surprised it wasn't a little more recent. According to the document, he had the standard airman's Servicemen's

Group Life Insurance Policy with a $400,000 payout, another policy obtained through American Express with a $300,000 payout. He also had around $750,000 under management. I scanned both policies—neither payout was affected if the policyholder committed suicide. So the guy was worth way more than a million. The amount surprised me. According to the will, there were two beneficiaries—the relative in Gainesville, though what was coming to him looked to be nothing but family memorabilia. Everything else went to Amy McDonough.

I gave the Post-it that Lyne had passed me a closer look: *Amy McDonough, 42 West Lincoln, Pensacola.* Lyne was catching on fast—there was an employment address, too: *Elmer's Sports Store.* That name rang a bell. I checked the receipts from Ruben's gym equipment. It had all come from Elmer's, where Ms. McDonough worked. I wondered what sort of discount she'd given him.

Pensacola was a long drive, roughly seventy miles, from Laguna Beach where I'd seen her last night. A long way to drive for a margarita, no matter how big they made it. I remembered the conversation she was having with Butler, like they were having a lovers' tiff.

"Here are those calls," said Lyne, placing a couple of sheets of paper on the desk, pulling me out of the daydream. I put my feet on the desk and looked them up and down. The animal growling in my stomach told me it was feeding time. Dinner. I'd run out of pencils and my mouth tasted of number two lead. I tried not to think about food and concentrated on the list of calls instead. Wright didn't use his cell much. Over a period of two and a half weeks he made just eighteen calls. There was nothing in the cell's SMS in-tray or out-tray. Most of the calls were made to McDonough, the balance to phone numbers in Pensacola. One of the numbers looked familiar. I picked up the will again. It was drafted on letterhead from a law firm in Pensacola called Demelian and Partners, and there it was—the familiar phone number. The call he'd made was a brief one: fourteen seconds—long enough to listen to an answering machine, perhaps. So maybe Ruben had called his lawyer, and the guy wasn't in. I checked the received-calls folder in the cell's memory against the phone company's records. Most had come from McDonough, her home phone or cell. Ruben's lawyer had called back twice, and there was a call from a number with an area code that placed it in Atlanta. It was after eight P.M.—too late to get anything other than a recorded message, but I thought, what the hell, and phoned anyway. Thirty minutes later I was more puzzled than when I started.

"I said, are you taking calls, Vin?"

"What...?" I snapped out of it. Lyne's head was craned around the door.

"Calls," he repeated. "Are you taking any?"

"Is it my ex, her lawyer, or her new husband?"

"It's Colonel Selwyn."

"Then sure."

"Line three."

I pressed the button.

"Agent Cooper?" said Clare Selwyn.

"Ma'am, how you doing? What's up?"

"Oh, you know...blood, guts—the usual. Actually, it's pretty quiet here, for a change. How're you doing?"

"Good. Nice climate, holiday atmosphere, a little murder..."

I heard a feminine snort. "Those lab results came through. But getting them out of me is going to cost you dinner."

"I thought the results were going to take a week?"

"Seems the lab's not too busy. It's coming up on New Year's...Maybe all the local killers are on vacation."

"So where do you want to meet for this dinner I owe you?"

"You know The Funkster, the place I told you about in Destin?"

"Yeah. Friendly tourist crowd."

"There's a restaurant two doors down called Salty's."

"Sounds bad for the arteries."

"Actually, for seafood it's the pick of the bunch around here. They do these amazing soft-shelled crabs. Just do me one favor?"

"Name it, Colonel."

"For Christ's sake, lose the shirt."

TWENTY-TWO

The restaurant was jammed. Fortunately Colonel Selwyn had left a reservation with a guy at the front desk who could have been Mr. Salty himself—beard, squint, tattoos. Popeye the Sailor had a doppelgänger. I was ten minutes early, the colonel was twenty minutes late. I ate my roll. Then I ate hers.

"Hey, sorry I'm late," said the voice behind me.

I felt a light hand on my shoulder as Clare Selwyn surfed past on a wave of French perfume and took the seat opposite. Her blond hair was loose. She wore a green top tied at the waist over a white T-shirt, a swishy white skirt that ended below her brown knees, and leather sandals. Her toenails were painted red. Selwyn's makeup was minimal, the way I liked it, and she glowed with life.

"No problem. I passed the time with your roll."

"That's OK—I don't do carbs," she said.

An old woman arrived and poured glasses of water. She might have been Salty's wife, or maybe his twin sister. The beard gave it away. "Get you folks drinks?" she asked.

"Thanks," said Selwyn, looking up at her. Candle-light danced in her eyes. I cleared my throat.

Mrs. Salty placed menus for food and alcohol on our table and walked off to baby-sit a rowdy table nearby.

"You've changed your shirt," said Selwyn as she picked up her napkin and smoothed it across her legs.

"It was about time. The girls were starting to play their ukuleles."

"I like the one you're wearing better."

"This old rag?" Actually it was new, bought from the BX. It was fitted and vaguely khaki.

Selwyn smiled approval, then said, "I know what's good here. Should I just order for us?"

"You're a colonel. I'm a major. I'm not arguing."

"Good," she said.

The bearded lady returned to get our order. Selwyn chose a Napa Valley Chardonnay. I had a glass, for the sake of politeness, then switched to Moosehead. The food came fast—a couple of clam chowders followed by soft-shelled crabs, plus scallops and prawns. Selwyn ate her fair share. Nice to know her trim figure didn't come from eating with a calculator, counting calories. Nice also to have dinner out with a woman, any woman, even one who outranked me. It had been a while. Months, in fact, not including the surprise takeout with Anna in my apartment. Suddenly, thinking about Anna made me feel uneasy. Why? This was just dinner, wasn't it? And Anna and I were . . . well, what were we? On the rocks, founder-ing, a hole in the keel, great whites thrashing about for the pickings, our relationship's blood in the water? I snapped out of it. The colonel was talking.

"... Selwyn's my maiden name, by the way. As I was saying, Manny stays with his grandparents, my parents. He goes there every second Thursday night— overnight. They moved to Panama City from Seattle when Dad retired. They said they always intended to settle down there, but I'd never heard them mention the place—ever—and then suddenly they're living there."

"Any other grandparents helping out?"

She hesitated. I sensed that if not for the wine, Selwyn would have left it at that. "You really want to know?"

"Only if you want to tell me."

She took a breath and let it out. The flames on the candles twitched and swayed, shifting the shadows across her face.

"Getting married was the one truly dumb thing I've done in my life. Now I realize it was just an attack on my parents. They resented the fact that I took my medical degree and joined the Air Force. My dad was a thoracic surgeon, and pushy about me following in his footsteps."

She took a sip of her wine.

"Anyway, the guy I married was a developer. My folks had visions of me marrying a doctor, of course, or at least a dentist. I met him on vacation in the Caribbean. We flew to Vegas at the end of it and tied the knot. Three months later I was pregnant. We both knew it wasn't going to last forever. We weren't talking much toward the end, but he loved Manny. We were pretty much done when he was killed in the plane crash. His parents were divorced and remarried and didn't want to know about their grandchild." Selwyn lifted the glass to her lips again. "What about you—I notice you're not wearing a ring. You single, or just traveling in disguise?"

"Divorced six months ago. We just ran out of steam." I was happy to skip the details.

"What about a girlfriend?"

"I'm not sure. We've been bouncing around. She's in Germany."

"Oh, right, one of *those* relationships."

"Meaning?"

"Long distance. It's a killer."

I was anxious to move on and I was unlikely to get a better opportunity. "Which reminds me, you had a toxicology report for me?"

"Yeah, that pill. I can tell you what it is and what it's for—but I can't tell you whether it was medication Ruben Wright was taking. Unfortunately his remains have been cremated and we don't have the appropriate tissue samples. As for the dead roaches, they weren't significant. The sugar coating on the pill wouldn't have killed them. They might have recently checked out of a nearby roach motel and come to die where it was nice and warm. And, like I said, an earlier tenant could have dropped it."

"I get you. There are caveats. What is it?"

"A four-milligram serving of Tizanidine hydrochloride."

"Taken for . . . ?"

"It's used to relieve spasticity in the muscles."

"Who takes it?"

"Someone who's had a stroke or a spinal injury . . ."

"So it wasn't Wright's medication. He couldn't have jumped with—"

"It's also taken by people with MS—multiple sclerosis," she said.

Multiple sclerosis? That could put a spin on a couple of calls Wright had made to certain numbers in Pensacola. "I'm not exactly sure what MS is," I said.

"It's bad."

"That much I know."

Mrs. Salty cleared our plates as Selwyn poured the last of the wine into her glass. Those big brown eyes of hers weren't quite so big now, I noticed, but her speech was still sharp and without any hint of a slur. "It's a degenerative disease of the central nervous system, where the nerve pathways are gradually destroyed. The symptoms, which get progressively worse, are vertigo, muscle spasms and weakness, loss of coordination, numbness, loss of memory. Speech is affected, as is vision. There's no cure, but drugs like Tizanidine can ease the symptoms. MS attacks its victims in different ways, but it's often debilitating and can be fatal. There are better ways to die."

"Like cutting yourself out of your parachute harness?" I wondered how Wrong Way would have taken the news that he was going to take a long, slow journey into a pine box, most of it either on crutches or in a wheelchair. I also wondered, if he did have

MS, where he kept his drugs. None were found in the house after his death.

"If Sergeant Wright was suicidal because he had MS, and he'd decided to jump to his death, as I said when you first arrived, why wouldn't he just pass on pulling his rip cord? Why go to all the trouble of cutting through the harness?"

Yeah, it was still a good point. In fact, it was the crux of the investigation. I thought back to the Ruben Wright I knew: Mr. Invincible. He was strong, self-assured, athletic, and very hard to kill. MS seemed unlikely, every bit as unlikely as suicide. If he had it, he'd be trying his damnedest to beat it into submission. If I had to put money on how he died, I'd still be betting on murder. But for the first time there were, I had to admit, faint fluffy clouds of doubt on the horizon.

Tables were being reset for the morning's breakfast trade. We were the last patrons to leave and already, at the periphery of the restaurant, lights had been turned off. A waiter swept the floor nearby, noisily shifting chairs around. I could take a hint. "Looks like we've outstayed our welcome," I said.

Outside, the night air was cool and still. The distant traffic sounded like waves, or maybe it was the waves arriving on the beach nearby sounding like traffic. There weren't many vehicles in the parking lot out front. One was my SUV. I wasn't sure which one was Clare's.

"Do you mind giving me a lift home?" she asked. "I think I've probably had too much to drink."

I detected the first signs of slurring. "Where's home?"

"Other side of Fort Walton Beach."

I deactivated the SUV's alarm and opened the door for her. She climbed up and I noticed the colonel's calves. I liked what I saw: slim, tan, and toned. "You spend much time at the beach?" I asked, keeping it light.

"Yeah, the sea is one big playroom. Manny builds things out of sand; I like to run on it."

I couldn't help but admire her. I knew plenty of couples bringing up kids. It appeared to be a tough enough job when the parenting was a double act. Going it alone was close to heroic in my book.

"So, what's next?" she asked as I accelerated into the traffic.

"There are a few people I need to see in Pensacola."

"No, I mean tonight. Between you and me?"

"I'm going to drive you home."

"And then?"

"You're a lieutenant colonel and I'm a major, ma'am. The Air Force has rules."

"I don't see any uniforms."

"Are you going to order me?"

"There's an idea."

I smiled at her and she returned it.

"Single moms can have sex, Vin. We're allowed, you know. In fact, it has been so long this particular single mom is climbing the walls."

"How long is so long?"

"Too long. Anyway, the house is empty, the bed is

warm, your maybe-on-maybe-off girlfriend is on the other side of the planet, and what goes on tour stays on tour, right?"

"Are you always this pushy?"

"Does pushy scare you?"

I glanced across at her. She was leaning against the door, warm air from the dash vent blowing through her hair. One eyebrow was arched so that she looked playful, seductive, and hungry all at the same time. Her hand slid into her lap. I couldn't help noticing that her legs were apart, outlined by the sheer fabric of her skirt.

"You're making it hard for me to drive," I said, my throat suddenly dry.

"Good," she said. "Hold that thought. Better still, let me hold it."

I smiled. "Why me?"

"Do you want your ego stroked, too?"

"If you think it'll help."

She laughed. "OK, I've thought about this—about you. To start with, I like you. Also, to be honest, you're just passing through. It can be uncomplicated—no rumors, no bullshit, no games. You won't want a piece of me, or my life, so I can concentrate on my son. And, if you haven't noticed, there's an over-preponderance of macho types here. I've been watching you. I like a man who has a brain as well as a penis."

"Yeah, well, pity they gave me only enough blood to operate one at a time."

That earned another laugh. "Take the next left, after this set of lights."

I took the turn and Clare directed me through a maze of side streets. The house we eventually pulled up outside was a seventies prefab. The front yard was painted silver by the moon; a silver tricycle nosed into a bush, a silver station wagon parked in the driveway.

"Are you going to come in for coffee?" she asked.

I shook my head. "Coffee keeps me awake."

"Then I'll make sure it's brewed strong." Clare reached across and took a handful of my shirt. She pulled me toward her and we kissed. Her mouth tasted of wine. Mine tasted of Moosehead. Fair trade.

*   *   *

Clare's bedroom smelled of fresh flowers. Her head was on my shoulder. I listened to her breathing as she slept, and felt her breath ruffle the hairs on my chest. We'd skipped the coffee. Her body was lean and long, hard in some places, soft where it counted. She obviously spent plenty of time running on that sand. Perhaps it was to work off the excess energy she would otherwise have expended between the sheets. She'd told me that it had been "a while." Going into the second orgasm, I'd begun to think of that as maybe a warning. Heading into the finishing straight of the third, I was damn sure of it.

Groggy with sleep and sex, I stared at the ceiling, where events of the past couple of weeks were playing like the broken cuts of a movie trailer: I saw the probes blasting from the end of a Taser; I watched

Anna close my apartment door as she left; I saw the disk pushed under the door; I imagined I saw Sergeant Wright the moment before he hit the ground, curled into a ball; I saw the fine blond hairs between Clare's legs and recalled her salty sweet taste; I saw a pile of cigarette butts mashed into the steel deck of the *Natusima*; I saw a monster shark, bloodred water streaming from its gills as it snapped off Tanaka's head and shoulder from the rest of his body; I saw Amy McDonough and her firecracker hair; I saw a panda armed with a carving knife attack a woman on a park bench; I saw a silver station wagon parked in the driveway; I saw Tanaka's hand grasping for Boyle's wallet as it slipped twirling into the shark's wake.

*   *   *

My eyes opened. My body clock was linked to Air Force time and it told me to wake the hell up. I checked my watch: 0530. I must have spent the night unconsciously processing the pieces I had on the Tanaka case because the fitful sleep had brought me to some kind of conclusion about what had happened to him. I still didn't know why he was killed, but I'd woken up with a hunch about the "who." I hoped the feeling wouldn't evaporate as the day wore on.

It was still dark and Clare was asleep, but there was enough light to turn her hair into molten silver. It flowed across the top of an exposed breast that rose and fell with her breathing. I was aware of my erection an instant later, at precisely the moment Clare stirred and her hand brushed it. "Good morning," she said sleepily, stretching, purring, full-stopping her stretch in the middle of it with a playful squeal when she realized what was beneath the sheets, waiting impatiently.

"Morning," I replied.

She faced me, her eyes closed. "I see you have a little something for me down there," she said. I felt her hands wrap around my shaft.

"Little?" I said.

*   *   *

We showered separately but had breakfast together. The sun didn't rise till nearly a quarter to seven. I wanted to be out long before it did. Part of the reason was the full day I had ahead. The other part had something to do with the curiosity of Clare's neighbors. I didn't want to give them something to talk about. When I'd mentioned this, Clare said, "Jesus— I'm not a nun. Don't worry about it. The woman on my left is an old widow. Doesn't go out much—give her something to talk about in her chat room. The people on the right are even older—the lady's deaf and her husband can't see past the weeds in his lawn."

We finally had that coffee. "I know you planned it," I said after the first grateful sip.

"Planned what?" she asked.

"This. Having me stay over."

"What makes you say that?" she asked, in uniform, leaning back against the kitchen counter, her fingers interlaced around a mug.

"You told me last night you'd had too much to drink to risk driving. Your vehicle's in the driveway. You left it here so that you could get a lift."

She put down her mug and took the two steps across the kitchen and gently cupped my testicles. I felt the heat of her hands, warmed by the hot mug, seep through the fabric of my pants. "So, what you gonna do about it?" she whispered. "You wanna pull me in for questioning, Special Agent? I promise I'll come quietly. On second thought, maybe I'll scream a little—you seem to have that effect on me."

Old faithful stood to attention. Again.

She whispered in my ear as she undid my fly and slipped her hand inside. "And I seem to have a certain effect on you."

*   *   *

In order to keep up with Lieutenant Colonel Clare Selwyn in the sack, I figured I'd have to run at least fifteen miles a day. We kissed and I said I'd call her later, exhaustion permitting.

It was light, but the sun still hadn't cleared the pines on a distant low hill. I decided not to drive back to Hurlburt Field, but to keep on going to Pensacola. I had the addresses and phone numbers in my notebook, and a bunch of questions in my head.

TWENTY-THREE

Pensacola lay on the far side of the Pensacola Bay Bridge. A brisk early-morning wind was pulling at the gray water, dragging up little white triangles all over the bay and blowing them into spindrift.

According to the digital display on the dash, it was only 8:45. I was too late to catch Ms. McDonough at home. Elmer's Sports Store was a ten-minute drive away, so I headed there. It wasn't hard to find, a shop in a mall off Pensacola Boulevard that looked like it had seen better days. Or maybe these days were the best it was ever likely to see. Or maybe it was just being punished by progress—there was a newer, bigger version a couple of miles back up the road. The place looked blackened and eroded by road grit and exhaust fumes that had been blowing off the adjacent multilane since the day the mall's foundations were laid. Faded "SALE" signs hung askew in almost every window. Paper cups, burger wrappers, straws, and plastic bags from the fast-food joints that had refused to read the writing on the walls of this shopping Alamo had gathered in the corners of the buildings and perimeter cyclone fencing like discarded ammunition boxes on a battlefield where the fight had moved on. The parking lot, which was so vast as to seem more an exercise in wishful thinking, was dotted here and there with vehicles in not much better condition than the buildings, most of which were closed, shuttered, and barred. The aforementioned writing on the walls was everywhere—black, angry, aggressive, and mindless. I wondered how many tennis rackets Elmer's was selling these days.

I walked inside and found a joint selling coffee to early-bird shoppers and retail staff. I bought a cup—strong and black, no sugar—and a cheese-and-bacon sandwich. The food was surprisingly good. I ate the sandwich and ordered another. A few of the shops were getting ready to open. Most of the salespeople were no more than kids, and were either lardy or anorexic, depending on their chosen eating disorder.

I sat on a bench outside Elmer's, drank the coffee, ate the second sandwich, and waited for Amy Mc-Donough to make an appearance. More shoppers were starting to arrive. They were a listless bunch. All the fight had gone out of them. Several stood outside the shops, waiting, staring, waiting.

I noticed movement inside Elmer's. I went to the window and had a look inside. A guy in a blue tracksuit-style uniform was at the counter, on the phone, one of his arms waving about like he was bronco busting. He was yelling. Good soundproofing stopped me from hearing what he was yelling about.

Five past nine. No sign of Ms. McDonough, but there was a chance she'd arrived early and I'd missed her. The shutter rolled up on Elmer's. I went inside and had a walk around, making like a shopper nosing for a bargain. Elmer's was basically a large rectangular room with an office at the back. I knew this because there was a door behind the free-weights section with the word "Office" on it. Posters showing various athletes achieving greatness and others depicting women who looked like they were in the middle of an orgasm while they worked out hung on the walls. The showroom smelled of new rubber, cardboard, and old dust. Elmer had a large selection of running shoes. He also specialized in jogging machines and home gym equipment like the machines Ruben had bought.

The guy in the blue tracksuit stayed behind the counter and leaned on it, studying an old *Sports Illustrated* swimsuit issue. He didn't look up. Maybe he didn't *want* to look up in case he found himself standing behind the counter in a run-down sports shop. He was in his early twenties, baby-faced and big. Not in an athletic way, but in an extra-cheese-and-giant-fries way. He had white, greasy skin, pimples, and a fine black mustache that looked like it might come off in the wash—if he ever had one. The way he flipped over the magazine's pages, every few seconds and violently, suggested there was nothing in the issue he hadn't seen a thousand times already, and that something had pissed him off. Maybe it was the phone call; maybe it was the fact that there was nothing in the magazine he hadn't seen a thousand times already. His name tag said I should call him Boris.

"Yeah," he said when I approached, looking up from the mag with a look of flat boredom.

"I'd like to speak with Amy if she's in."

"Related to something you want to buy or return?"
He said this like he was reading it off a card.

"No."

"Then it's private business. Private business may not be conducted during business hours. Company policy."

Spoken like a true dipshit. "Then she's here?"

"Perhaps you didn't hear me, sir."

It was obvious Chuckles didn't know this great nation of ours was built on the idea of service with a smile. I headed for the office.

"Hey!" he called out to my back as I opened the door. Behind it was a small room with a desk, a computer, a filing cabinet, and an old Pamela Anderson calendar on the wall. It was March 2002—ancient history—and Pammy was playing with a python. There was no Amy McDonough.

"Turn around real slow, mister."

I turned. Boris was armed with a baseball bat. A wooden one. It was old by the look of it—didn't want to abuse the stock, most likely. Elmer himself had probably put it behind the counter thirty years ago in case of folks coming in and asking questions about things other than sports. "Baseball season's over, sonny," I said.

Boris had fifty pounds on me, maybe more. He was working through the odds. I could see it in his face, in the curl of his lips, the narrowed eyes, the flared nostrils, the pupils dilated by the adrenaline surging through his system. I could tell he'd come to the conclusion that the odds were in his favor. He swung the bat to get a feel for it.

"Y'all want to tell me who you are and what you want?"

"Not unless you say the magic word."

This confused him. He had a weapon; I didn't. Why wasn't I scared, or at least conciliatory? The reasons had a lot to do with experience. In fact, I wish I had a dollar for every weapon I'd taken out of the hands of drunken airmen and soldiers. Mostly those weapons were either broken bottles or bar stools rather than baseball bats, but the principle was the same.

"Please," I told him. "The magic word is *please*."

He swung the bat again—a ranging swing—and took a step forward.

I didn't move. "Look, I just wanted to talk to Amy. She's not here? Fine. I'm happy to walk out."

He seemed happier with this apparent appeasement. He misread it. "You came in all abusive. I have the right to protect myself and my customers."

"More company policy?" I asked.

Boris answered by suddenly rushing in, swinging. I ducked under the bat and kept low. His momentum kept him going past me. We both turned and he came back for another go with a few more wild swings. He missed—I knew from his eyes and the shift in his body weight where the swings were coming from, like he was sending me e-mails on his next move. When he'd finished this flurry, I put a leg-extension machine between us. Boris's face was red with splotches of white. He was breathing heavily with effort.

I was getting tired of the game as well as concerned that he might just get lucky anyway and connect with my head. I said, "If you swing that thing at me one more time, I'll take it off you and teach you some manners."

Boris smiled. He was enjoying himself; perhaps for the first time in a long time he was getting a little serious job satisfaction. Perhaps he was also thinking about how his boss would call him a hero for subduing this here abusive noncustomer as per company policy. He raised the bat high over his head and rushed forward. Instead of retreating and giving him room for the downward swing, like he expected, I stepped toward him. The bat was still behind his head, pointing down toward his ankles, when I grabbed it and pulled it all the way down behind his back. I wrenched it from his hands as his knees buckled and he fell backward. He lay on the floor, hands in front of his face, waiting for me to teach him those manners.

"Get up," I demanded.

He rolled onto his side, got to his knees, and then staggered to his feet. The sneer on his face was gone, replaced by a quivering chin.

I propped the bat against a triceps machine. "Boris, it's no wonder the folks around here are choosing to shop somewhere else. Now, ask me again and this time use the magic word."

"I-I forgot the question," he said.

"You asked me who I was and what did I want."

"Who-who are you and what do you want?"

"Please."

"P-please."

"Now, was that so hard?" I asked.

He shook his head.

I pulled my badge and held the shield where he could see it. "Vin Cooper, special agent with the United States Air Force, and I already told you what I wanted."

"McDonough called in sick. I'm only supposed to be on a half day and she called in sick."

I actually felt sorry for the slob. He'd be replaying this little scene with me in his mind for the rest of his life, replaying it and no doubt playing it forward differently.

"Is that a reason to try improving your batting average on potential customers?" I asked.

"No, sir."

"Special Agent."

"What?"

"You don't have to call me sir. Is that who you were on the phone with?"

"Yeah. McDonough said she had to go to the doctor's."

"I don't suppose you know who that doctor is?"

"Nah. She said she might not be back till tomorrow. But, like, fuck, you know ... I've got things I need to do, too," he said. The quivering chin had mutated into anger. His humiliation was Amy McDonough's fault, my fault, Elmer's fault, anyone's fault but his own.

"This is my card." I took one from my wallet and held it out to him. He reached for it with a long arm like it was going to bite him. Or maybe blow up. "She calls you back, you don't tell her I came to see her."

"No, sir."

"You find out where she is and you call me. Please."

"Yes, sir."

"Where's Mr. Elmer?"

"Died ten years ago."

"Who's the boss now?"

"His nephew—never comes in."

There were still no customers in the store. The place was atrophying, heading for life support. Or maybe the nephew wanted it DNR, for tax reasons. "Don't you go losing that card, Boris."

"No, sir."

"Special Agent."

"What?"

"Never mind."

I walked out into the parking lot. My cell rang. The screen told me it was a private number, which I usually don't answer. In a rare moment of cell generosity, I pressed the green button. "Special Agent Cooper," I said as I watched three guys take their anger and frustration out on a wall with cans of orange spray paint.

"Hello. My name's Erwin Griffiths. You left a message to call."

"Sorry, sir," I said. "What did you say your name was?"

"Erwin Griffiths."

"Where you from, Mr. Griffiths? I've left a few messages around town lately."

"Sure. Ah, I'm from a company called Neural Paths."

Neural Paths—I remembered. "Yeah, Erwin," I said. "I'm investigating the death of a man you called at the beginning of last week—before Christmas." I leaned against the Explorer and watched one of the graffiti artists throw a rock at the one last unshattered pane of glass. He missed.

"Oh, sorry to hear that. Dead? Can you tell me who it was that died? Don't mean to be rude here, but, like you, I call a lot of people."

"Ruben Wright."

"Ruben Wright, Ruben Wright, Ruben . . . Oh, yeah, got his file right here. Dead? Hmm . . . that's a shame."

He made it sound like it was a shame Ruben's file was on his desk rather than on someone else's.

"Can you tell me what kind of company Neural Paths is, Erwin?" I asked.

"Sure. We do, like, credit card fraud."

"Credit card fraud. You mind giving me an overview?"

"OK . . . Well, let me tell you something about yourself you probably aren't aware of. You're predictable. Most people don't like being told this, but it's true."

He continued. "You . . . everyone, in fact, spends money in a manner that software can now predict. That's because you spend money in a pattern that's highly regular. As I said—you're predictable. If you deviate from that spending pattern, either in the type of things you buy or the amount you spend—sometimes both—the program pops your name up on screen and someone like me gives you a call to check that your erratic spending isn't the result of card fraud—that your card isn't being used by a person, or persons, unknown to you." I heard him take a breath.

I didn't know Erwin, but I sensed he was the kind

who found the word "brief" beside the word "impossible."

"You called Ruben Wright because of his spending patterns?"

"Yep, textbook. He'd suddenly gone from being a pain-in-the-ass customer who never used his plastic to the kind of customer the credit card company wanted on its gold rewards program. Like, if it was really Mr. Wright spending all that money, which I was calling to confirm, then the credit card company would have asked him if he wanted to increase his limit."

The Ruben I remembered kept a family of moths in his billfold. Spending bags of money? Not the Ruben I knew—and obviously not the one the credit card company was familiar with either.

"So Wright's dead?" Erwin asked, the voyeur in him coming out for a look around, hoping to catch a glimpse of something truly nasty—the way drivers slow down for a traffic accident, eager for a glimpse of blood.

I cut off his enthusiasm. "Yeah. So I doubt he'll want to take up that rewards program."

"Oh. Well, then...thank you," he said, miffed, sounding like I'd shortchanged him.

"Glad to be of service," I said, hanging up. I was intrigued. There was something going on here—an erratic pattern that the software between my ears had picked up.

TWENTY-FOUR

I like Pensacola. Not too big that you don't know anyone, and not so small that everyone knows you. Home to the U.S. Navy's Blue Angels, and also to Amy McDonough. I drove out to her house. It was off a busy road and it was small and mean. I stood in the driveway and looked around. The house across the street was black with mildew, one corner sinking into the soft earth. An old oak with a limp beard of Spanish moss threw a pale gray shadow across the veranda. The house was a twin to the one McDonough lived in, except that the oak in her yard was reduced to a gray stump, the rest of the tree having been sawn off three feet from the ground a long time ago, its ancient dry roots breaking through the concrete drive here and there.

Amy's red Chevrolet Cavalier was not parked in the driveway. I went to the door and knocked. No answer. The place felt empty. I checked the fuse box. Something inside was drawing power, a low drain. Probably a clock, a radio turned down low, a computer on sleep. There were a couple of reasonably fresh oil drips on the driveway. The mailbox didn't hold the usual junk that might have indicated a long-term departure.

Amy was just out. If I believed Boris, she was out paying her doctor a visit. I didn't have the resources at my disposal to ring the one hundred or more doctors in town to find out which one was hers. This made me reflect, for an instant, on how different police work is from that shown on TV shows and how, in reality, some cases actually take longer than forty-four minutes plus commercials to resolve. I wondered when Agent Lyne would get impatient with me and demand to have his house back.

I parked the SUV down the road a respectable distance and waited for Amy's return. Two hours later, she was still a no-show. I called Boris on my cell. He said she hadn't come back to work and hadn't called in again. It was time to move on. I had a doctor's appointment of my own I didn't want to miss.

*   *   *

Dr. Murray Mooney shared his waiting room with five other doctors in the medical center, a rambling, prefab fortress that reminded me of a pile of blocks stacked by a two-year-old. The doctor was behind schedule, but then so was I. As I ran the usual gauntlet of forms at reception, he came out to walk me into his office.

Dr. Mooney's age was impossible to guess, anywhere between thirty and fifty. What was more certain, however, was that he was short and hairy—coarse black wire sprang from his ears, nostrils, and up and over the collar at the back of his neck. Alsatians had less hair than this guy. But in a joke played on him by his genes, his noggin was as smooth and brown as a polished walnut. He wore pants and a striped blue-and-white business shirt without a tie.

I followed him into his office. I took the seat indicated with a sweep of his hand, along with a moment to get my bearings. Hung on one wall was the chart I'd seen in every doctor's office I've ever visited. It showed a man with a placid look on his face whose skin and musculature had been peeled back from his belly so that the correct position and size of his organs could be seen. When I was a kid, I wondered if doctors had this poster in case they needed reminding where everything went should someone walk in spilling their guts on the carpet. Mooney was a general practitioner, not a specialist, so there was an array of interesting models scattered about: a tower made from half a dozen vertebrae of the lower spine, the workings of the inner ear, a partial bust of a flayed head showing the muscles of the face, jaw, and eyes. In another corner of the room was an eye chart. Beside it, a human skeleton hung from a pole. His desk was littered with numerous items for the probing and prodding of human orifices, as well as items such as pads and pens and gimmicky bits of junk all carrying the logos of various branded drugs. The place looked like the aftermath of a medico's rummage sale.

"So, Vin Cooper," he said, glancing at the card I'd filled out at the front desk. "What can we do for you today?" He leaned toward me, his hands clasped together in the space between his knees, his face wearing its professional smile—affable without being friendly. "Special Agent," I said.

"Sorry?" He took another look at the card, confused.

"Special Agent. Special Agent Vin Cooper." I showed him my badge. "You were the doctor of a friend of mine who—"

The smile vanished and he sat back in his chair. "I'm sorry, but I thought you needed medical attention. I cannot discuss—"

". . . A friend of mine who is now dead."

"Who . . . ?"

"United States Air Force Master Sergeant Ruben Wright."

"*Sergeant* Ruben Wright?" His larynx was working like a piston.

I nodded. "Yeah, sergeant. You didn't know Ruben was in the Air Force?"

"No. I . . . I would've handled it differently."

"Like, for instance, you'd have notified the Air Force that Sergeant Wright had MS?"

Mooney stared at me. I watched the wheels turning behind his eyes. *Do I come clean? Do I claim doctor-patient privilege?* I gave him a nudge.

"There're no liability issues here, Doc. He jumped out of a plane and hit the ground. I'm looking into why."

"He committed suicide?"

"That's one possibility," I said.

Mooney shook his head, stood up. "I thought he was a fitness instructor." He turned to his computer and pulled up the relevant file. "Yes, a personal trainer," he said, reading the screen. "He was a very healthy man."

Was. Ruben must have known something was very

wrong with him to have picked out a doctor fifty miles from the base. If the medical staff at Hurlburt Field had known of his condition, they'd have had him discharged as fast as the clerks could cut the paperwork.

The doctor sat, breathed deeply, and expelled his next breath with a hiss. "Ruben Wright's MS came on fast. Do you know much about the disease, Mr. . . . er . . ." He checked my card a third time.

"Special Agent will do," I said. "And, no, not much. You prescribed him Tizanidine?"

"I prescribed him a long list of medicines to control the disease and its symptoms. He had to take pills all day long. The Tizanidine was for the spasticity, yes." He swung round in his chair, faced his computer again. "MS is a disease that attacks the myelin, a fatty tissue that helps nerves in the brain and spinal cord conduct electrical impulses. Ruben came to see me about three months ago with a range of symptoms. I sent him off to have an MRI and it came back conclusive. MS has a wide range of symptoms and not all sufferers run the gamut of them, because the attacks on the myelin range in severity and location from one sufferer to the next. Ruben's presentation, though, was classic. Let me see . . . the first time he saw me he complained of the spasticity, and the fact that the right-hand side of his face was numb, along with his right foot. Two weeks later he was back with the numb face, a numb hand, vertigo, and . . . er . . . yes, erectile dysfunction. That's when I sent him off to get the MRI. He had what's called the progressive-relapsing type of MS, the type that gets steadily and quickly worse."

"How did Ruben take it when you gave him the good news?"

"He reacted the way most people do—he went into a kind of denial and shock spiral, followed by depression. Depression, incidentally, is another feature of the disease."

"Sounds like a barrel of laughs. Is the disease fatal?"

"No, not usually. Not in the sense that it will kill you."

"What other sense is there?"

Mooney massaged his chin. "In the sense that MS can put an end to your life the way you've always known it, especially if you're a physical person, the sort of person Ruben Wright obviously was. There's no known cure for the disease, either."

Yeah, Ruben was that kind of guy. He'd have taken the news of the steep slide into atrophy ahead of him hard. "Was he suicidal, do you think?"

"I hope not . . . but I can't say for sure. I'd prescribed an antidepressant called Effexor to help him cope. I also gave him the name of a very good psychologist I know."

"Would her name be Judith Churcher?" I asked.

"Yes, that's her. How did you know?"

"Nokia," I said. The doctor didn't seem to understand, but I was beginning to. "Well, thanks for your time, Doc."

"Seems Ruben wasn't so honest with me."

"I guess he thought he had a lot to lose," I said, and left.

TWENTY-FIVE

Judith Churcher, psychologist, had her office in a place called The Sunshine Clinic, which turned out to be a rambling old house surrounded by a garden that was part manicured, part jungle. Artfully hidden throughout the garden sat painted fairies and frogs cast from concrete. The front door was daubed in the colors of the rainbow. My nostrils detected incense on the air currents. If you weren't depressed when you arrived, The Sunshine Clinic would fix that.

I pushed the rainbow aside on its squeaky hinges and walked into the reception area. It was unattended and no customers were waiting, patiently or otherwise. Judith Churcher shared the house with a kinesiologist, an expert in Reiki, and another psychologist, like herself, who specialized in anxieties. There was a rack of printed materials on one wall. Among an array of titles instructing on how to detect and repair your aura and how to release your inner life-force energy was a book titled *Have a Nice Flight*.

"Is there anything I can help you with, sir?" said a voice behind me.

The guy who it belonged to was a painfully thin

hippie type with stringy arms, wild, wiry gray hair, and a cracked and weathered face that called to mind old window putty. He wore a loose purple cheesecloth shirt, pants of a similar material tied around his scrawny waist, and sandals. A wave of patchouli enveloped me, causing me to fight for oxygen. "I'm here to see Dr. Churcher," I said. As with Dr. Mooney, Churcher had every reason to believe she had an appointment with a new patient. In this way, I was reasonably sure that the people I drove fifty miles to interview would be in.

"The doctor should be here any moment. Take a seat."

I nodded and took up his suggestion, one beside an open window.

Almost immediately, a woman in her late forties bounced in the front door. She was wearing a beige linen skirt and matching jacket. Her hair was cut in a short bob and dyed strawberry blonde. The PTA mom type. She walked into one of the rooms and closed the door. Thirty seconds later, she opened it again, sans coat, ready to counsel. "Mr. Cooper?" she inquired.

I stood and walked into her office. She closed the door behind me. "Sit, sit," she insisted. "Obviously we don't know each other. So, why don't you tell me a little about yourself. Start wherever you like." She knitted her eyebrows together in concentration, like she was determined to memorize Each And Every Word.

"I'm an investigator with the OSI—an Air Force cop," I said.

She blinked a couple of times and tilted her head, a combination that communicated her deepest understanding and sympathy for this situation I found myself in. I wondered what was really going through her mind. White noise, most likely. "I'm looking into the death of someone you were counseling. His name was Ruben Wright." She blinked again, this time with confusion.

"But I thought . . . Do you mind if we start again?"

"Sure, I'm Special Agent Vin Cooper." I pulled my badge and gave her a good look so there was no mistaking what variety of Vin Cooper I was. "Sergeant Ruben Wright died a little over a week ago when his parachute failed. I'm looking into his death."

"Ruben's dead?" She frowned and took a breath, her red lipsticked lips thin and pursed so that they looked like a cut. From the way she took the news, I gathered it wasn't the first time she'd heard one of her paying customers would no longer be making contributions to her beach house. "I called him only last week," she said.

"I know," I replied.

"He missed an appointment."

"Yes."

"He was in the Air Force? I thought he was a personal trainer." I sensed real disappointment, almost hurt. Judith Churcher believed she'd had a deep and honest rapport with Wright.

"He didn't let anyone know the truth, Dr. Churcher," I said, giving her a break, letting her off her personal hook. "He couldn't, otherwise he'd have been bounced out of the Air Force. We don't let people with MS jump out of planes. He came to see you precisely so that *we* wouldn't know."

She nodded and allowed herself to relax a little.

"I want to ask you about his mental state."

"You're thinking he might have killed himself?"

"We're just closing down options," I said ambiguously. "I've already spoken to the referring doctor—"

"Dr. Mooney."

"Yeah, so I know he was on medication for depression. You were helping Ruben come to grips with his new reality, easing him through the grieving process of losing the life he'd lived."

She nodded. "Yes."

"In your opinion, do you think he was capable of suicide?"

This was a difficult one for Churcher to answer, and I could see by the lines in her forehead that she was wrestling with it. If she believed it was a possibility, why hadn't she done something about it, even if it was only to warn Mooney? And if she hadn't seen Wright's suicide coming, what did that say about her ability to do the job? In the end, Churcher came down on the side of her own professional defense. "Suicide? No. I didn't think he was at risk of that. He was unhappy about the MS, which is only healthy—and natural. But the Effexor seemed to be getting on top of the depression, and the other prescribed drugs were helping him manage his symptoms. Most days, he said, he was actually feeling pretty good." She glanced up at the ceiling, hunting for a summary. "No, I'd say his state of mind was positive—realistic, but positive. Did you know Ruben?"

I said that I did, that we'd worked together some years back.

"Then you know the kind of person Ruben was—a tower of strength. He was coping well—better than well, in fact. He knew what he was in for, that there were speed bumps ahead, but he appeared to be prepared for them."

That all sounded like the Ruben Wright I knew, but I also knew that the bigger folks were, the harder they fell. And Ruben had fallen hard. I'd seen the photos. "Were you aware that he was throwing money around like water these past couple of months, pretty much from the time he was diagnosed with the MS?"

Churcher appeared disappointed with the news. She looked at the floor. "No, no, I wasn't."

"Now that you know, what do you think?"

"I know what *you* think," she said.

Amazing, I thought. A shrink who makes statements rather than asks questions. "So tell me."

"You think he was spending all his money because he intended to kill himself."

I shrugged. "You can't take it with you."

"Look, it's possible. I just . . ."

"Just what?" I pressed.

"I just don't . . . he wasn't the type. He wasn't suicidal."

"But it fits."

"Yes, it does. I have a few MS patients. It's an expensive disease. You need a lot of drugs to control the symptoms, and when the disease advances, earning an income gets difficult. There aren't many jobs around for people with memory loss, right?"

There was always politics, I thought.

Churcher continued. "The point is, securing your financial situation should be one of your first priorities—there's a long and bumpy road ahead. Instead, he began frittering it away, wasting it. That's a pretty big signpost."

That was the way I figured it, too.

We sat around for another forty minutes, going well past the booked hour. I rehashed the interview with her—asked the same questions different ways, in case anything I'd missed popped out, but I seemed to have picked everything up on the first sweep. At the end, Churcher asked, "Do I have to worry about any repercussions because of this, Officer?"

"If you're worried about the Air Force—no. Hiding a medical condition from the military is not unheard of. You're not responsible for Ruben's actions—he was."

She nodded, but I knew she wasn't totally satisfied. Like every shrink I'd ever met, Churcher believed she could look into a patient's soul, locate the hidden truth, and help the patient find it, too. It was a big blow to her ego to realize that—at least in the case of Ruben Wright—she'd looked into his soul and failed to spot the lies. I handed her my card and told her she could call me if anything we hadn't covered came to mind, which was pretty much the way I concluded every interview. I took a few steps into the reception area. Two men in business suits and a woman in a hoodie and sweatpants grazed among the medical paperbacks and pamphlets. The woman picked up something about the inner child and flicked through it. That reminded me. I went to the rack and lifted out the *Have a Nice Flight* booklet. Maybe a little self-help wouldn't hurt. I turned to Churcher and said, "How much do I owe you for this?"

"Have trouble flying?" Churcher checked the title, her smile turning vaguely knowing, in the everyone-has-issues way you get from people who make their living convincing the rest of us that healthy self-doubt is a sickness.

"I think it's more a problem with crashing."

"Nineteen ninety-five," she said.

I gave her the money and took a receipt. I had at least one more stop to make, and I was late.

TWENTY-SIX

It was mid-afternoon by the time I reached the offices of Wright's attorney. The guy sat in a one-room office over a chemical-supply warehouse. The room smelled of unwashed-body odor and bleach. Under Juan Demelian's arms, half-moons of perspiration had stained his yellowing business shirt gray. He chewed gum aggressively while his right leg vibrated with nervous energy under the desk. A pack of NicoDerm patches lay open on top of a collection of folders. An ex-smoker near breaking point.

Demelian looked South American, perhaps Uruguayan. His brown eyes bulged with what looked like a thyroid condition, the gray skin beneath them wrinkled with lack of sleep. He was the compact type, small and swarthy. I didn't need a sixth sense to know business was going no place for Juan Demelian, except down the drain. Maybe that accounted for the bleach smell.

"Wright, Wright, Wright...yeah...File's here someplace. Got a reading of the guy's will next week," he said as he chewed, staring at the voice recorder in my hand, its red light flashing. He sifted through the desktop sea of paperwork with his fingertips. I sat back and let him get on with it, feeling the vibration of his jiggling leg through the floorboard under my foot. Demelian and I had already gone through the prelims. He knew who I was, where I was from, and what I wanted. This wouldn't take long.

I made use of the time by checking it; it was after 3 P.M. By now I'd hoped to have received a call from Boris down at Elmer's, letting me know that Amy McDonough had arrived for what was left of her day's work. Maybe she hadn't come back. Maybe Boris was holding out on me.

"Okay, here we go." Demelian lifted a pair of bifocals onto the end of his oily nose. He picked out a folder that had been used many times over, earlier titles scribbled on it in black pen and subsequently crossed out with red. He flipped it open and scanned the contents. "Yeah...Notes here say he called seven weeks ago, made an appointment that was rescheduled a few times. He was on my calendar for an appointment ten days ago. Next I heard, he was dead."

"Who told you?"

"The Air Force."

"So you knew he was in the Air Force."

"Of course."

"Do you know what Ruben Wright wanted when he called you?"

He shrugged. "I handled the guy's will—that's all. I can only assume it had something to do with that."

A reasonable assumption. "Is this the will you handled for Sergeant Wright?" I took a copy out of my pocket, unfolded it, and then passed it to him across his desk.

He took it, scanned it, then compared it with a copy in the folder that had Ruben's name scrawled across it. "Yeah, that's the one." He handed it back.

"What might he have wanted to change, do you think?"

"Do I look like a mind reader?"

"Guess."

"The law doesn't guess."

"Humor me."

Demelian rolled his goldfish eyeballs. "As I said, I only handled his will. He might have wanted it altered, even just a change of address, for example. He might have wanted to change the beneficiaries—maybe leave everything to a Romanian orphanage, or something. After I got the call about his untimely demise, I sent a copy of the will to Hurlburt Field by registered mail."

"You think it likely he made an appointment just to change his address?"

"Nope."

I wasn't getting far. "Was there anything you noticed about his will that was at all unusual?" I asked.

"Like what?"

"I don't know. You do wills; I don't. Use your imagination."

"I don't have an imagination; I'm an attorney—I have process and precedent."

I stared at him like I had all day to do this.

Demelian took a resigned breath and shook his

head. He pushed a pellet of gum from a blister pack and dropped it in his mouth. "An unusual will? No. As you know from reading it, Wright had a distant relative in Gainesville. He left a few family photos to the guy, but everything else he had he was going to hand over to an Amy McDonough, who I assume was his squeeze. She lives here in Pensacola. You should go talk to her; maybe she knows."

"Good idea," I said. "I'll keep it in mind. Had Wright changed his will before?"

Demelian thumbed through his notes. "No. Not in the last two years."

"What did you change back then?"

He called up a file on his laptop. "Um . . . made McDonough the sole beneficiary."

"Nothing from him after that?"

"Not a peep until seven weeks ago."

"Did you know Wright had been diagnosed with MS?"

"Wright had multiple sclerosis?" asked Demelian. "Shit . . ."

"You didn't know?"

"Nope."

"He was diagnosed a couple of months ago, about when he called you for the first time in two years. Is that the kind of news that prompts people to change their wills?"

Demelian shrugged. "Beats me. Why don't you ask him?"

The attorney's concern for his late client's health and state of mind was touching. I had to admit, though, my line of questioning was a reach—and I wasn't even sure what I was reaching for. Two years ago, Ruben Wright made a new will that gave everything he owned to Amy McDonough. And then seven weeks ago, he wanted to make another change, not long after discovering the spasms in his legs were the first signs of MS. Coincidence? Or was there another reason for the decision to alter his will?

"Well, thanks for your time," I said, standing to leave.

"Don't thank me. Just pay my bill when you get it."

"The name of your firm—Demelian and *Partners*..."

"Having partners gives clients a sense of security."

"Where are they?"

He gave me a snide twist of his lips, which I took to be a smile. "I got three partners—Me, Myself, and I."

"Have you ever been in a bank with a lawyer buddy while it was being robbed?"

"No, why?"

"Never mind."

TWENTY-SEVEN

I parked a block from Amy McDonough's house, and walked the rest of the way. Her place still looked and felt every bit as empty and deserted as it did that morning. Nevertheless, I went to the front door and rang the bell.

Nothing.

I took a step back, stood on the porch, and wondered where she'd gone after the doctor's appointment she'd told Boris about—assuming she even had a doctor's appointment in the first place. It was 4:47. On the walk back down the path, I called Elmer's. After six rings a recorded voice message clicked in and told me my call was important to Elmer's and that I should try ringing during business hours, which were between nine A.M. and five P.M. Monday to Saturday, and nine A.M. to two P.M. Sundays and public holidays, except for Christmas Day, New Year's Day, and Thanksgiving when they weren't open at all, and my call would be happily handled by their expert trained staff. I wondered in what field Boris's expert training lay. Maybe it was in finishing up early.

Despite my earlier belief to the contrary, I was reasonably sure Boris took me seriously enough not to piss me off. I believed he would have called had Amy turned up for work, even if just to get revenge on her for leaving him alone in that wasteland of weight machines for the day. I got to the SUV and wondered what to do next. It would be dark in an hour. If I drove to Hurlburt Field, I'd only have to drive back out to Pensacola in the morning. My cell rang. Another blocked number. I answered it anyway.

"Hey. I thought you'd have called, or maybe sent flowers."

"Ma'am . . ."

"It's Clare to you now, OK?"

"OK."

"Anyway, now you've made me call you. Where are you? It's New Year's Eve, for Christ's sake, and I've got the night off."

"New Year's? Jesus, when did that happen?"

"At least *try* to sound enthusiastic, Vin. You might give a girl a complex."

"Sorry, Clare. Last night was amazing—you're amazing . . ."

"But something's wrong," she said. "Yes, you've had an attack of the guilts—haven't you?—and now you don't want to see me because seeing me will remind you of your pathetic weakness for truly beautiful women."

I laughed. I'd forgotten how to do that with a woman—laugh.

"So, what are you doing tonight? Mom and Dad have Manny. I've bought a bottle of vodka, the cutest underwear ensemble you've ever seen, and some whipped cream."

"Whipped cream?"

"You'll never know unless you come over."

"I'm still in Pensacola."

"Really?"

"Actually, I'm parked a block away from the home of a woman by the name of McDonough."

"Who's she?"

"She was Wright's girlfriend, and maybe Butler's, too."

"Did Wright know that?" Clare asked, turning instantly into a cop.

"I don't know. That's one of the things I want to ask her."

"So what's going on at her house?"

"Nothing. She's not home. Went out this morning and hasn't come back. I'm going to sit in the SUV and wait for her to turn up."

"Now there's a New Year's Eve to remember. How has the rest of the day gone? Dig up anything interesting?"

"Yeah—bits and pieces." I gave her a rundown—she was still the DI on the case.

When I'd finished, Clare said, "And you're hoping Amy will provide the piece that makes it all fall into place?"

"That'd be convenient, wouldn't it?"

She agreed that it would. Having gone through everything with Clare, I realized I now had a pretty good picture of Ruben Wright on his last jump. To begin with, he was not the man I knew. He was sick, his face and hands possibly numb, his legs possibly spasming as MS attacked the nerve endings in his brain. He was also more than likely to have been clinically depressed, and jumping in the company of a man he despised, not least because he probably knew the guy was boning his girlfriend—something Wright was more than likely no longer capable of doing. That would have been hard for a man like Ruben—at least, the man I knew—to take. In my first conversation with Clare on this case, her view, as well as my own, was that the circumstances surrounding Ruben Wright's death were, at the very least, suspicious. They still were, only now I was equally suspicious of Ruben Wright. He at least had the motive to take his own life. What was Butler's motive? He had the girl, didn't he? The guy might have been an asshole but he wasn't a psychopath—the type who killed just for the sake of killing. The picture didn't make a hell of a lot of sense. I had Butler's version of events, a little interesting forensic evidence, plus a few conflicting interviews. Was it possible the facts could be put together to form a different picture, one that made total sense?

I was aware of the silence, but it wasn't an uncomfortable one. It was almost as if the discussion about the case we'd just had was the small talk buffering the major issue still to be resolved—namely, were we somehow going to overcome the tyranny of distance between us and get together for some serious action with her bottle of whipped cream, or what?

"Where are you going to stay?" Clare asked, finally.

"Well, I currently have a room at the Ford Explorer, but the room service sucks."

I heard her laugh. "What if McDonough doesn't show?"

"Then I'll try to find the complaints box and leave a note."

"Why don't you just go to a hotel and make sure you're up early enough to catch the worm?"

It didn't take much to convince me that this would be a much better idea.

"I know a place just after you cross the bridge, coming into town. It's clean and the rooms don't smell of old sex," Clare said.

"Okay, you've talked me into it."

"Great. I'll see you there in an hour and a half. Wait up." There was a pause. And then she added, "On second thought, have a quick nap. Might as well get some sleep while you can."

*   *   *

I found the place Clare recommended. As promised, it was clean and fresh—more in the country bed-and-breakfast mode than hotel-style accommodation—and run by a tough little granny in orthopedic shoes whose thinning hair was dyed chestnut. As she handed over the key she informed me that I was lucky to be getting a room, it being New Year's Eve with folks down from the colder northern climes to enjoy the warmer weather. The old lady had apparently had a last-minute cancellation.

I ordered a club sandwich in my room, and took a

shower. The sandwich arrived just as I was toweling off. Perfect timing. I had no fresh clothes, so I put on the robe supplied, ate the sandwich, and tried not to think too much about the case at hand. I succeeded, but only because I couldn't shake the feeling that I still had work to do on the Tanaka/Boyle case. Under my skin was that feeling I'd had in the morning, the one I'd woken up with. I wanted to call Arlen. I wanted him to check on whether Al Cooke's faxed statement had turned up. I wanted him to look into the guy's bank account for me. Cooke was on deck the same time as Tanaka. He'd told me it was Boyle who'd murdered Tanaka. But what if it'd gone down another way and he was more involved in the murder than he was prepared to admit? Boyle was the only other person who could have verified his story, and now Boyle was dead. I picked up the phone, then put it down. New Year's Eve was New Year's Eve. My crap could wait twenty-four hours. And anyway, I knew what he'd say: "That's not your case anymore."

I turned on the television for company. The screen filled with some local doll presenting the news. The lead stories were still related to the hit on the Transamerica Pyramid building and the Four Winds apartments. Rescue efforts were about to end, the emergency crews standing by, engines idling. There was a piece shot on a set of steps in downtown San Francisco, the President noting with thanks the condolences sent by a host of nations and angered by some that hadn't, most notably Pakistan's new anti-West government whose thinly veiled message in their statement about the bombing basically said we deserved it.

The President's general displeasure with Pakistan dovetailed with a report about Islamabad announcing the resumption of nuclear testing. Apparently, they had one ready to go. India had reacted by placing its military on high alert, and rushing reinforcements through midwinter blizzards to defend the disputed patch of high-altitude dirt and ice in Kashmir.

Meanwhile, elsewhere in the world, various religious nutcases were trying to turn the clock back to around the year A.D. 600—a great time to have been a Muslim, apparently—and blowing up their fellow Muslims who dared to want to live in the present.

Eventually, CNN got around to the real news that, once again, it was almost certain the Redskins would fail to make it into the divisional playoffs. They had to win the next three of three. I hit the off button in disgust.

I twiddled my thumbs—still had an hour to kill. The book I had bought earlier caught my attention. I lay on the bed and leafed through it. The miracle cure for my flying issues could possibly be just a few chapters away. *Have a Nice Flight*. Pictured on the cover of the book was a supermodel seated on a plane pointing out the porthole at something below, her partner looking over her shoulder with interest. Both were beaming with happiness and relaxation. In reality, I bet the plane probably hadn't even taken off. It probably hadn't even left the hangar.

I told myself to keep an open mind—if nothing

else, the book had cost me nearly twenty bucks. The first chapter gave an overview of the kind of people affected by "aviaphobia," the name of this particular anxiety disorder. It informed me that aviaphobics fell into three categories: worriers by nature; people who'd just been through an emotional trauma like divorce; people who'd had a bad experience in a plane. Generally speaking, I wouldn't have classed myself as a worrier, and, although I'd also been divorced, that particular event was more joyous than traumatic. I was firmly in the third category. I flipped through the chapters, getting a feel for how the cure was going to be effected. Instead what I found were plenty of the detailed experiences of my fellow phobics—how and why they became fearful in the first place, and then how they managed to overcome their fear. There were chapters on the physics of flying—how planes have to fly, have no choice in the matter, and so on; chapters on how pilots are trained and retrained to handle disaster, which I found contradictory. If flying was so goddamn safe, why the hell was there so much emphasis on what to do *when*—not *if*—the thing ceased to stay aloft and came screaming to earth in a disintegrating ball of flaming aluminum?

I put the book down, lay back, and stared at the ceiling. There was a fan up there, its three blades reminding me of an airplane propeller. Outside, a couple of cats growled at each other. My problem was that I'd been in a number of pretty hairy flying situations. I'd also lost plenty of good friends to plane crashes, accidents with rotary and fixed-wing aircraft being a primary cause of noncombat death in the military these days.

I picked up the book again and read the same paragraph three times about a guy whose fear of flying sprang from his being knocked unconscious by the drinks cart as it rolled out of control down the aisle. There was a joke in there somewhere, but I was too damn tired to find it. I closed my lids for a moment, just to moisten my eyeballs. The next thing I was aware of was a thumping sound. I rolled off the bed and opened the door.

"Hey, sleepy...taking my advice about the nap, huh?" said Clare.

"Hi. Come in," I said, rubbing my face. "Sorry about that."

Clare was dressed in jeans, sneakers, a tight, light blue T, and a light green cardigan with embroidered daisies scattered on it. It was a cool night and her nipples were giving a couple of those daisies a little extra definition. Her hair was loose—she'd done something different to it so that soft blond curls framed her face. A little black eyeliner accentuated her blue eyes, and lip gloss gave her lips a pink, wet look. She carried a woven hemp bag, the sort people often take to the beach.

"What's in the bag?" I asked.

"Supplies. There a fridge in the room?"

I pointed.

"Sorry I'm late, by the way," she said as she transferred the contents of her bag to the small refrigerator.

I checked my watch. She'd taken close to two hours. "That's OK. It's nice of you to come."

"Nice? Nice? I'll show you nice, buddy-boy." She turned and took three running steps toward me. She took me by surprise, knocking me back so that I fell on the bed. I grabbed hold and took her with me. Her hair fell over my face, smelling of wildflowers. She kissed me and nearly took my tongue by the root. She lifted my hand off her ass and brought it to her breast and whispered, "You really should fuck me, Vin." Then she sat up and took her cardigan and shirt off, revealing a delicate white lace bra, a fine white mesh fabric cradling her small breasts. "You like?"

"Yes," I said. I traced the shape of her nipples with my fingertips.

Clare closed her eyes for a moment, savoring the sensation, then went down on all fours over me, running her lips and her tongue down my chest. "Close your eyes and keep them closed," she ordered. "And no cheating."

"Yes, sir."

She kissed me again.

Then I felt her get off the bed. "Where're you going?" I asked.

"Nowhere. Keep them closed."

"Yes, sir, Colonel, sir."

I felt her untie the sash of my robe and her tongue lick the length of my erection. The blast of pleasure that resulted was like an electric shock.

"Now, no cheating," she said again.

As a game, this beat the hell out of Scrabble. I heard her light a match, smelled it in the air, heard the wick crackle, and then smelled the hot wax. I heard her loosen her belt and listened to the sound of fabric on skin as her jeans came off. My breathing was hard, as was the rest of me, my whole being concentrated in a rod of steel between my legs.

I heard her open the fridge and fill a glass with ice. Next came the sound of running water.

"Keep them closed, or you'll be in big trouble," she warned.

"No, it's you who's going to be in big trouble," I replied. Every nerve ending in me was now raw and craving sex.

"Yeah, I can see that," she whispered in my ear. "Nearly ready."

I heard the glass tinkle. Then she took me in her mouth, which also contained ice, and a shiver rocketed down my thighs. A tingling sensation bounced up and down my spine. She cupped my balls with a hand that had been wrapped around a hot mug. The heat and cold caused me to gasp.

I wasn't going to protest. Clare ran her fingernails along the skin of my legs as she knelt between them and then took me in her mouth, her now scaldingly hot mouth. I felt as though I was melting between her lips.

"Jesus, stop, stop..." I whispered in order to prevent the explosion welling up inside me.

Clare slid off the bed. She stood beside me, armed with a melting ice cube, a dribble of water rolling down toward her wrist. The flickering light from the candles glimmered across her flawless golden skin and a spark danced in her eyes and in the gloss of her lips. She reminded me of Tinkerbell, a very bad Tinkerbell.

I think I must have swallowed, because she said, "You like?"

"Uh-huh," I said. "Is that what you mean by 'cute'?"

She answered by removing her bra and running the ice around a nipple. "You want a turn?" she asked.

Clare gave me her best *Playboy* bunny pout.

"What, and spoil the show? Come here," I said.

She took half a step toward the bed, which brought her within range. I reached up and grabbed her wrist and pulled her onto me. We kissed long and slow, exchanging the ice cube a few times until the heat within us dissolved it. When our lips parted, she informed me, "Like I said, your turn. I promise I won't look."

Clare lay back on the bed, her eyes closed, her hands above her head as she stretched catlike. For the first time I noticed, lined up on the bedside table, that can of whipped cream she'd mentioned, as well as a bottle of honey, a block of dark chocolate, a mug of hot water, and a bowl of ice cubes.

"I thought you were joking about the whipped cream."

"I never joke about food."

"Um . . ." I said, considering the lineup on the table.

"Use your imagination, Vin." Clare sighed as she rolled over on the bed, lifting her ass high, toward me. "Just start with the honey and move on to the chocolate," she purred. "Happy New Year, big boy."

TWENTY-EIGHT

It was still dark outside when the cell started ringing, dragging me from a sleep so dark and deep it was like I had to crawl up from the bottom of a coal mine. I stumbled around the room, barking my shins on various bits of furniture and swearing until I located my pants and pulled the goddamn thing out of a pocket. "Jesus H. Christ," I muttered under my breath. The ringing stopped. The screen announced one missed call. Who the fuck would be ringing at five A.M. on New Year's Day, for fuck's sake? The question was enough to vaguely awaken my curiosity, which was still more asleep than the rest of me, and every bit as grumpy. "It had better be the goddamn Pope," I said aloud.

Half asleep, Clare asked, "Who is it?"

"What? Don't know yet. Missed it."

The cell suddenly buzzed in my hand. I stabbed the green button. "What?" I snarled at the caller.

A recorded voice informed me that I had a new message. I hit the button.

Sounds of a party spilled out of the earpiece. "Special Agent Cooper? You there, dude?"

It was a familiar voice, but I couldn't place it.

"Happy New Year! Hey, I found out why that slut, Amy fucking McDonough, didn't turn up for work today." Boris—Boris from Elmer's—with a head full of ecstasy and booze from the sound of it. "She's in Pensacola General, dude. She went to see her doctor and ended up there. Just heard the news from some bimbo friend of hers at this shindig here. Hey, sorry about what happened yesterday. That was, like, totally rude of me, you know? Anyway, like, Happy New Year. Have a nice life."

"Everything okay?" said Clare, rising onto an elbow, now fully awake.

"Yeah. Might have a lead on Ruben Wright's girlfriend."

"That's good."

I wasn't sure what to do—go back to bed, or get an early start.

"You coming back to bed?"

"Thought I might take a shower."

"Sure. But first, let's get you all dirty."

Clare sure knew how to settle an argument.

*   *   *

The first of January was shaping into a fine day. At breakfast, Clare and I ate enough for four. The old lady in the orthopedic shoes approved, a healthy appetite being, so she said, akin to a healthy mind. If only she knew. Maybe she'd give it some further consideration when she changed our sheets and wondered why we appeared to have baked a cake in bed.

Clare headed back to Fort Walton Beach with her

bag of tricks, looking forward to picking up her son and hanging out with him for the day. I went the opposite way—into town and Pensacola General Hospital. I'd called beforehand to make sure Boris wasn't pitching me a curve ball. An Amy McDonough had indeed been admitted.

I made my way to the front desk and badged the person sitting beneath the word "Reception." She was a petite, small-boned woman wearing frameless glasses on the end of her nose and a thin blue cardigan around her shoulders. She reminded me of a frightened bird. The woman checked the computer screen after pecking at a few keys. Yes, Amy McDonough was a patient, but not for too much longer. She told me the computer expected that Ms. McDonough would be checking out in the morning, once the doctors had done their rounds. I asked what McDonough had been admitted for and was told I'd have to speak with a doctor. She also gave me a ward and directions to help find it.

Even with the directions, locating the ward wasn't easy. The hospital was a rabbit warren of additions piled on carelessly over the years with little thought given to the whole. Once I got to the ward, though, Amy McDonough's red hair made her easy to spot. She shared the room with a woman who was lying on her side, a fluid the color of butterscotch flowing through a tube attached to her gut into a plastic bag hanging below her bed. She was snoring lightly. Amy was sitting up flicking through an old *Vanity Fair*. The Hollywood couple on the cover were embracing and smiling ferociously for the camera. It was the same couple who'd recently battled through the divorce courts, ripping into each other and each other's bank accounts.

I held up my badge. "Ms. Amy McDonough? Special Agent Vin Cooper. I'm with the Air Force Office of Special Investigations. I'm looking into the death of Master Sergeant Ruben Wright. I believe he was a friend of yours."

McDonough bit her lip. Her eyes watered and then plump tears plopped onto her cheeks.

"Can I help you, sir? It's a bit early for visiting hours."

I turned. A guy—who looked too young to get a driver's license—wearing a doctor's coat with a stethoscope over a shoulder was standing behind me, hands on his hips, head at an indignant angle. I showed him the badge, which, I hoped, would have the effect of automatically extending visiting hours. "I'm inquiring into the death of an associate of Ms. McDonough's," I told him. "I have just a few questions for her."

The doctor motioned me to follow him around the corner, out of earshot. "I won't be releasing the patient today. I'm concerned about her mental state. She's in shock."

"Can you tell me what her medical problem is?" I asked. The look he gave me let me know I was about to get the old doctor-patient-privilege lecture. I headed him off at the pass. "Look, Doc, I'm just here to ask a few questions about the deceased. Your patient's not a suspect. I'll be sure to tread carefully." The doctor appeared to wrestle with this spray of half-truths. The moment of indecision lingered, and then he said, "She's anemic—lost a lot of blood."

"You want to tell me why?" I was thinking maybe a gunshot wound, or maybe a—

"She came here after having her pregnancy terminated at a clinic. Started bleeding and wouldn't stop."

An abortion. That wasn't on my mental list. Maybe it should have been. I kept the surprise out of my face.

"You have ten minutes," he said.

I walked back into the ward, feeling a little like the clouds had thinned to reveal a hazy sun. Amy McDonough was now sitting up, legs over the side of the bed, blowing a puffy red nose into a wet wad of tissues. "I'm going to ask you a few questions," I said, using my most soothing tone, the doctor observing my bedside manner from around the door. I gave him a brief reassuring smile. He frowned and walked off down the corridor.

I dropped the act and sat on the bed opposite the redhead. "Did Ruben know you were pregnant? And that Butler was the father?" I asked.

McDonough sniffed, and avoided eye contact. "Yes. I didn't tell him, but he knew."

"Who told him?"

"I don't know."

I did. Wignall's comment about Butler came to mind: *He's the type who likes to get the business done quick so he can get down to the pub and brag to his friends about it.*

"Did you know Ruben had multiple sclerosis?"

"What?"

"You weren't aware of that?"

She shook her head. Her chin quivered.

"He was diagnosed with it a couple of months before he died," I said.

She shook her head again.

"Did you know one of the symptoms of MS is impotence, Ms. McDonough?"

"God, I didn't know . . ."

"What was your relationship with Ruben Wright?"

"We were f-friends."

"I thought you were more than friends—lovers, perhaps."

"W-were . . . Our relationship had changed." She took a deep breath and shuddered.

"Was *he* aware of that change?" I asked.

McDonough nodded.

"Do you think Ruben was suicidal?" I asked.

"I don't know."

She didn't appear to know a lot.

"How long have you been seeing Chris Butler?"

She looked at me like I'd just stepped on her foot.

"What did Butler say when you told him you were pregnant?"

"He said, 'Get the little bugger cut out.' " Her face crumpled as she began to sob. I gave her a moment. I remembered the night down at Laguna Beach, her and Butler across the bar, watching them drink a cocktail of anger, regret, and sadness—the way couples do when they're in a spiral dive with no hope of recovery.

"Did you know Ruben may have been trying to have you removed as a beneficiary of his will?"

"No," she said, regaining a little composure.

"But you knew you were a beneficiary?"

She grabbed a couple of tissues from the box and loudly blew her nose. "We talked about it. Years ago."

"So you knew how much Ruben was worth?"

"No."

"When he told you that you were to be his chief beneficiary, he didn't tell you how much would be coming your way if he died?"

"He tried to. I didn't want to know—like it was bad luck or something. I didn't want to jinx him, us."

Ironic, I thought, given what had happened to "him, us." I had to hand it to McDonough; if she was lying, she was a pro.

"Have you had a conversation with Ruben's lawyer about the will yet?"

More shakes of the head. "Never spoken to him, you know, not one on one. But I received a letter from him. There's a reading next week."

I was just getting into my stride on this Q & A when I heard, "Your ten minutes are up." It was the minor-impersonating-a-doctor. He pulled the chart at the base of the bed and examined it as a nurse entered the room and began to fuss, herding the patient back under the covers. The sheets billowed as she pulled them over McDonough's legs. The nurse then turned her attention to the curtain beside the bed. She gave it an aggressive tug and it raced around the overhead rail, cutting me off from McDonough. End of interview.

*   *   *

I drove back to Hurlburt Field, putting it together in my head. There were big holes. Butler told me he wasn't having an affair with McDonough, but McDonough hadn't backed him up. She'd just aborted his child. When the issue of paternity could have been settled with a test, it had to be Butler who was lying.

Butler had also said he didn't know where McDonough lived or worked. Was that an attempt to stall me from talking to Amy long enough for her to have the pregnancy terminated? Had he hoped I wouldn't find out about her condition before he went back to England?

As for the pregnancy itself, Amy had apparently learned of it seven weeks ago. Around the time that Ruben made the call to his lawyer to—it was still an assumption—have his will changed. Was the timing of the two events significant? Had to be.

And what about Ruben's MS medications? Where were they? If he'd destroyed them before the fatal jump, what would that say about his death? That he intended to commit suicide? Maybe, but if he was intent on taking his own life, why bother hiding them at all? If Butler took him by surprise that night, wouldn't his drugs have been reasonably easy to find? Hmm . . . perhaps, perhaps not. I reminded myself the MS was a condition Ruben was intent on keeping a secret from the Air Force. According to Dr. Mooney, he required a cocktail of drugs taken at regular intervals during the day, and that meant having ready access to them. I found myself back at the start: Where did Ruben keep his stash? And, given their relationship, was it really possible McDonough didn't know about his MS?

The weather had changed. The Gulf had become a sheet of blue glass beyond the Pensacola Bay Bridge, rippled here and there by puffs of wind. It was the kind of day that caused me to think hurricanes were a figment of the collective imagination. But I knew that was not the case. The seeds of destruction were buried somewhere out in the Gulf, just waiting for the right conditions to germinate.

As the SUV chewed through the miles, the same thoughts kept going round in my head: Sergeant Ruben Wright, my old CCTs buddy, was not the kind of guy who'd take his own life, but he was most definitely the type who'd take the enemy with him, especially if he thought there was no way out. How would he face up to the challenge of knowing his mind and body were deteriorating and, with it, his career and the relationship to the woman he loved?

Enter Butler—young, fit, and virile, three realities his girlfriend was experiencing firsthand behind his back, and on hers. Learning that Amy was pregnant and Butler was the father would have been hard for Ruben to take. And when he found out, would that have been catalyst enough to change his will? I knew his condition was deteriorating rapidly. What about his mental state? Was that crumbling, too?

It could have gone down exactly as Butler said it did. Ruben was depressed, jealous, and angry. When the SAS unit came out of the C-130 all messed up, it wasn't just one of those things. Ruben made sure it happened that way by stumbling into the other guys and breaking up the formation. He'd then slammed into Butler in midair with the full intention of causing him some significant damage. Then he cut his own thigh strap with his knife and pulled his rip cord. Gravity and Newton's Laws of Motion did the rest, separating him from the chute. The unlikely method of his suicide, coupled with the significant bruising Butler would have suffered in the collision, the smashed flashlight . . . What investigation wouldn't put those things together in a light that would make Butler look bad? Ruben Wright's sweet revenge. The last desperate act of a desperate man.

Before I was aware of it, I'd driven fifty miles and the sign for Hurlburt Field appeared. I turned into the base, showed the security detail my shield, and drove to OSI. I slotted the Explorer between another SUV and a late-model Harley-Davidson.

My cell rang. I pulled it from my pocket as I passed Agent Lyne. Lyne glanced up from his desk and called, "Vin, there's a—"

With Lyne spinning in my wake, I walked into the room I'd been using as both an office and a warehouse for Ruben Wright's effects. A staff sergeant I didn't know, dressed in immaculate Class As, was standing among the trestle tables. Under one arm was his cap. In the other was an envelope, all official. "Special Agent Vin Cooper?" he asked.

I nodded as I pressed the cell's green button.

"Orders for you, sir."

In my ear, I heard a familiar voice. "Vin? Arlen."

I accepted the envelope from the sergeant. "Hey, Arlen. What's—"

He cut me off. "You know that little vacation you've been having down there at Uncle Sugar's expense?"

"What?"

"It's over."

TWENTY-NINE

Vacation?" I asked. I glared at the handset then put it back to my ear.

"Trust me," Arlen said. "Having your toenails pulled one by one would be a vacation compared to D.C. right at the moment. How's the case going?"

"Fine. Why do you ask?" I said.

"It's not me asking."

"Who is?"

"I'm channeling for the boss."

"What does he want to know?"

"Whether the Butler did it."

"I've already used that one, Arlen."

There was a sigh. "Jesus, you make it difficult sometimes."

"I'll take that as a compliment," I said.

"What I'm trying to ascertain here is whether you think the Limey's guilty."

"He's guilty of being a serious asshole."

"He's English," he said. "They're born that way. What about murder?"

I frowned at a spot on the wall. I suddenly realized Arlen's interest in this case the last time we spoke might have been more than idle curiosity. "What's the deal, Arlen? What's up?"

"I don't know. The boss wants to know—asked me to ask you. There's no sinister intent here, Vin. The Brits are our allies and the general's just being a politician—you know how they are."

I was prepared to take Arlen at his word. Having a member of the British SAS up on a murder charge would create a bunch of headaches for a range of people who'd rather be on the golf course. "I can't say definitively, but the more I look into it, the more it seems . . . you know . . . I'm just not certain which way it's going to go."

"How much more time do you need?"

"A week, maybe two."

"I've been told to tell you you've got a day, Vin. Your orders should be there by now."

I looked at the letter that had just been deposited in my hand. "Yeah, got 'em." The sergeant who'd delivered them had already departed.

"You're wanted here for a briefing the day after tomorrow."

"Where's 'here'?"

"The Pentagon."

"The Pentagon? Who with?"

"Chip Schaeffer."

Schaeffer, my CO back at the DoD? I sat in the chair, rocked back, and put a foot on the corner of the desk. "Do you know what it's about?"

"Nope. I've just been told to make sure you turn up looking eager and interested."

Hmm...maybe one of Schaeffer's fish had died and he needed me to lean on the pet store for a refund. I changed tack and asked about something Arlen might have an answer for. "Any headway made on the Transamerica hit?"

There was a pause.

"Yeah, as a matter of fact," he said. "Remember there were two Arabs who rented the van?"

"Yeah."

"They turned out to be Pakistanis."

"Pakistanis don't look Arabic," I said.

"No, but I'm guessing the witness at the rental company wasn't no anthropologist. All she knew was that the guys who rented the van weren't white, black, or Korean. FBI is hunting down the sleepers who helped them. But don't expect to hear about it on CNN until they have them all under lock and key."

"What about the disk—the one I sent you an MPEG copy of?"

"The FBI found Dr. Spears's DNA all over the envelope's seal. I heard someone say it was almost like she'd gone down on the thing. If she didn't want people to know she'd sent it, you'd think someone with her experience would have been a bit more careful."

"Yeah, you would," I agreed. "Have they located her?"

"Don't know."

I let all this sink in. There was silence on the line. After a few moments, I said, "Has a statement from Al Cooke turned up yet?"

"Who's Cooke?"

"The cook on the *Natusima*. You remember, Dr. Tanaka—"

"You're not on that one anymore, Vin."

"I knew you'd say that, Arlen. Has it turned up?"

"I don't know."

"Listen, can you get some bank statements—"

"No."

I told him whose statements I wanted. Arlen was surprised, but he agreed to see what he could do.

"You're a pal," I said.

"I know. And, by the way, Happy New Year," he said.

"Thanks, Arlen. Back at you."

"So, what did you end up doing last night to see in the New Year?"

"Went to this noisy little restaurant in Pensacola. You?" I enjoyed a quick flashback to Clare on top, rocking back and forth, massaging my naked torso with honey as she licked her fingers.

"Sat at my desk along with everyone else in Washington and made phone calls."

"Any of them involve heavy breathing, at least?"

"No. So, did Anna get through to you? She said she'd tried and was going to try again later."

Anna had tried to call? I didn't believe it. The hotel I'd stayed in wasn't in a dead zone—the call from Boris before sunrise proved that. Was she just paving the way for an excuse? "I didn't hear from her."

"Oh, yeah, the other big news . . . my promotion came through. You can call me Lieutenant Colonel now."

"That's great, buddy. Congratulations."

"Sir . . ." said Arlen.

"What?"

"Congratulations, *sir.*"

"Blow me. *Sir,*" I said.

"No thanks," Arlen said.

"So, how's Anna doing?" I asked, fishing.

"Good, I think," Arlen said. "We didn't talk much. She said she wanted to talk to you. Told me to tell you that if she didn't get through to you, she'd call again in a few days."

"Uh-huh."

"Everything OK?" he asked, picking up on something in my tone. Crushing guilt, most like.

"Yep, all copacetic," I said.

"OK. Hey, gotta go," said Arlen, distracted. There was the sudden noise in the background of several people in the room with him, all talking at once. "Drop by tomorrow."

"Will do. See you then."

"Sir."

"What?"

"See you then, *sir.*"

"Fuck you. *Sir.*"

I hit the off button, but not before Arlen beat me to it. He was enjoying himself.

Hand-delivered orders, a call from Andrews in the form of Arlen to make sure I got them—something big was up. I glanced at the envelope in my hand. I tore the side off it, removed the folded sheets of paper, and ran my eye over the legalspeak. As usual, much of the letter was a form, reminding me that as I held a commission, I had numerous legal responsibilities to my commander in chief, the President. Basically, these were that I had to do what he said. Distilling out all the wheretofores, therebys, and hereins left me with the demand to get my ass to the Pentagon no later than tomorrow, where I was to present myself in Class A uniform to Captain Charles Schaeffer at my old Pentagon address. OSI, DoD, OSI, and now back to DoD. I was going back and forth like a badminton birdie. What gives? I wondered. And why make such a big deal about the dress code? Chip and I weren't exactly strangers. The written orders held no clues. There was no point giving it any thought—as Arlen had said, I'd find out soon enough. That didn't stop me feeling annoyed. I'd been yanked off the Tanaka case before bringing it to a successful conclusion, and it looked like the Ruben Wright case was going to go the same way.

I tossed the paperwork on the desk and leaned back in the chair, a number of competing thoughts running through my head. I wondered why Anna said she'd called me when she hadn't. Was her intuition picking up on my movements, particularly the ones beneath the sheets with a certain colonel?

I needed some air. I picked my way through the electrical gear and the records spread around that were all that remained of Ruben Wright, and went outside. While the early-afternoon sun had begun its downhill slide to the horizon, it still held some warmth out of the breeze. I thought about Freddie Spears. She must have wanted to be connected to the disk. So why the theatrics?

I walked out into the parking lot. The Harley-Davidson caught my eye. I rode one for a few years out of school. Mine had been held together with gum and wire, so it was nothing like this one. This baby was low at the back with raked forks out front and just enough chrome to ensure the job of keeping it all polished up was never quite finished. Its bright crimson gas tanks reminded me of hard candy and looked good enough to lick.

There were plenty of Harleys running around the base, but something about this one told me it was Ruben Wright's. Maybe it was the two thousand miles on the clock. Or maybe it was the fact that I'd seen the paperwork for it in his files. Seeing the bike reminded me that I had a single day to resolve, as much as I was able, what happened to Ruben and why.

I went back inside to hunt for a few specific items I'd seen listed with the bike on the breakdown of Ruben's effects. I found some of the items in the third box I opened. One was a digital Handycam. The batteries still held some juice. I fired it up and checked its folders. Empty. The other item was an Apple Power-Book. I pressed the start button and waited for it to boot up. I don't know what I expected to find, but whatever it was it wasn't there. Aside from a bunch of old nineties hits burned into iTunes, it was completely devoid of documents, e-mails, photos, movies. There was nothing.

I replaced the Handycam and computer in the box,

disappointed. I wandered out of my office in search of
Agent Lyne. I found him in a back room.

"Do you know if Colonel Selwyn's around?" I
asked, leaning on the doorway. I had some news for
her she might not like. Or maybe that was my ego
talking. Would she care that I was leaving town?
Maybe she'd strike up the band.

Agent Lyne ignored me. I called louder. "Yo, Lloyd!"

Nothing. I became aware of a distant sound that reminded me of chipmunks rioting before I saw the little white iPod buds in his ears. He had the volume
turned way up. I tapped him on the shoulder, which
made him jump. He turned and pulled out the buds.

"Don't think much of your old pal's taste in music,"
he yelled. "Full of nineties crap."

I gestured at him to hand it over. He shrugged and
pulled the unit from his breast pocket. It was new, of
course, and top of the line. I toured the playlists—
Aerosmith, Metallica, Hootie and the Blowfish, LL
Cool J, U2, Matchbox 20. I didn't share Lyne's problem with Ruben's music taste. On a hunch, I checked
its settings. It didn't contain many songs—one hundred at most. Not enough to account for all the memory used. I checked the video folder. Empty.

I backtracked into my office, restarted the Power-
Book, jacked in the iPod, and waited for everything to
fire up. The icon for the iPod appeared on the computer's screen. Ruben had titled it "Sgt. Rock." Cute. I
double-clicked it and a window appeared. Inside the
window there was a folder titled "Bitch." In the folder
were a large number of MPEGs and JPEGs. Each MPEG

was dated. Ruben must have stored them here so they couldn't be played on the iPod's screen. I opened the MPEG with the earliest date, taken close enough to seven weeks ago. The clip opened on a slow pan along a beach, empty except for a few joggers. It was not a sunny day by the looks of things. Then the camera zoomed in on something a long way in the distance. After what seemed a moment of hesitation, the camera had come in for an even closer look. I could now make out more detail. It was a couple making out on the sand. They were dry humping each other. The person on top rolled off. I recognized the person on the bottom first. The red hair gave her away. Her dance partner turned briefly toward the camera. It was Staff Sergeant Butler. He unzipped his fly and extracted his erection, which McDonough shoved down her throat with the gusto of a plumber trying to unblock a drain. The show ended prematurely. Counting back the weeks, the recording would have been made at around the time Ruben first tried to change his will. Given that I don't believe in coincidences, the timing was at least suggestive.

I watched the other MPEGs and opened the photos. The dates on the files indicated Ruben had his girlfriend and Staff Sergeant Butler under close observation for the ensuing eight-week period leading up to his death. There were even a couple of MPEGs taken through the lens of a night-vision monocle, McDonough and Butler looking as green as tree frogs as they slid around on each other in the backseat of her Chevy.

So which hypothesis did this discovery support?

"The colonel is in, sir," said Lyne, breaking in on my train of thought.

"What? Sorry, who?"

"Colonel Selwyn. You asked earlier whether the colonel was in. Well, she's in."

"OK, thanks," I said. I had to tell her I was leaving town. And there were also the discoveries found on Ruben's iPod. The old good-news, bad-news thing. I wondered what she'd want to hear first.

THIRTY

Give me the bad," Clare said, a realist. Her hair was pulled back off her face in a tight ponytail, accentuating her strong cheekbones. She was dressed in BDUs. I found it impossible not to think about what she might be wearing under them. A framed photo of her son sat on her desk, his innocent, big brown eyes following me. Sorry, kid.

"I'm leaving tomorrow," I said, straight out. "Orders."

"And the good?" she replied, without the slightest flicker of regret evident. Clare Selwyn wasn't the type who'd be standing on a train platform waving anyone good-bye with a tear-sodden hanky, unless it was her son.

"That doesn't bother you? The fact that I'm leaving?" I said.

"Of course I'm disappointed. The sex was pretty good, but this is the Air Force." She shrugged. "What can you do?"

The sex was pretty good. *Pretty* good? I'd have said *amazing*.

"So, the good news?" she asked again, this time with a frown.

I took her through the discoveries on Wright's iPod by showing her, loading the QuickTime MPEGs up on her computer. "So what do you think?" I said when we'd gone through them all.

"I think you should spend your last evening in Fort Walton Beach with me," she said, using that command tone of hers.

"For some more of that *pretty* good sex?"

"Who said anything about sex, Vin? I'm just talking about a home-cooked meal. You're probably not going to get one of those for a while. And maybe we can talk about the case."

"Sure," I said. She was toying with me. Cat-and-mouse might be another of Clare's little games. The thought of having dinner with her was a distraction. It took a moment or two to lift my head out of her pantry and get back to Ruben Wright. "The further I get into this case, the more I'm wondering about the other side," I said.

"What other side? What do you mean?"

I stood and walked to the window. There were clouds in the sky now, white on top and gray beneath as if they couldn't decide which sort to be. "Right from the get-go we both believed the most likely scenario was that someone who jumped with Ruben cut him out of his harness. Butler seemed our best suspect because of the flashlight and his injuries."

Clare nodded. "I've just completed the tests on that flashlight, by the way. The red lens material you recovered near the crime scene belonged to it."

"So no surprises there," I said. "On the face of it, you'd have to say Butler's our man. Except..."

"...except for what we now know about Master Sergeant Ruben Wright."

"Yeah." I made the points on my fingers. "One: He had MS, a fact he'd kept from the Air Force. It was the aggressive variety, so he didn't have long till the Air Force evened the score and had him medically discharged. Two: He'd discovered his girlfriend was saucing Butler's sausage. Three: The ultimate insult to a guy like Ruben—he discovered that McDonough was pregnant with Butler's kid. My guess is that it might even have been Butler who gave him the news. Four: Amy McDonough was the sole beneficiary of Ruben's will, a will he tried to change at a time that roughly coincided with the date of the first home movie of Butler and McDonough making like turtles up the beach."

"So now you think that perhaps Ruben Wright, to get back at his cheating girlfriend and the English staff sergeant, killed himself in such a way as to frame Butler in the role of perp?"

"A reach, isn't it?"

Clare gave a noncommittal shrug. "Like you, I think I'm almost convinced enough not to be totally convinced about murder."

"There are a couple of other issues I don't have answers to," I said.

"And they are?"

"Ruben never did get around to changing his will. It would help to know why. I also want to know where he kept his MS drugs. The fact that we haven't found them means that he either disposed of them on the morning of the day he died, or they were kept someplace secret and we just haven't located them yet."

"What would be the significance of him getting rid of them?"

"If he dumped his medications, then a reasonable conclusion would be he knew he wasn't coming back. The fact that we haven't found them could also mean that he didn't want anyone to know he was on medication for MS. We might never find them."

Clare nodded. "Hmm . . ."

"Would an autopsy have told you he had MS?" I asked.

"Perhaps, if we knew we were looking for it," Clare said. "But a human body that hits the ground at around a hundred miles an hour ain't pretty. Organs are practically liquefied on impact. Finding something as subtle as reduced myelin on cranial nerves would be kinda iffy."

I put my hands behind my head and looked out her window. A file of trainees triple-timed past on the roadway, heads down, looking inside themselves for something extra. I said, "I dunno . . . it's real unlikely a healthy CCT hotshot would cut his own harness."

"But it's also conceivable that a dedicated soldier who sees his career in the crapper and himself in a wheelchair might," she said.

"You really think it's possible Ruben killed himself to set up Butler?" I asked as I watched a young airman using a toothbrush to paint the rocks marking the edge of the road white. I wondered if he'd be expected to clean his teeth with it later.

"It's possible," Clare said. "You're the investigator, Vin. The question is, which of those answers would *you* want to lock in?"

Neither of us said anything for a few moments while we both chewed over the options. Then a question unrelated to the current investigation rose out of my subconscious the way a body stuffed in a trunk and sunk in a river can pop to the surface. "You mind answering a question related to another case?"

"Sure, if I can."

"You had much experience with badly burned bodies?"

"Depends. What do you want to know?"

"Is it possible a body can get so badly burned that identification through DNA ceases to be an option?"

"How was this particular body burned?"

"Major gas fire."

She nodded. "DNA is not invincible. It fact, it's pretty easy to destroy, and fire is as good a means as any. Gas burns at over a thousand degrees Fahrenheit. If the fire is sustained, and the temperature is high enough, like in a gas fire, the body ends up deep-frying in its own fat. Eventually, if this cooking continues, the body broils away happily like any piece of meat left in the oven too long, and it gets turned into carbon. If that happens, there's no DNA left. In a fire like that, you probably won't get dental records, either, because the head will have been burnt off. The same with the hands, arms, and legs. Fingerprints will be the first things to go. Identification is going to have to come through some other means. Does that help?"

"It's going to help me turn vegan."

"So," said Clare, "where do you go from here?"

"The Pentagon."

"Not you, the case . . ."

"Which one?"

"Which one do you think?"

"On this one? That's it for me, Clare. I'm done. It's up to the next guy."

"What next guy?"

"My replacement."

"This one's going to end up in the freezer; you know that, don't you?" Clare gave me the how-could-you? look.

"You know, I don't want that to happen, either. I've got a couple of thoughts, but you'll have to see them through, if you can."

"Such as?"

"You'll need the local PD and maybe a court order or two."

"We've got a reasonable relationship with the local cops. What you got in mind?" Clare asked.

I told her about a few of those things—phone and bank records for Amy McDonough and Juan Demelian, Ruben's attorney. Others I kept to myself on account of they had more to do with what was on tonight's menu over at her house.

I returned to the train wreck that was my makeshift office. I had quite a bit to do before leaving Hurlburt Field, a major task being the rationalization of my expenses onto a DD Form 1351–2 for e-mailing to the GAO. For one thing, my wallet was so stuffed with receipts it felt like I was sitting on a shoe. For another, I was almost broke. I also had to see that Ruben Wright's effects were packed back into storage, and write up my notes on the case for that next guy, if there was a next guy.

I was repacking the stereo into its box with foam blocks that wouldn't go back in the way they came out when the cell rang. I should have checked the screen before answering it. "Special Agent Vin Cooper."

"Vin."

That familiar voice. Hearing it was like being in an elevator that had just had all its cables cut. "Anna. Hey—how's it going?" I said as I dropped through the shaft.

"Good. And you?"

"Good. Happy New Year, by the way."

"And Happy New Year to you," she said. "I tried to phone you."

"Yeah, Arlen told me." I didn't call her on the lie.

"So, how was your night?"

"Pretty good," I said. *Pretty good? Jesus!* "Yours?"

"It was okay. Vin, I . . . I've got some news."

"Yeah, Arlen said you—"

"Vin, I've met someone."

I should have seen it coming. She'd said she had some news. *Some* news usually meant bad news with nothing good to counterbalance it. I knew for certain she hadn't tried to call, though she'd probably been thinking about doing so quite a bit. "You've met someone?"

"Yes. Someone I like."

"How much do you like him?"

"Vin, don't make this more difficult than it already is."

I could have made it easier and told her about Clare. That would have let her off the hook, but it would also have left me hanging on it.

"I just needed to be honest with you," she said.

There you go again, Anna, reading my mind, I thought. "So, how long have you been seeing this guy?" I asked. "It is a *guy* you've been seeing...?"

"Vin..."

"It could be a chimp."

I heard her make an impatient *tsk* sound. "He's JAG. A lawyer."

"Oh, right, so that would make him a chump."

She went on to say she'd been seeing the guy for a month. A month? A JAG lawyer? It was like a joke with a really unfunny punch line. She'd been seeing the guy since long before she'd paid me that impromptu visit before Christmas. I felt my Clare-guilt absolved. What had that trip to my bed been about, anyway? Was she maybe comparing us, deciding which way to jump? Or who she was no longer going to jump?

"Vin, I'm sorry this has hurt you."

I didn't say anything on account of there was nothing to say.

"You know it wasn't working—the distance, the bad phone calls, the silences..."

"The piano principle," I said.

"Piano principle?"

"Your friend Steinway and his postage stamps."

"Yeah, right..."

"I guess this makes it official, doesn't it?"

"I guess it does," she replied.

Even though we'd already called time, a part of me was still hanging on to the improbable. She and I had history. We'd worked the toughest case of my career—and hers—together. The slow death of separation had finally done what bullets and a car crash had failed to do.

"You there, Vin?...Vin...?"

"Yeah, I'm here...So has this JAG lawyer got a sense of humor?" I asked.

"I...I don't know...well, yeah, he does."

"You don't sound too sure about it. You need to tell him my favorite lawyer joke and watch for a positive reaction," I said. I gave her the two-lawyers-in-the-bank joke, which got a laugh. I hung up and stared at the phone a while.

THIRTY-ONE

The C-130's interior smell was a mélange of hot kerosene, grease, and gasoline. Up at the front of the aircraft, not too far from where I sat, a battered, tied-down Humvee leaked fluid onto the bare aluminum floor. I knew how it felt. My bladder was on the verge of doing likewise. I had the pins and needles in my fingers along with the sweats and the shortness of breath. I was well aware of the classic symptoms of aviaphobia even before reading about them in my new flying companion, *Have a Nice Flight*, on account of the only time I experienced them was when I sat in an aircraft. And the fact that these symptoms were "classic" didn't make me feel any better about having them.

The aircraft lurched, bucking forward as the pilot tested the brakes. And then the engines screamed as only engines in C-130s can, and we turned onto the strip and accelerated. I did what the book suggested I do when in an aircraft heading down the runway. I pedaled, just like Fred Flintstone in his Flintstone car pedaled. This, according to the book, was to give me a feeling of control over my situation. It was supposed to help. It did. It helped me feel like the village idiot, especially as I only noticed the smirking loadmaster strapped into the troop seats on the opposite side of the aircraft after we'd taken off. He began flapping his arms like bird wings, which is one of the ways people lose their front teeth.

Driving a rental back to D.C. wasn't an option. The fact that I had to get my ass up to the captain's office by 1300 hours didn't give me the chance to dick around on the nation's highways. As is often the case at an Air Force base, there happened to be a flight leaving and headed my way. Lyne got me and my well-thumbed copy of *Have a Nice Flight* on it.

The book didn't recommend getting comatose with a bottle of single malt as a means of overcoming my fears, a suggestion that would have suited me just fine. Instead it recommended distraction. In the lexicon of modern weaselspeak, the book called this "thinking positive thoughts." I put my cynicism away and gave it a go. There was the bust-up with Anna— nothing positive there. I thought about Ruben's last few months and couldn't see much good there, either. I thought about dinner the previous evening at Clare's. And I thought about how wrong I'd read it. After the night in the hotel, I believed she'd been having fun with me when she'd said I was being presumptuous about sex being on the table, or words to that effect. But no. In fact, we ate fried rice with her son, Manfred. One of the things I learned about Manny was that he wanted to be a rotary-winged pilot, ironic given what had happened to his dad. Or maybe not. Maybe it was the kid's way of conquering the loss: He couldn't beat 'em, so he was going to join 'em—or would when he grew big enough to reach the pedals.

Manny was a good kid, but laying carpet would have done more for my libido.

The closest Clare and I came to sex was dessert. She fixed us each a banana split. Given what I knew of her proclivities, this was practically pornographic.

When dessert was finished, it was bedtime—Manny's. Clare read him a story. Afterward, we sat on her back porch, listened to the frogs in the marsh beyond the fence, and talked shop—about the case, about past cases. The conversation ran its natural course until there was only one topic left to discuss. Clare sipped her glass of wine and said, "I meant it when I said just dinner."

"OK," I replied.

She picked a small bug out of her glass that was beating its wings furiously, swimming in panicked circles on top of her wine. She flicked it away. "It's been fun."

"Yes, it has."

The frogs croaked in unison somewhere in the darkness until one of them missed its cue. "You were just passing through, Vin, and that made what we were doing possible. Remember?"

I remembered. "But now I'm so passed through I'm out the other side?"

"Yes," she said. "I'm really going to miss you."

"The feeling's mutual."

She gave my hand a squeeze. "So we've had a nice farewell dinner. I don't want to ruin it."

"Can't we ruin it just a little?" I asked.

A short while later, we shook hands at her front door—buddies. It seemed the right thing to do at the time. But now, sitting in a climbing C-130, when I needed a positive distraction, I had none. So instead I focused on a spot on the floor, ground my teeth, fought the pins and needles, and wondered why the hell I hadn't studied accounting.

*   *   *

Flying time to Andrews AFB in Washington, D.C., was a little over three hours. I stepped off the C-130 with my ears ringing, feeling like I'd spent a couple of hours rolling around inside a steel hubcap with a handful of gravel. I took a cab to my apartment. It was exactly as I'd left it—quiet and empty. The übermold in the fridge hadn't even managed to regroup for a renewed assault. I had a quick shower, threw on my Class A uniform, and walked out the front door half an hour after I arrived. The sky was gray and so low I could almost touch it. The fingers of my left hand ached—a sure sign that snow was in the air.

It started coming down as the cab climbed the ramp on to the Beltway. It fell slow, like white ticker tape. In between songs, the radio warned a big storm front was headed D.C.'s way. A little snow was OK. Too much and the only people who'd benefit from it were the kids who might be forced to skip school if the drifts got too deep.

The cab slowed along with the surrounding traffic as the snow became heavier and the temperature kept dropping. Nevertheless, I arrived outside Chip's office with two minutes to spare. I had enough time to release two buttons on my coat when Schaeffer's door burst open. He was in his Class As, too. "Fall in, Major," he said as he strode past. Perhaps I was being unfair, but striding was something I thought he was incapable of. Schaeffer's face was red and he didn't look pleased. I was pretty certain he wasn't going to wish me Happy New Year.

We climbed a level and walked to the other side of the building. I followed Chip through an unfamiliar section, took some more turns, came through several doors requiring the swipe of his security card, and through another couple needing his card as well as a ten-digit code punched into their touchpads. One set of doors even required a scan of Chip's retinas. While he was being scanned, I kept a lookout for Tom Cruise and his Mission Impossible team.

Thirteen minutes after we set off, and, disproving Arlen's seven-minute theory, a female naval officer with the rank of lieutenant snapped open a set of double doors as we approached. Once inside, I could see there was a bunch of people sitting around a large, rectangular table. Flat-screen computer monitors faced each chair at the table, and the room was ringed by large television monitors at standing height. The light wasn't good as it was provided only by table lamps and the flat-screens. I took all this in at a glance, my synapses popping away like corn on hot steel. Although I couldn't see exactly who was who, I caught enough stars to know there was a who's who of high-ranking brass in the room. However, it was the presence of three people dressed in civilian clothes that gave my pulse rate a push: the U.S. Secretary of Defense; one Bradley Chalmers, now back from his little trip to Guam; and Dr. Freddie Spears. The doctor didn't look up when Schaeffer and I walked in, which told me I was expected. For a second or two I thought the smile on Chalmers's face meant he was pleased to be in my company again. When I looked again, I saw it was a snarl.

"So this is your man, eh?" said the SecDef, leaning back in his chair, appraising me like I was a suit on the rack that might possibly fit.

Chip Schaeffer said stiffly, "Yes, sir, Mr. Secretary. Major Vincent Cooper, currently assigned to OSI, formerly a special tactics officer in the CCTs."

"At ease, gentlemen," said an Air Force four-star who, like the admiral, was one of the people I didn't recognize.

At least the order to wear Class As now made some sense, even if the rest of it didn't. An Army four-star got to his feet and walked up to and around me. "Are you fit, Major?" he asked.

"He looks fit," said a voice from the shadows down the end of the room.

The general was short, with big fleshy ears that reminded me of Yoda's. He smelled strongly of breath mints and cigar smoke. Those three words—"Are you fit"—gave me a tight feeling in my gut. Since when did physical fitness have anything to do with an ability to investigate crime? The Air Force had a basic fitness standard for its cops. Basically, you had to be fit enough to stand for ten minutes on line at a Krispy Kreme's.

"Reasonably, sir," I said.

"Reasonably, eh?" the general said, half turning to the audience seated behind him.

"Get on with it, Henry," said some rear admiral.

"Your record says you're thirty-four, Major."

"Yes, sir."

"Hmm," the general said, sucking in his top lip and then chewing on it. I read the name tag on his chest: Howerton. I knew the name. Henry Howerton was Chairman of the Joint Chiefs, which explained who the rest of the brass were. The gray hairs of his eyebrows were long and met above the bridge of his nose where they tangled like a kid's shoelaces. He was thinking hard, frowning. "Major, I want to see if you can do the APFT push-up requirement, plus eight to round it up to fifty," he said.

"Jesus, Henry..." said the unidentified admiral.

Howerton turned and said, to no one in particular, "If the guy's not in shape, we can sort that out here and now and move on if we have to. Do we have time to screw around?"

"No," said the SecDef.

"Well, then...Fifty push-ups, son," Howerton said, speaking to me with his hands on his hips. "I don't reckon you can do 'em, and neither does Ulysses S. Grant here." He pulled his wallet from a back pocket, lifted out a fifty-dollar note, and slapped it on the table.

Whatever I might have been expecting, it wasn't this. The APFT was the Army Physical Fitness Test. I'd done it before for reasons I didn't want to think about.

"Go on ... take his money, Major," said the admiral from the shadows.

I found myself undoing my overcoat buttons, not because I wanted the fifty bucks but because majors don't say no to generals, not unless they enjoy a good kick in their performance reports and mine were already bruised enough. The room was cool but I was sweating anyway. I took the coat off and put it over the back of a chair.

"Make 'em good ones, Major—straight back, chin up," said General Howerton.

A little voice in my head told me this might be a good bet to lose. I got down on the floor and saw my nose reflected in the mirror shine of Howerton's shoes. With all the adrenaline in my system, I did thirty-five easy, without feeling them, Howerton keeping count, but I made the last five look like I was bench-pressing three years of pancakes with extra cream, and stopped at forty-eight, spent. It was a great performance. I got to my feet slow, sucking in the O_2. "Sorry, General," I said, shaking my head. "Hit the wall."

"That's OK, Major. I get to keep my money. This is what's known as a win-win." He said all this with a broad grin.

My eyes narrowed.

"Like I said, the APFT says you only need to do *forty-two*, son. I just wanted to see with my own eyes. Satisfy myself and these good people here. See that you could do 'em."

"Gotta hand it to you, Henry; you read the Major right," said the admiral with a chuckle. "The way you started out, Major, looked to me like you could go all the way to a hundred."

Someone else said, "You sure about this, Henry?"

"Look, he's got the necessary experience. We can get him an Army Regulation 40-501 flight physical examination that falls within the specified time limitations. He meets the height and weight standards as set down in AR 600-9. He scrapes in with a few years to spare for age, he's a good thirty inside the two-hundred-forty-pound weight limit for MFF, and he's security-cleared for black ops. We can get him waivers for the rest. In other words, gentlemen, for the purposes of this exercise, Major Cooper here is good to go."

The APFT? *MFF!* Hang on a second, good to go the fuck where? And for the purposes of *what* exercise?

"You look confused, Major. Don't worry, you won't be for too much longer." Howerton put his hand on my shoulder. "Your orders will be cut this afternoon and given to Captain Schaeffer. Dismissed. Oh, and, Vin . . . good luck."

THIRTY-TWO

The woman behind the counter had lost her figure a long time ago and what was left had about as many curves as a desert road. Her gray eyes were blank and the airborne fat combined with her own perspiration to oil up the skin on her face, causing it to shine. She asked me what I wanted with a raise of her eyebrows.

"Coffee, thanks," I said. "Black, no sugar."

She ambled off and pressed the button on the machine after placing a cardboard cup under the nozzle. I surveyed the food behind the glass. I was hungry, but not hungry enough to risk eating what at least a thousand customers before me had decided to pass on, and for good reason by the look of it. I'm not a food snob—in the military, you can't be—but I don't eat what I can't identify. The woman put the coffee on my tray and turned what little attention she had left on the customer behind me. I took a Snickers bar, put it on the tray beside the cup, and moved one place closer to the cashier. The cafeteria was still crowded, despite it being after 1400 hours. I found a vacant table.

I didn't want to think about the briefing, but, at the

same time, I found it impossible to think about anything else. MFF, Military Free Fall, jumping out of a
plane at high altitude. Given my issues with flying,
that was bad enough. Worse would be the reasons for
being made to do the course. What was I good to go
for, exactly? Obviously, it had something to do with
Chalmers and Doc Spears and so there were clues
right there. Worrying clues.

I ate the Snickers and watched people come and
go. The guy I was hoping would turn up arrived, even
before the coffee I bought to make occupying the
table legit went cold. He stood in the line, ordered,
and eventually found a table, maneuvering through
the crowded area with some difficulty. He sat, and I
made my way over. "How was Guam?" I said as I took
the seat opposite.

I interrupted his lunch—light coffee, and something in a Styrofoam tray that looked like it had come
from the sump of a blown engine. Chalmers looked
across the table at me with flat lids drawn across his
eyes. No Happy New Year from him, either. "Go fuck
yourself, Cooper."

"Do I look like a hermaphrodite?"

"What do you want?"

"How'd you break your leg?"

"None of your goddamn business."

I took a breath and tried again. "Guam. I meant it.
How did it go? You caught up with Al Cooke and ran
him through his statement about the night Dr. Tanaka
died, right?"

"This is how it went, asshole." He tapped a crutch with his knife.

"You broke your leg on Guam?"

"Disappear, Cooper."

"I'm sorry about your injury."

"No, you're not."

"Al Cooke—tell me about him," I said, trying to break the cycle. In fact, I was interested in finding out how he broke his leg, but only because I wanted to know whether I could claim some credit for it.

"Why should I?"

"Because everyone keeps saying we're on the same team?"

"Jesus, Cooper," he said, laughing sourly. "What goddamn shower did you come down in?"

"OK," I said. "If you won't tell me what you know, I'll tell you what I think you found."

"You sent me off on a fucking wild-goose chase, asshole," he said, all the preppy Ivy League crap peeled back, revealing the genuine plastic core beneath.

"Can we talk?" I asked.

"Put a dick in your ear."

"You got to Guam and found Al Cooke gone."

"What makes you think that?"

I ignored the question. "Did you check his bank account?"

Chalmers chewed and pointed to a cheek with his knife, indicating he wasn't going to speak with his mouth full.

"If you did, I'm guessing you'd have found a large unaccounted-for sum of money, recently deposited."

He swallowed. "Why would we check the man's bank account? Cooke was a potential witness, not a suspect."

"You did read his statement? The one I provided with my case notes, the one he provided over the phone, the one you went all the way over there to check? Didn't the statement strike you as odd?"

Chalmers shrugged and shoveled what appeared to be engine parts in brown grease into his face. "You got somewhere else to be, Cooper?" he said. "I can think of a few places, if you can't."

"Does CIA want to know what happened to Tanaka, or not?" I said. I tried to ignore the tough-guy act. I had to remind myself that Chalmers was CIA, not a cop. Unless the subject wore a hand towel or a trench coat, he probably wouldn't know what to do.

"Not," he said. "We're after bigger fish. What makes you think you know more now than you did before Christmas, Cooper?"

A reasonable question. "Because I've just been in a room with you and Dr. Spears and a whole bunch of brass. That tells me a few things right there. One of those things has to do with a certain DVD. It scared Spears bad enough to make her pass it on to me and then get the hell out of Moreton Genetics. She came to that decision after I interviewed her about the relationship between Boyle and Tanaka. I saw it in her face."

"Did you read her palm as well?" Chalmers shook his head and wiped his mouth with a napkin, which he tossed into the remains of his lunch. "Now, if you don't mind, fuck off." He pushed his chair back and made like he was going to stand up. "Are you finished? Because I am."

I was banging my head against a wall with this guy. His mind had the flexibility of a retiree with rickets. "I'm going to take another guess," I said.

"My food tray can hardly contain its excitement. It's going to sit there all afternoon and listen to your bullshit," he said, pulling himself up onto his crutches.

"That wallet found at the Four Winds supposedly belonging to Professor Boyle—five will get you ten Forensics have said it wasn't burned in the same fire that torched everything else around it. And that calls into question not only the identification of the body it was found under as being Sean Boyle's, but also makes me wonder who planted it."

The slight hesitation in Chalmers's determination to leave told me I was right. Professional pride wouldn't let him ask me where these conclusions of mine had come from. I stood and tucked my card into his top pocket. "Just in case you get stuck," I said as I walked out.

As I reached the exit, the cell buzzed against my leg. I pulled it out and reviewed the number before answering. "Arlen."

"Hey, Vin. Where are you?"

"On thin ice, skating."

"Well, bud, when you've stopped playin' around, you need to pay us a visit over here."

"Andrews?"

"Yeah."

"Why?"

"Your orders came through."

"Already?"

"Yeah."

"Shit."

"Your old boss brought them over personally."

"Chip Schaeffer?"

"Yep."

Schaeffer must have left the Pentagon meeting and gone straight there. "I need to go home and change."

"Chip told me to tell you to get ready to deploy immediately."

"You know where to?" I asked.

"The orders are SPECAT."

"SPECAT . . ." Special Category—no names, no destinations, lots of secrecy. Obviously Arlen knew, but he wasn't saying. A bad sign.

THIRTY-THREE

This time I was in and out of my apartment within twenty minutes. There was nothing to say good-bye to, except maybe the fridge mold. I didn't bother checking the e-mail, or the mailbox stuffing. I wasn't expecting anything anyway.

I saw that Kim and The 38th Parallel were still a week away from reopening, but there were signs of life in Summer Love, the vegan joint. A hippie, Summer herself probably, was mopping the floor. She glanced up and waved. I waved back. She had great legs and was attractive in an unshaved kind of way. Maybe I could get to like tofu burgers. Maybe I could take the tofu out. Maybe it was time to move.

The snow had stopped falling, though my fingers still ached, an indication the halt was only temporary. As I walked on to the street, a cab conveniently stopped a couple of doors away and a customer got out. I made the driver's day by taking him back into the city. Watching my breath condense on the window beside my face, I wondered what poo the Air Force had polished and put my name on. *MFF? Jesus.* I closed my eyes and settled in for a slow ride.

Forty minutes later I was sitting in an office at

Andrews AFB, waiting for Arlen, staring at his gray filing cabinet. He walked in looking way too perky. "Having a good day?" I asked.

"Vin—how you doin', bud?"

"Having a ball. Before I forget, can you lodge this for me, please?" I put my will on his desk and said, "I'm leaving the Vegas casino to you."

"Great, I could use one. You been in your office yet?" He picked up my will and put it in a tray with a bunch of other papers.

"No, why? What's in there?"

"A couple of suits over from the GAO, and they didn't look happy."

I wondered if it was the same two guys. "Is one of them Asian?"

He nodded. "I take it you've tangled with them before?"

I nodded. Could this day get any worse?

"Man—you're a game son of a bitch. No one takes those General Accounting Office people on."

"You got those orders there?" I asked.

Arlen opened a drawer and pulled out a thick envelope.

"You read them?"

"Nope."

"Heard any talk?"

"No."

The seal on the envelope was unbroken. I fixed that with my thumb. Inside were copies of the orders, six in all. I'd had to present six copies of orders only once before in my career with the military, though back then I was green and keen and no one had shot my ass out of the sky, or any other part of me, for that matter. I skimmed the paperwork in no particular order. Sweat beads popped on my forehead and my shirt felt clammy as I read and then reread the paragraphs that weren't pure template.

"Well?" Arlen asked.

"Well, what?" I said, breathing, trying to stay calm.

"What do they say?"

"To pack extra underwear."

"So I heard right," said Arlen.

"You said you hadn't heard anything."

He put his hand on my shoulder and gave me the sort of look you might give someone who'd just experienced a death in the family. I got up and made it to the head just in time to park the contents of my stomach.

I had a drink of water and headed for my office. I needed to have a few moments on my own to think the orders through. I'd forgotten I had guests.

"Cooper," said the Asian guy with the familiar New Jersey accent as I walked in. "Good of you to drop by."

"Yeah, the Gulf agrees with him, wouldn't you say?" said his partner. The Asian guy nodded.

"Wu and De Silver, right?" I said. "But it has been so long, fellers. I'm going to need some help. Which one's which? You're Wu, right?" I said, pointing at the guy who was about as Asian as spaghetti and meatballs. The real Wu was sitting in my chair, doing a good job of appearing constipated. I took a couple of steps toward my desk, which was bare except for a phone, an in-tray, an eraser, a mug stuffed with pens, and Wu's boots. "You mind?" Wu swung them off, stood, and then meandered around the other side, squaring up my in-tray with the side of the desk as he passed it. Accountants. The guy was so anal his shit probably came out symmetrical. I sat in my vacated chair. "Good of you to warm it up for me. Now, what can I do for you gentlemen?" I said, resting my chin on a pyramid of fingers.

"We told you we were going to keep an eye on you, Cooper," said De Silver, his hands loose in front of him like door security before they start brawling. His head was even cocked at the tough-guy angle. I almost laughed, but then I thought I'd better not if I wanted my expenses for the past few weeks reimbursed, an amount close to two thousand bucks. And all of it on my government Visa.

"Yeah, I remember you saying that the last time. And what has that eye you've been sharing seen, exactly?"

Wu and De Silver exchanged a glance. De Silver nodded. Wu stepped forward and leaned over the desk. "Uncle Sam is not your private bank, soldier." He produced a copy of the expenses form I'd filled in over the net when I was down in Florida and banged it on the desk. "One man does not consume two clam chowders, a basket of soft-shelled crabs, a couple of pounds of shrimp and scallops. And then there's the wine."

"The meal was a legitimate expense incurred in the performance of my duty," I said, parrying the thrust. The dinner at Salty's came back to me, unedited. Clare and I had discussed the Wright inquiry at length before going back to her house to play consenting adults. A snapshot of Clare came to mind. I saw her on top, holding me with both hands, the silver moonlight spilling through the bedroom window and flowing all over the bed.

"Something funny?" asked Wu.

"No, not funny."

"Then why are you smiling?"

"None of your damn business, sonny," I said.

Wu scowled.

De Silver droned on. "Also, there's the form itself. The DD 1351–2."

"What about it?"

"You're *AF*, pal. That means you fill in forms with an *AF* prefix," he said.

"The upshot is, Cooper, that we're not paying your expenses," said Wu, more confident now.

"Y'know," I said, "that's really great news."

"And why's that?" said Wu, frowning, disappointed. Perhaps he'd been expecting that this bulletin might upset me.

" 'Cause I just got SPECAT orders from a four-star by the name of Howerton. You might have heard of him?"

Both nodded involuntarily, pure reaction to hearing the name of the Chairman of the Joint Chiefs. "I'm supposed to be leaving tomorrow," I continued. "But in order to fulfill this latest contract I have with both the President as well as the Constitution of the United States, I'm going to need a card that isn't frozen because of nonpayment. But if you bold warriors are game enough to prevent me from following my orders, I can only admire you, and thank you. Means I'll live longer. Of course, I'll have to notify General Howerton about your problem with the number of soft-shelled crabs I ate as being the reason for my inability to follow his orders. I just know he'll want your serial numbers for verification purposes." I pulled a sheet of paper from a drawer and a pen from the mug. "Why don't you just write them down here? I'd hate to make a mistake and get a couple of innocent clerks castrated in your place."

I watched as De Silver chewed something off the inside of his cheek. SPECAT orders were classified, which meant they couldn't ask to see them and I would be breaking the law even giving them a peek. I could be bluffing, but, then again, maybe I wasn't. Also leaving an unpleasant taste in their mouths was the realization that on the expense form I would submit at the SPECAT mission's conclusion, only the amounts column would be filled out. There'd be no receipts provided, no details recorded or able to be verified. This was the GAO's worst nightmare—goddamn unsubstantiated expenses. I mean, just how many soft-shelled crabs would I be eating unchecked on the job this time? And then there was the wine . . . Both men glared at me, at the paper and pen, and back at each other. Wu finally spoke. "Then let's all just hope you don't make it back alive, Cooper." As they stomped out of my office, Wu slammed the door shut. I almost felt sorry for their next victim.

THIRTY-FOUR

An hour into the seven-hour bus trip south to Fayetteville, North Carolina, I was still staring disbelieving at the acronym soup that was my orders. There were two parts to the mission. The first part was not SPECAT. I was to get to Fort Bragg, North Carolina, by 1500 hours the following day, whereupon I was to report to a Major Jay Cummins, B Company, 2d Battalion, 1st SWTG (A)—Special Warfare Training Group (Airborne)—for the purposes of attending MFFPC.

The second part was as vague as only SPECAT orders could be. The paperwork merely said I would be required to attend a JMAP, or Joint Military Appreciation Process, at the successful completion of the MFFPC, at a place and venue TBN. TBN, of course, meant NFI for no fucking idea. Knowing the Air Force, the NFI was as much theirs as mine.

I considered my immediate future, feeling like I'd been sucked into the maw of something carnivorous. MFFPC was the acronym for military free fall parachute course. Specifically, an MFF is conducted from anywhere above 10,000 feet—and sometimes as high as 30,000 feet. In MFF, the paratrooper free-falls—

without the parachute deployed—to a specific altitude. The rip cord is then pulled so that the chute opens, ideally within two hundred feet of the designated height. In order to do this, I would be jumping out of a perfectly good airplane, not that there was any such thing. Also, I'd read *Have a Nice Flight* from cover to cover twice, but I'd failed to locate the chapter covering this particular scenario. I kept telling myself that it wasn't falling I had a problem with; it was crashing. But that didn't seem to help a whole lot. I pulled the book from my carry-on and fed it to a trash can at the Greyhound terminal.

All the way to Fayetteville the differential under my seat whined like a spoiled kid in a candy store. I got about as much sleep as the guy with a head cold sitting across the aisle, which is to say none. I told myself the bus was still better than flying and got no argument.

The weather in Fayetteville when I arrived was cool without being cold, the skies a simpatico gray. The Army shuttle buses out to Bragg were regular but didn't begin till ten A.M., so I found a diner and had breakfast—a double serving of bacon with two eggs, two servings of toast, two cups of black coffee, and a toothpick. The food helped my mood; must have helped the skies too, which were clear and blue by the time I walked back out on the street and took a seat on the service to Bragg.

The bus was empty but for two guys and three women—all 82nd Airborne—coming back from leave. My fellow travelers knew each other and chatted easily.

I didn't have to talk to anyone, which suited me fine. The bus meandered through farmland and pine forests. Nothing had changed here in forty years, except maybe for a few more subdivisions.

The base looked like every other one I'd ever seen, seemingly designed by the same slide rule in the Army's planning department. Columns and squares of young men and women sang in cadence while noncoms flogged them through another day designed to make them fit, hard, and willing. I saw myself among them, years younger and dumber, back before Afghanistan and Kosovo when I was on my way to joining the combat controllers. As I remembered it, this place was no picnic. The passage of time had done nothing to make me in the least nostalgic about the physical pain I went through back then to get jump wings. Usually the sight of America's youth muscling up made me feel good, but this time it didn't. This time I knew what lay ahead.

*   *   *

Jay Cummins was a major in the Army and he had an office at the SWTG HQ. He'd had bad acne as a kid and he'd inherited early-onset male-pattern baldness from his parents, whom I'm sure he thanked for it every waking day. The major also looked extremely fit with a broad chest and bazookas for arms.

I knocked on the door frame. The guy was hunched over his keyboard, elbows tucked in, shoulders bunched up like he was squeezed into a box. "Major Cummins? Special Agent Vin Cooper," I said.

Cummins glanced up from whatever he was concentrating on—losing a few more hairs, maybe—then stood and walked over to greet me with an easy smile. We shook hands and his grip was firm. On the breast pocket of his BDU was the badge of a master paratrooper.

"Cooper. You're early," he said with a southern drawl so that "you're" sounded like "yower," full of hospitality and grits. "That's good. We don't have much time with y'all. I was just going over your details. Take a seat." He stuck his head out his door and called out, "Randy, you want to go get Uncle down here for me. Let him know Major Cooper's in the house."

From behind the wall of another office, I heard Randy answer, "Yes, sir."

"Have yourself a good trip down, Major?" Cummins asked.

"Yes, thanks," I answered.

"You got your orders there?"

I nodded and handed over the thick envelope. He pulled out the paperwork and went through the copies one by one. "Good," he said. "All six copies. At least we know someone in Washington can count. Also proves D.C. can haul ass when it has to. We were only told 'bout you yesterday, and here y'all are."

"Uh-huh," I said, distracted. On his desk was a photo of his wife and a woman I guessed was his daughter. Both were pretty. The daughter looked like her mom, rather than her father. Lucky for the daughter, I thought. I glanced around the office's gray walls.

There were plenty of pictures, highlights from his career. Looked like he'd spent some time in Afghanistan and Iraq. He'd also jumped out of quite a few planes. Willingly, too, by the looks of things.

I tuned out while Cummins brought himself up to speed on a bunch of waivers designed to counter various regulations tripped, in the main, by my lengthy time out of special ops. There were also the physical examinations and qualifications I knew I had, most of which I also knew were out-of-date. My records had been doctored so that the rank and file wouldn't question my fitness and preparedness to train for and undertake the SPECAT part of my orders. The question I still wasn't sure about was, would I? At least in the short term, I'd play along. This MFF refresher was connected to Dr. Spears and, through her, somehow to the murder of Hideo Tanaka. The investigator in me was itching to know how and why.

"Just a little housekeeping, Major, before we get you started here..." He picked out a form from one pile, and put it on another. "So... we've got you staying on post. And the government will also be covering all your meals."

Gee... All of them?

"Your gear has also been forwarded."

"Gear?"

"Airborne Battle Uniforms, running shorts, PT uniform..."

"Any idea how long I'll be here, Jay?" I asked.

"Our advice from SOCOM is ten days. And you've got a lot to pack into it."

SOCOM—Special Operations Command. Cummins had just supplied another piece of the puzzle. SOCOM had been responsible for putting me behind enemy lines on a number of unpleasant occasions in the past. Unpleasantness was SOCOM's specialty.

"Do you know what SOCOM has planned for you here, Vin?" asked Cummins.

Something told me it wasn't beach volleyball lessons. I shook my head.

Cummins rifled through the paperwork again. "Says here you've logged over three hundred jumps, around seventy of them MFF, fifteen of which were into hot combat zones."

"Sounds about right," I said.

"I read something in *Stars and Stripes* about you. Weren't you the guy shot down in a CH-47, rescued in another CH-47, and then shot down again, all in the same action?"

"Uh-huh."

"That was a good job you did."

Except that everyone but me died. "Thanks," I said.

"Well, with your record, we ain't gonna make you go back to square one here. Our job is to get you fit, and get your head into free-falling again so you're not a danger to either yourself or those around you. We're going to start you in the VWT to get your orientation right, skip the jump phase out at Yuma, and pretty much go straight for daylight jumps here, gear-free, starting at ten thousand feet. Assuming everything goes to plan, we'll get you out of a C-17 at around twenty-eight thousand by day six in a packet, ready to kick ass as you hit the DIP. How does that sound?"

"You got a bathroom somewhere nearby?"

When I returned ten minutes later, a couple of pounds lighter and with color splashed into my face by cold water, I explained away my sudden exit on a bad slice of bacon I'd eaten for breakfast. The truth was that I didn't exactly know whether I was going to be able to pull this off. Cummins's précis of the curriculum had rattled me. There was a tap on the door behind me.

Cummins glanced past my shoulder. "Come on in, Uncle," he said.

"Uncle" turned out to be an Army E-8 whose name, according to the patch on his chest, was Fester. Uncle Fester. Figured. Fester was short, dark, and built strong with narrow hips and broad, heavy shoulders that somehow became his head without bothering with a neck. His nose had been broken a couple of times, and put back together with a few pieces missing. He looked the type who could lift a couple of times his body weight—a human flea. The major and the master sergeant appeared to get along well.

"OK, Sarge. This here's Major Vin Cooper. Be nice to him, like we discussed. He's yours for the duration. You might start by showing him where he'll be sleeping."

"Yes, sir."

"Y'all need anything, Major Cooper, just let me know."

A bus ticket out came instantly to mind.

"Kindly change into your running gear, sir," said Sergeant Fester as he led the way down the hall.

"I thought we were going to see where I'll be sleeping."

"Yes, sir. But first, we run."

So the guy wanted to run. Most likely that would be running Fort Bragg–style—over lots of hills and through leech-infested marshes. That was OK. I'd been to this place before, and I was ready for it this time. In fact, I was pretty sure I could show Uncle Fester here a little about running.

Five miles into what was to be ten miles of pure hell, I hated the sergeant as much as any person I'd ever met, on account of he made me run carrying a wounded pilot across my shoulders who very closely resembled a duffel bag full of sand. Every step was a lesson in pain and humility that brought tears to my eyes.

THIRTY-FIVE

I slept the restless sleep of a dead man fighting his way back to the light. I didn't dream, I just wrestled with my adrenal glands, coming half awake with a racing heartbeat and aching muscles, and then falling back into the pit, exhausted. I finally woke in the dark to a voice that said, "Let's go, Major." It was Sergeant Fester. "We got us some running to do."

The following three days were a blur of sweat, lactic acid burn, and a desire to drown Master Sergeant Fester. There was no room for talk in the schedule—just running, climbing, swimming, crawling, marching, and swearing.

On the morning of the fourth day, I was waiting for Fester in the dark, laced into the Nikes and ready to go. All the work done to regain some strength after the long stretch in rehab had been a big help. The investigation into the deaths of Tanaka and Wright had put me off my schedule, but now I was getting on top of things. I waited but Fester didn't show, so I went off on a run anyway—just for the hell of it.

I'd showered and just put on a clean ABU when the sergeant finally arrived, pulling up in a Humvee. I wasn't sure what he wanted. I pointed to myself and then at the door on the off chance he wanted me to get in. The sergeant gave a nod. Mystery solved.

"Where'd you get to this morning, Sarge?" I asked as I got inside. "Sleep in?"

No answer.

"You know, you make it damn hard for a guy to get a word in edgewise," I said.

"You haven't had the breath to waste on talk, Major," he replied. After a while, he said, "Yesterday in the pool. Saw you'd been wounded."

"Afghanistan and Washington."

"Washington?"

"Don't ever get between a congressman and his re-election contributors," I said.

Fester gave me a look like he'd just whacked his thumb with a hammer. I realized he was smiling, something he didn't seem to do much of. "I also served in Washington." He pulled up his shirt. There was a chunk out of his ribcage the size of my fist.

"You got that in D.C.?" I asked.

"No. Somalia. But I've done a tour of Washington." The sergeant smiled again. Twice in one day. Maybe Fester was losing control.

"So, what's going on?" I asked when he'd regained a little composure. "You decided to go easy on me because I've stopped a few slugs?"

"No. You passed the physical. Now it's time for a change."

"Passed?"

"You're on the edge when it comes to your age, sir.

Major Cummins and I wanted to make sure you were up to the job."

"What job?"

Fester shrugged.

I knew I wasn't going to get any further. Even if Cummins or Fester knew what job they were training me for, which I doubted, they'd never let me in on it. "So, where're we going?"

"You'll see."

Around half an hour later I was wearing a black jumpsuit—my watch and all loose articles stowed in a locker—and I was standing in an octagonal-shaped room. I could hear my breathing and my heart beating because, for one thing, the room was heavily insulated for sound, and, for another, my ears had plugs in them. The place reeked of leather and sweat.

Five other people in the room were similarly dressed. Another five, the instructors, wore bright pumpkin-colored suits. Above us, in the ceiling, the seventeen blades of the 3500-horsepower Babcock fan began to rotate and an ominous vibration came up through the floor. Within minutes the room was filled with the roar of a column of air screaming toward those rotating blades at close to 150 miles an hour. Fester took a couple of steps forward and launched himself into the center of the Sergeant Maj. Santos Alfredo Matos Jr. Military Free Fall Simulator, otherwise known as the VWT—the vertical wind tower. Seeing it in action still made me gawk. Fester flew. The newcomers were openmouthed. The sergeant immediately assumed the classic high-arch position and maneuvered about the space by altering his body shape and using his hands and fingers to steer in the same way a bird uses the feathers on its wingtips. After a couple of minutes of demonstration free-falling, he exited the column of air, rolling on his back and letting the thick cushioning around the circumference take his fall.

He tapped me on the helmet. My turn. I did what I'd been briefed to do—took a step and dived out into midair above a wide mesh safety net, arms and legs spread-eagled. Unlike Fester, I kept going, the hurricane wind spitting me out the far side. I hit the padding like a fastball smacking into the sweet spot of a catcher's mitt. Nice bit of demonstration flying there, Streak, I told myself as I rolled off the padding.

I got back on my feet and adjusted the helmet a notch tighter. From across the chamber, Fester told me with hand signals to do it again, only with a little less this time. So I took a step and jumped. This time I managed to stay caught in the roaring column, my body arranged in the high-arch position as it had been trained to do so many years ago, the forces of gravity and wind resistance in balance.

The air pressure rushing past my mouth and nose made breathing difficult, just like in a real free fall. In fact, the overall sensation was almost identical to falling through the air at terminal velocity, which is to say, it didn't feel like I was falling at all; more like lying on top of a few hundred fists pummeling away on the underside of my legs, body, and arms. I used my hands and fingertips to spin, and then altered my body position to rise and fall in the column. MFF—it was all coming back. I was having fun. Too much, apparently. Fester was gesturing at me to come on over. I noticed Major Cummins had made an appearance and was standing beside him, wearing the kind of scowl he might have worn if I'd just told him I was dating his daughter. He was in the process of biting off a fingernail which he then spat out. I landed a little less like a gooney bird in a storm the second time around. Cummins and Fester were already heading for the exit. Fester motioned at me to follow.

Outside the chamber where it wasn't so noisy, Major Cummins shouted, "We just got word from SOCOM. There's been a change of plan."

THIRTY-SIX

Cummins drove me to the strip and didn't spare the horses. An Air Force C-21 executive jet from the VIP squadron was keeping its fan blades warm. The loadmaster pulled me almost bodily into the plane and we were rolling before the hatch closed. Inside, I was shown to a leather, executive-style chair. Some senator had used the plane before me and the drinks cabinet was stocked. It appeared the senator and I had a mutual friend by the name of Glen Keith, and the two of us were so damn pleased to see each other I almost forgot I was flying until the loadmaster put the cork back in the bottle.

Less than half an hour later, I was on the ground at Andrews AFB, getting into a blue car with a driver. Forty-five minutes after that, I was being shown into a room at the Pentagon. If I were a home-delivered pizza, I'd still have been hot. The room was darkened—too dark for me to make out faces until my eyes adjusted. Up on a multitude of screens, various maps, intelligence reports, and satellite images of terrain and weather systems were being discussed. I was taken to a seat at the table and ignored by the shadows seated around it. I figured I was there to listen.

The country I was here to listen about, according to all the intel up on screen, was Pakistan. Somehow, I wasn't so surprised. A woman I didn't recognize was in the middle of giving a briefing on the nuclear warheads sitting atop Pakistan's Ghauri missile, which, I learned, was theoretically capable of hitting every major population city on the Indian subcontinent. An admiral asked a question about the Chagai region of Pakistan, where previous atomic devices had been tested.

I shifted in my seat, unable to get comfortable. Pakistan was behaving like it had a hand full of aces, and letting everyone at the table know it. The new revolutionary government in Islamabad was cocky, dangerously so. I could feel the pace accelerating like a runaway steamroller.

I heard someone ask someone else by the name of Willard a question. I recognized the voice of the person asking as belonging to General Henry Howerton. I recognized the guy being asked the question when he stepped into the light bouncing off a screen. Willard F. Norman, Deputy Assistant Director, Directorate of Operations, CIA. He was slight, sedentary, and pear-shaped, with delicate hands that looked soft. Rumor had it he washed them a little too often. Norman looked like the kind of guy you wouldn't leave alone with your niece. His small, pale eyes were nervous. They flitted about the room like finches escaped from their cage. A thick clump of dyed brown hair above his left ear was combed over his skull and oiled enough to stick there no matter how hard the wind blew. I remembered he'd come up through CIA ranks, making a name for himself in HUMINT—spying, basically, though on whom and to what benefit were unknown and would most likely remain so for a long time to come. Whatever he'd done, it was enough to land him in a corner office at Langley.

Willard F. Norman's voice was high-pitched and, even if he sounded like a mouse caught in a trap, he spoke with the authority of someone who knew what he was talking about, even if he didn't—a surefire way to get ahead in some parts of D.C. "These are file photos of the town of Phunal, Pakistan," he said. The monitors rolled through a series of pictures of an ancient town, built mostly from rock, mud brick, and dung, shot in the setting sun. Discovery Channel stuff. While I'd never been to Pakistan, I'd seen plenty of towns like this one just across the border in Afghanistan, perched on a knife edge between life and death, settlements where the people had nothing in their lives except for war, a few goats, and a lot of religion. "It's roughly a hundred and fifty miles northwest of the city of Quetta, a Pashtun stronghold," Norman said. "Phunal is of great interest to us because it's the town closest to a major nuclear weapons research facility. It's also rumored to be a local black-market weapons bazaar frequented by Taliban and al Qaeda forces bouncing in and out of Afghanistan. We think it's being run by former Pakistani Inter-Services Intelligence Directorate people, the very same people who funneled weapons to the mujahidin fighting the Soviets back in the eighties.

"It's for these reasons that we've tried damn hard to keep assets on the ground there. With the recent political upheavals, that policy seems to have been an excellent piece of foresight. As you're all aware, since the coup, Pakistan is now the world's only fundamentalist Islamic nation equipped with atomic bombs and the missiles with which to deliver them. For once we find ourselves reasonably well prepared..."

My initial discomfort was turning into a full-blown case of the cold sweats. I was having a serious attack of the I-think-I'm-on-the-wrong-train syndrome. I didn't do this kind of shit anymore. Yet here I was, doing it. This was a JOPES, or in longhand, a joint operation and planning exercise. It was the kind of briefing I used to get back when I was an STO, jumping into the following day's headlines with lunatics like the late Sergeant Ruben Wright.

"Recently," Norman said, "our sources took the following series of photos of a convoy stopped in Phunal." He let the pictures do the talking. The file snaps were replaced by more recent shots. Falling snow had replaced the gold leaf beaten into the town by the late-afternoon sun in the previous snaps. The shots showed a column of military trucks pulled to a stop outside a cluster of buildings. Maybe it was a public john and a couple of the drivers had needed to stop to take a leak. The photos kept reeling off, two a second. It played like an MTV video clip, the action jumping forward in fast motion. The photos zoomed in closer to pick out various individuals milling about the trucks. One of the men had walked a few yards away from the others. He wasn't dressed in military fatigues and parka as most of his comrades seemed to be. He was wearing the clothing of the local Pashtun—a flat-topped woolen cap called a *pakool,* and a kind of rough quilted jacket over his *salwar kameez*—the name given to the long shirt and baggy trousers worn by the men thereabouts. He removed the pakool to scratch his head and . . . I was suddenly looking at a very familiar pudding bowl. I blinked. Goddamn it! Professor Sean Boyle.

On the screen, Professor Boyle was frozen, staring down the lens of the camera. The photographer would have used a very long lens—no way would Boyle have known at the time he was going to be a poster boy for Uncle Sam's security machine—but the guy's stare right into the camera was unnerving . . .

And that's when it hit me. Oh, Jesus, the body in the makeshift morgue down at the Four Winds that was supposed to be the professor. I hadn't believed at the time that it really was Boyle, but I also hadn't had the nerve to carry that suspicion to its final terrible conclusion—that if Boyle's death had been faked, then someone, or some organization, had done the faking. So many people dead and injured . . . Pakistan had set up the explosions purely to cover Boyle's disappearing act. Whatever Boyle had, they must have been pretty damn desperate to get their hands on it.

The residual image of the dream I'd had at Clare Selwyn's place swam before my eyes, the one of Dr. Tanaka's outstretched hand spinning in an eddy as the shark dove beside him, Boyle's wallet clenched firmly in his white fingers. Jesus, the wallet! How did it get there? Who planted it on the body?

General Howerton's voice snapped me out of it. "Dr. Spears, if you wouldn't mind?"

Dr. Freddie Spears. I hadn't seen her in the gloom.

"Certainly," Spears answered, standing. The doctor made her way around the table and an admiral held open the door for her. She flashed the general a smile as she left. I figured the briefing was about to roll into operational issues that didn't concern her. By this time, my eyes had adjusted to the low light. I was sitting at a desk only a little smaller than the state of Rhode Island, populated by a full bench of heavy hitters, one of whom was, again, the SecDef. He said, "Do we have a military option yet, Henry?"

I was right about those operational issues.

"Yes, Mr. Secretary," said Howerton. "Nigel? You wanna take over?"

I didn't know who Nigel was, and I wasn't given an introduction. He was British Army, though, and from the single crowns on his epaulettes and the sand-colored beret in front of him, an officer with the rank of major in their Special Air Service Regiment. "This is the facility itself," the major said, pressing a button on a touch screen in front of him. The pictures up on the monitors changed. There were views of a large walled compound containing a number of buildings, followed by blueprints of one of those buildings. There was one road in. The major cleared his throat. "We, that is to say, a British construction company, built this facility for Pakistan in the mid-eighties. Because of that, we have available to us an intimate knowledge of it. This knowledge gives us a unique edge. As you may or may not be aware, we've had a number of men from the British Special Air Service Regiment Mountain Troop training in the States over the past three months, learning cooperative operational techniques with the U.S. Army and Air Force. For the past week, however, since Boyle's existence has been confirmed, this troop has been training for the specific intention of storming the Phunal facility—"

The door to the room opened. A soldier walked in and hopped to attention. This guy I did know. We'd met.

"Ah, Staff Sergeant Butler," said Nigel. "Good of you to join us. You can stand easy."

Chris Butler removed the poker from his butt.

"Have a seat, Staff."

Butler took the one next to me. He avoided eye contact.

"Why don't you bring us up to speed, Staff? How are things progressing?"

Butler said, "Sir, the Air Force Special Ops squadron we've been training with is confident of being able to get us into the sky over the target covertly. And, thanks to the excellent intel provided, we're confident of being able to capture and remove the target from the facility. But there are a number of variables, weather being of concern. Winter is harsh in those hills, though that could also help shield our arrival and make pursuit, once we've secured the target, more difficult. The plan is to air-drop three Ski-Doos and two team members five clicks to the south in an area that's comparatively flat and unpopulous. The attack force will continue in the aircraft, which will climb. We will then HALO down to the ridge on the high ground above the facility..." Nigel handed Butler a small laser pointer, and a shaky red dot appeared on an area up behind the high wall that surrounded the facility. "We're going to need a diversion. We'll blow the propane gas tanks here. That should make a bit of noise. In the confusion, the power will be chopped at the main junction box here. We'll cut through the wire here before the auxiliary power can be fired up, and make our way to the accommodation block here in the darkness and confusion." As Butler spoke, the small red dot flitted over the satellite photos of the research compound. "Sir, does intelligence still have the target quartered in the block?"

The question was addressed to Major Nigel Whoever, but the CIA boss chipped in instead. "Yes, but that's why we've had to move things forward," said Willard F. "Assets on the ground have informed us there might be a pullout to another compound closer to Islamabad, or maybe south to Dalbandin, where the weather's a little more predictable. They've had a hell of a winter there this year."

"The timing change shouldn't affect our schedule adversely, sir," said Butler. "With the target secured, we'll rendezvous with the Ski-Doo team, and then drive for the Afghanistan border. It's not far from the facility. There we'll rendezvous with U.S. Special

Forces. We'll be ready to go in a couple of days, once we've had time to work in with the arresting officer."

"Excellent. How about your man, General? How's he coming along?" asked Nigel.

"I don't know," said Howerton. "Let's ask him, shall we? So, Special Agent Cooper. How does it feel to be jumping into hot water again?"

THIRTY-SEVEN

Something had caught in my throat and it wasn't a chicken bone. It was the phrase, *"Are you fucking kidding?"* It eventually found its way out, modified a little to "I'm not sure, sir. I haven't seen the mission planning."

"Well, keep your ears open, Cooper, because that's what we're here to discuss," said the SecDef. He leaned forward and looked down the table. "So what's the legal position on all this? What does JAG say?"

The discussion moved on while I felt as if a hurricane had just passed overhead leaving me battered and bruised in its wake. *A mission with Butler to snatch Boyle from a military facility in Pakistan?* I dialed back into the meeting on the lawyer's summation. He was saying, "What you're suggesting here breaks U.S. law, international law, and a raft of agreements we had in place with the former government of Pakistan. This is kidnapping, and, if that's not bad enough, you're doing it on foreign soil. My advice would be to find another way."

"OK, so we'll just cancel the mission," said the SecDef. This comment removed sound from the room as effectively as a drain hole sucking water from a bath.

Silence.

Several sets of eyes shifted around the room, searching for more dissent. A few throats were cleared. No one for a moment believed the SecDef meant it. I focused on the JAG lawyer. His face had more lines on it than a used bus ticket, and all of them were headed in the general direction of a scowl. He knew the SecDef didn't mean it, too. His hair was thick and polar-bear white, his skin newborn-baby pink. I figured he was around a year off settling into a condo, probably down in Florida, maybe Naples, someplace rich and effortless where the hired help manicured the grass with nail scissors and the mosquito population was held in check with regular aerial spraying. His recommendation to abort meant nothing that happened in this room would touch his retirement benefits if things went to shit. He'd done his job. I was having trouble concentrating. The situation seemed surreal. I thought about Boyle's wallet. I also wondered whether the JAG general personally knew the lawyer swapping body fluids with my girlfriend.

Objection. Former girlfriend.

Sustained.

OK, *former* girlfriend.

There were quite a few lawyers in the military these days—which said a lot about the military—so maybe not. I wondered whether the JAG general would appreciate my two-lawyers-in-the-bank joke. If not, I had others.

"Special Agent Cooper? Cooper?"

Howerton. He was talking, leaning across the table

toward me. "Yes, sir," I said. The hurricane had dou-
bled back like they've been known to do on occasion.
I was doing a lot of wondering. Now I was wondering
what I'd missed. A couple of the officers were standing. Butler and Nigel were in a huddle, talking about
something. The JOPES was concluded.

"Like I said, son, we don't have anyone in the OSI or
the Army's Criminal Investigation Command with your
particular skill set," said Howerton. "With your time in
the CCTs working with Special Forces from coalition
countries, coupled with your experience working with
the law . . . Well, you're uniquely qualified."

After hearing the doubts expressed by the staff
judge advocate, maybe they needed someone who
knew less about the law and more about how to take
a fall. Nevertheless, I replied, "Yes, sir."

He handed me another thick envelope. "What we're
talking about here, Cooper, is a snatch op. Usually, with
this kind of situation, we'd offer the country development grants and low-interest loans, which, of course,
would subsequently be forgiven. They'd roll the guy
over to us and that'd be the end of it. But that's not possible in this case. Pakistan reminds me of Iran in 1980
when Khomeini's revolutionary guards booted out the
Shah and took over the country. And just like Iran,
anti-U.S. sentiment is rife. CIA says the place is high on
its own revolution. Your job is to get Boyle safely back
to the U.S. embassy in Kabul. The FBI, armed with a
warrant issued by a U.S. federal judge, will arrest him
there. All nice and legal. In the packet are your orders
to Kandahar. Three days is not a lot of time to get your-

self prepared for this. Rely on Staff Sergeant Butler and his men. They come highly recommended."

Yeah, Staff Sergeant Butler and his men. Here again was a twist of fate confirming my opinion that fate was one twisted son of a bitch. Why me? I didn't get it. In three days, fate was going to send me up in a plane and then he was going to make me jump out of it into the Pakistan night with the very same guy I was investigating for possible murder. Ruben Wright, his wrecked parachute harness, and his even more wrecked remains flashed through my head. Then I thought about Butler's smashed flashlight and broken ribs. Howerton had told me to trust Butler. But, with all the doubt still swimming around the Ruben Wright case, could I do that? Seriously?

*　　*　　*

The temperature dropped through the floor as I closed in on the exit. I had a few things on my mind jostling for attention with the impending mission: the hit on the Transamerica and Four Winds buildings; Al Cooke; Dr. Freddie Spears's resignation from Moreton Genetics and then her presence in heavyweight Pentagon meetings; the charred corpse; Boyle's wallet . . . all of it swirled through my brain like snow flurries.

If I was right about the wallet, and I believed I was, that meant it had to have been planted, only the people who detonated the truck bomb and set the device in the basement of the Four Winds wouldn't have had the opportunity to do that. So who did?

Outside, the snow was still falling, playing havoc

with the traffic. Vehicles were sliding around on the ice and slush. I made my way to the cab rank and joined the line. I looked down the length of it, trying to judge the wait, when I saw Doc Spears climb into a cab at the head. And suddenly I was running, weaving through the crowd of people coming and going. Spears's cab was pulling forward, sliding around. I jumped off the curb and half-stumbled as I landed in a ridge of knee-high brown-and-black icy crud pushed to the side of the road. Ahead, Spears's cab had stopped, waiting for a gap in the stream of slow-moving traffic. I got up and sprinted. I dived for the rear passenger door handle and pulled it open, just as the cab began to move. I hauled myself inside and the driver jammed on his brakes, shouting, "Hey!"

I pulled the door shut with a thud. "Jesus, it's cold out there," I griped.

"Cooper!" exclaimed Spears.

"Everything all right, ma'am?" asked the driver, a skinny black guy in a leather hat with woolly flaps that covered his ears. From behind, he looked like a cocker spaniel.

"Er . . . y-yes," she said, not a hundred percent certain about it.

He shrugged, muttered something, and turned back to get on with the driving.

"So," I said, "what's it all about?"

"What's what all about?"

"I don't know. Start wherever you like. Tell me what you know about Tanaka and Boyle. Tell me what they were working on. Tell me about the DVD you slid

under my door. Tell me why you resigned from Moreton Genetics after I interviewed you. Tell me when you
think the weather will clear up. Your call. Where are
we going, by the way?"

"My hotel."

"Which one?"

"The Sofitel."

"That's on Lafayette Square, isn't it?"

She nodded.

"Nice." Nice was an understatement. The Sofitel
had a view across the square into the front sitting
room of The White House. "You've lost weight, Doc."

"I've been under a lot of stress."

"I would, too, if I had to pay for a room at the
Sofitel."

She gave me the thinnest of smiles. The cold had
burned red circles into her cheeks. "Care to unburden
yourself?" I asked.

"I can't," she said.

"OK, well, I'll go first. Let me tell you how your
friend died."

"That's not necessary," she said.

I ignored her. "The weather was calm and it was a
moonless night. It was peaceful out on the *Natusima*'s
deck. There was a party going on below deck, celebrating the end of a successful expedition. Nearly
everyone was there. Your friend Hideo had drunk too
much. You can thank the guy who kept filling his
glass for that—Professor Boyle. Feeling queasy, Hideo
went out on deck to get some air. Big mistake."

Doc Spears wasn't looking at me, but I knew she

was listening. The cab pulled onto the 359, heading toward D.C. over the 14th Street Bridge. Our speed went down to a crawl as the weather worsened.

"He might have been leaning over the side of the boat," I said. "Perhaps he was puking because of the alcohol, but then a guy by the name of Al Cooke came up behind Hideo, lifted him up over the gunnel, and threw him overboard. He did this for two reasons: He was a sadist who just wanted to see what would happen; he was also paid to throw him overboard. Exactly what happened next, who can say? The water was cold, Doc. You ever been in water that cold?"

Dr. Spears didn't respond to the question.

"It would have been a few degrees below freezing. The gag reflex produced by the sudden cold would have forced Tanaka to take a breath underwater. If he was lucky, he'd have drowned right then and there. But let's say he didn't. Let's say he fought his way up to the surface, treading water, the cold knifing into his skin. He would have called out. Maybe he called out a few times for help. None came. But then something else arrived, brought by the vomit and the urine and the fear. It was a great white shark that had been trailing the boat for days. From the tooth found in what remained of Hideo Tanaka, the giant fish was between nineteen and twenty-two feet long. A fish that big weighs over two and a half thousand pounds, and has one seriously healthy appetite. The coroner believed it took Hideo—all of him from the neck down—in a single bite. We know this because Hideo Tanaka's head ended up being sucked into the ship's engine-cooling system."

Freddie Spears turned toward me, her eyes wet.

"Doc, I need to know *why* it happened. It has something to do with what they were working on. What was it?"

"I can't tell you."

"Jesus, Doc, you can and you will. Goddamn it, it was you who slid that DVD under my door. You did that because you wanted me to know something important. Something relevant to your friend's death."

"The people at the Pentagon—Defense, CIA. They know."

"Yeah, but they won't tell me. So you tell me, Doc. There's no one following us in this weather, no helo overhead keeping an eye on us. And no undercover agent would be seen dead in a hat like that one." I nodded at the driver.

"You sure you're all right, miss?" he said, glancing over his shoulder at his paying passenger, who was now sobbing.

"She's fine," I said. "Tears of release."

The driver glanced at me next, unsure. I gave him a big smile to keep him that way. Doc Spears blew her nose and regained some composure while I looked out at the highway. A horse and cart could have moved faster. I'd pushed the doctor as far as I could. She didn't have to tell me anything, would be breaking a federal statute or two if she did. But I was getting close to panic. Some military planning committee was fixing to have me jump out of a plane and it was all somehow connected to the murder of Hideo Tanaka. If I could figure it out in time, maybe the mission would get canceled.

"Do you know what Mad is?" I heard her say into her tissue. At least, that's what I thought she said—the sentence didn't seem to make sense.

"Do I know who what is?" I asked.

"Mad. Do you know what Mad is?"

Maybe I'd pushed Doc Spears a little hard, after all, and she was just a touch unhinged. I said, "*Mad*—yeah, sure. Alfred E. Neuman. A great magazine. You gotta love their movie spoofs. They did such a number on Schwarzenegger in *Terminator 3*. Did you—"

Spears looked at me with her red-rimmed eyes like *I* was mad. "No, the acronym: M-A-D."

All I could think was that the military was acronym-mad. I shook my head.

"M-A-D. Mutually Assured Destruction."

"Oh, right, you mean *that* MAD. Yeah, I remember. It was a Cold War thing, right?"

"Mutually Assured Destruction was peace by stalemate back when the world was divided into armed camps: Communism versus the West. It was the theory of nuclear deterrence—that if you launched a nuke at me, I'd massively retaliate. Things would escalate and we'd all die, so what would be the point?"

Spears gave a final sniff and put away her tissues. "MAD prevented that first strike. Whether anyone believed in the theory or not, something worked because we're all still around, even if the Soviet Union isn't." She glanced out the window, collecting her thoughts, carefully wiping the mascara on the bottom of her eyes with a finger.

After a handful of impatient seconds, I said, "So here we are, Doc, both with our fingers on the big red button..."

Spears took a breath. Then she continued. "Hideo was an expert on deep-sea environments that technically should not have been able to support life. He was searching for a particular form of extremophile—"

"A what-o-phile?"

"An extremophile. An organism found in a hostile environment at great depths. Hideo isolated an extremophile—a bacterium—in the gut of a particular worm that could digest human feces. He—"

"What?"

"The environment around a hydrothermal vent is rich in hydrogen sulphide. Hydrogen sulphide is extremely caustic, poisonous, and is one of the toxic components of human sewage. Hideo was searching for an organism that would consume it."

"He was looking for a bug that would eat shit?"

"You have a way with words, you know that?"

Now I really had heard everything. I must've appeared skeptical because Spears said, "Think about it. Something like that would be worth millions, even billions. The sheer volume of human waste is a huge problem. Have you any idea how much sewage a city the size of New York alone produces in one day?"

I visualized eight million New Yorkers sitting down at the beginning of the day with their newspaper. "Lots?"

"In layman's terms, Professor Boyle's role was to

look at the organism's genetic makeup, to manipulate it to see if it could be made to live in nonpoisonous environments."

"But something went wrong."

"Or went right, depending on your point of view. Boyle created an ionized bacterium that actually secreted hydrogen sulphide."

"In layman's terms, you've lost me."

"The DVD you saw was the result of one of Boyle's experiments. He modified the organism so that the airborne bacterium was attracted to electric fields. Where you find an electromagnetic field, these days you'll eventually find computer chips. Once this organism gets onto a printed circuit board, it secretes hydrogen sulphide that literally eats the chip away. The bacterium got into the air-conditioning and shut the building down—every computer chip in MG was turned to mush."

I got it. "In the wrong hands, that would be some weapon—a biological computer virus."

"A virus is not a bacterium," she informed me.

"Whatever."

"Once the potential of this weapon became apparent, our government became interested. Even if only to make sure no one else got the technology. On the battlefield, if you had the delivery system sorted out and ensured your own systems were hardened against attack, you could win without a shot being fired."

"A war where no one died. That wouldn't be such a bad thing, would it?"

"You're looking on the bright side, Special Agent. I didn't take you as a glass-half-full sort of person."

"I'm not," I said. Pakistan had Boyle, which meant it also had this meltdown bug. "So, Islamabad is lining up India for an atomic weapons strike? That's what all this is about?"

I didn't need to see Spears's nod to already know the answer. That was where Butler and I supposedly came in. "So, this bug—it's ready to go?"

"We don't know. Boyle took everything when he left. But I do know that the delivery system was always going to be difficult. The bacterium was highly successful at digesting our computer systems because, when it got into our air-conditioning, its lethality was pretty tightly directed and controlled. When the NLW is released into the atmosphere, control is lost."

"Did you just call this thing a nonlethal weapon?"

"Um, yes . . . why?"

"Something that lets one side launch nukes against another is a *nonlethal* weapon? That doesn't sound a little oxymoronish to you?"

"That's what the DoD was calling it."

And all this time I'd been thinking the DoD didn't have a sense of humor.

"A quick lesson in geopolitics, Agent Cooper. Asia is unstable. Not only is there the standoff between Pakistan and India, there's the Korean Peninsula, with the North and South still deeply mistrustful of each other on many levels. There's the considerable friction between the two Chinas—the People's Republic and Taiwan. And then there's the Muslim world to consider.

Like Iran and Syria, for example. What would the re-action be if Pakistan attacked India with nuclear weapons?"

"Most likely plenty of backslapping from other Muslims."

Doc Spears had her face turned toward me. I could see this was one deeply concerned former CEO.

"What's your security like at MG?" I asked her.

"Are you going to question me about those Tasers again?"

"No, but given what I now know was being devel-oped at MG, the fact that your people weren't armed with something that made a more permanent point now seems just a tad restrained. Also, I was wonder-ing how Boyle got the bacterium out of MG." I knew it was a dumb question as soon as I asked it. "He got it out the night he let the bug loose, didn't he?"

Spears nodded. "I think he let it loose with the in-tention of knocking out the security. With all our sys-tems down, he could have just walked out with it on a petri dish. And there's another possibility, some-thing no one wants to think about."

"This can get worse?"

"The genetic changes Boyle made allowed the bac-terium to reproduce—multiply. There's the possibility that, released into the atmosphere, the bacterium could rapidly find its way around the globe."

"And . . . ?"

"Well, that could put every computer chip in the world at risk."

"Oh, you mean like Y2K?" If the rest of it wasn't so serious, I'd have stifled a yawn.

"No, Y2K was a great marketing exercise—it sold a lot of computers and helped a load of companies sell a mountain of dusty stock. If this does get into the atmosphere . . . worst-case scenario? It'll take the world back to the age of steam."

The cab pulled up at Spears's hotel in Lafayette Square and a porter in a monkey suit ran to hold open the car door. "Good afternoon, Dr. Spears," I heard him say.

I watched as she said hello back and climbed out onto the sidewalk. She and the doorman knew each other.

"You've got the gist of it now," Spears said, paying the driver through his side window—too much, from the look of the wad she pressed into his gloved hand.

Something occurred to me. "Doc . . . the CIA man— Chalmers. Do you know how he happened to break his leg?"

"Yeah, I heard someone say it happened aboard the *Natusima*. He slipped on a pile of soggy cigarette butts or something. Seemed unlikely to me." Spears shrugged.

"Well, you know smoking—dangerous habit."

The monkey suit slammed the door. I gave the driver directions to my apartment. Then I made the guy wait while I changed out of the Class As, and had him drive me across to Andrews AFB.

THIRTY-EIGHT

B y the time I made it back to Bragg, my nerves felt like they'd been rubbed with crushed glass. I'd bought a fifth of single malt to keep me company on the return flight, but I left it unopened in my carry-on. Instead I found myself churning over the past few weeks, the brief investigation into Tanaka's murder, and the equally brief inquiry into the death of Ruben Wright. Neither investigation had been concluded satisfactorily. Time was proving to be my biggest enemy. I hadn't had enough of it to resolve my caseload. And now the world was under the gun. If Boyle had perfected his biological weapon, a nuclear war was imminent. Boyle had to be stopped. Only, I was having trouble dealing with the irony that Butler and I were the ones who were going to be working together to stop him. I recalled the phone conversation I'd had with Arlen, the one where he'd sounded out my view on whether Butler was guilty or innocent of murder. I'd told Arlen that doubt about him being the perp had crept in. Had that been enough to clear Butler for this operation?

I picked over the investigation into Tanaka's death. That case might have been easier to resolve—a hell of a lot easier—if I'd been cleared to know exactly what Tanaka and Boyle had been working on. If I'd been aware they had something so valuable, and as relatively easy to sell as a biological weapon, that would have been a plausible motive for Tanaka's murder right there. Boyle wouldn't have been able to move with his research partner hanging around, so he had thrown him to the sharks. I could have—would have—seen it from the start. I might even have been able to nail Boyle before the people paying the bills in Pakistan had pulled off his vanishing act in downtown San Francisco, an act which had cost hundreds of lives. But that was the problem with hypotheticals. Stewing over what might have been did no one any good—not me, and least of all the family and friends of the people who had died in the explosions at the Transamerica and the Four Winds.

I mulled over the Ruben Wright investigation some more. If I'd had another couple of days, I'd have paid Amy McDonough another visit, even if just to ask her the same questions over again to see if she gave the same answers. And there was Ruben's lawyer, Juan Demelian. He seemed about as straight as a paper clip. Something was going on there that didn't ring true. Demelian's answers seemed to be more like deflections. Maybe it was my gut talking, and not just because it was churning with the start of the descent to Pope AFB, Fort Bragg.

There were angles I'd asked Clare Selwyn to follow up for me in my absence—obtaining phone records and so on for McDonough and Demelian. While she wasn't, strictly speaking, in my line of work, I hoped she'd had the inclination—and the time—to carry through on my requests. The big question for me was this: What if Butler really had murdered Ruben Wright? It could be that I was about to parachute into harm's way with a guy itching to make a habit out of slicing the chute harness off of people he didn't get along with. And without doubt, Butler and I did not get along. Searching my memory, I couldn't recall reading anything remotely like this scenario in *Have a Nice Flight*.

I decided I wouldn't be going on so much as a Coney Island ride with Butler until we talked a little more about Ruben Wright's death. I wanted a few more answers on his relationship with Amy Mc-Donough, the woman who was both his lover and sole heir to the Wrong Way fortune. One and a half million give or take might not be a king's ransom these days, but I've known people killed for twenty bucks and change.

I made it back to my quarters in the dark. It was late and I was beat. There was a note under the door. *Be ready at 0500.* It was signed with the letter *F.* That would be Fester. I cracked the seal on the fifth. There were no rocks in the small bar fridge so I chipped some ice clogging the freezer coil with a knife and put it in a glass with a couple of slugs of bravado. I watched the glass for a moment or two, wrestling with something inside that told me not to drink. The something lost. It tasted like I imagined fermented sock water might taste, so I guess the something also won. Maybe booze wasn't the path. I pulled a card from my wallet and dialed the number scribbled on the reverse side. A familiar voice came on the line.

"Hello?"

"Hi, Clare."

"Who's that?"

How soon they forget. "It's Vin."

"It's late, Vin."

"Sorry, what's the time?"

"Forget it. It's good to hear from you. How's it going?"

"Like a house on fire . . ."

"Great."

". . . where everyone's trapped in the attic."

"Oh. What's up?"

"Guess who I caught up with today?"

"The Queen of England? I don't know . . . can you at least give me a short list?"

"Staff Sergeant Butler."

"Really? Did the meeting go well?"

"We didn't get to talk. Listen, have you got onto those things I asked you to follow up for me?"

"Vin, I haven't had time."

There it was again, the enemy—time.

Clare continued. "Also, I have to go through civilian channels and all of them are on vacation. The judge I wanted to see got back to town this afternoon. I've got all the paperwork sorted out. I'm seeing her first thing tomorrow."

"Clare, would you mind seeing her tonight?"

"Tonight?"

"Tonight."

"Tonight's almost over," she said.

"It's important," I said.

There was a pause, the sound of reluctance.

"She's in Pensacola."

My turn for a pause, the sound of I-don't-care.

"You really expect to turn something up?" she asked.

"I'm following my gut here, Clare."

"No, *I'm* following your gut, Vin."

"I wouldn't ask if it wasn't important."

I heard a sigh. "I know."

"How's Manny?" I asked.

"Asleep."

"Oh."

"Vin, it's past ten P.M. and he's only five. We're not exactly going to be sitting around playing cards at this time of the night. Perhaps when he turns seven."

"Yeah. Sorry. I don't have kids."

"That you know of."

"Very funny."

I heard her sigh. "It's OK, I'll throw him in the car. It'll be an adventure. And maybe I can use him as a little emotional blackmail with the judge when I get there. She's got kids of her own."

"Atta girl. Listen, Clare . . . thanks."

"Vin, if I'm going to do this, I'd better get moving."

I waited for her to hang up the phone. She didn't. She said, "So . . . is everything all right with you, Vin? You seem a little, um, distracted."

Yeah, Boyle was helping Pakistan get ready to hurl

nukes at India. I said, "That's because I am distracted. Listen, when you get those phone and bank records for McDonough and Ruben's attorney, call me. It's important. If you can't get through on my cell, call Colonel Arlen Wayne, OSI, at Andrews. He'll know how to reach me."

"Will do."

There was nothing more to say that hadn't already been said, if not in this conversation then in previous ones. As we'd agreed before I'd left for D.C., it'd been fun, and fun was all either of us had wanted.

"Be safe," she said.

"You, too, Clare. Now . . . fly like the wind."

"Will do," she said, and there was a smile in the space between the farewell and the dial tone.

THIRTY-NINE

I dreamed of silent mushroom explosions, puffed-up orange balls of dust and flame, but the specifics had gone by the time I opened my eyes, a damp sheet wound around me clinging like Gulf seaweed. Before Sergeant Fester's Humvee rumbled up to the front door, I'd showered and dressed and inhaled a large can of beans I found in a kitchen cupboard. It was cold and wet and miserable outside. I threw on a jacket and walked out into the rain.

We drove in silence out to Pope AFB, pulling up to a building I knew from the old days. Seeing it again made my nuts go light and my feet heavy. I walked into supply. Other men and women were being issued equipment; most were eager, a few quiet, shitting themselves. I was handed a flight suit, helmet, O_2 bottle, and the MC-5 ram-air chute. I'd used MC-5s before on numerous occasions and, unlike Ruben Wright, had walked away every time.

I sat through the one-on-one briefing Fester conducted via a whiteboard and took mental notes in silence. Emergency procedures—malfunctions, cutaways, entanglements . . . all the things that could go wrong and sometimes did. Fester covered off jump commands as well as the oxygen system. There was also a nav board refresher—the instruments strapped to the chest that facilitate navigation at night and in all weather conditions.

I'd done almost as many jumps as Sergeant Fester but there was no apology for the spoon-feeding. The first jump would be from 10,000 feet with minimal equipment. The second—if everything went well with the first, he informed me reassuringly—would entail a group exit from 25,000 feet with a full hundred and seventy-five pounds of equipment, including survival gear, M4 carbine, plus ballast to simulate ammunition. On this and all subsequent jumps, I'd be required to land within twenty-five yards of the group leader—Fester. This was leapfrogging the course. I knew that and so did Fester. If he knew why we were in such a big hurry, he wasn't saying and I wasn't offering.

A group of us walked across the apron to the rear end of a C-130. On this first jump, Fester and I were the only pair exiting at 10,000 feet, and so we entered last.

The ramp at the back of the plane came up, blocking out the natural light, and a low growl grew from somewhere, from within my belly, in fact. After a minute or so, the plane's turbines joined in. No escape. My fingertips were going numb, there were pins and needles in my toes, and my mouth filled with saliva that tasted metallic. My body was going through its own preflight checks. My breathing became shallow as my heart rate soared. A bead of sweat rolled down my forehead into an eyeball, causing my eyelids to blink rapidly. The loadmaster seated opposite blew me a kiss.

On the flight deck, the pilot edged the throttles forward and we began to move. A few twists and turns later and we were screaming down the runway on the takeoff roll. The aircraft rotated and climbed away at a steep angle. My stomach reacted: I vomited into the O_2 mask.

The Hercules continued to climb, leveling off at 10,000 feet. Ten minutes later, the red light began to flash as the ramp came down and the aircraft filled with the roar of its own jet blast and slipstream. I felt a slap on my helmet. From the corner of my right eye, I saw Fester's boots. The sergeant was standing beside me. I didn't think I could move.

I heard Fester scream in my ear, "Get up, mister!" I felt a hand under my armpit, lifting. I stood and swayed while he checked my gear again. "You can do this, sir," he yelled. "You've trained for it. You've done it."

I thought for sure my legs were going to crumple beneath me. I took a step and then another, walking backward toward the edge of the ramp, knowing nothing but air lay behind if not this step, then the next.

*   *   *

"You're not fit for this," said Sergeant Fester over a Heineken in the club.

I didn't reply.

"You might get to where you have to go but then

you're going to freeze up." He looked me straight in the eye, searching for clues. "What do you want me to do about it?"

"Whatever you think you have to do about it."

Fester didn't answer right away. He thought about it, drank his beer, and thought about it some more. Waiting for enlightenment, I guessed.

"What if I do nothing?" he asked.

"That's an approach."

"You need to see someone."

"When the job's done."

"That's the point, ain't it? What if you can't get the job done?"

Fester had seen the yellow bile bubble out from under my oxy mask and streak my webbing and BDU. He'd seen my hands shake. For a moment up there, my knees had almost caved. I thanked the God of Clean Underwear that He had at least heard my prayer.

Fester said, "Jumping when every part of you says don't takes a lot of guts." He had another long conversation with his beer before getting back to me. "I'm going to pass you," he said, wiping his mouth with the back of his hand, "even though you've got a mountain of fear to climb every time you get in a plane." He ordered another round by pointing his chin at the enlisted man behind the bar. "I'd still get help if I was you."

"I'll buy a book," I said.

FORTY

Pakistan was closed to U.S. aircraft. Therefore, the C-17 ferrying me and five U.S. Army engineers into Kandahar, Afghanistan, had to take the long way round. Refueled in flight, we flew nonstop via Turkey, Armenia, Azerbaijan, and Turkmenistan. I spent most of the flight time grinding my teeth or filling a paper bag on my knees with yellow slime from my stomach. I finally got some fitful sleep but then the plane began its descent, a wild descending corkscrew. I braced myself against the fuselage and waited for the crash. There was a rumor circulating that the local Taliban operating around Kandahar had somehow managed to get their hands on a bunch of late-model Stingers. The C-17 twisted and writhed, either to avoid being shot down by the aforementioned rumor, or because the pilots were a couple of sadists.

A series of rapid explosions erupted, the vibration from them pulsing up through the floor and the fuselage. Keeping time with this, a strobing staccato of white light flickered through the sky outside, close to the aircraft. The pilots had banged off flares and chaff to confuse and divert inbound infrared and radar-guided missiles. Maybe the missile threat was genuine. Whatever, we were thrown around like kids on a fairground ride designed to make people sick. It succeeded. I threw up as usual, along with two of the engineers. With all this puking, I was starting to feel like a bulimic. I glanced at the loadmaster strapped in opposite to get some clues about the wild approach. He was yawning.

The aircraft felt like it was slipping sideways out of the sky as the flaps deployed and a rumble below my feet told me the landing gear was now hanging in the breeze. And then suddenly the aircraft pulled up and the turbines screamed and my earlobes almost kissed my shoulders under the weight of the G-forces driving me down into the seat. There was a massive *thump* as the tires smacked onto the runway. Thank Christ. Touchdown, Afghanistan.

*   *   *

It was sleeting out on the runway. The icy water stung my face, but I needed the wake-up. I turned my head into the wind and took the punishment for a full minute. Veils of rain and sleet hung below licorice-colored clouds lumbering in from the south. The familiar mass of Zaker Ghar Shomali, a hill away to the northwest, looked like a white roll of sugar. I'd only seen it once before when it was a drab gray-green, the color meat turns when left to the bluebottle flies too long. My hand ached. More snow was on the way. That wasn't so bad. Snow would bury the powdered rock that settled on everything here and blew into ferocious dust storms capable of stripping paint from steel.

I was processed through the APOD, the aerial port of debarkation—the military's version of immigration and arrivals. This was housed within the structure of Kandahar Airport, a series of high, sixties-style egg-shaped arches butted up against each other. The place reminded me of a Wild West wagon train set in a defensive circle, waiting for the Indians to attack, which, given what was going on in Afghanistan, was not an inappropriate metaphor. Neighboring Pakistan had turned its sociological clock back to around the time the Magna Carta was signed, and the Taliban and al Qaeda units were rubbing their hands together with glee because of it. According to various Web sites known to host prime-time decapitations, the coup in Islamabad was an omen from God that the struggle to make everyone's life small, mean, and miserable was destined to succeed.

The APOD was packed, the buildup announced three months previously still going on. I hoisted my gear over my shoulder and walked over to a big-framed USAF sergeant who was seated behind a desk playing a computer keyboard like it was a baby grand. The group Nickelback was on the comeback trail and their latest track blared through the airport's speaker system. I came up beside the sergeant and saw that he was in the middle of some kind of shoot-'em-up game. "Oh, damn it!" he said when the leg of the character on screen got blown off. He glared up at me, annoyed, like it was my fault. "Sir . . . ?"

I said, "Can you tell me where th—"

"Special Agent Cooper. You're in serious danger of looking like a soldier."

It was a familiar voice behind me, though not one I'd have considered friendly.

"Hey," I said, with not a hell of a lot of warmth.

It was Sergeant Butler and Corporal Dortmund. "If you're looking for the welcoming committee, boss, we're it. Good flight?" asked Butler.

"Nope."

"We're out the front," he said as he led the way through a swirling sea of brown, desert-patterned DDUs.

I followed.

"Nice to see you again, Mister Cooper," he said over his shoulder.

"Really," I said. The conversation had the easy flow of a glacier.

"You seen the dailies, by any chance?" Butler asked.

I wasn't sure what he was talking about. He straightened this out by handing me a folded copy of the *Trib*. One of the headlines sharing the front page said, *Pakistan Announces Bomb Tests. Closes Borders.*

"We've just had the word from SOCOM—they want us to pull our fingers out. There has been some movement at the facility. Intel is suggesting an imminent move."

"What's the schedule?" I asked as we pushed through a door and into the sleet. I wondered how

Butler had managed to keep the tips of his hair so perfectly blond.

"This way, sir," said Butler. The two SAS men made for a nearby Land Rover. I recognized the driver—Lance Corporal Wignall. When we arrived at the vehicle, Butler said, "The schedule is that we go tomorrow night."

"Tomorrow night?" A little fear escaped along with my words.

"Yep."

Tomorrow night? *Jesus!* While I'd long since passed the point of no return, it still felt like I was in a car heading down a hill with the brake lines ripped out. Dortmund took my gear and threw it in the back.

"You first, Agent Cooper," Butler said, as he opened the door for me. I climbed in and he followed. Dortmund took the seat beside Wignall. The Land Rover coughed into life and moved off slowly through the ice rink the parking lot had become. "We're ready," Butler said, continuing where he'd left off. "We've got a good setup back at the safe house. We've got a scale model of the facility, we have the blueprints of the place, the transport squadron has given us the thumbs-up. The weather's not playing by the rules, and the report for tomorrow night looks iffy, but we knew that would always be the case at this time of the year, right?"

"Uh-huh," I said. The vehicle stank of diesel oil and sweat.

"We've been doing quite a bit of work with the Ski-Doos—got 'em modified the way we want 'em—and we've managed to pack in quite a few practice jumps with them. How about you, guv? If you don't mind me asking, when was the last time you jumped? I mean, you might have been Special Forces once, but you're a copper these days, right?"

The vehicle's windows fogged. I didn't wipe it away. There wasn't much to see—the snow shower had turned into a serious dump, and, besides, seen one parking lot crammed with U.S. Army light infantry vehicles, seen 'em all.

"Yeah, as a matter of fact, I do."

"Do what?"

"Mind you asking," I said. "But, since you've asked, don't worry about me." *Yeah, 'cause I'm doing enough of that for both of us.* "I jumped up and down with excitement for days when this job came up."

Butler smiled. "Have we got issues, Special Agent? You and me?"

"That depends on whether you killed Ruben Wright," I said.

Butler shook his head. "I wondered whether those bollocks would come up...No, actually, I was *sure* they would. I told you already—I didn't kill Sergeant Wright. Got anything else on your mind, guv?"

"Nothing that can't wait. Where are we going?"

"Safe house," said Butler, sitting back, wiping away at his window. Apparently, a sudden desire to do some sightseeing had overcome him.

I kept my eyes on the windshield framed between Wignall's and Dortmund's ears. The snowfall had ended. Snow in Kandahar was unusual. The city was in the southern part of the country, away from the high mountains. It sat in the middle of the farming belt, where the weather was a little less malevolent. Today, the more usual browns and tans of Kandahar were hidden beneath a layer of soft whiteness. The place reminded me of a Christmas card. The image was reinforced when we turned down a narrow street and Wignall slowed to give three Afghan men leading donkeys a little room. I wondered if they were on their way to visit a newborn king. If so, they were late: Christmas was over. Maybe they were on their way home. None of the men looked at us, though one of the animals snorted, raised its tail, and dropped a couple of pounds of crap onto the ground. Or maybe it was myrrh. The men leading the donkeys were hunched over as they kicked through the freshly fallen snow, their bodies wrapped in tan capes and their heads wound up in light-colored turbans— protection from the elements.

Wignall accelerated through an open square. Across the far side was another Humvee. I could see American Army engineers building a snowman with a bunch of local kids. One of them pitched a snowball at an engineer. It exploded against his Kevlar. The guy returned fire. The battle escalated. Based on this evidence, I was prepared to believe we were winning at least a few hearts and minds, though the Afghans were a wily bunch, as they'd proved to every uninvited visitor since the days when an iron sword was state-of-the-art in military high-tech.

I received a thumbnail history of this country the

last time I was here. It went something like this: Over the past couple of thousand years, after having a crack at it themselves, assorted kings, emperors, and generals usually put the job of subduing the Pashtun Afghans on the things-to-do list for their successors, just to give their next-in-line a lesson in humility. I'd witnessed the lesson myself on my last tour, and the fact that we were still here, years later, fighting the same people we were fighting back then, didn't bode well. And this time, the enemy had learned lessons from their buddies fighting the insurgency in Iraq. No way were they going to come and slug it out toe-to-toe with us like they did at Tora Bora. Not when it was so much fun to kill us slow. It's said the Pashtuns are only happy when they're at war. If this was true, they'd had something to keep them chuckling pretty much continuously since the time of Alexander the Great.

I wasn't too familiar with Kandahar. I'd been here before, but only in transit on the way to someplace else. The town was an important transport hub in support of our effort here, and so a lot of attention had been paid to making the place as secure as possible. Occasionally, though, shoot-and-scoot squads still sent rockets or mortar rounds in from the surrounding countryside, or an improvised explosive device blew the lid off a light armored vehicle, or charbroiled a Humvee, just to keep us on our toes.

Wignall slowed again to pass men herding a few donkeys and camels across the street and into a wide square that stank of unwashed animal and dung fires.

A few homes and businesses were lit by electric lights but most burned oil or kerosene or wax for light. The temperature was hovering around the freezing point and there weren't a lot of people out. I figured most were indoors, hugging their stoves.

Wignall took a sudden left turn. We dived through a small dark lane and into a largish courtyard. A tent was pitched in the corner of the open space, taking up one third of it. "Be it ever so 'umble," said Dortmund with a smile after the vehicle squealed to a stop.

"Billy, grab the Special Agent's kit," ordered Butler as he got out. I did likewise.

Damian Mortensen appeared from behind the Land Rover. He gave me a nod by way of hello.

"I'll show you around," Butler told me. "Norris is the only one of our lads not here. He's inside. The other people wandering around are CIA and NSA. They're here to make sure we've got intel hot off the sats."

I looked for and found security cameras watching all entry points and common walls. I noted a number of claymore mines hung up high on the walls with command detonation wires taped together and snaking off toward one of the buildings. Maybe they were expecting a visit from unfriendlies—maybe from the GAO.

Knowing the CIA's paranoia, there were probably also motion sensors buried inside and out, as well as other external cameras. The devices were small, and hidden or disguised. But our enemies weren't fools. Hidden cameras or not, we'd just driven into this place in a Land Rover. We might as well have been preceded by elephants on their hind legs playing trumpets. "Safe house?" I inquired.

Butler cleared his throat and spat onto the snow. "The neighbors are all on our payroll."

I followed the SAS men across the courtyard. Beneath a small shelter with a corrugated-iron roof sat a couple of Honda generators, one of them purring softly. Corporal Dortmund lifted the tent flap. The floor was raised and made from interlocking metal planks. Inside, parked against the far wall, was a compact forklift, welding gear beside it, and a bench with a small lathe and drill press. Trooper Brent Norris was sawing the barrel off a Remington 870 pump. He looked up and gave a nod, which I returned. Painted white and strapped down onto pallets were three Ski-Doos. An M249 squad automatic weapon was mounted on the back of each. Two of the machines were equipped with trailers.

"They're getting picked up shortly," said Butler. "Ever driven one?"

I shook my head. The only thing I'd ridden in the snow was an inner tube.

"How about a motorbike?" he asked.

"Yep."

"Same deal, only easier. Select forward, twist the throttle grip, and go," said Butler.

Next stop was a large room with a fireplace. A gas heater filled the room with orange warmth. The walls were covered by maps, floor plans, and photos—some taken on the ground, some from altitude. The subject matter was limited to the facility. Various lines of entry and egress were drawn on the plans, then duplicated on the photos. Radio frequencies and call signs were printed on sheets of paper and hung on the wall. Set up on a large table in the center of the room was a model of the facility. The roofs of various structures within it had been removed so that the squad knew where to find stairwells and elevators.

"I'm thinking you shouldn't take part in the assault phase, Cooper. We haven't worked together and there isn't time for you to learn our tactics and methods. We wouldn't want any accidents now, would we?"

That depends who has them, I thought. I reminded myself that very few special-ops missions went like clockwork, and there was no reason to assume this one would be an exception to that general rule—especially given the truncated planning and rushed schedule.

"We're going to leave you with a Ski-Doo and all nonessential gear half a mile from the facility, at this point here," Butler said, landing an index finger on a cross already marked on an aerial recon photo, "and rendezvous with you once we have Warlord under control."

"Warlord?" I asked.

"Yeah, Professor Boyle—Warlord is Washington's code name for the target. We'll go through the specifics of the op later. We've got another rehearsal planned tonight, with a follow-up in the morning."

"Uh-huh," I said. Sean Boyle, Warlord? An impressive title for a murdering dweeb with stupid hair.

"C'mon, I'll show you where you can throw your kit," said Butler. "You're sharing with one of the CIA guys."

"That would be me."

Another voice I recognized. I glanced at the open door where my least favorite spook was leaning on his crutches. We could crack open a case of Bud and call it a reunion.

FORTY-ONE

I didn't realize this was a physical therapy session," I said.

"One day I'm going to fuck you right up, Cooper," replied Bradley Chalmers.

"You two know each other?" asked Butler.

"Not in the biblical sense," I said, "though it sounds like Chalmers is eager."

"Part of the reason I'm here is to ensure Cooper doesn't poison this mission with his usual failure rate."

"So, another member of your fan club?" Butler said.

I'd lost interest in sparring—Chalmers wasn't worth the breath. He and Butler could swap notes, stick pins in Vin Cooper dolls; do whatever made them happy.

"Where's my gear?" I asked.

"Let's keep moving." Butler continued to lead the way.

I followed Butler through the rest of the building, stopping at the mess to throw down some chow. The tour came to an end in a room where Dortmund, Wignall, Mortensen, and Norris were checking and rechecking various items laid out on the floor. Butler showed me to a couple of duffel bags. A name tag on each read "Cooper." I added my own bag to the collection. I watched as Butler opened a steel locker. He pulled out a rifle as well as webbing stuffed with magazines. "Not sure what your preferred shooters are, but, being a septic tank an' all, I thought you'd at least be familiar with these."

"Septic tank?" I asked.

"A Yank. Rhyming slang," explained Dortmund.

Butler removed the magazine, pulled back the Beretta's slide, and checked the chamber. It was empty. He reinserted the magazine and handed me the weapon, butt-first. Next he picked up the rifle and went through a similar routine. I repeated the investigation of both weapons. I preferred the heavier Colt .45 to the Italian-made 92F Beretta, which since 1985 had been the pistol of choice of U.S. Armed Forces. No issues with the M4A2 carbine, however: light and idiot-proof—some would say my kind of weapon. It was, however, equipped with a thermal telescopic sight I hadn't seen or used before.

Butler told his men to go eat and they all filed out, leaving us alone. As they left, he informed me, "The ammunition for the M4 is the new Bofors armor-piercing variety. It'll punch holes in twelve-millimeter armor plate at one hundred yards, and does a good job of turning masonry into rubble at the same distance. You've got eight magazines loaded here with a tracer round three shots from empty. The scope is an ELECAN SpecterIR. It's a thermal job—be more useful and reliable than night-vision technology where we're going. It's only two times magnification, but it picks out heat sources like you wouldn't believe, especially against ice and snow. It's a great piece of kit—I'm also using one. The armorer has centered it, by the way. I know that doesn't mean much—normally you'd want to do that yourself, but there's no time left to get it done. For what it's worth, with the barrel warmed, it'll drop an inch over two hundred and fifty yards, three inches over three hundred yards, and, unless you really know how to shoot, forget about it after that. We've got a smorgasbord of antipersonnel grenades, smoke, whatever you want, and there's a box of nine-millimeter ball for the M9. I'm assuming you've brought your own handcuffs?"

I had. I examined the carbine as he spoke. It was brand-new. I said, "Did you know Ruben Wright had MS—multiple sclerosis?" I switched on the scope and looked into the eyepiece. As we were inside in a room with no windows, there was nothing to see in the eyepiece except gray.

"Jesus, you're not still going on about Wright, are you?"

"The case isn't closed. So . . . did you?"

"No. I didn't."

"And Wright's ex-girlfriend never mentioned it?"

"Not that I recall. Did *she* know he had MS?"

I ignored Butler's question. "So, Ruben Wright never seemed off-color at all? Not even a little?"

"I guess the reason you're asking me these questions

is because you don't think he committed suicide. You think I had something to do with his death."

I didn't answer. All I knew for sure was that I hadn't given Butler a good shake, and so I didn't know what might or might not fall out. Like most people, Butler wasn't comfortable in the silence, so he filled it. "Wright and I didn't get on—that's no secret. You could even go as far as to say we were barely civil to each other. But that doesn't mean I killed him." He picked up an M4 from the table, removed the bolt, and gave it an inspection.

His denial meant dick. Murderers don't usually admit to killing their victims. I'd even known killers who'd sworn they didn't do it even after being found with their bloody hands still holding the weapon. "Did you know your girlfriend was his heir?"

"Girlfriend?" said Butler.

I let out a sigh. "I visited McDonough in the hospital. She'd had an abortion, which I'm sure you knew about. Lying about your relationship with her makes me wonder what else you're lying about."

Butler licked his bottom lip and scratched his head, weighing the odds. He said, "OK, I lied about Amy and me."

"Why didn't you tell me the truth the first time?"

Butler shrugged. "Broken ribs, smashed flashlight, shagging the dead bloke's bird...wouldn't have looked good for me, would it?"

"And still doesn't," I reminded him.

"I didn't kill your buddy," Butler insisted again.

"Did you know Ruben Wright had taken a number of intimate videos of you and McDonough?"

"Dirty bugger," said Butler, almost proudly.

"Is that a yes or a no?"

"Yes; I mean, no—I didn't know."

"I suppose you also didn't know Amy McDonough was first in line to collect?"

"Collect what?" he asked.

"Framed butterflies. Money. What do you think?"

"How much, then?"

"Plenty."

He shook his head. "No, I had no idea." He leaned against the bench, folding his arms.

Just like McDonough, it seemed to me Butler didn't know, or didn't *admit* to knowing, much of anything. Did I believe him? The SAS were the cream of the cream of the British Army. These guys were handpicked for their intelligence and resourcefulness. They were committed and self-reliant. The way Butler talked, I had trouble believing he was capable of remembering how to tie his own shoelaces. "Have you been in contact with Ms. McDonough since Wright's death?" I asked.

"Yes, I saw her once. To call it quits."

"Was that at a place at Laguna Beach called Miss Palm's?"

Butler fixed me with a look that could break rocks. "You been following me?"

"Just happened to be out for a drive," I said. "It's a small world. Did you break up because Ruben's death spooked you? Or was it after McDonough told you she was having your kid?"

Butler's ears went purple. Full of indignant anger, like I'd suggested something that had breached his code of honor, he said, "Amy told me she was on the pill. I was surprised to hear she was up the duff."

"So she tricked you into getting her pregnant? Or did you make her promises you had no intention of keeping?"

Butler pushed out his chin. "Get off your fucking white horse for fuck's sake, Special Agent. Men have been tricking women into licking their dicks since we all climbed down out of the trees. Don't tell me you've never lied to a bird?"

Okay, he had me there. I kept the acknowledgment out of my face. "Maybe that meeting down at Laguna Beach went the way it did for different reasons."

"Like?"

"Like maybe you misjudged Amy? You were both after Ruben's money, and it was all going along nicely until Amy got pregnant and she told you she wanted to keep the child."

"Is that what that slut told you?" Butler's voice dropped to a whisper. He took a step into my personal space so that we were toe-to-toe. "Cooper, in less than twenty-four hours, we're jumping into a hostile country. I'm done with your questions. If I were you, I'd forget about Ruben Wright for a few days. I'd concentrate instead on how to avoid joining him. I'd also be checking my kit, especially the condition of your MC-5." Butler pushed past, bumping my shoulder.

The MC-5—the ram-air foil chute. It was sitting on the floor, propped against the wall. I'm not great with hints, but I did have the vague feeling that I might have just been threatened.

*   *   *

I packed and repacked the MC-5 twice, paying particular attention to the harness and suspension lines. I also thoroughly examined the oxygen system and mask. I then stripped the M9 and M4 several times each, and replaced the manufacturer's gun oil in both with a silicon-based type. I checked the M4's magazines, all eight, removing all two hundred and forty rounds and then replacing them, shifting the tracer to the fifth-last shot in each.

At some stage in the evening, Butler and his men returned to go through their gear again. There wasn't a lot of small talk between them. I wondered whether that had anything to do with my presence, because there was absolutely zero small talk between us. Wignall, especially, went out of his way to have no contact with me—eyeball or otherwise. I wondered if Butler could sense that Wignall was the Judas in his ranks.

I tested the batteries of the GPS I'd been issued, as well as the spare set, and did likewise with all other electrical gear I'd be taking in, from the Iridium satellite phone to the SpecterIR thermal sight. Everything appeared to be in order. Despite Butler's parting comment, I didn't expect to find anything amiss. Maybe he was right—I needed to stop being a cop for a while and start thinking like Special Forces. He was also right in saying that my survival would depend on all my gear being present, accounted for, and in good working order.

Aside from ammunition, weaponry, electrical equipment, and the usual survival gear like a hook knife for cutting tangled suspension lines, I made sure I had enough water-purifying tablets to last an extra four days in the field, as well as MREs—meals ready to eat—to last an extra day. I also threw in a dozen chemical hand-warming packs, half a dozen nylon cuff locks, and, finally, my lucky Smith & Wesson stainless-steel, double-locking handcuffs. I held the reassuring weight of them in my hand and couldn't decide who'd I'd rather slap them on—Boyle, Butler, or maybe even Clare Selwyn. I dispelled the happy thought. The sack called and I slept like a cadaver till after sunrise. When I woke, I was relieved to find Chalmers's bunk unslept in.

⅄   ⅄   ⅄

After breakfast, I again checked and repacked all my gear, except for the MC-5, which I didn't want to disturb, having taken extra special care with it twice already. I then spent three hours in the briefing room with Butler and his men, running through the op with the latest intel from CIA and NSA, as well as getting the latest atmospheric conditions from CWT—Air Force Combat Weather. I keep hoping these people from CWT will look like network weathergirls, but they never do. Today's report was delivered by a couple of dumpy guys with dandruff. They promised nil wind, but low visibility with heavy snowfalls and cloud at 22,000 feet down to 7000 feet, the altitude of Phunal. Temps, of course, would be subzero. Ordinarily, conditions such as these would have guaranteed an abort. But, as it was only a matter of time before Pakistan killed a few million people on the subcontinent, I had the feeling we'd be going in anyway.

The briefing progressed and I was again told I'd be having very little to do on the ground in the assault phase, though Butler had decided to bring me in closer. My role would be limited to keeping the Ski-Doo's motor running and maintaining overwatch on the snatch through the SpecterIR, looking for Hajis who might want to get trigger-happy in behind the SAS unit. From what I could see, Chalmers had even less to do—except perhaps to pick his nose a couple of times.

The assault itself still looked pretty much like Butler's presentation to General Howerton back at the Pentagon. After the color and movement provided by the blowing up of the facility's propane tanks, and while the Pakistanis were racing around yelling "The sky is falling," Butler and his men intended to just stroll into Boyle's billet and grab him. We'd all then simply drive across the Afghan border into the arms of a waiting company of U.S. Army Rangers, who'd then escort us to the U.S. Embassy in Kabul. Plans were best kept simple, but this one seemed a dime or two short of a quarter. For example, there were no backup escape routes if things fell to pieces. Weather would prohibit emergency extraction by a chopper. Our safety was up to us. There was, however, one interesting modification. SOCOM informed us by sat link that we didn't necessarily have to bring the professor back alive. If things went into the crapper, we just had to bring him back. Or return with evidence that he'd never be coming back. I had the feeling SOCOM would have been happy with Boyle's head on a stake.

FORTY-TWO

A little after 1500 hours, a group of parachute riggers from U.S. Army Special Forces arrived and readied the Ski-Doos for the drop. They rigged them onto aluminum platforms with a sandwich of paper honeycomb to absorb the landing shock. Dortmund supervised the loading. I heard one of the Army guys say, "We've hooked 'em up to G-12D cargo chutes. These babies have sixty-four-foot canopies, so your toys will fall like snowflakes."

I went back inside and repacked my gear yet again—anything to keep the flight and the night drop out of my head. I had something to eat, and tried to get some sleep. I woke several hours later with an ominous feeling in my gut, my watch alarm beeping, and Chalmers standing over me on his crutches.

"Yeah? Can I help you with something?" I said, sitting up, wiping the crud from my eyes.

"NSA passed this to me. Some OSI lieutenant colonel back at Andrews seems to think it's relevant to the mission. I want to know why."

Chalmers passed me a couple of sheets of printout on OSI letterhead. I glanced at the familiar signature at the bottom of the page. The lieutenant colonel Chalmers referred to was Arlen Wayne. I gave the contents a quick scan and said, "You mean, how."

"How, what?"

"*How* it's relevant, not why."

"You ever stop being an asshole, Cooper?"

"Most important organ in the body, Chalmers. Don't believe me, have yours sewn shut and see what happens."

Chalmers looked confused. "Hurry, ass—dipshit. The train leaves the station in twenty minutes. Maybe I'll see you in Kabul. Or better still, maybe not." Chalmers hopped away on his sticks, the look of victory on his face, leaving me with the printout. I lay back for a moment until all my gears meshed, wondering what the hell Chalmers was doing here anyway. What use to anyone was he on crutches, unless it was to keep an eye on things, or maybe just to supervise me? He'd said as much. I'd thought he was just indulging in a little unfriendly banter; perhaps I should be taking him at his word. Whatever. Chalmers was in the wrong job. He was even too much of a shithead for CIA. I could see him working out just fine with Wu and De Silver over in the GAO, which gave me an idea. Maybe the three of them should meet up. If I did make it back in one piece, I decided I'd do a little matchmaking.

I read Arlen's note and a choir of internal alarms went into meltdown. Clare Selwyn had come through. She'd filled in some of the holes I'd left behind in the Ruben Wright investigation. Phone company records revealed Amy McDonough and Ruben's lawyer, Juan Demelian, had been calling each other regularly before Ruben died. Why would they be doing that? Demelian wasn't her lawyer and they weren't friends. All they had in common was Ruben. Moreover, both insisted to me that only one call had been made to the other, and that was *after* Ruben had died. The reason for these calls, according to what Demelian had told Clare after she leaned on him, was that he had been trolling for business. He'd simply forgotten that he'd made the calls. Yeah, right.

I pieced the case together with this new information and the *how* went something like this: Ruben found out about McDonough and Butler, and called Demelian telling him he intended to change his will. Demelian stalled him and immediately informed McDonough of Ruben's intentions. Demelian told her he couldn't put Ruben off indefinitely. I wondered who had the idea first to kill Ruben. It didn't matter. Demelian's payment for betraying his client was for Amy to agree to cut him in on Ruben's estate. Her side of the deal was to come up with a method of doing the deed that wouldn't incriminate anyone. Enter Staff Sergeant Chris Butler. All three obviously knew about Ruben's MS, and also knew how important it was for him to keep it a secret.

Butler stuck his head in the door. I flinched like I'd been caught in the act of something distasteful. He said, "Let's go, then, guv."

"Yeah," I mumbled. "One minute."

"Hurry," said Butler, disappearing.

I reread the last page. Clare had also obtained a search warrant for Amy McDonough's home, including the sewerage pipes. She'd had the lines at Ruben Wright's accommodation checked out, too. While Ruben's came up clean, old tree roots clogging McDonough's pipes had snagged a range of medicines used to control the symptoms of multiple sclerosis. Clare had cross-checked the list of meds with Dr. Mooney and was of the opinion Ruben kept only a small portion of his pharmacopeia at McDonough's—a backup emergency supply, perhaps. In a statement to police, Amy said she'd tried to get rid of the drugs after he died—in fact, right after she'd returned home from identifying him at the morgue. She said that when she discovered them she was worried no one would believe her story about her not knowing a thing about Ruben's condition, and that this might somehow connect her with his murder. Damn right. There was no way to check she wasn't lying about the timing, but she'd lied about practically everything else, so why not this? I was convinced that McDonough had simply flushed the drugs down the head on the day Ruben died.

I recalled the trip to her house and the stump of what must once have been a very big tree in her front yard. I wondered whether its roots had been the ones responsible for clogging her drains. If so, its revenge for being turned into firewood had been sweet.

The search of Amy McDonough's home also turned up a spare key to Ruben's on-base accommodation—the quarters I'd been occupying. Amy could quite easily have gained access to the base with someone carrying a DoD ID—someone like Butler, for example—and not have had her name recorded at the base's entrance security checkpoint. No one would have raised so much as an eyebrow.

While it was pure speculation on my part, I was convinced Amy had planted that single pill under the fridge after Ruben's death, knowing it would eventually be found when the investigation got under way. The discovery would lead to the fact that he had MS, then to Dr. Mooney, on to Ruben's therapist, Judith Churcher, from there straight to a plausible theory that Ruben Wright had been unstable enough to take his own life. I asked myself why had it been important for Amy to lie about her knowledge of Ruben's condition. The plan had been to give the impression that Ruben was depressed and secretive, cut off and alone—suicidal—and it had worked, at least up till now. Her ignorance allowed her to play dumb on the question of his condition, which reinforced her assertion that her relationship with Ruben was over.

I dragged myself off the cot and scratched my head. So what about the other theory, the one that had Ruben killing himself and making it appear that Butler had done the job? Aside from the fact that I knew for sure Amy and Butler had been lying from the start, what did I have? Nothing concrete, though I now had a solid lump in my gut telling me that when Ruben jumped out of the aircraft with Butler and his men that night, he had every expectation of walking away from the landing.

I took a breath and stared up at the cracked and peeling ceiling plaster, looking for something. Maybe it was for a way out. I couldn't see one.

FORTY-THREE

W e rode out to Kandahar International Airport in the back of a banged-up covered truck left behind by the Soviets that smelled like an old barn. We were all in our gear, half a dozen or more layers of it, plus body armor and helmets, weapons, ammunition, food, water, electronics, batteries, survival gear, first-aid, oxy supply and mask, MC-5s, reserve chutes, nav boards, and so on. There wasn't enough room left over in the truck to squeeze out a fart. The mood was tense; at least, mine was. I had a list of questions for Staff Sergeant Butler, but they'd have to wait. Some eyes were shut, others were focused on their feet as the truck bucked and rolled down the ancient roads of the city.

Ten minutes later we turned into the airport access road and the ride immediately improved. The truck eventually pulled up with a grinding shriek of Soviet metal on metal. We got out into cold night air heavy with the smell of jet fuel and snow. My boots crunched on a mixture of gravel and ice. I took a look around. To the west, the lights of the distinctive Kandahar International "wagon train" terminal blazed white and yellow on the far side of the open field.

Spill from the lights bounced off the sky, turning it the yellow of stomach slime. A little to the north, over against the perimeter razor wire, a snowplow was clearing a taxiway, but I couldn't hear its engine. We'd pulled up fifty feet from a C-17 Globemaster, and its auxiliary power unit was screaming, drowning out any ambient sound, keeping the plane ready for a quick start.

Behind the C-17 sat a low-vis gray U.S. Navy EA-6B Prowler. I could see its four-man crew through the Plexiglas, small flashlights in their mouths, going through the preflight. The Prowler's job was to precede us into hostile air space and blind the enemy's radar with waves of microwave energy so that, while the Pakistanis were stumbling around in the dark, we'd just glide on in and then float on down. At least, that's how a major from the transport squadron explained it in his best Chuck Yeager drawl.

Issues and problems splashed around inside my head like the contents of a cocktail shaker. Boyle murdered Tanaka—Cooper failed to crack case. Butler murdered Wright—Cooper failed to crack case. Cooper, failed investigator, sent with murderer Butler to capture and perhaps kill murderer Boyle. One failed cop and two monsters mixing it up together. Hell, all we needed was an olive.

There was no time to think about that mountain of fear, as Sergeant Fester described my flying phobia, although my fingertips were suspiciously numb and my heart rate was racing like a bilge pump in a sinking ship. We assembled behind the C-17's ramp and organized our gear. I kept my distance from Butler. In my mind's eye, I kept seeing Amy McDonough back in the hospital, after the abortion. Her getting pregnant by Butler gave Ruben a powerful motive to set the SAS staff sergeant up for his murder. Following this thought through, it occurred to me that maybe Butler and Amy had been going at it like rabbits so as to make the pregnancy as likely as possible. And if *that* were the case, then perhaps terminating the pregnancy was also part of the plan.

I recalled that meeting between Amy and Butler at Miss Palm's. Could the unhappiness between them—along with the subsequent rift—have been caused by her announcement that she intended to go through with the pregnancy?

I wrenched my concentration back to the job at hand, gave my oxygen bottle and mask a final inspection, tested the tactical radio set, and then checked that the goggles sitting atop my helmet were still clear and clean. I attached the heavy para-ruck carrying most of my gear onto the front of my chute harness, making sure the rip cord handle wasn't fouled, then clipped in the M4. I felt myself being checked over and suddenly I was looking into the eyes of Staff Sergeant Butler. They were smiling eyes, confident eyes, the eyes of a winner. I fought the urge to poke them. It was a complete fuck of a situation. I'd had the opportunity to have Butler taken off active duty, and I'd blown it. But I intended to set that right when this mission was concluded.

I followed the SAS up the ramp and into the C-17.

The Ski-Doos and trailers were sitting on pallets down the center of the aircraft, their drogue chutes linked by static lines to a cable running down the side of the fuselage. The loadmaster pointed to seats he wanted us to take on either side of the Ski-Doos. Butler sat opposite; his deputy, Corporal Billy Dortmund, beside me; Mortensen on his right. Brian Wignall sat beside Butler. Norris sat on Wignall's other side. All nice and cozy.

Coming from a long way off, but more precisely from somewhere beyond the skin of the C-17's fuselage, I could hear the Prowler roaring down the runway on its takeoff roll. The Globemaster's ramp came up and the interior of the aircraft was bathed in red light that wouldn't mess with our night vision. My small and large intestines twisted themselves into clove hitches. I followed Butler's lead, pulled my goggles over my eyes and fully attached the oxygen mask. I listened to my own Darth Vader breathing, and closed my eyes.

I tried the technique of focusing on all the good things going on in my life to get me through the takeoff, but they only took me as far as the first taxiway. And it was a short taxiway. So instead I thought about how I would keep myself alive on this mission. It wouldn't benefit Butler if I somehow ended up dead. With the facts Clare now had, a ten-year-old kid could piece together the case against him, McDonough, and Demelian, and Clare was a lot older than a ten-year-old, thank the Lord. I had the feeling Butler thought he'd outsmarted us all. If he intended to kill me, handing me the task of standoff sniper was going to make that task more difficult than it would otherwise have been. That thought worried me. Why had Butler given me the job of watching his back? In a sense, it meant he was turning his back on me. I sure as hell wouldn't do the same to him.

The C-17 seemed to go vertical as it left the runway. It climbed hard, turbofans angry, or maybe frightened. The pilots were eager to get as far away from the ground as possible. I knew the reasons—those missile rumors—but I'd rather I hadn't. I felt the landing gear seat home and the flaps retracting. The power dropped back a little and the nose came down. I sensed the continuous climbing turn to the left somewhere in my ears. I knew from the briefing that the Globemaster would reach its cruising altitude of 24,000 feet over Afghanistan.

The minutes ticked by.

In their goggles and oxygen masks, Butler and Wignall looked like a couple of flies. I got nothing from them, and gave nothing back. It wouldn't be long till we crossed into Pakistan's airspace, the flight time to the drop zone just twenty-five minutes. With the EA-6B Prowler somewhere out front, radar screens from Quetta to Peshawar would be snowed under by electron blizzards.

*   *   *

The plane had stopped climbing. The red light came on, the signal for us to switch on our oxygen supplies. The ramp came down and the aircraft filled with a swirling partial vacuum. It might have been cold, but the gear I was wearing made me impervious to it. The noise, though, was deafening. More minutes ticked by. I watched Butler stand. I saw him throw something down toward the flight deck. I wondered what. And now there was a Beretta in his other hand. I asked myself why. I watched him push the muzzle into Wignall's neck. I saw the gun jolt.

Wait . . . what? I blinked a couple of times. Was this a hallucination of some kind . . .

Half of Wignall's neck and shoulder were now plastered all over Norris, the man to his left. Red blood on white. I didn't understand. And suddenly, everything forward of the wings was engulfed in a fireball. Grenades. That's what Butler had thrown—grenades. I felt movement to my right, or sensed it. It was Dortmund, shooting. Everything above the bridge of Mortensen's nose disintegrated, flipped back like the top of a hard-boiled egg removed with a knife.

The plane's wings folded. The plane was breaking up. I was thrown to the floor. I saw Butler. He was shooting. He was shooting at me. The slugs slammed into the Ski-Doos as they slid past, going backward. They dropped down the ramp, out of what was left of the C-17. The shifting weight caused the floor to tilt vertical. I fell backward, after the Ski-Doos, through burning wreckage. The aircraft's fuel had caught fire. Aluminum and composite materials were burning. Fire, intense heat, dripped like orange rain through the blackness around and above me.

I dropped away from the worst of it. Falling. Escaping. It all happened so fast, I wasn't even sure what had happened. Butler and Dortmund. They'd completely lost it. Snapped. Killed everyone. Everyone except me.

I fell through the night. The altimeter on my wrist read 20,000 feet. I had survived. I had a chute. I wondered who else had made it out, if anyone. Maybe I could—

A huge weight suddenly slammed into me, punching the air from my lungs. I'd been struck by something, maybe a piece of plane. No, it was one of the men. Something gave way beneath me. I looked into the face of a giant black fly. It was Butler. I knew it was Butler because he held a long thin dagger in front of my face, where I could see it, so there'd be no misunderstanding, no doubt. A Fairbairn-Sykes. Wright's missing knife. *Ruben Wright.* That sensation—the one of something giving way beneath me? Butler had cut through the thigh straps of my chute harness. A flash of memory took me back to Clare Selwyn's office and her explanation of exactly what had happened to Ruben—how he'd died.

And then Butler continued with the practical demonstration of how he killed Wright. He reached for my rip cord, and pulled it.

I only had a few seconds. The drogue chute snapped out of the bag and crackled in the slipstream behind my back. It began to pull the main foil out of the bag. I grappled with Butler, fighting, grabbing, clawing for straps, webbing, anything. My hand found something as my main chute deployed, coming open with an almighty *bang*. The sudden deceleration ripped me out of the chute harness, just as Ruben Wright had been ripped out of his. It also nearly tore my hand off, the one holding on to Butler. I tumbled, spinning, disoriented, for a thousand feet or so. When I regained control, I saw Butler in the high arch close by, following me down. Behind the oxy mask, I'd be willing to bet he was smiling that smile, the one I saw as he checked my gear earlier. Now I knew what the smile meant. He waved good-bye as he pulled his rip cord, just like he did when he left Hurlburt Field—the "fuck you" wave. I watched his drogue chute appear and drag the foil out of his chute bag. It opened with a *bang* and Butler instantly disappeared somewhere into the black sky above, while I was left alone to plunge without a chute toward certain death.

FORTY-FOUR

The altimeter told me I had around thirty seconds of free fall, plenty long enough for the life flashing before my eyes to go into reruns. Somewhere below, the big end was rushing toward me at around a hundred and twenty. No way to fight it. Nothing to do but wait. This was it. The Death Fall that powered my flying phobia had arrived.

The seconds dragged by like the wind tearing at my helmet and filling my ears with a roar. When it happened, it would happen quick. I'd be alive, then not. Solid, then liquid, a splash on the earth. I was falling through cloud, buffeted by windborne snow. Ten seconds left. Dying's not so—

*　　*　　*

As I swam in and out of consciousness, I became aware of a series of loud bangs nearby—gunshots—then familiar voices. I tried to speak, but then the blackness welled up from beneath and dragged me back to nothingness.

*　　*　　*

I was numb. Floating and, at the same time, sinking. Conscious, but not. A trickle of ice water ran down the back of my neck, between my shoulder blades. I was aware of the pain in my chest. Jesus, my hand hurt. And then the blackness gobbled me up.

*   *   *

Every muscle ached. I coughed the icy wetness out of my mouth and opened my eyes. The light hurt. White all around—above and below. I couldn't move my arms or legs. I lay there motionless until I recognized that the whiteness above was cloud. In fact, it wasn't white. It was low and gray, and full of snow. I lifted my head and discovered I was encased in snow. I couldn't feel my toes. I tried to roll. The snow gave a little. I moved, rolled some more. The snow tomb collapsed, releasing me. I lifted my knees, then my arms. My face was numb, my oxygen mask ripped away. One of my hands was numb. I'd lost a glove. I looked at my fingers. They were blue; two were dislocated, poking up at odd angles like the broken teeth of a cheap hair comb. My brain was starting to function. I remembered the fall. I remembered Butler. My fingers had been mangled trying to hold on to him. Why wasn't I dead?

I pulled myself up to look around, feeling every bone and muscle in my body scream when I did so. I was on a high, treeless plateau. Snow met the horizon all round. With my good hand, I unclipped the M4 carbine from my webbing, followed by the para-ruck. The SpecterIR sight was smashed and the carbine's barrel was slightly bent. It—I—had taken a hell of a hit. Butler had made such a big deal about this weapon system, all that bullshit about the Bofors ammunition. He knew I would never get to use it.

My chest ached beneath the ceramic plate in my body armor. I opened the para-ruck and pulled out a couple of chemical hand-warmers and a pair of shooter's gloves. I broke the seal on the warmer and fed it inside the glove. Then I took one finger at a time and relocated them. Each went back into place with a wet *crack*. The numbing cold reduced the pain to bearable. I hoped the circulation hadn't been completely cut—I wasn't enthusiastic at the thought of losing them to frostbite, or to anything else. They were the same two fingers I'd broken on my last case. Unlucky fingers, both of them.

I carefully slid the shooter's glove on. I felt the glow of the hand-warmer on my palm, but nowhere else. Maybe it was too late for those fingers. I gave myself an examination, patting down my legs and arms with my good hand. There didn't seem to be any other broken or otherwise damaged bones. I was overcome by a feeling of total, all-consuming amazement. How had that happened? How had I managed to walk away from a fall of at least 20,000 feet? I'd heard of people surviving high falls by landing in hay bales and deep snowdrifts, but from what I could tell, there weren't any hay bales around and the snow a couple of feet down was hard and compacted.

I sat up on my knees and took in the surroundings again, searching for clues to this miraculous escape.

The plateau was featureless except for a mound of roughly piled snow a hundred feet away. I stumbled toward it. Halfway there, I found part of a large chute. I grabbed hold of it with my good hand and pulled. Some more of it lifted out of the snow and I used it to haul myself forward. I arrived at the mound and scraped away some of the snow. Beneath was one of the Ski-Doos. The handlebars were bent and broken, the windshield cowling smashed. Something heavy had landed on it from above. Me?

I sat with my back to the mound of snow, cradling my injured hand. I didn't remember hitting anything during free fall, but then, I wouldn't have. Traveling at a hundred and twenty miles an hour, I'd have been knocked instantly unconscious. I struggled to piece it together. My survival had something to do with these machines—had to. I remembered the Ski-Doos sliding out the back of the plane. Their chutes had not deployed—not immediately, anyway. I remembered seeing the cable to which their static lines were attached get ripped away from the fuselage and follow them down the ramp. I'd fallen free of the aircraft shortly after. The Ski-Doos' enormous equipment chutes would have opened very late. Maybe I'd fallen into one of these vast nylon canopies while it was still inflated; all sixty-four feet of it. If so, it would have acted much like a giant airbag as it collapsed, breaking my fall without breaking me. Maybe I then rolled off it and fell, crashing into the Ski-Doo, hitting it with my chest, before continuing the remainder of the journey to earth riding it, unconscious. All this was a million to one. Ten million to one. I could see the T-shirt: *"I free-fell 20,000 feet without a parachute and all I got were these two broken fingers."* Which reminded me. They were starting to throb and the pain was getting through the frozen nerve endings. I laughed and gave a whoop. Fuck, I was alive. If surviving a fall like that didn't cure me of the flying phobia, I should transfer to the Navy.

After five minutes of sitting and thinking about just how goddamn invincible I was, I decided to inspect the Ski-Doo. Maybe my luck would hold and I could jury-rig a pair of handlebars and just ride the thing out of here, back to Afghanistan. I scraped away more snow to inspect the engine. It had been shot up. Shit. This puppy was going nowhere. Butler had to have been here. He'd found this Ski-Doo and shot half a dozen rounds into it, put the thing out of its misery. I had a vague memory of hearing gunfire and Butler's voice when I was drifting in and out of consciousness. The other two Ski-Doos were gone. Maybe Butler and Dortmund had taken them. I glanced around. There were no tracks—a light snowfall had covered them. The landing must have thrown me free and into snow deep enough to hide me from Butler's SpecterIR. Obviously, Vin Cooper was one lucky guy who the gods obviously thought was way too handsome and clever to be cut down in his prime. Obviously, I was getting delirious. Hypoxic, even. I checked the altimeter on my wrist, just in case. It was smashed.

Movement at the edge of the plateau caught my attention. I started to stand, to move. I heard a hard crack and a bullet whistled past my Kevlar, trailing a mini sonic boom. *What?* Men on horseback were trotting toward me, yelling. I had the M9, but I'd never get it out of the holster in time to do anything other than get myself shot dead. I heard another couple of cracks and the snow at my feet kicked up. I raised my hands above my head. Maybe I'd used up all my luck.

I counted around twenty men, all on horseback. They surrounded me, yelling. I heard the words *kafir* and *aspai*—"infidel" and "dog." They swirled around me, the horses turning and snorting steam. The men were mostly wrapped in dark or black wool blankets. Some wore Afghan *pakool* caps, others had black fabric rolled loosely around their heads. At a guess, I'd have said the band was Taliban with some al Qaeda mixed in for added nastiness. There was nothing "maybe" about my luck having run out.

One of the men slid down off his horse, shouting at me. He was carrying an AK-47, coming toward me with the stock raised, yelling. I was about to—

FORTY-FIVE

Ruben Wright and I were sitting in a slit trench dug into a snowdrift, the air around us swirling with frozen ice crystals that reflected the available light like diamonds. The cold had numbed my ass so completely I wasn't even sure I had one anymore. I was so cold I'd crack if I tried to move. Ruben was sighting down a Squad Automatic Weapon, an M249 machine gun, his left cheek wrinkled with deep clefts beneath an eye clamped shut. He was aiming at a far ridge over which we knew the enemy would be charging. It was just Ruben and me, alone in the snow. He looked good for a dead guy and I told him so. Perhaps being dead he wasn't affected by temperatures frigid enough to freeze skin to exposed metal. "Death agrees with you, buddy," I said.

"Nice of you to say, Vin. In return, I'd like to tell you that you're kinda stupid."

"Oh, yeah? Why's that?"

"Did you really think I'd committed suicide?"

"It looked bad there for a while, Wrong Way."

"Would I cut myself out of my own harness?"

"There were conflicting signs."

"Goddamn it. So I had MS. I could still do what I

needed to do—jump out of planes, kill the bad guys . . ."

"Knowing you, I wasn't sure how you'd have handled it—wasting away slowly . . ."

"I was handling it fine, for Christ's sake. Just another challenge."

"What about Amy and Butler?"

"Yeah, well, shit happens."

"You were stalking them."

He nodded. "Yeah."

"I found the MPEGs."

"Always knew they'd turn up."

"I know you. At least I thought I did. I looked at the facts. They told me it was possible you might have decided to take Butler down with you—leave while the party was still happening, and get in a little revenge of your own."

I turned to face him. His gray eyes were clear and his skin glowed pink with health. He was going to say something, but he appeared to change his mind and instead commented, "You don't look well, Vin."

"I don't feel so good," I agreed. Indeed, I was pretty sure I'd reached the point of no return. My blood was so thick with cold my heart couldn't pump it around my body. I noticed that blurred black-and-white shapes had appeared over the far ridge, a wave of them. The enemy had returned. Behind them, giant mushroom clouds from an earlier dream blossomed and reached far into the upper atmosphere, and this time they were white rather than orange. Ruben let off a burst of fire from his SAW. I started firing my weapon at individual targets, my trigger finger the only part of me that I could move. I hit nothing. Ruben hit nothing. The enemy kept coming. The rifle bucked and jumped in my hands over and over. No hits. I managed to change mags and then flicked the selector to full auto. The rifle reared and sprayed its deadly load. I glanced to my right. Ruben was no longer beside me. Just like I'd suggested, he'd had the good sense to leave before the situation climbed into the toilet.

I woke shivering so hard my top and bottom teeth were banging away at each other like a couple of castanets. I was lying on a hard, dirty floor. My head hurt with a pounding pain. My hands were locked behind my back. I licked my lips. They were cracked and bloody and swollen. One of my eyes wouldn't open. Maybe it didn't want to know what was on the other side of the lid. My captors had stripped me down to my BDU. No shoes, no gloves. Everything ached. I craved water. I rolled onto my side and sat up and tried to get my bearings, stop my shivering. I couldn't feel my hands or toes.

A door kicked open, letting in so much light it was almost blinding. Several dark shapes entered. When they came closer, I saw the shapes were a couple of men leading horses. They came past, close. Both animals lifted their tails and dropped piles of steaming shit in front of me. I accepted the invitation, wriggled forward on the bones of my butt, and dug my toes into the crap. Delicious warmth surged through my feet and up my legs. Someone yelled something and slapped my face a few times. I was numb so it didn't hurt too bad, although it changed the rhythm of the headache between my ears, shifting it into four/four time.

Another man bent down, grabbed my hair and yanked my head back. "You are American," he said in heavily accented English.

There were no identifying patches on my uniform or gear, but I had to have come from somewhere. "American," I said.

I earned another slap. *Whack.* "I hate Americans," he said. "What are you doing in Pakistan?"

I didn't answer. *Whack.*

"What are you doing here?"

"Tourist," I said.

I knew what was coming. I wasn't disappointed. *Whack.* My brain bounced around inside my skull.

"I will kill you if you do not answer my questions. Will you answer my questions?"

"Yes," I said, though I made no promise to answer them truthfully.

There was a discussion going on between the guy slapping me around and someone else I couldn't see. They were arguing excitedly in Pashtu.

"Do you know what this is?" the man demanded, suddenly back in my face. His eyes were green, his skin olive. Up close, he reminded me of a badass-biker type. A wild, light-brown beard began somewhere inside his nose and ended raggedly mid-chest. He didn't seem in a particularly good mood. I glanced down. My Beretta sat in the palm of his hand.

"Yes," I replied, keeping it simple. I knew what it was.

He pulled the slider back to chamber a round, lifted my head, and put the muzzle against my forehead. My good eye watched his finger squeeze the trigger. I watched as the skin on his dirty index finger between the second and third joint whitened with pressure against the metal. The trigger moved. I couldn't. Any moment the hammer would hit the—

Clack.

"Next time, American, there will be a live round behind the hammer."

I saw him raise the gun like he was going to use it to chop wood, saw the downswing, felt—

FORTY-SIX

There were no dreams. There was just nothingness, then awareness. During this awareness, mostly what I was aware of was my own shit. I'd been moved blindfolded from the stable to a small one-room storehouse. Maybe all my groaning was bothering their animals. My hands were secured behind my back, and they in turn were tethered to a ringbolt set in the wall by a length of thin, rusting cable. There was enough free play in the tether to get me to a bucket on the floor. I'd knocked it over a couple of times trying to use it.

I was fed water and food at reasonably regular intervals—a little dried bread, rice, and some kind of slop. And for my main course, knuckle sandwiches. It was warmer, at least, in the new place. I was shivering less. My dislocated fingers throbbed continuously. They were swollen but I knew that, under the dirt, they were pink with circulation.

My captors asked a lot of questions about my government and said they didn't like it. I replied they weren't alone and that around half of America, give or take, felt the same way. They thought I was joking, giving them lip, and beat up on me some more.

I gave up nothing of a military nature, which caused them a lot of stress and anger, which they then took out on my face. I didn't know whether these beatings made them feel better because I was mostly on the floor, thinking selfishly about the mess I was in.

But I had to give them something. Eventually, they got my name, rank, place of birth, and my mother's maiden name. I figured that if I could give out that information to a cable guy to get connected, what could it hurt giving it to them? And my captors felt at last that they were getting some cooperation. The beatings lessened.

My captors pulled the pistol trick twice more. On the last of these occasions, they fired off the M9 a couple of times and then put the pistol to my head. I smelled the burnt powder, the gun oil, and some kind of spice on the guy's fingers that reminded me of curry. He pulled the trigger again on an empty barrel. Everyone thought this was a lot of fun and there was plenty of laugher. Yeah, sidesplitting. Afterward, they dragged me back inside and urinated on me.

"Abu Ghraib," they said a couple of times as they wove yellow figure eights on me.

At least the urine was warm. See, I said to myself, you *can* be a glass-half-full guy. The allusion made me laugh, which brought on another beating.

I was right about there being two distinct groups within the party, and probably right about the Taliban/al Qaeda mix. One set was Afghan; the other, Arab. The Arabs hit harder, but were in the minority. I got the impression the Arabs thought they were in charge, but I don't think the Afghans agreed with them on that point.

The chief inquisitor, an Afghan who occasionally translated questions for everyone else in the band, wasn't putting his shoulder behind the hits after what I estimated were a couple of days of softening-up. I liked to think it was because his hand was starting to hurt after I smashed my face into it repeatedly. But then I began to wonder if there wasn't another reason. Like if they were going to video my execution and broadcast it, for example. It wouldn't be great PR if my face resembled a strawberry shortcake dropped on the sidewalk. I thought about this in a distracted way, like it was happening to someone else.

Religion was another favorite question-time subject. Did I realize, for example, that there was only one true God and that his name was Allah?

I kept it simple and said yes to this. I wasn't sure about the name, but I reminded myself a rose by another name smells as sweet, or however that saying goes. The question got me thinking. I knew a bunch of guys in a club who thought the one true God was Camaro, probably a '69 model—metallic blue—with a manual box. I had the good sense to keep this to myself, protecting it. They wanted to know if I believed in God. Tricky. There were times when I did and times when it seemed there wasn't one, or if there was that He was plainly psychotic. Mostly, I told them what they wanted to hear. When I told them things they didn't want to hear, the sessions ended, which was good. They ended because usually I was unconscious, which was also good but for the brief, painful period leading up to it. This was one of those times when I thought there was no God, but I told them otherwise.

There was always one man standing guard at the front door, or sitting at a bench warming his hands against the glass of a hurricane lantern, the wick turned way down. I noted the job rotated through half a dozen different men, a shift lasting a few hours each. I realized I was looking for a way to escape. There didn't seem to be one.

I passed the time by spending a lot of it in my head, replaying conversations I wished had gone another way. Surprisingly, second on the list of the ones I spent most time re-editing were the phone conversations I'd had with my ex-wife, Brenda. I didn't want the outcome of our divorce turned around, just the mood of it improved. It was a regret. So I called her in the life I was having in my head. The call went well. All was forgiven.

First on the list of conversations to re-edit were the ones I'd had with Anna. She forgave me, too. She also forgave me Clare, and I forgave her the JAG lawyer. We made up and had make-up sex. I went through this make-up over and over. The people in my head were far more pleasant and forgiving than the ones keeping me chained to the wall.

After a break of a month, but it also could have been days or even hours, the beatings started again. This time, rods of wood were often used. They mostly kept the hits away from my face. Once, a couple of Arabs came in and spent some time sharpening long knives and machetes and making movements with the blades across their own necks. I was hoping they'd slip.

Questions usually, but not always, accompanied the beatings. On one of these occasions, it was me who was given some answers.

"Where are you from?"

"America. You know that."

"In Afghanistan. Where did you take off from?"

"Kandahar."

"What was your mission?"

"Transport flight."

Whack.

"Liar! We know this is a lie. What was the snow car for?"

I assumed he meant the Ski-Doo. "I don't know."

Whack.

"You are commando. You were going to raid _____."

His heavy accent got in the way of me catching the name, but I knew he meant Phunal. I wondered how he knew. "No," I said.

Whack. Whack. "Liar!" *Whack.* "You were heavily armed. You had sniper scope. You had GPS, radios, supplies for a week."

Three days in all, but I didn't correct the error.

"We shot down your plane," he bragged. In the words of the movie *Top Gun,* this guy's ego was writing checks his body couldn't cash.

"We know where you were going because _____ was attacked that night. You will pay for the many brave lives lost there."

I shook my head and said, "Transport flight."

Whack.

And so it continued along in this general vein. As an interrogator, this guy was an amateur. To start with, he'd said "snow *car*." "Car" meant singular. So they'd recovered only one Ski-Doo. More important, Phunal had been attacked. Butler and Dortmund and maybe others had gone on to complete the mission—captured or killed Boyle and put an end to the nuclear threat. That didn't make any sense and I wondered whether all the whacking had addled my brains.

*   *   *

I wasn't sure how much time had passed since my capture. I felt myself withdrawing, building a room of my own deep within and hiding away there. I knew what my mind was doing. The Air Force had prepared me for this a long time ago with a course in capture and torture.

One morning, or it could have been afternoon, I sensed plenty of activity outside. There were many horses stamping and snorting, and voices. There was also cheering. The commotion died down and nothing much happened for the rest of the day. No interrogation, no punishment, no threats. I was hoping they had all decided to move on and had forgotten about me. I was about to try to stand up when my cell filled with people. My eyes were swollen almost shut, so I couldn't see too well. I felt a hand under my chin that smelled of horse sweat and dung. The hand lifted my head and I looked into a face. I knew this guy. He was an old friend. He'd aged a little since I last saw him, and grime was pressed into the pores of his skin, but his eyes were soft and brown and his lids drooped a little like he was tired. Maybe he was. Hell, I was. "Hey," I said. "How you doin'?" My voice cracked, and it came out as a whisper. I gave him a smile, too. I wondered what this friend of mine was doing here in this place and whether he'd come to get me out. I thought I should warn him he was in danger of ending up a punching bag. Those kind, sad eyes looked into mine, but I saw no recognition in them. I was a stranger to him. "It's me. Vin," I said, again in a whisper. This was a funny situation. Finally, here was someone come to take me home, a familiar face, a buddy, and he didn't even recognize me. I must look like shit. The hopelessness of it made me laugh. It was funny. It was dumb.

The laughing earned me a beating.

FORTY-SEVEN

It was day or night, I wasn't sure which but I knew it had to be one or the other. I felt my shoulder being shaken. "Come on, wake up. Time to go."

I wondered where this stranger was going and why he was telling me. It didn't occur to me to wonder who "he" was.

The owner of the voice shook me again and said, "Here, drink this." I felt the pressure of a cup against my lips, and smelled heaven inside it. I tasted warm coffee, full of sugar. The flavor was exquisite, powerful. My shaking hands spilled some as I tried to get it all in my mouth, past my swollen lips, and I nearly wept. Next came a small chunk of soft cheese. He put the end of a bag in my mouth and cool, clean water flooded my throat. I coughed, hacked.

"Shhh . . ." said the man, putting a finger to his lips. He whispered, "Put a sock in it, buddy."

Put a sock in it, buddy? That threw me. The words were said with what sounded like a broad New York accent. I was also thrown because this guy was one of the Afghans, one of the people who'd beaten the crap out of me when I hadn't given the right answers.

I heard the familiar light tinkle of key against stainless steel and my hands were released. The blood surged through my shoulders, down my arms, and out to my fingertips, which throbbed and burned and felt as if they would burst like a couple of balloons overfilled with water.

While I was trying to adjust to this sudden change in fortune, the guy fiddled around behind me, unwinding the end of the cable from whatever had secured my hands. He held up my handcuffs and set them on the floor beside me. "A souvenir," he whispered.

I picked them up and pushed them into a thigh pocket. Smith & Wessons—the bastards had used my own handcuffs on me.

"I'm gonna take a look at your feet. OK?"

I nodded.

He checked them out. "I'm gonna put these on you." He showed me a pair of old socks and boots that appeared to have been resoled countless times.

I nodded.

The socks and shoes went on and the sensation was strangely reassuring.

"Can you stand?"

Another nod.

He helped me to my feet. "You've been here nine days. They haven't tortured you. You should be OK."

Haven't been tortured? Easy for you to say, pal, I thought. Nine days. It had felt like nine months. He threaded my hands through the sleeves of a thickly padded, coarse, knee-length coat, and then fastened the front buttons. The coat was far from tailored, but it was warm. I sagged against the wall while he wound a length of black wool around my head and face, and then a dirty blue wool cape around my shoulders.

"These are your gloves," he said under his breath, holding them in front of my face. "Can you put them on?"

More nodding. The knuckles of my formerly dislocated fingers were swollen up like golf balls, but I could wiggle the digits and they didn't hurt as bad as they had a right to.

"Take this," he said. "Feel free to use it if you have to. But use it quietly, OK?" He wiped the weapon on his cloak and handed it to me.

It was a knife, a long, thin, lethal knife, the edges modified—honed razor sharp. I knew this knife. I ran my gloved fingertip down the inscription on the blade, wiping away some of the crimson coagulated blood clogging the letters. There wasn't enough light by which to read the words, but I knew what they said: *And the American Way*. This was Ruben Wright's knife, the one Clare Selwyn and I both thought was lost close to where Ruben had died. *Truth, Justice* on the one side, *And the American Way* on the other. Ruben Wright's personal motto, the last line of the theme song from the original *Superman* TV show.

"Where'd you find this?" I asked.

"Same place we found you. Can you walk?"

This must have been what my fingers found when Butler and I had grappled in midair. "Who are you?" I asked, taking a couple of unsteady steps.

"A guy who's about to blow his cover. Come on—

the window of opportunity's small. We get this wrong, we're both dead."

He helped me to the front door. I slipped and almost fell. There was something on the ground, hidden in the night shadow from the flickering orange light of the hurricane lamp. It was one of the Arabs. His throat had been cut and his blood had leaked out, making a hell of a sticky, slippery mess. His clothes had been stripped off him and his feet were bare. We stepped over his sprawled legs, through the door, and into a densely black night. Snow was falling. It was utterly quiet, all sound absorbed by fat, ghostly flakes the size of flower petals drifting down from above.

My rescuer pulled out a pair of night-vision goggles from somewhere and put them on. "This way," he said, nudging me in an uphill direction. We made our way up through what was a small village cut into a rock face that was close to vertical. Somewhere, a mutt barked halfheartedly, the sound muffled by the falling snow. I was lucky. Everything in the village was made of stone and mud brick and even the smallest sound would usually bounce around amplified in a place like this, especially in the thicker night air. Nevertheless, we stopped moving occasionally, my guide making the gesture of silence with his finger pressed against his lips. Once, I was pushed back against a wall and into a deep shadow as two men with AKs strolled past. They were both smoking. I knew from experience the glowing tips would register in the NVG's lenses like a pair of usher's flashlights.

We climbed over a couple of low walls and left the

black silhouette of the town behind, then climbed a steep hill through soft, knee-deep snow. I guessed we were well above 10,000 feet. I had a headache that reminded me of my heavy-drinking days, and my lungs were searing with effort. I couldn't get enough air into them, and what air I could get was frigid, which made my nose, throat, and mouth feel like they'd been sliced up with a straight razor. When I tried to stop to get my breath, which happened every half-dozen steps, my rescuer gave me a push. Eventually, the climb lessened and we dropped over the ridge into another valley. My hands and feet were again numb with cold, the shooter's gloves not providing a lot of protection against the elements and the snow having found its way inside the boots. I had questions for my savior and guide, but I was too cold and tired to ask them.

"Not much further," said Mr. Mystery just when I was thinking that lying down in the snow would be better than going on. It gave me strength, but he lied about the further bit. I figured I was still in Pakistan. Wander around an Afghan village at night like this and we'd have stepped on land mines.

After an eternity of being dragged through the snow, we arrived at a cleft in the rock with hard-packed snow forming a roof over the top. I got the "Ssh" signal again. I kept still, thinking there might be more Arabs wandering around, when I heard a familiar snort.

"Here," I heard the guy say.

He led the way through the cleft. I saw a big horse

and a little horse with big ears—a donkey. The horse stamped a hoof and shook its head and snow went flying. The guy talked to each animal softly, and then pulled heavy blankets off each. The animals were saddled and ready to go. Whoever this guy was, he'd done his homework. "Can you ride?" he asked me.

"Which side are the gears on?" I replied.

He turned the NVG on me.

"Just kidding."

In fact, I'd only ridden once before. I'd been eighteen and a girl I wanted to get to know without her clothes on was into horses. I went away with her on a riding weekend. I had this fantasy that all the bouncing up and down in a saddle would make her eager for sex. It did, and she was, only not with me but with the guy from the stable. I went home empty-handed. The girl went home pregnant and never rode again. And neither had I. Until now. I took a tentative step toward the horse.

"Uh-uh, buddy. The little one's yours," he said as he gave the donkey a pat on its rump, which made its ears twitch. "It'll follow the horse." He handed me a long stick. "If it decides it doesn't want to go forward, give it a jab like this." He demonstrated, a stabbing motion down into the side of the beast's neck. I must have looked doubtful because he added, "Don't worry, you won't hurt it."

I gave the animal a pat on its neck. The muscle there was like a sheet of hairy iron. My guide gave me a hand up and the animal took a step forward and twitched its ears at me.

We rode through the night in silence. Like the guy said, the donkey followed the horse. I just hoped the horse didn't step off the mountain. I gathered we were in a hurry, even though pursuit was looking less likely by the hour. It continued to snow till just before dawn, covering our tracks. When the low sky finally lightened to a slate gray, we were making our way down a ridge and into a valley. The mountain on the other side—slabs of ice and black rock—rose into the clouds and disappeared.

"Down there is the border with Afghanistan. Beyond is the pass we have to take," said the man.

"You from New York City?" I asked.

"That obvious?" he replied.

"Uh-huh. I'm from New Jersey," I said, now with enough strength to exercise my curiosity.

"I know."

"Is that why you hit me so hard?" I asked.

"No, I hit you hard so that I could come back another day and rescue your ass. And I didn't use a closed fist."

"I don't remember the details."

The animals beneath us picked their way down the slope the way Clare's kid, Manny, removed green things from his fried rice—with infinite care.

"How're you doing?" he asked.

"Good." There was a bag of food attached to the saddle and I'd been eating my way through the contents—cheese, flat bread, and olives. My strength was coming back fast.

"Cool," he said. "So, what were you doing? Did it have something to do with the raid on Phunal?"

"Maybe," I said. "Maybe not."

"That's OK. You don't have to say."

"What do you know about Phunal?"

"The night you were captured, we saw an explosion in the sky. It was close to the village we were occupying, so we investigated. We came across you while searching for the wreckage. You can find all kinds of useful things in plane wreckage. Anyway, we found you and located your gear. A lot of it was damaged. You must have come down hard."

"You could say that," I agreed.

"What did you do with your parachute? We looked everywhere for it."

"I got hungry, so I ate it."

"Come on, really . . . what'd you do with it?"

I told him what I thought happened, but he didn't believe me. He seemed to prefer to believe that I had, in fact, eaten the damn thing. Hell, I still had trouble swallowing the truth myself.

We traveled in silence, huddled into our blankets, trying to keep out the bitter cold. My body ached like it had never ached before. I believed I could actually feel the bones beneath my skin and it felt like blades of frozen steel had scraped them. I huddled down low on the saddle and tried to get into the donkey's rhythm. I watched the animal's neck, the snow melting to ice and crusting its coarse hair, and tried not to think about the thousand or so feet of sheer drop to the valley below, just a couple of steps to my right.

Eventually, my animal came to a stop beside the horse. The guy turned toward me, steam coming from his mouth when he opened it. He said, "We heard a couple of days later, after we recovered you, that Phunal was attacked. It's some secret test base or something, right? A lot of people were killed. Some scientist was kidnapped. From the way it went down, sounded like coalition Special Forces at work. The feeling is, you were supposed to be one of them, but something went wrong with the plan. Allah's will. So, they were going to hand you over to the new revolutionary Pakistan government and make trouble for Washington. But then, as you know, we had an unexpected guest. But I suppose you're wondering what a nice boy from New York is doing in a place like this?"

"Yeah, had crossed my mind," I said, but in truth I was thinking about Butler and Dortmund. They'd killed everyone on that plane. And then they had still followed through on the mission. Why? What the hell was going on?

"Like I said, my cover was blown getting you out anyway, so I guess I can tell you."

He didn't get around to letting me in on his secret for a little while longer. We'd reached a treacherous part of the road cut into the side of an almost vertical granite face. We dismounted and walked the animals across. My traveling companion had to help me down. I couldn't move—my body had locked up solid.

"As I was about to say, I am Lieutenant Ibrahim al-Wassad, at your service," he said as we mounted up again with what I hoped was the most dangerous section behind us.

"Pleased to meet you, Lieutenant," I said through frozen lips burning with cold.

"I was U.S. Army infantry, then U.S. Army intelligence, then CIA, then, hell, now I'm not sure what or who I am. Someone in a back room somewhere found out I had American-Afghan parents, could speak Pashtu and a fair smattering of Dari, worshipped in the Islamic faith, and did pretty well at West Point. Before I knew what was going on, I was given a whirlwind course in spycraft at Langley, then counterterror at Quantico, and rotated into Afghanistan.

"Three months after that, I'm working deep cover as a schoolteacher in a town up north in the heart of the Pashtun region, saying all the right things about what a great idea jihad is. Two months later, I'm recruited by a remnant of the Taliban. I join the band, and go touring. Over the past six months we've played up and down the border between Afghanistan and Pakistan, looking for action, but not too much action, because the people I'm with at least have the good sense not to go head-to-head with coalition forces. Hit-and-run stuff, mostly. I've done some bad things in the name of this mission . . . then you drop in and make life difficult."

"Why difficult?"

"Because you arrive a couple of days before Bin Laden."

"What?" I was so surprised, even my donkey stopped.

"Yeah, the unexpected guest I mentioned—the man himself."

"Jesus." The donkey snorted and moved off.

"He just walked into town out of nowhere—him and twenty other al Qaeda heavy hitters. I recognized a lot of them."

"Shit," I said.

"Don't you remember? He paid you a visit. He looked right into your face. You laughed at him." He chuckled. "They didn't like that. They were going to cut your head off in the morning."

Christ, my memory was in serious sleep mode, but al-Wassad had just given it a massive jolt. I suddenly put the friendly face and the name together. I'd seen so many pictures of Bin Laden that he was intensely familiar, like a Hollywood or TV star is familiar. In my weakened, addled state, I'd thought I knew him like a buddy rather than as Osama Bin Laden, leader of al Qaeda, Emperor of Terror, Sultan of Slaughter, King of Killers, Monarch of Murderers, Serious Thorn in Three Presidential Asses, et cetera and so on.

"So now," Lieutenant al-Wassad continued, "I've got a stack of problems. The guy we've spent trillions looking for is having hot tea with the imam down the road, and I have no means of contacting anyone to tell them about it because, of course, I have no means of communicating with the outside world."

"Why not?"

"Because the batteries on the Ericsson R390 satellite phone would have run out six months ago. There's no means of charging them out here. And then there's the fact that I never deployed with one in the first place, because I'd have kept my head about five minutes if the Taliban had found me on it chatting to Washington. So, the only way to get word out is to do it in person, on foot. And then there's you. I can't just walk out of the place and leave you behind, because, pure and simple, they're gonna kill you at sunup."

"We need to get in contact with SOCOM," I said. "And in a hurry."

"Yeah. Only two problems with that. One, we're going as fast as we can, and two, Bin Laden isn't going to hang around where we last saw him. When they trip over the dead guard, find you gone and me missing, and discover they're eight legs short in the transport department, they're going to smell a rat. And they're going to run."

"Hmm..." Of course al-Wassad was right, only, as far as I knew, this was the first time in many years someone other than those within Bin Laden's inner circle knew for certain, down to the square mile, where he was holed up. It was information one side would die to have, and the other would die to keep secret.

We'd just about reached the valley floor, a deep gash in the surrounding walls of granite and basalt filled with new snow, tendrils of cloud, scree, and capillary-sized rivulets. I didn't know much about horses and donkeys, but I knew ours were tired and hungry. Soon we were going to ask them to carry us over a mountain and we couldn't afford to have them go lame on us.

I was about to suggest we stop, even if only just fifteen minutes to give them a rest, when there was sudden movement all around us. Our animals skittered and wheeled about, snorting and grunting, wild-eyed with fright. Men covered in snow with occasional splashes of tan and gray camouflage had popped up seemingly out of the ground, surrounding us. Their M4s were raised to their shoulders, trigger fingers twitching. I recognized the brown-and-tan flag patches on a couple of shoulders not covered in snow, on account of it was also my flag. Some advice I was once given in this part of the world popped into my head: "*Either you dress like an American soldier, or you're a target.*" We'd walked right into an ambush and, with the *pakool* caps and dark blue cloaks over the padded jackets and salwar kameez, we were probably looking a hell of a lot like a couple of bull's-eyes. One of the soldiers, a lieutenant whose face was blue with cold, shouted, "*Odriga! Lasona jakra. Kanh zadi walm Aspai!*" I did the rough translation in my head: "*Stop or I'll shoot, loathsome smelly dog!*"

I did as I was told, and al-Wassad followed my lead. I said, loud and clear, "I am Special Agent Vin Cooper, a major in the United States Air Force. This man is a lieutenant in U.S. Army Intelligence." One of the soldiers spurted a load of brown chewing-tobacco-stained saliva onto the snow at his feet.

Those M4s didn't waver an inch.

A lieutenant answered, "Yeah, and I'm Snow

White and these are my seven dwarfs." He suddenly pointed his weapon at the clouds and his dwarfs followed suit.

"So which one's Dopey?" I asked.

"That'd be Stephenson," said one of the men with a snigger.

"Shove it, dipshit," came the reply.

The men relaxed a little, though most still eyed al-Wassad and me with suspicion. The lieutenant removed a glove and searched in a thigh pocket. He pulled out a small pad. Checking it, he said, "You say your name was Vin Cooper?"

"And still is," I replied.

"You look pretty beat up, sir," he pointed out.

"I'm not a morning person."

"You were involved in the raid on Phunal."

It wasn't a question. "I was, but I didn't quite make it. You guys Airborne?" I asked.

Someone spat.

"Rangers, sir. We were supposed to rendezvous with you and the SAS assault team. We've been out a few times looking to run into you guys, in case any of you survived. We've got a Global Hawk UAV up there working the border—picked you up coming across the pass."

"Lieutenant," I said, "we have vital information and we need SOCOM to hear it. You packing comms?"

"Latest and greatest, sir."

As he spoke, I heard the deep flat snarl and thrum of a large helo making its way through the hills.

"That's our transport, Major. We're heading back to

Bagram and a hot shower. And with respect, sir, you sure could use one."

*   *   *

The helicopter banked sharply around a wall of blue ice clinging to a sheer granite face. We were so close I was pretty sure the rotor tips were going to raise sparks against the rock.

Through my headphones came the voice of a colonel who was probably sitting in a nice warm room at Bagram Airbase. "You positively identified Bin Laden and al-Zawahiri?" He sounded like a man who'd just been told he'd won the lottery—thrilled on the one hand, disbelieving on the other.

"Yes, sir," said al-Wassad. "I can even give you his cell phone number."

"You what . . . ? Tell me this ain't no crank call, soldier."

"I've got a witness here, sir, a Special Agent with OSI—Major Vin Cooper."

I gave the lieutenant a reassuring thumbs-up.

The colonel sounded like he was talking from a mouth occupied by a fat cigar. "You got *who* there with you?"

"Special Agent Vin Cooper, sir."

Lieutenant al-Wassad gave the astonished colonel a quick overview.

"Son, if you're right about this, they'll give you a ticker tape parade from LA to Times Square and name a street after you in every goddamn town in between. Osama Bin Laden and Ayman al-Zawahiri? Shee-it!

You wanna give me those coordinates? Did you say you had Bin Laden's phone number?"

Al-Wassad reeled off map reference numbers while the chopper copilot showed me on a ground map display that the village I'd been held in was ten or so miles inside the Pakistan border. I wasn't sure what the Army would be able to do with the information, but, now that they had it, I was equally sure they wouldn't sit on their hands with it.

The Black Hawk was old and noisy and shook like a jalopy in serious need of a wheel balancing. I glanced out the door at the walls of snow-laden granite flashing past. The old nerves were chained to a metaphorical ringbolt set in the wall with a bucket on the floor. Surviving the fall from the C-17 had given me a whole new perspective on flying.

FORTY-EIGHT

Two weeks after I arrived back in Washington, I took the bandages off my hand. I removed them in the bathroom down the hall from the briefing room at the Pentagon. I didn't want anyone there thinking I was incapacitated in any way. I checked myself in the mirror. "You've still got it," I said to my reflection as I straightened my tie, and indeed my face was looking less like a ruined piece of fruit with every passing day. If an attempt was going to be made to put things right, I didn't want to be sidelined. Butler and I, to use a euphemism I never liked much, needed closure.

Apparently, this Pentagon briefing I'd been summoned to had followed two others with the President, the SecDef, the SecState, the Chief of Staff, the Chairman of the Joint Chiefs, the heads of CIA and the FBI, the British Ambassador, British military attachés, various military ops personnel, and so on. A course of action had been decided on and now, presumably, the talking was done. Everyone was in a hurry.

I'd seen yesterday's *Post*, and a couple of reports on CNN revealed that a chunk of the detail was already in the public domain: A renegade British SAS soldier had apparently run amok and killed a number of his own countrymen, as well as U.S. personnel and Pakistanis. He'd also destroyed several millions of dollars' worth of C-17 aircraft. The press wanted to know why coalition forces were conducting operations inside Pakistan. Parallels were being drawn with the CIA operating in Laos and Cambodia during the Vietnam War. As yet, the media didn't know why all this had happened, but I was sure everyone in the briefing room knew they'd find out eventually. Someone somewhere would get sick of not being able to sleep or eat with the pressure of The Truth burrowing into them like a tick and would then breathe the clues to "the wrong person." The trail would eventually lead back to the disaster at the Transamerica and Four Winds buildings in San Francisco, and forward to the reality that Pakistan intended to leave India a black smoking hole in the ground, and perhaps set off a global nuclear war in the process. In all of this, the murders of Hideo Tanaka and Ruben Wright wouldn't rate a mention.

In the words of the Chairman of the Joint Chiefs, General Henry Howerton, Operation Warlord had been a cluster fuck of monumental proportions, rivaling the disastrous Tehran hostage crisis of three decades ago. Rumor had it the President was sitting in his office with the door locked, sucking his thumb.

At the moment, though, the media was diverted from the investigative angle by the political fallout: The revolutionary Pakistani government was demanding an apology as well as financial compensation and reparations, and had moved every unit in its Army up to the border with India; the United Nations General Assembly was screaming about U.S. and British imperialism and laying blame for what appeared to be snowballing into a global catastrophe; the Russians and Chinese were exerting the usual pressure for loans and trade deals if a full censure in the UN Security Council was to be avoided.

All this made me think back to the original JOPES where the political situation in Pakistan had already been likened to the overthrow of the Shah of Iran. Someone who got paid a lot more than I did should have read the signs and pulled way back, maybe taken a different approach.

In the briefing, intelligence assessments held that Butler and Dortmund had snatched Boyle and simply driven off on the Ski-Doos—not to Afghanistan as planned, but to India. From there, the trail had gone cold. Why? Because, the experts believed, Butler was out scouting for a buyer for Boyle's secrets. No one in the briefing room asked what those secrets might have been—if you didn't already know, you weren't supposed to know. I wondered how many of the people sitting at that table actually *did* know about Boyle's meltdown bug.

I figured that with twenty years in the military serving all around the world, Butler's little black book of contacts would be around the size of the Yellow Pages. General Howerton, along with everyone else in the loop, was no doubt hoping like hell Butler wouldn't find that buyer in the People's Republic of China. Or, for that matter, North Korea, Iran, or Syria.

If this was, in fact, what Butler had done, I wondered when it was that he'd decided to abduct Boyle and sell the guy and his technology to the highest bidder. Perhaps when someone told him how valuable Boyle was. I could think of only one person who would have spilled those beans. Giving Butler an added push toward this insanity might have been the conclusion that it was only a matter of time before he was nailed for Ruben's murder. To hide, he would need *a lot* of money. The motto of his own SAS regiment was "Who dares wins." If the intelligence assessments were true, as operations went, the one he'd conducted on his own behalf to get rich quick was as big and as daring as they came.

There was in all of this gloom, though, at least one bit of sparkling news, and the media was all over it—the story of a Hellfire missile launched from a Predator drone that had hit a group of al Qaeda terrorists fleeing from a village on the Pakistan/Afghanistan border. One of the men believed killed was Bin Laden's right-hand man, al-Zawahiri. Bin Laden was missed in the attack, but al-Zawahiri was a major scalp, and the administration would take whatever it could get. At least the rumor about Bin Laden lying low and maybe running a curry takeout somewhere in London had been dispelled.

The hope that all the talking had been done was an example of wishful thinking on my part. I sat at the table for two hours listening to speculation and rebuff. Nothing concrete was decided on because no one knew where Butler and Boyle had gone. It was a waiting game. But at least with Butler out of Pakistan, the threat of all-out war with nuclear weapons had receded, though Islamabad had announced that the first test in its renewed program would be the detonation of a bomb with a very large yield. India threatened to do the same.

As far as locating Butler and company went, the CIA's Willard F. Norman reassured General Howerton and the SecDef in his peculiarly squeaky voice that everything possible in terms of stones not being left unturned was being done. There was a little more speculation about motives and the mental states of both Boyle and Butler. I was also questioned about my captivity and, of course, about Bin Laden and my impression and observations of the man. My impression was that he had a kind face and warm eyes. My observation was that I wished I'd somehow managed to get the guy's autograph—it would fetch a fortune on eBay. I thought it wise to keep these impressions and observations to myself. Instead I told them all I could remember was that his fingers smelled of horse shit. The briefing was called to an end, and I went home.

*   *   *

In and around my apartment block, a couple of things of interest had happened in my absence. Kim's 38th Parallel had reopened to again do battle with Summer Love for take-out supremacy. The vegan joint, though, was hitting below the belt. Stuffed in my letterbox was the usual flyer promising that no animal products were used in its cuisine, either as ingredients or in the cooking process. Admirable though that was, I bet it all tasted like warmed up papier-mâché. And, besides, I like eating animal. I figure if you weren't supposed to, they wouldn't be made of meat. I turned the flyer over. On the flip side, it was personally signed by Summer—the woman with the mop and the sensational, though hairy, legs—with the invitation to give her a call. Her cell number was included plus a coupon for a veggie burger. Summer was going all out. I stuck it on the fridge.

Meanwhile, inside said fridge, the resident mold had invited over quite a few buddies. I announced the party was over with the aid of a brush and a spray that made me feel like my sinuses were bleeding. In the middle of this cheery domesticity, the phone rang. "Vin Cooper," I said.

"Agent Cooper, there's a car with a driver headed your way. It'll get to you in ten. Don't keep it waiting." Dial tone. General Howerton. Man of few words. I glanced at my watch and wondered what had happened in the three hours since I was last at the Pentagon.

FORTY-NINE

It was a different room this time, smaller and better lit, though it, too, was buried somewhere within the Pentagon's lower bowel area, a region I seemed to be spending an increasing amount of time in. Howerton was at the head of the table, CIA Deputy Assistant Director, Directorate of Operations, Willard F. Norman beside him. Opposite Norman sat the white-haired staff judge advocate, the general with the lined face who'd provided the legal thumbs-down on the original mission to Phunal. Beside him was Brigadier General James Wynngate, my CO at OSI, and beside him the British SAS Major First-Name-Nigel.

"Ah, Vin," said Howerton, glancing up as I entered. "Take a seat."

I took the one opposite Norman.

Howerton continued. "You've already met or know everyone here, but just in case..." He went through the introductions. I learned that Major First-Name-Nigel's surname was Overton, and that the staff judge advocate went by General William Weildon.

There weren't a lot of smiles going round the table.

The heavy entrance door slid open again, accompanied by a rush of air. It was Bradley Chalmers, accompanied by his crutches. His arrival was not acknowledged, which led me to believe either he'd arrived earlier and pleasantries had already been exchanged, or he was unimportant. I tried to think charitably about which might be the correct answer, and failed.

"Bringing you up to speed, Special Agent Cooper," said Howerton, "Butler and Boyle have been found, along with Dortmund. News came through an hour ago. CIA located them in Seoul." Howerton glanced at Norman, who looked like he would have preferred to be somewhere else. "CIA found them yesterday, and then lost them," added Howerton. That explained Norman's discomfort.

"Something that hasn't been determined," said Norman, "is whether Boyle is in Butler's company reluctantly; whether he's being held against his will. We're assuming the worst—that they've become partners and that North Korea is top of their shopping list."

Christ! North Korea!

"Just so I've got this straight," said the SecDef, leaning forward, "our radar system the South Koreans use, the, ah . . . the . . ."

"The Aegis Ballistic Missile Defense System, sir," said Howerton, helping the guy out.

"Do we know for sure it's vulnerable to this, er, technology, Henry?"

"We believe so, sir," said Howerton grimly.

I wondered if I was perhaps the only guy in the briefing who didn't officially know what *this* technology was. As if reading my mind, General Howerton cleared this throat and stood. He then gave a halting overview of the project developed by Professor Boyle at Moreton Genetics for the DoD. That explained Howerton's discomfort.

When he'd concluded, there was silence while everyone let it all sink in. As if things weren't bad enough, North Korea was hoping to arm itself with a weapon that could knock out South Korea's defenses, negating the very latest deterrents we had on the ground there. And the North was just nutty enough to try it.

"Vin," said Howerton, once again catching me off guard, "I want you on the ground in Seoul, ASAP, in the event these three turn up again. A CIA operative, handpicked by Assistant Deputy Director Norman, will join you there."

I hoped like hell the person picked wasn't Chalmers.

"Bradley?" said Norman, gesturing at Chalmers with his chin.

I held my breath.

Chalmers said, "You'll be working with Special Agent Haiko Rossi..."

Exhale.

"...Italian American father, Japanese mother. She spent five years in the Marines developing the skill set we need, speaks Japanese—and English, of course—as well as Korean and a couple of European languages, including Italian and Portuguese..."

Hmm, Portuguese, I thought. *That's sure to come in handy.*

"By the time you meet up with Special Agent Rossi in Seoul, Agent Cooper, we should have a lead on the targets. I'll accompany you to Seoul for a joint briefing on the ground with Rossi when we get there."

Christ, I hoped he didn't expect us to actually sit together on the plane over. I had to hand it to Chalmers, though; he was a smooth operator when he wanted to be. Watching him work the table, full of cautious confidence, I could see why he'd gotten so high in an organization that truly embraced bullshit.

I knew why I wanted in on this mission. What I didn't know was why Howerton wanted me involved. There were other federal agents around in better shape than I was. I could only assume the people above me wanted to keep the circle as small and as tight as possible to avoid leaks. I wasn't complaining.

Howerton spread it on a cracker for me. "Cooper, your role will be to keep Boyle and Butler under surveillance until we can determine exactly who is in the market for the NLW."

There was that term again—NLW, nonlethal weapon; in this instance a genetically engineered neoform that allowed one side to kill potentially millions of people on the other side without the fear of immediate retaliation and retribution. There was enough irony in calling the death bug an NLW to swing a compass needle.

"Anyone got anything to add?" asked Howerton.

I hoped not. I wanted to leave, get some air. Heads were shaking like they were at a game of tennis with everyone watching a different ball.

Brigadier General Wynngate, my CO, said, "Colonel Wayne has a hard copy of your orders, Major."

"Yes, sir," I said, standing. I had to take a moment to think who Colonel Wayne might be. Arlen—the "colonel" bit still hadn't sunk in.

General Howerton followed me to the door. He pressed a button on the wall and the door came ajar with a hiss. "A moment, Vin," he said as I stepped into the hall. "I read your interim reports on the Tanaka case, and the Wright inquiry. Good work on both."

"Thank you, sir."

The general hesitated, then asked, "Is it true what I heard?"

"I'm not sure, sir. What did you hear?"

"About you falling twenty thousand feet and landing in the cargo chute canopy as it collapsed. Did that really happen?"

I'd given plenty of thought to that Houdini-like escape of mine. Whatever I hit knocked me unconscious, so all I could do was speculate on what had saved me from digging my own grave in the snow. "Sir, the truth is I'm not sure, but it can't have been anything else," I said.

The general shook his head. "You're one lucky SOB, Vin."

"I'm expecting a call from the *Guinness Book of World Records* anytime now, sir."

FIFTY

Chalmers and I didn't sit together on the plane. We didn't catch the same bus from Incheon Airport to the city. We didn't stay at the same hotel. So I was happy. I believed I'd finally figured Chalmers out. He was involved in the mission in such a way that if it turned out well, he could grab a hefty measure of credit. If not, he was far enough away to avoid any career-lethal shit from sticking.

As for the flight itself, I ate the food, watched the movies, and, like most other passengers, tried to get some sleep. No sweats, no tingles, no fear—just the apparently far more normal searing boredom. I made myself a mental note to write to the publishers of *Have a Nice Flight* and give them another surefire method for overcoming aviaphobia.

Like just about everywhere else in the world, it seemed, it was snowing in Seoul, and about twenty-five degrees. There was no wind. That had apparently been and gone, leaving the place rattled, a vicious Siberian squall that had moved on to Japan to terrorize the island of Kyushu.

I took a cab from the bus terminal to the Hilton. I'd been to Seoul once before, but only for a few days and it was quite a few years back. My memory of the place was that the people ate a lot of pickled cabbage called *kimchi,* and not enough breath mints. They were also excruciatingly polite, mostly went by the name Kim, and used writing symbols that reminded me of crop circles.

Night had fallen, though the city's love of neon was doing a good job of keeping things lit up. The cab pulled into the hotel drive. I signed into my room and received an envelope with a message inside. I tore it open. It was an address and a time and an offer to meet up. The note was signed "Rossi." The clock on the wall told me I had an hour and ten to get to the address.

An hour and five later, my cab pulled up outside a Korean BBQ joint in a relatively quiet street. I paid the driver his fare and went inside. The place smelled like the foyer of my apartment back in D.C. The restaurant was way too hot, around eighty degrees, causing a burning sensation on the tips of my ears. The lighting was on the moody side of dark. Most of the male customers seemed a lot older than the women accompanying them, which probably accounted for the lack of watts.

"Cooper?" said a voice behind me. I turned and a woman held out her hand to shake. "Haiko Rossi."

We shook. Her hand was small, but the grip was firm. It was like shaking hands with needle-nose pliers. "You hungry?" she asked.

I looked around, searching for some sign in English. "They do *bulgogi* here?"

"Specialty of the house."

"You eat here a lot?"

"Never been here before."

"How do you know it's a specialty?"

"It's a specialty of every Korean restaurant."

I followed Rossi to a booth. I couldn't place her accent. Midwest, probably, but the edges had been
ground away by a long absence. Haiko Rossi was petite, maybe five six, anywhere between twenty-five
and thirty. She wore tight, low-slung faded jeans and
a fitted top with some kind of graphic on it that
looked like an ink stain. Her boots were black polished leather. Her straight black hair was almost blue
in places, except where she'd had it dyed dramatically
blond. It was cut in layers and short enough on top so
that it stuck almost straight up. Down the back, it was
layered so that it followed the curve of her neck.
There was a diamond stud in her nose, and one high
up on the left ear. Her features were Asian, but European at the same time, her makeup expertly applied.
Rossi was attractive, if the whole Eurasian/exotic-
beauty thing worked for you.

"Want to eat something?" Rossi asked, as I took the
seat opposite, squeezing into the narrow booth.

"Sure. I'll have whatever, just as long as it's not
tofu."

"Don't worry; tofu's a dirty word in this place."

"My kind of restaurant then," I said, as a waitress
appeared with menus. Rossi waved them aside and
instead spoke rapid-fire Korean. The waitress scribbled and disappeared.

I felt Rossi's eyes appraising me. She said, "Your file photo doesn't do you justice, Special Agent. They either spent a lot of money on retouching it or the light here isn't doing you any favors."

"Thanks," I said. The light had nothing to do with it. My left hand was bandaged and the skin around both eyes and left cheek was alternating between purple and yellow. At least most of the stiffness and soreness from my forced stay in Pakistan had left my body. Basically, I looked worse than I felt. The waitress arrived with a couple of plastic bottles. "What's this?" I inquired.

"Beer," Rossi announced. "This is the way the locals like it. Doesn't look like beer. Come to think of it, doesn't taste much like beer, either."

I took a mouthful. Rossi was right on both counts.

"So, what happened to you?" she asked.

"I fell out of a plane without a chute."

She looked at me, took a sip of her beer, and said, "Don't want to say? Sweet, I can dig it."

I noticed she also had a silver stud in her tongue. "What's with all the body piercing?"

"The ones in my nose and my ear were for me. And this one," she said, poking out her tongue and rolling the stud back against her teeth, "this one's for my boyfriend." This seemed to quell our curiosity about each other, or maybe it was the arrival of the food that did it. The waitress slid the steaming bowls onto our table. "So, what about Chalmers?" I said. "Will he be joining us?"

"No, don't think so."

"Because?"

"Because something's come up."

"You wanna spare me the twenty questions, Ms. Rossi?" I said.

"We got confirmation twenty minutes ago. The package has turned up in Bangkok. The Company is working with the Thais, keeping them under surveillance. We have to leave."

"When?" I asked.

She looked at her watch, then said, "Put it this way. Forget dessert."

FIFTY-ONE

I was wrong about the world having frozen over. In the town of Mae Sot, a flyspeck up on the western border Thailand shares with Burma, the night air was hot, moist, and heavy, like inhaling soup. It had rained earlier, a rain so heavy it could have been a shower of polished nickels. Now the rainwater was evaporating, the eternal cycle on the upswing. I took a deep breath and caught the scent of lemongrass. I gave my eyes a rest from the monochrome picture presented by the SpecterIR scope and glanced up at the night sky. It was the color of black coffee and starless except for a constellation of flickering orange stars that reminded me—if I was to get poetic about it—of a snake coiling languidly.

"Beautiful, aren't they?" said Rossi, putting a bowl of something on the table, which explained the smell of lemongrass in the air.

"What are?"

"Those lights. They're candles carried up there by bags of hot air. The adults send them up as a tribute to Buddha," said Rossi. "The kids do it for fun."

I made a noncommittal noise in the darkness that surrounded us. In this business, I found it was sometimes easy to forget that most people actually did lead normal lives.

We had around ten minutes of moonlight left. Once it set, darkness would be total. I turned the scope back on the villa across the valley. If Mae Sot wasn't the last place on earth you'd expect the fate of the world could be decided, there weren't too many below it on the list. "Do you have any thoughts on why here?" I asked.

"Why here what?" she replied.

"Why would they choose this place to make the exchange?"

Rossi thought a moment before answering. "It's not really so unlikely. Not far from here is the Freedom Bridge. Across it, over the Moei River in the Burmese town of Myawadee, I'm told several high-ranking North Korean army officers have estates given to them as payment for helping Rangoon modernize, train, and arm their military. Our intel says one of these North Korean officers might be brokering the deal."

"Okay, but why couldn't it be hammered out in Bangkok, or Seoul, or even Pyongyang?"

In the receding moonlight, Rossi was rapidly becoming no more than a faint gray shape. I could imagine her shoulders rising and falling with a shrug, but I couldn't see them. "Maybe Butler or Boyle or one of the Koreans doesn't like Bangkok. Or maybe it's not suitable for the same reason Seoul isn't—too many agents from the wrong side hanging around. And as for Pyongyang—if I had something the North Koreans wanted badly, I wouldn't go anywhere near the place, at least not until the terms of the deal had been thrashed out. Those North Koreans don't play fair. And then there's the fact that this area is famous for gem and drug smuggling. People here don't see a thing and haven't for years, if you know what I mean. Or maybe I'm wrong on all counts. And why ask me anyway? I just work here."

In my opinion, Rossi had made fooling people into believing she didn't know much into an art form. It was an effective disguise. I warned myself not to take her for granted.

"Well, I believe it's time for my watch," she said. "And I bought you some food. Any movement over there?"

"No," I replied. "Do we know yet who owns that villa?"

"Some big-shot local fisherman has his name on the paperwork—rented out two weeks ago to a dummy company in Bangkok owned by a South Korean import/export corporation, which is probably a front for North Korean interests."

"Sounds sketchy," I said.

"Yeah," agreed Rossi.

The reality was that we weren't sure who was in that villa. The local CIA station believed it had spotted Boyle, Butler, and another Westerner, who could have been Dortmund, at a Muay Thai tournament in Bangkok two days before. But supposedly positive identifications of Boyle, Butler, and Dortmund had

also since been made in Belfast, Rio, Mexico City, and
Hong Kong.

"What does the colonel want to do?" I asked.

"Storm the place. Or bomb it. Or maybe bomb it
then storm it."

Colonel Samjai Ratipakorn from the Royal Thai
Airborne Regiment was ostensibly in charge. It was
his country, after all. But he'd been leaned on heavily
to take advice from CIA—Rossi and Chalmers. Ratipakorn didn't like it, especially given that Rossi was a
woman and Chalmers was an asshole, but he didn't
have much choice. At least Chalmers hadn't made
the car trip up from Bangkok—according to Rossi,
Chalmers was strictly a rear-echelon jackass.

Colonel Ratipakorn headed up the Thai antiterror
forces. He stood about five and a half feet tall in his
boots and had less fat on him than a Thai free-range
chicken. I knew this because his uniform fit like a seventies body shirt. He never removed his Ray-Ban Avi-
ator sunglasses, even at night. I hadn't seen him
smile, either, and he didn't so much talk as yap. Like
most Thais, he was Buddhist. Maybe in a former life,
he was a chihuahua.

The hut Rossi and I were occupying was one of half
a dozen scattered around the valley. It wasn't the closest to the villa we were staking out, but not the furthest
away, either. It was small with an enclosed veranda, a
bedroom with a double bed and two singles, a kitch-
enette, and a bathroom barely big enough for a generous Western-sized butt. A squad of Ratipakorn's
heavily armed antiterror specialists was standing by,

suited up and ready to roll three hundred yards up and over the ridge behind us.

"Hang on," I said. "Movement."

"What you got?" asked Rossi, moving catlike across to the other side of the window and settling behind the thermal camera.

"How do you do that?" I asked.

"Do what."

"Move without making a sound?"

"I float," she said.

I watched as a huge Asian guy in a shiny suit opened a shutter on a double window, and scoped the trees from left to right. Behind him, I caught a glimpse of another sumo-sized guy, also in a polished suit.

"Shit," I said. "There he is."

"There who is?"

"The man seated with his back to us. You ever seen a worse haircut in your life? That's Sean Boyle."

Rossi answered by reeling off a couple of dozen snaps for the CIA photo album, and then said, "Jesus, that's really him, isn't it?"

"Yup."

"You sure?"

"No doubt in my mind."

"What do you make of the muscle?"

"Gotta be North Korean. They're the only country who get their suit patterns from old *Dallas* episodes. Get a load of those shoulder pads."

I heard Rossi snort in a delicate Eurasian-beauty kind of way. "You should be on the stage, Cooper."

"You think?"

"Yeah, the first stage out of town."

"We should pass on the positive ID to Ratipakorn so that he can do his thing," I said.

"No, not yet. You know he'll just charge straight in there."

"Isn't that what we want?" I asked.

"We first want to make sure everyone's present and accounted for. We don't know yet whether Mr. Big is there."

"No, we don't," I agreed. "Who's Mr Big?"

"The guy they're waiting around to meet."

Rossi paused to take another look through the scope. "Like I said, it's my watch. You've been at this four hours now. Why don't you catch a little sack time, Cooper. If anything happens, I'll wake you."

I didn't need to hear the suggestion twice. "Okay, the Starship Enterprise is yours." I got up and stretched. Then I left the veranda, leaving behind the food. I needed sleep more than I needed noodle soup. I lay back on the double bed fully clothed and counted the lumps in the mattress...

*   *   *

My eyes came open with a start.

I tried to lower my arms and realized I couldn't. I tried to pull them down but all I got was the sound of a rattling chain. "Hey, what the...Have you cuffed me to the bed?"

"See what happens when you bring sex toys to a stakeout," Rossi said as she walked out of the bathroom. I moved the cuff chain around the headboard and realized pretty much immediately I wasn't going anywhere in a hurry. Shit! I wished I'd followed my own advice not to take this woman for granted. The darkness hung like coal soot in a bunker. I couldn't see Rossi but I sensed her presence nearby. A small flashlight came on, its bloodred light peeling away the blackness in a cone in front of her face. She was kneeling on the floor, the flashlight in her mouth. I noticed she'd changed into black, urban assault-style gear. She didn't even glance in my direction and was leaning over a rectangular box that I didn't remember seeing among her gear. Rossi opened it, unfastening two clips, and pulled out a long length of pipe—a barrel, in fact—and began to assemble a rifle.

"What are you doing?" I said, asking the first truly dumb question of the day. I knew it was dumb on a number of levels, the least obvious being that I suddenly knew this was Rossi's mission—to kill.

"My job," she replied, not looking up.

"Then what was mine?" I had believed—or been led to believe—that it was to assist the Thais in taking Boyle, Butler, and Dortmund into custody, so that they could then be extradited to the States to face an array of charges, and then spend the rest of their miserable lives in prison. Instead, I would be a witness to a state-sponsored execution.

"Probably not what you think."

"Then set me straight."

"Positive identification. You'd actually met the package. You pointed him out to me—confirmed the target's ID. That was your job. Mine's to show him the exit."

"I didn't realize the CIA was still in the assassination game."

"Don't use that word."

"What, assassination?"

"No—game. My mother's maiden name was Tanaka. Ring a bell?"

Yeah, it did. "Dr. Tanaka didn't have a daughter."

"No. But he had a sister," said Rossi.

"You were his niece?" I tried to remember the briefing in D.C. What had Chalmers said about Rossi? That she had an Italian American father and a Japanese mother?

"As part of my briefing, I got a look at your case notes on the investigation into Hideo's death. Uncle and I—we were close. I think I was the only person he had any kind of relationship with. He had a problem with people. He liked fish."

"What sort of problem?"

"It's not that he didn't like people. He just couldn't handle them. Some sort of phobia. You probably wouldn't understand."

"Try me."

"He would sweat, feel sick—look, I don't have time for this now."

A people phobia. That didn't stack up against Dr. Spears's claim that she and Tanaka had been buddies. "Did he ever mention anyone aside from Professor Boyle at Moreton Genetics? A Dr. Spears, maybe?"

"Who? Not that I remember."

Killing people in cold blood for a paycheck isn't easy. It helps if the killer is a psychopath, or a religious fanatic, or if the target has somehow been dehumanized. None of these profiles fit Rossi. But if she knew how her uncle had died and who'd helped him on his way . . . well, revenge was also a powerful motivator when it came to killing someone. And the CIA was a master at leverage—it would use whatever it could get. I watched her mate the barrel to the trigger mechanism with oiled proficiency. They came together with a *click*. Rossi was no novice.

"I thought Hellfire missiles were the preferred assassination weapon these days," I remarked.

"Burma stopped throwing ordnance across the border at the refugee camps here years ago. Langley figured a bullet would be easier to hide."

"I was told you learned your skills in the Marines."

"Two tours in Iraq."

"I didn't think the Marines used female snipers."

"They don't, not usually. But then, I'm not usual."

I didn't buy the Marines legend, although I was sure she would have all the right paperwork to support it. Nope, Rossi was a Company creation, through and through.

She slid a five-power day/night scope onto the rail, pulled back the bolt, cocking it, flicked the safety off, and checked the action. The firing pin smacked into its seat with a metallic ring that seemed to hang suspended in the darkness beyond the red spill of the flashlight. I watched her feed the magazine into its slot after checking each round.

"So what about all that crap you gave me about waiting for a Mr. Big?"

"There's only one Mr. Big here—Boyle. His is the only scalp the Company wants. You can't un-invent technology, Vin, which is why Boyle's secrets have to die with him." Rossi stood. "No one wants this genie of his let out of the bottle. No one wants what he's selling in anyone's arsenal—not even ours, not anymore." The rifle was almost as big as she was, but Rossi had its measure—resting it comfortably balanced in the crook of her arm, muzzle pointing toward the ceiling. "You're probably wondering what's going to happen here—to you."

I was. "Now that you mention it."

"In the morning, Ratipakorn's people will find you. You'll be handcuffed to the bed, which weighs a ton, by the way."

"How does Chalmers think this will play when I get back to the States?"

"Think about it, Cooper. Boyle is already dead, remember? He died in the fire at the Four Winds. Deputy Station Chief Chalmers told me you were there when he took possession of Boyle's wallet. No one will seriously believe that whole mess in San Francisco was merely a smokescreen created by Pakistan's new revolutionary government to cover Boyle's disappearance. And no one will believe that he died twice, either. As for the North Koreans, they won't make a peep. And the Thais are on our side. Why do you think they're pulled back behind the ridge? Nothing happened here. This op is as black as it gets."

Jesus, the damned wallet. I kicked myself for not putting it all together sooner. The lump of charcoal that was supposed to be Professor Boyle, his lightly charred wallet found beneath it. I'd known it wasn't Boyle from the start, but that wallet's presence had been a real puzzle. The Pakistanis couldn't have planted it there. That had to have been someone else's doing. Now I had a pretty good idea who that someone was.

"This operation falls under the subhead of mopping up." Rossi pulled a ski mask over her head, stuffed two extra magazines into thigh pockets, and threw a small pack over a shoulder. "Gotta go. Duty calls." The flashlight beam disappeared, and she with it. A handful of red and orange floaters drifted downward in the blackness. I strained my ears to hear her moving around, but heard nothing. I suddenly felt her lips brush light as a feather against mine, her breath sweet like cinnamon. "Bye, Vin," she whispered. "It's been real."

I saw the door open and caught her silhouette move against the black and grays of the night beyond the hut. The door closed and I was again dipped in total darkness.

"Fuck, shit, fuck!" I said, frustration dialing up the volume on those words so that they escaped louder than I'd intended. I rolled off the bed onto my knees beside it. I used my teeth to push the button on my watch, to illuminate the face. The time was 0505. The predawn light would soon throw a pink blush into the clouds.

The watch's illumination switched off automatically after ten seconds. I bit down on the button again, and used the glow to assess my situation. The bed's headboard was steel pipe, painted, with warts of rust poking through here and there. I used my weight to try to drag the bed across the floor toward me. It was a heavy fucker, but I was able to shift it a few inches. The legs squealed against the concrete floor like stuck pigs. The watch's blue glow went out. I sparked it up with another bite. I noted that the base and headboard were not bolted together. One slotted into the other, and the joins were caked in balls of rust. The light went out again, but I didn't need it on to know what I had to do. I pulled the bed out as far as I could from the wall. I got down low and lifted it up like I was doing a clean and jerk. After a couple of tries, I managed to get it up so that it pivoted around the legs on the far side, and held it on the balance point. Feeling with my fingers, I made sure the chain between the cuffs wasn't going to get hung up on anything and break my wrists when I pushed the bed over. When I was satisfied, I let it fall. The bed crashed hard against the wall and floor simultaneously, pulling me with it, and, despite my caution, practically jerking my arms out of their sockets. I toppled blind into a tangle of screeching metal, barking my shins and head-butting something with an edge on it.

I lay on the floor, dazed, listening to my breathing, tangled up with springs and braces, the copper taste of blood in my mouth from a cut somewhere on my head. The sound of crashing metal echoed in my ears and through my brain. Silence closed around me in waves and, when it finally arrived, the hum of a lone mosquito came with it.

Though surely no more than a minute had passed, a little morning light had managed to push through under the eaves and turn the room into a collection of shapes that shimmered like images in old grainy black-and-white photographs. Bottom line, I could now at least see the outlines of things. My wrists were still cuffed to the headboard, which had separated from the rest of the frame. I stumbled to my feet, feeling vaguely nauseated, and hoisted the headboard out of the wreckage.

FIFTY-TWO

I didn't have much time. Rossi was working with the dark. I had to get to her before the sunlight did if I was to stop her killing Boyle. I wanted him arrested and behind bars, not dead. The bush was coming alive with the sound of various unseen animals sparking up to embrace the new day. I noticed when Rossi had assembled the rifle that it was suppressed. Even so, it would still make a muffled crack when she sent a round humming toward Boyle's skull. So far, I'd heard nothing of that nature.

As I moved, I thought about where Rossi might set up. Logically, she'd take a position that'd provide an unobstructed view of the villa, as well as cover. That meant the high side of the valley. I had nothing else to go on. I worked my way around, climbing, hoping to stumble across her, wrestling the headboard through what was mostly scrub, alternately dragging, ripping, and carrying it through the dense foliage.

After fifteen minutes of this, through a small clearing up ahead I saw a ledge formed by an old fallen tree. I scoped the area down to the villa. It was an obvious hide for a sniper, providing a clear, unobstructed line of fire to the target 2300 feet across the valley. Fish-in-the-barrel distance for a trained sniper like Rossi. I took the last hundred and fifty feet slowly and quietly, coaxing some cooperation from the hundred pounds of steel pipes tucked under my arm. What I found when I finally arrived at the ledge didn't make my list of ten-things-most-likely.

Two Koreans—one I recognized, one I didn't—were standing in the small clearing. They'd swapped their suits for Adidas warm-up pants and T-shirts. I thought maybe they were out for their morning jog or something. I wondered where Rossi was. Perhaps this wasn't such a great hide for a sniper after all and she was elsewhere lining up Boyle in her crosshairs.

Then one of the Koreans, the one I recognized, did something that seemed odd. He took a turnip out of his pants. At least I thought it was a turnip—it was long, pale, and thin. That's when I saw Rossi. She was lying at his feet, the rifle kicked off its bipod. The other Korean rolled her over onto her stomach with his toe like she was roadkill. Her head lolled to one side. She was unconscious. The Korean kneeled and began cutting off her jumpsuit with a pocketknife, slitting the seams up the inside of her legs.

The Korean holding his turnip glanced over his shoulder and spotted me even before I began to move. There was no time to consider strategy. I charged forward out of the bush into the clearing, dragging the headboard. The man on the ground kneeling over Rossi went for a gun I saw tucked in the small of his back. I spun around like a discus thrower as I stumbled forward, and swung the headboard. It strained at the Smith & Wessons as it accelerated through the arc, rapidly gaining speed and momentum. Perhaps they'd never been assaulted by a man wielding half a bed before, because both men were standing openmouthed with surprise when the collection of rusting steel piping caught them full in their faces. The crunch of breaking teeth and bone was underpinned, if I wasn't mistaken, by an almost perfect middle C.

FIFTY-THREE

I stood panting and sweating, the Koreans and Rossi all tangled at my feet. Rossi was beginning to stir. She rolled slowly onto her back with a groan. Her left eye was bruised and swollen and there were two rivulets of blood flowing from both nostrils. The asswipes had busted her nose. She spat blood. Said asswipes also began to move, and that was a surprise. After the clout I'd given them, I fully expected them to be counting stars for another half hour at least. I figured they were either a couple of tough hombres, or stupid. I tossed a mental coin on the question and, based on the theory of no-pain-no-brain, came up with stupid.

Situation awareness dawned on Rossi slowly at first, and then with a rush when she saw the Korean's naked, spotty, twig-plastered butt and her pants sliced up. She stood uneasily, trying to find her balance, her fists clenched into tight balls, the skin on her knuckles white with the pressure.

"Rossi," I said, hoping for some acknowledgment. I got none. My instinct was to ask her whether she was OK, but I knew she was OK so that would have been trite. I'd come to the conclusion that Rossi only *looked* like a woman, a handy disguise in her line of work. A millimeter below that feminine exterior I believed she had all the warmth of a razor strop. "The keys. Where are they?" I asked her instead, holding my cuffed wrists toward her.

I didn't need to be a clairvoyant to see Rossi wanted to kill someone, maybe even me. Her eyes were flat, and it wasn't with shock. I didn't even think she'd heard my question. Her small pack was at my feet, so I picked it up, undid the zip, and shook out the contents: underpants, toiletries, a little makeup, and a couple of keys attached to a familiar Michelin Man key ring. My keys for the S&Ws. I unlocked the cuffs and transferred them to the Koreans' wrists. One of the men was attempting to sit up. He was groggy and spitting bits of tooth, gum, clotted blood, and mucus onto the ground between his legs. He was still a long way from giving trouble. I patted him and his buddy down. Both had binoculars, walkie-talkies, Colt .45s—my personal favorite—and a couple of spare magazines to go with them. I examined the pistols quickly. Their front sights were ground off and the magazines for both were full. I stuffed one of the weapons in the back of my pants and the other in a pocket with the spare magazines. Stupid they may have been, but I had no doubt these guys were professional enough to have radioed their observations back to base before approaching Rossi's hide too closely. I stomped on the walkie-talkies. The sets were no more than kids' toys and they shattered into chunks of plastic and printed circuit board.

"Borrow these? Thanks," I said, taking a pair of binoculars and not waiting for permission to be granted. I brought the lenses into focus on the villa. The image of Sean Boyle danced and shook with my adrenaline-charged breathing. I caught the last moments of my target being stuffed into the back of a black Lexus 4x4 by a clone of the two boys by my feet who, I noted absently, were now easily distinguished from him by the orthodontic work I'd just performed with what turned out to be a hundred-and-twenty-pound tuning fork. "They've made us," I told Rossi. "Boyle is on the move." I wasn't too concerned. There was only one road out. Colonel Ratipakorn would head them off at the pass, access blocked by a couple of Humvees topped with Mr. Browning's gift to the world—big, black fifty-caliber machine guns. Through the binoculars, I followed the vehicle as it bounced and rocked over the rough dirt road hacked through the bush on the valley floor. But where the ribbon of gray dirt cut through the green scrub and turned left, the 4x4 went straight ahead, cutting its own path. No. More likely, it was following a private road that wasn't on any map. "Shit," I said.

Behind me, I heard Rossi shout something I didn't recognize as being English. I turned in time to see her point the rifle at one of the Koreans' feet. I saw the barrel recoil and heard the *bang* and a couple of the guy's toes disappeared in a spray of atomized red mist that drifted across his buddy. The big man screamed. Rossi slid back the bolt like she had all the time in the world and then moved it forward, chambering another round. The injured guy rocked back, screaming in an animal kind of way, holding his shattered foot in the air. His tracksuit pants slid down his leg, revealing skin that had gone white with shock, the black hairs raised. His foot didn't start bleeding right away. The muscle fibers in the exposed flesh quivered.

Rossi altered her aim, burying the suppressor on the end of the long barrel in the pubic hair of the man's crotch, at the base of his now shrunken turnip. She asked whatever she'd asked before, only politely this time, confident of getting the right answer.

The man blubbered something, his formerly narrow almond eyes now as wide as any I'd ever seen.

"The airport," said Rossi, translating. "That's where they're going."

"You see how far a little politeness will get you?" I replied.

Rossi shrugged. I doubt her pulse cracked sixty. She could've been buttering bread for all the emotion she exhibited. "Now, before I blow off this guy's dick, did he touch me with it?" She nudged his penis with the steel finger of the suppressor. He whimpered.

I shook my head. "No."

I saw the slightest movement in her trigger finger. The guy saw it too and cried out. Rossi hesitated. She could pull the trigger. She could turn the weapon on me. She could start singing "Rhinestone Cowboy." She could also remove the suppressor from the Korean's crotch, which was in fact what she chose to do. The movement was reluctant, like it took considerable willpower. If I hadn't have been a witness, she might well have taken another option, and it wouldn't have been the karaoke one.

"We can leave these guys here—they're not going anywhere." I recuffed them after feeding one end of the S&Ws through the bars of the headboard. Between its bulk and the fact that they only had eighteen and a half toes between them, I was reasonably sure on that point.

I turned my back on Rossi and the Koreans and jogged back into the bush, heading to the stakeout hut. I wondered where Boyle and Butler were really going. The airport was crawling with Royal Thai Airborne troops. Their most likely destination had to be toward the soft mud banks of the Moei River, which weren't more than a thousand feet from the villa they'd been occupying. It'd be easy for them to have planned for a back-door exit, take a boat across to Burma, and vanish into the teak forests. Smugglers had supposedly beaten that very same path to bare earth.

The going on the way down was much easier than climbing up. Through my own footfalls and a cloud of mosquitoes humming furiously around my head, I could hear Rossi close behind. The sun was up, which meant there was plenty of light to see. I stopped to get bearings. And then I heard something else, something familiar, but I had no idea where it was coming from. Suddenly, a Humvee burst from the bush not fifty feet away. The driver swerved to avoid me. Another followed close behind. It was a posse of Colonel Ratipakorn's people joining the chase. So much for keeping station behind the ridge. Despite what they told us, the Thais must have had their own forward observers keeping an eye on developments.

Rossi overtook me on the trail, trotting effortlessly along, holding her rifle by its handle. She disappeared around a bend. Our hut was maybe two hundred feet away. I stood and listened to the Humvees as they smashed their way through the foliage, until the sound faded into the background. I was pretty stiff and sore. I'd walk the rest of the way. And then I heard the gunshots up ahead.

FIFTY-FOUR

I broke into a run. I slowed only when our stakeout hut came into view. The gunshots came from inside. I stopped at the edge of the cleared area, dropped to the ground, listened and watched. Nothing. The hut was dark and quiet. I considered how to approach it. If the people inside had the angle right, they'd be able to see me coming while I wouldn't be able to see squat.

My hand went automatically for the butt of the pistol in my pocket. It felt good, reassuring, a friend. I massaged my palm against the roughness of the checkering on the handgrip while I figured out a plan. I didn't have much to work with. I had no radio, no backup. I removed the Colt and gave it the once-over. All the blueing seemed intact. My thumb found the safety and satisfied itself that the weapon wasn't going to go off unexpectedly. I popped the clip. Seven rounds plus one in the chamber—.357 semi wad cutters. Make a hell of mess of someone. WCs reduced the weapon's effective range. And they didn't so much as put holes in you as turn you inside out. The choice of ammunition said something about the guy who packed this weapon—the word "fuckhead" came to mind. Perhaps the Korean assholes now sharing a headboard back up the valley weren't soldiers. I pulled back the slide. It was a well-oiled, well-maintained piece. The ground-away front sight...now, that was the sort of modification someone who regularly pulled a gun from a holster would make. I wondered how many tickets this piece had punched. Perhaps the owners of these weapons were bad asses from North Korea's Research Department for External Intelligence. NK's CIA equivalent. Who or what was inside our hut? More RDEI hitmen?

I'd heard two shots and they hadn't come from the same weapon. One, I was reasonably sure, had come from Rossi's. It had made a sound like a phone book smacked with a broom handle. The kind of sound a suppressed weapon might make. The other shot made a straight-out *bang*—a handgun sound, not unlike the one warming up my right hand would make when it went off.

There was no way to approach the hut except through the front door, which wasn't even a door. The windows were too high, and there was no way to get under the floor on account of it was a concrete slab poured onto the earth. I doubted the roof would take my weight. Even if it could, there was no way up there other than by pole-vaulting and, typically, I'd gone and left my vaulting pole in my other pair of pants.

The front entrance was it. No other option than to walk straight up and press the doorbell. I approached from an angle, running crouched over. It was quiet, too damn quiet. I figured whoever was inside wanted me inside with them. I sat down against the side of the hut, adjacent to the opening, and counted to three before rushing it. I thumbed off the safety, cocked the hammer. *Click*.

One . . . two . . . three . . .

I went in low. I managed to get three paces into the main room—the bedroom—before what I saw made me stop dead.

"You just won't fuckin' die, Cooper, will you?" It was Butler. He was sitting on one of the beds. There was a smile on his face. I could almost have believed he was happy to see me, except for the Glock 17 in his hand pointed straight at me. Curled up on the bed beside him was Sean Boyle, groaning. From the position the professor was lying in and the sounds he was making, I was reasonably sure it wasn't food poisoning. The blood oozing from a stomach wound was also a dead giveaway. His face was squeezed into a grimace. On the floor, beside the entrance to the bathroom, lay Rossi. She wasn't moving. There was a lot of blood on the floor beneath her face and neck. It was seeping out of her chest, which told me her heart was still pumping. She was alive. Only, for how much longer?

"How the fuck did you survive the fuckin' fall? Sprout fuckin' wings or something?" Butler asked, shaking his head.

"I think you should put the gun down," I said. I had the .45 in a two-handed assault grip, Butler's nose bobbing in the space where the front sight would have been. I thought about the last time we'd been face-to-face, dropping through the troposphere at one hundred and twenty miles per hour and him sawing through my chute harness. Oh yeah, I wanted to squeeze a couple of pounds of pressure into that trigger finger.

"And why should I do that?" he asked.

"Because otherwise I'm gonna have to give you a really bad nose job."

The professor moved a little and cried out in pain.

"He looks bad," I said. "Doesn't sound too good, either."

"Thank your friend for that," Butler said, with a nod at Rossi. "She walked in on us. Shot him, just like that. So I shot her. The prof will live, even if it's with only one kidney. As for the bird, you shagging her?" Butler changed target. He swung his arm and lowered his hand so that the gun pointed at the back of Rossi's head. "You should. She's got a wicked arse *and* she can handle a gun. Makes me horny just thinking about it. She's alive, but one more bullet—not even a well-aimed one—would probably finish her off. Lost a lot of blood, as you can see. I think it'd be a shame myself, but the call's yours."

"Where's Dortmund?" I asked.

"He let us off down the road. At the moment he's taking a tour group to the airport. With any luck, he'll be along later." I pictured Dortmund behind the wheel of the Lexus, Ratipakorn's machine-gun-toting Humvees in hot pursuit smashing through the jungle.

"How did you know which hut we were in?" I

asked. I was playing for time, hoping some interesting plan might pop into my head. Also, I was genuinely interested to know, just in case I ever had to do something like this again.

"I don't get it with you, Cooper. You're here, which says you're good at some things, though only God knows what, exactly. Maybe it's just being able to stay alive. Anyway, it's like this: There are nine huts scattered up the hillside. All except three were lit up at night. So either these unlit huts were unoccupied, or occupied by people who didn't use lights. We'd reconnoitered two of the darkened huts. They were empty. That left yours. According to my new Korean pals, there seemed to be movement coming from inside. Now, when people move around in the dark without turning on any lights, there's usually a good reason, isn't there?"

Yeah, I thought. Good point, even if it was made by a patronizing Limey shithead.

"Our patrol came across your friend here, and called it in. We just put it all together and dropped in to say hello . . . Hello."

"You're pretty relaxed about things," I said, annoyed at my own tactical stupidity. Goddamn it, it's not easy sneaking up on the SAS—that's why they're the SAS. "I get the feeling you think you're just going to walk on out of here."

"Actually, sunshine, I think that's exactly what I'm going to do."

"And I'm just going to let you?"

"You won't have a choice."

"And why is that?"

"Because you're going to be dead, Cooper. That's why I'm here."

"You came back, just to kill me?"

"Had to. Had three good reasons to."

"You need three?"

Butler smiled like he was enjoying himself. "Pride. I wanted to prove to myself that killing you could, in fact, be done. Also, it's clear you just won't give it a rest until I do. And finally, I promised a mutual friend. So there you go—had to."

"We have a mutual friend who wants me dead?" A mutual friend? I was glad whoever it happened to be wasn't an enemy. Who could that be? Boyle groaned.

"Don't for a moment think I'm going to tell you who," Butler said. "I've said too much already. I'm going to enjoy sending you off to hell guessing. So, what's it going to be, Cooper? Shall I put a bullet in your friend here, or do you want to give her a fighting chance?"

I didn't have a whole lot of choice. My arms, stretched out in front of me, were beginning to cramp. I glanced at Rossi. She was continuing to lose blood. She needed a hospital and she needed one now.

I nodded.

"So, what? I just surrender?" I asked.

"We put our guns down and we go at it, hand to hand, man to man. Remember this?" He kept his gun on Rossi, I kept my gun on him. Mexican standoff. His moves were slow, deliberate, and very careful. I shuffled into the room a little further and took a couple of

steps off to the side. I didn't want Dortmund, if he arrived, coming up behind me. Butler reached under a
fold in a bedcover and pulled out a long, slender, and
very lethal blade. Yeah, I recognized it all right. Ruben
Wright's Fairbairn-Sykes.

"You been going through my gear?" I asked.

"What can I say?" he said with a shrug. "I'm bad."
He held the blade up and read out the inscription on
it. "And the American Way." He glanced from Rossi to
me. " 'Truth, Justice, and the American Way.' Wright
was a right bloody nutcase, he was. The twerp really
thought he was Superman. I couldn't believe it. He
even had that dumb *S* symbol tattooed on his shoulder, remember?"

I remembered.

Another snort. "I used his own knife to cut him out
of his harness. I wonder if he was surprised to discover he couldn't fly."

I didn't say anything. Butler was reminiscing. So
was I. In fact I was reminiscing about him doing the
same thing to me.

"I was fucking his bird senseless because he couldn't
get it up anymore. Some Superman. I don't think he
liked it much, me fucking his missus. But Amy did. She
was a screamer. Couldn't get enough pork sausage, if
you know what I mean. There was nowhere we didn't
fuck, and I'm not talking about venues."

"So what do you want, Butler? Seen too much?
Can't take it anymore? Looking for a nice retreat in a
closed country where they hang people up by their
toenails?"

Butler's eyes narrowed. "Let me answer that by asking you what you're going to do when your government decides it's time for you to retire?"

"Become a marriage counselor—I've got it all figured out. But before then, I've got a nice set of nylon cuff ties in my bag. You probably saw them when you were going through my gear. I'd like you to just slip a pair on."

"I don't know about you, Cooper, but nothing I've done or been involved in over the years has made half a snot's bloody difference. I've seen brave men killed and cowards win. I've helped monsters get rewarded and had a hand in taking down good men. The heroes I know aren't anything more than PR fantasies—creations for recruitment drives. None of it has meant shit at the end of the day, none of it. I want something for all the hard work, for the failed missions, and for the ones that came off. I've risked, and now I want return. Something more than a pension—"

"I'm not sure what you're selling, but I'm not buying, Butler. You killed a buddy of mine. You tried to kill me the same way. And the people who pay my salary don't like you all that much, either."

"What is it you Yanks say? Wise up? You look like you've been around the block yourself a few times, Cooper. You know the score."

He was right, I did know the score. And mostly it was 10–0 in the other guy's favor. But that's life, isn't it? I'd never known it any different. Not when I was a kid growing up in Shit Hole, New Jersey. Not in my first marriage. Not now. It'd be great if it was different.

But it never would be. For some reason, I thought of Anna and the fact that she was now seeing some JAG lawyer. Yeah, 10–0 in the other guy's favor all the way. "So you're overworked and underpaid. Join the human race," I said. "But, before you do, put down the gun and the knife."

"Do it your way, and the girl dies, no question," said Butler. "Do it mine and she might live. Depends on whether you're up to the challenge." He raised Ruben's dagger in his right hand, like he was going to throw it at me. I crouched, bracing to shoot him, arms tensed. He lowered the blade and tossed it across the rough concrete floor. It clattered to a stop by my front foot. I picked it up, moving slow, not taking my eyes or gun off Butler.

Butler pulled his own knife from a scabbard attached to his thigh. He held it up, giving me a good look. If I wasn't shitting myself, I might have been impressed. The weapon was a variation of a Ka-Bar military combat knife, though it was longer and meaner than any Ka-Bar I'd ever seen. It had to be around sixteen inches in length. The blade was hollow ground, tapered carbon steel that came to an end in a fanglike swept tip. One edge was serrated, the other honed sharp enough for a surgeon.

"I pop the girl in the head, or you and I resolve our differences hand to hand. You've got five seconds to decide, Cooper. One."

I hesitated.

"Two."

I had a clear shot. If I took it, would Butler still be able to squeeze off a round into Rossi's brainpan?

"Three."

Could his trigger finger beat the bullet, a simple muscle contraction that—

"Four."

I didn't like Rossi—her profession, her organization, or her methods—but that really didn't matter. I had no options.

"Five."

I said, "You first. Gun down."

"That's the problem with the world today—no trust."

"Nope."

"We do it together," he said. "Our pieces go on the floor. Put your foot on it, kick it toward that corner." He indicated which corner with the point of his chin. "Make sure it goes all the way there."

I bent at the knees and put the Colt on the floor, mirroring Butler's moves. Removing my hand from the grip felt like saying good-bye to a buddy. Butler and I stood up, each with a foot on a handgun. We both kicked at the same time and the weapons tumbled together with a clatter into the corner and came to rest there.

My breathing was short and sharp. Sweat soaked my armpits and ran down my forehead. My pulse throbbed in my temples. Every sense was heightened. A couple of mosquitoes hummed somewhere close. Being a federal agent, I'd removed plenty of weapons from the hands of unwilling servicemen over the years. Most of them had had a skinful at the time, or didn't know what they were doing, like Boris and his baseball bat back at Elmer's sporting goods store. Disarming Butler would be a completely different proposition. SAS guys knew how to use a knife. He proved me right by holding the blade so that the steel ran back down the inside of his wrist and forearm. There was no way either of us could get out of this without being cut. I just had to hope that, in my case at least, it wouldn't be anywhere vital. There was a good chance we'd end up killing each other—our own personal Mutually Assured Destruction. I swapped the dagger to my right hand and crouched, poised. Butler did the same.

Sean Boyle groaned. Rossi shifted her weight a couple of inches.

A dribble of sweat rolled down Butler's forehead, ran into another droplet, and gained speed. An instant later it hit another droplet, accelerated, and fell into his eye socket. He blinked. I thrust. Not a slash. No back swing. More of a jab. He caught it, steel on steel. Tang to tang. No advantage. We disengaged. Separated.

I feinted to the left. He covered the movement, exposing his front leg. I kicked him in the thigh with my right shin, driving it into him with all my body weight. It was a heavy hit, but Butler shrugged it off, merely hopping on his good leg a couple of times as we came apart. At least I'd let him know it wasn't just the knife he had to watch out for.

Butler switched his blade to his left hand, letting

me know it wasn't just his right *I* had to watch out for.
He swung the knife at my face. I felt the change in air
pressure as the tip swept by an inch away from my
eyeballs.

Butler suddenly leapt toward me and tried the
same slash again. I moved into him this time, stepping
inside his range, and smashed my forearm down on
his arm as he brought it through. This inside move
caught him by surprise. His neck was exposed to an
elbow strike, but Butler was ready for it. He dropped
to the floor before I could hit him and he rolled away,
coming up in stance, perfectly balanced, ready to kill.
We moved in toward each other, circling. I thrust with
the Fairbairn-Sykes, hoping to open up his gut. Butler
moved, and I missed. My momentum carried me forward, a little out of control, and I slipped on my own
sweat. I fell forward. I tried to roll as Butler had, but
slipped again. Butler was all over me like cheap aftershave. He stabbed his knife down toward the back of
my head. I sensed this and moved. The point of his
knife tip slammed into the floor beside my cheek and
I felt a small concrete chip ping off my ear. I twisted
away and came up on my knees before he could repeat the thrust. Butler saw his opportunity. He
jumped forward and stood on the Fairbairn-Sykes,
jamming it against the floor under his boot. I was vulnerable to a slash across the body, which would have
opened me up like a ripped trash bag. I had no choice.
I caught the blow with my arm. His blade buried itself
deep in my deltoid, the muscle below the shoulder
ball joint, almost cutting through to the bone. Oddly,

I felt no pain. I watched it happen like it was someone else's arm. Butler ripped the knife out, cutting, tearing, and small hunks of muscle and skin clung to the knife's bloody serrations as he brought it away.

I fell back against the wall before he could bury the knife in my guts, the blood surging from the severed blood vessels in my arm. I had nowhere to go. Butler had my knife as well as his. He came toward me, grinning, waggling them—one in either hand as if to say, "Now, which one will I use to finish you off?"

I had no weapon, but I had a belt. The belt had a buckle on it. I struggled to my feet, unfastened it, and pulled it through the loops. A weight suddenly fell down through the inside of my pants and clattered onto the floor. I was so surprised I kicked it accidentally with my heel as I moved, and it flew across the floor. Goddamn it, the *second* .45 confiscated from the NK patrol, the one I'd jammed into the small of my back, held there by the belt. I'd completely forgotten about it. It spun into the pool of blood around Rossi. She suddenly lifted her head and picked it up. She had my full attention. Butler's, too. She thumbed off the safety. Aimed the gun. *Bang!* I opened my mouth. She shot Sean Boyle as he lay on the bed, clutching his stomach. The slug, a wad cutter, entered beneath his chin, smashing through his palate and turning the bone there into splinters that continued on through his brain, changing it to the consistency of mousse, and then blowing the top of his head clean off. Clumps of Boyle's brains spattered across Butler's face, momentarily blinding him.

I threw myself forward into Butler as he clawed the gray matter out of his eyes. My knee slammed into his ribcage and I felt it cave in like rotten wickerwork. We both fell backward and I came down on top of him, his Ka-Bar sliding away out of reach. He brought up his leg. That's when I saw the small-bore revolver in a holster strapped to his ankle. I reacted, kicking his leg away, but he was determined to get to his gun. Life. Or death. I went for his neck, wrapping my hands around it. His skin was slick with brains, which oozed between my fingers like gray mud as I squeezed. With the busted-up knuckles of my left hand, I couldn't get a grip. Strangling the guy wasn't an option so I used my elbow, mashing it into the side of his face, twisting his brain stem, giving him something to think about. Butler's head rolled about, but he was still conscious, still going for that goddamn gun.

I was exhausted. So was Butler. I kicked his leg away from his hand. I moved to hit him again. He moved his head to avoid my elbow, and that's when I saw Ruben's dagger—the Fairbairn-Sykes. It was under Butler, pressed between his body and the floor. I reached for the handle and pulled. It came away. The diversion gave Butler the chance to reach for his revolver.

I had no time to think about what I did next.

I slid the blade through his shirt, beneath his skin, between the bone fragments of his broken ribs. The cold steel blade sliced through small then large intestine. More pressure was needed to carve up through the tough muscle wall of his diaphragm. Butler gasped like he was wading into icy water. I heard the click as his thumb cocked back the hammer on his gun. I pushed up on the hilt, the blade's edge overcoming the resistance of muscle and tissue. *Bom-bom-bom*...I felt his pulse through the hilt when the tip of the dagger came to rest up against the wall of his throbbing heart. I was ready to call it quits. I didn't want Butler dead. I still had questions, and maybe this was the only guy left alive with the answers.

Butler's mouth was open, his eyes wide. I heard the gun he was holding clatter to the floor. I relaxed. Suddenly, I felt his hands on mine around the knife's handle, slick with blood, sweat, and brains. Tears streamed from the corners of his eyes. With a final burst of strength he drove the blade higher, deeper into himself. And then, transmitted through the steel, I felt his heart explode, impaled on the tip of Ruben Wright's Fairbairn-Sykes.

FIFTY-FIVE

When I got back home I spent a couple of days relaxing in a hospital bed, if such a thing is possible, while various people in white coats sewed me up, stuck me with hypodermics, and generally poked and prodded me. I told them there was nothing wrong with me that a few days off and a few servings of Kim's *bulgogi* couldn't fix, and even managed to get a cute nurse to go pick me up some takeout on my last night there.

Lying around with nothing to do except trouble the aforementioned nurse gave me time to put a few things together, and get some action happening on a few others. I needed to find out who Butler might have been referring to as "our mutual friend."

I gave Bradley Chalmers a lot of thought too and decided to make good on an earlier promise I made to myself to put him, Wu, and De Silver together for their mutual benefit. Assigned to that Senate oversight committee, Lieutenant Colonel Wayne was uniquely placed to help with this, if he was inclined to.

When they released me from the medical center, I went straight over to OSI.

"Yo, Vin, 'sup?" Arlen glanced up from his keyboard

when I walked in. He came around his desk, wearing a big smile, holding out his hand.

I held up my right hand where he could see it, but not shake it. It was bruised and swollen, and that was the good one. The left was in plaster, those knuckles finally getting the attention they deserved. "OK with you if we also skip the friendly, welcome-home pat on the arm?"

"Oh, right. I forgot. How many stitches?"

"Enough to knit a scarf."

"Shit . . . How's the CIA woman?"

"In bed with a drip."

"She hitched to a Company man?" said Arlen with a grin.

I looked at him.

"I know, I know. Sorry, Vin. Poor-taste humor. Been around you too long, I guess." His grin vanished as his eyes examined my face, taking in the damage. "You gotta stop putting your body on the line, buddy. You ain't gonna go the distance."

"That's for damn sure," I said.

"I kinda heard a little of what's been going on. You did an amazing job," he said, shaking his head.

I gave him half a smile, which probably looked as uncomfortable as it felt. I'm not great with compliments.

Arlen brightened and took a seat on the edge of his desk. "Got a call from a Lieutenant Colonel Clare Selwyn a couple of days back."

"Oh, yeah? Any message?"

"Sends her regards. Told me to tell you that local

law enforcement have taken one of the suspects into custody."

"Did she say who?"

Arlen checked a pad on his desk covered in graffiti and numbers. "A Juan Demelian. That's your Ruben Wright investigation, right?"

"Yeah. Selwyn say anything else?"

"Wants you to give her a call."

"OK." That was something I'd intended to do anyway.

"We've got all kinds of people from upstairs—starting with General Howerton—leaning on us for a written report."

"It's coming."

"How much time will you need?" he asked.

"Can you get me till the end of the week? Still got a loose end or two."

"See what I can manage, but don't count on it. And I got the note you sent through about the security-camera footage at the cafeteria. The bank statements you asked me to get have come through, too. All that have anything to do with those loose ends?"

"That's them," I said.

"Well, Pentagon Police's idea of security is not to let anyone look at anything, ever. Crude, but effective. I've been promised the disks will get here in about an hour. The proviso is that they're returned tomorrow oh-eight-hundred sharp, and that no copies are made. Can I ask what you're hoping to find?"

"Once and for all I'm going to nail the criminal responsible for the coffee in the Pentagon cafeteria."

"Vin . . ."

"If it turns out my hunch is right, you'll be the first to know, *sir*. Where've you set me up?"

"Your office."

"Thanks." I turned to go.

"And again, good job in Thailand," he said.

I wasn't so sure. I'd helped stop that genie leaving its bottle, which was something. But it was a genie my tax dollars helped fund into existence in the first place. The realization reminded me of the World-According-To-Staff-Sergeant-Butler speech. Maybe, if I found what I hoped I'd find on those disks, I could prove Butler wrong.

"Before you go, those ass-lickers from the GAO have been asking about you again and I don't think it's to see your vacation snaps. And here's that code you wanted. Took some doing." He glanced conspiratorially left and right, then whispered, "You didn't get this from me, OK?" He handed me a folded sheet of paper laser-printed with a long line of numbers and letters on it. "Careful, Vin," he warned. "That there's dynamite. Make sure it doesn't blow up in your face, or mine."

I nodded. "Thanks, buddy."

"The bank statements are on your desk. Also, like you asked, we sent someone over to the Sofitel to see if anyone recognized Sean Boyle. Your hunch was right. Only seems they knew Boyle by a different name. Makes for interesting reading. The report's on your desk, too."

"A different name?"

He nodded.

I left his office and walked into mine down the hall. Fluorescent tubes hummed in the false ceiling. A few things had changed since I was last here. There was a fine layer of dust on the folders in my in-box. And on a small stand with wheels on its base there was a compact color monitor that looked like it had sat in a pawnshop for years. The shelf beneath it held an equally decrepit CD player.

The report Arlen mentioned lay waiting on the desk. I sat and read the three pages written by the special agent who'd paid the Sofitel a visit, then spent half an hour reviewing those bank statements. Everything was pointing me in the one direction and I shook my head at the audacity. I needed one more piece to be certain of the woman's involvement. That, I hoped to find on the Pentagon's security recordings.

The disks still hadn't arrived so I turned on my computer. There were forty-seven unread e-mails. I isolated the ones from the General Accounting Office—nine in all. I pulled up the expense form and filled it out, loading it with every possible expense and doubling a few while I was at it. While I was doing that, a brown package the size and shape of a shoebox arrived. The delivery guy, a cop in plainclothes, dropped it on my desk. I signed the form he waved under my nose, which sent him on his way. I ignored the package for the moment and returned to the expense form. I referred to the line of code Arlen had given me and copied the string of numbers and letters into the box. Then I hesitated. How much did I dislike Chalmers?

"This much," I said softly, clicking send. The processor made a sound like a beetle scratching on a wooden floor and the e-mail scuttled on its way.

I trashed the rest of the e-mails, most of which were the usual banal office circulars pertaining to the proper requisition and use of stationery, which photocopier was down, et cetera. And then I gave Clare Selwyn a call. She answered on the fifth ring.

"Colonel Selwyn."

"Clare. It's Vin."

"Hey, stranger. Where you been?"

"Here and there. You?"

"Same." There was a pause. "Vin, I heard through the grapevine a certain SAS sergeant went home in a box, and that you put him in it."

I didn't say anything.

"And I heard you got yourself pretty banged up, too. You OK?"

"I broke a couple of fingers but they've been glued back on." I changed the subject. "Hey, listen, thanks for following through on all those things for me. Made a big difference."

"That's OK—hope you didn't get it all too late."

"No—worked out fine," I said.

"Oh, did I tell you we found more of Ruben's drugs . . . no, I didn't. Agent Lyne found them."

"Oh, yeah? Where were they?"

"He took Ruben's Harley for a ride. Got a flat. Found them stuffed in a tube clamped to the frame."

"Was he looking for the spare tire?" I asked.

"Probably," Clare said with a laugh.

"Will you give him a pat on the back from me?"

"Will do."

"I got the news about Demelian being arrested," I said. "He confessed? Should be able to get him on conspiracy to murder, and fraud, too."

"Vin, there's a problem."

"What sort of problem?"

"Pensacola PD found Amy McDonough hanging from her kitchen ceiling two days ago."

"Jesus," I said.

"There was no foul play. She left a note."

"What'd it say?"

"One word—Sorry."

"Shit."

"With McDonough and Butler dead, there's no damning physical evidence that ties Demelian to Ruben's murder," she said. "He'll walk on this one."

"So he gets off free as a bird."

"Weeeell, maybe not quite. Pensacola PD checked him out thoroughly. Seems the guy's not really an attorney. Did two years of law school, then dropped out. Never passed the bar. Been taking people's money for years under false pretenses, and hasn't filled in a tax return for years, either. You know how cranky the IRS can get when you don't do that. The DA says even with a plea bargain, Demelian'll do time, and plenty of it."

It wasn't quite conspiracy to murder, but it was better than nothing. "Clare, if you were here, I'd buy you a...a...chocolate sundae."

"Vin, please—I don't do phone sex."

We both laughed. It hurt my face.

After we hung up I sat back for a minute and thought about Amy McDonough. I felt bad for her, but I felt worse for Ruben.

I took my mind off that whole painful mess by turning on the CD player and monitor. There was a plastic take-out knife in a drawer and I used that to slit the packing tape sealing the box. Inside was a letter and floor plan showing the footprint of each security camera in the areas I was interested in.

I read the letter and examined the floor plan. There were thirty-three security cameras covering the Pentagon's main cafeteria area, including the entrances and exits servicing it. Somewhere here in this box, there'd be evidence of a particular meeting between two parties.

I knew the day in question and could guess at the hour, but that would still mean thirty-three hours of recording to sift through to find it—if it even existed. If I was smart about it, less. I pulled a disk from the box. On its sleeve was written the camera's number, which told me where it was positioned and the area it captured on the accompanying floor plan, along with the date and time of coverage. I fed the disk to the player.

I was smart about it, but maybe not smart enough, which could be why it still took five and a half hours of watching the tops of people's heads to get through it all. At the end, I knew two things for certain. The first was that there were a lot of bald men working at

the Pentagon. The second put me on a plane to La-
Guardia to see that mutual friend Butler and I
shared—the one he'd said wanted me dead.

*   *   *

As everyone knows, John Lennon lived at the Dakota
Apartments building on Seventy-second Street in
Manhattan, before he got himself shot outside the
front entrance. If the place was expensive before the
killing, prices at the apartment block afterward were
murderous. Those New Yorkers, they love a gimmick.

I flipped my badge at the doorman, a big guy with
puffy cheeks and a soft, round belly that filled out his
uniform like a full vacuum cleaner dustbag. He
checked me over—MA-1 flying jacket, jeans, boots,
the remnants of a badly battered face, and a plaster
cast on my hand. Reluctance to let me in was written
all over him, but he had no choice. The badge of mine
told him so, as did the uniformed guys with their
hands on their hips leaning against the two federal
marshal Crown Vics parked in the street behind me.

"Who you wanna see?" he asked, not sure he
heard it right the first time. He cocked his left ear at
me. I saw the hearing aid.

I said it louder the second time.

"Does she know you're coming up?"

"Damn well hope not," I said. "You follow me?"

He gave me another uncertain look, then waddled
up the front steps. Hip problems. An old guy like this
should be propping up a bar somewhere, telling lies

about his youth, not opening doors for rich people. "How long you been doing this job?" I asked.

"Since a year after the battle of Chosin—that was a *real* war, son, not like this bull crap we're fighting today. I've been working this door since after I got out of repatriation. That's more'n fifty years." His nose was red with cold, his top lip slick with clear, running mucus. He inserted a key into a security board and gave it a twist.

"Thanks for your cooperation," I said. I couldn't afford the sympathy, but I dug the note out of my jacket pocket anyway and palmed it to him.

"Gee, ten dollars. Now I can retire," he said, examining it closely before stuffing it in his pants. With the clientele in this building, the guy probably earned three times my salary in goddamn tips.

As I waited for the elevator to arrive, I checked out the foyer. Like the building's exterior, it reminded me of food with too much garnish. There were cameras in the corners of the ceiling. Like so much about the building, I figured the old guy was just for show. After the John Lennon thing, the Dakota Apartments' residents would have taken their security a little more seriously. No doubt somewhere close was a bunker with a couple of young, bored guys, pieces strapped to their hips and a direct line to NYPD, watching folks come and go.

"You got the apartment number?" the doorman asked.

I had it written on a separate page in my notebook, which I showed him.

"Fourth floor," he said as he turned and waddled back into the brittle, cold air outside.

The ornate elevator door opened and I stepped inside. The air smelled of warmed rosewood. I pressed the button and rode it to the fourth floor. The doors slid back. An old couple stood in the doorway. The woman looked familiar, though I couldn't place her. A fifties movie star, perhaps. Whatever, they both looked at me disapprovingly then stood aside, allowing plenty of room to let me pass in case I had something they could catch—like poverty, maybe.

I stepped into the hallway. More cameras in the ceiling, and, like before, not too discreet. The carpet was thick enough to roll in. I walked up to the door number duplicating the one in my notebook, and pressed the button. There was no spy hole, no need—not with those guys in the bunker somewhere killing themselves slowly on coffee and doughnuts, eyeballing monitor screens.

The door opened.

"Mind if I come in?" I asked. I didn't wait for the answer, stepping inside. The woman's mouth dropped open wide enough to make a dental surgeon's day. The doorman hadn't phoned ahead, which made mine.

"Special Agent Cooper," she said unnecessarily. I knew who I was. And I had a pretty good idea who the woman holding open the door was too, though she was a somewhat different woman from the one I thought I knew. "You look awful," she added after a second look, once I'd walked past.

"I fell," I said, eyeballing the room. "Nice place." It

was, if you went in for expensive junk sales. Crystal chandeliers, silver candelabra, couches with carved claw feet, ottomans, Persian rugs, clocks, quilts, and old paintings of English fox hunts slugged it out for attention. Heavy burgundy brocade drapes hung above two vast ceiling-to-floor windows framing multi-million-dollar views of Central Park.

"I was just about to fix myself a drink," said Dr. Freddie Spears. "You care to join me? How's the mission going?"

I saw my favorite brand keeping company with a number of other bottles on a liquor cabinet beneath a painting that looked like the English countryside except that it wasn't—a group of Native Americans were handing over a few beads to a couple of European types. "Sure," I said. "Glen Keith with rocks. And I guess you could say the mission is still in the planning phase." I was relieved—not about getting a drink, but about the mission's integrity. Spears knew as much as the newspapers about what had happened in Thailand: nothing.

The doctor moved to the cabinet. She was dressed in beige slacks and a fitted white silk shirt. Her feet were bare, toenails carefully manicured and painted pink. She was looking relaxed, all things considered.

The rocks tinkled into the glasses. The sound was music to my ears—like Beethoven, only easier to play.

"So, what can I do for you today, Special Agent?" she asked, handing me the tumbler.

"You can tell me about the moment you decided to

make a killing on something other than the stock market."

"What?"

"You know, Doc, you're a smart businesswoman. No doubt about that. But, like a lot of smart business-people who go off the rails, you believe that the rules the rest of us follow don't apply to you."

"I'm sorry?"

"Gotta hand it to you, you were convincing. When I first met you at Moreton Genetics, you had me be-lieving you were concerned about your great friend Tanaka, the same Tanaka who got nauseous in your company unless you had gills."

Spears's mouth was open again like a fish suck-ing air.

"And you *were* concerned about him, but not in the sense I thought you meant at the time. What you were concerned about was that he might actually make it back from that expedition—other than in a box with the lid screwed down."

She swallowed. "I beg your pardon?"

"At first I thought perhaps you were just shaken up when you found out *how* Tanaka died. The whole shark thing—you weren't expecting it. Perhaps you were hoping for a simple drowning."

"I don't know what you're talking about." Spears put her drink on a side table and flopped on the couch beside it. She tucked her feet up beneath her, all re-laxed like I was a friend about to spill some interesting society gossip, or maybe to give her my thoughts on interior decorating. She was getting good at this, more confident—practice makes perfect.

"Does the name Al Cooke ring any bells?"

"Cooke . . . Cooke . . ." She stroked her chin and glanced at the ceiling. The gesture looked self-conscious. I wondered if she'd practiced it in the mirror.

"He was a crew member of the *Natusima*."

"Why would I know the—"

"He was the ship's cook. You knew him well enough to have thirty-six thousand dollars transferred into his bank account."

"I don't think so."

"I know so, Doc. Because of 9/11, banks these days are pretty cooperative when it comes to the transfer of large sums of money." I silently thanked Arlen for his persistence on my behalf. "It's the sort of activity indulged in by drug dealers and terrorists. You live well, Doc. Large five- and six-figure sums like that appear and disappear in your accounts sometimes on a weekly basis. Your record of spending and saving is consistently extravagant, so you don't look like a drug dealer or a terrorist to the system, and the computers that monitor these things skip over you. Only this particular thirty-six thousand dollars went to an account registered in the Caymans to one Sean Boyle. From there it was transferred to Al Cooke's account, an account that has rarely, if ever, been out of the red. It arrived in two chunks—eighteen thousand dollars one month, eighteen thousand dollars the next. To me, that makes it look like a half-now-and-half-after-the-job-is-done kinda transfer, especially when the arrival of those deposits bookended the day Dr. Tanaka got turned into fish food."

Doc Spears was frowning like she wasn't following my logic. More acting. "Are you saying Professor Boyle used money I loaned him to have Dr. Tanaka *murdered*?"

"Nice try, Doc," I said. "I don't believe you loaned Sean Boyle anything. I believe you conspired with him in the murder of Hideo Tanaka."

Spears picked up her drink and took a delicate sip. The glass wasn't shaking. "This is ridiculous," she said.

My turn to shrug. "When I first met you, you told me that you got on well with Tanaka, but not with Boyle. I've been doing a little fishing of my own, Doc. You'd been at MG sixteen months. Tanaka was twenty thousand feet under the water for much of that time, collecting specimens. You barely knew the guy. And while you did your best to keep it quiet, you got on real well with Sean Boyle—lovers first and then business partners. And you both wanted Tanaka a little closer to the surface, like only six feet under."

The doctor sucked in her top lip, and tapped her chin with her index finger like she was considering her next move.

"We've had a team going over your expenses," I said. This wasn't accurate. What I should have said was, we *will* have a team of experts going over your finances, shift it from the perfect tense to the certain future. But under the circumstances—the circumstances being that I wanted her rattled—I was sure even Chip Schaeffer back at the DoD would have approved of my grammatical license. "The bellhop at the Sofitel knew you by name. I could have believed the front desk or even the concierge might know the names of the hotel's paying guests, but the guy in the monkey suit who picks up the luggage? Unlikely. Unless of course you'd stayed there many times before. And that was certainly possible. On a hunch I had him shown photos of the professor. Seems I'm not the only one who never forgets a bad haircut. The bellhop figured Boyle was your husband. You always registered as Mr. and Mrs., didn't you? Except Boyle never signed the register, which meant he never had to show ID."

I waited for an answer, a reaction, but Spears's face remained a mask. She said, "Is that all you've got, Special Agent?"

A challenge like that is the cop equivalent of smelling blood in the water. I suddenly knew how the shark that ate Tanaka felt. I said, "Do you want to know what I think, or what I can prove?"

"I think you should leave," she replied, her plucked, arched eyebrows knitted in a scowl, the corners of her mouth pulled in the general direction of her manicured toenails.

"OK, if you insist, I'll go with what I know: Tanaka and Boyle's research came up with something interesting. Tanaka wanted to take it in one direction, perhaps as a sewage treatment; Boyle in another. Boyle came to you; you agreed with his point of view. You secured more funding from MG's old friend the DoD to develop the biotechnology for purely military purposes. Tanaka wasn't thrilled.

"I don't know yet where you and Boyle started banging each other's doors—the Sofitel was one of your favorite fuck pads. Maybe the close proximity to power, the White House being within spitting distance, turned you on. Somewhere along the way—perhaps right from the beginning—you both decided Tanaka had to be removed from the scene permanently. And then Boyle double-crossed you. You weren't a hundred percent sure about that until I showed up and started asking questions after the Transamerica/Four Winds explosions. At the time, I thought your distress was the normal concern one human being shows for another—the unfortunate and violent deaths of not just one but *two* of your employees, and so close together. But I read it wrong. At some point during our little chat at Moreton Genetics that day, you realized Boyle's death had been staged so that he could take his nasty little secrets to a new buyer—Pakistan—without having to split the profits with you. With scandal inevitable, and in order to protect the value of your stock, you resigned, but not before passing me a copy of the security-camera footage that showed Boyle stealing the technology—technology *you* helped him steal. That envelope the disk came in had your DNA all over it. By slipping me that disk, you were behaving just like the seemingly innocent who goes on television to beg the public for leads to a crime she herself has committed."

Spears's nostrils flared as she breathed.

"But then you got a break. The DoD called you in to consult on the mission to snatch Boyle. That's when you met Staff Sergeant Chris Butler."

"The British soldier?" Spears shook her head. "I had nothing to do with him. The only times I ever saw him were in those briefing sessions."

"Security cameras are everywhere these days, Doc. You of all people should know that." I pulled the small rented DVD player from my bag, flipped up the screen, and pressed play. The picture quality was poor, with lines and glitches. A code in the bottom right-hand corner identified the camera that had taken the footage, as well as a date and time. The subject matter was pretty dull—just a number of cafeteria-style tables occupied mostly by men of various ages, some in uniform, but most in business suits. Plenty of bald heads. In the top left of the frame, Spears was clearly identifiable, sitting alone at a table for four, with a paper cup full of what I assumed was coffee, or at least what passed for it at the main Pentagon cafeteria. No sound accompanied the pictures. Suddenly, Spears got up and left, leaving her coffee behind. The picture jumped to footage from another camera. It showed Staff Sergeant Butler standing in a hallway. The date was identical to the first view, the time pushed barely seconds forward. Spears joined him. They shook hands. A third view—same day but two minutes later—captured them getting in a cab together. The Pentagon Police would trophy my nuts if they knew I'd copied their disks and edited this little show together.

Freddie Spears took some ice in her mouth and crunched it. "I'm calling my attorney," she said.

"Relax, Doc, I can't arrest you. I'm OSI and you're not in the military. And even though you told Butler to kill me, I'm not the kind that bears a grudge."

Spears leaned forward, elbows on her knees, fingers laced. She'd dropped the act. If I wasn't going to arrest her, that left only one other alternative, didn't it? "So, what do you want?" she asked, very casually.

I leaned back and crossed one leg on top of the other. Bingo. "Fifty percent of what you left Moreton Genetics with," I replied. "According to my research, that makes my share worth around twenty mil."

Spears's eyes narrowed. "That makes Chris Butler and me minority shareholders. What do we get for that?" Her fingers were still laced, only now she was wringing them.

"With any luck, around twenty years."

"What?" she said, bewildered by the sudden change in direction.

Much of what I was saying was guesswork and gut instinct. No way could Boyle have pulled off the theft from Moreton Genetics without someone on the inside helping out. And then there was Butler. He was already a rotten apple, but someone had to have planted the seed in his head to turn the Phunal mission into an investment opportunity.

Spears was clever, and no doubt the team of lawyers she'd hire would be, too. All the evidence, even the bank transfers to Boyle and to Cooke, could conceivably be presented as something innocent. With Boyle and Butler both dead, there wouldn't be much of a case. The only way to nail her was to get an admission made freely to someone who wasn't an officer of the court—specifically, a *civilian* court. An admission made to someone like me.

The doorbell rang right on cue, making a sound like Big Ben.

I went to the door and opened it. I was surprised to see Chalmers standing there, leering with that stupid grin on his face, his crutches updated with a cane. Behind him were several FBI types; behind them my backup marshals; and behind them, the doorman with my ten bucks. "Special Agent Cooper," said Chalmers, stepping inside. "Bumbling along as usual?"

"What are you doing here, Chalmers?"

"Come to help collect the latest addition to the FBI's witness protection program—mostly to make sure there are no problems with you. And maybe, well, maybe to gloat just a little . . ."

A half-dozen humorless types filed in behind Chalmers, filling the expensive room like a flood in a blue suit. Along with the old doorman, the marshals kept to the outside hallway, but peered in to satisfy their inquisitiveness.

I checked this invasion with Spears, glancing over my shoulder as a black guy the size of a locomotive put his hand under her arm and hoisted her to her feet. From the look of uncertainty on her face, this was all news to her.

"You planted that wallet at the Four Winds," I said

to Chalmers. "And then you used my presence on the scene to legitimize its discovery."

He took a step toward Spears.

"We both know it couldn't have been the bombers, those Pakistani glassblowers; it had to have been someone who'd come along later," I said. "I might actually have fallen for it if you'd had the thing properly deep-fried."

Chalmers was still looking smug. If he'd had a nail file, he'd have pulled it out and used it. "The evidence could have been better prepared, I suppose," he agreed.

"So you going to tell me why?" I asked.

"Why what?"

"Playing dumb comes naturally to you, Chalmers."

I wanted to hit him, knock the supercilious smirk right off his face, but I resisted the temptation. "So now you've got Doc Spears over a barrel," I told him. "She'll have to cooperate with you or go to prison for a very long time." I wondered what Spears had that Langley wanted so badly. Then it hit me like a slap. "All the missing research on this bug. You people think Spears knows where it is."

Chalmers shrugged eloquently.

"Who wants it upstairs, Chalmers? Norman? Your boss is determined to do a little empire building, is he?"

The smugness fell away. "I'm through playing twenty questions with you, Cooper."

I'd hit a nerve. With Tanaka and Boyle dead, Doc Spears was the last link to technology the CIA wanted for reasons I didn't want to think about—a bargaining chip, or leverage, maybe. Or perhaps the intention was to sell it, like Boyle had tried to do. Hell, even as a sewage treatment it was potentially worth billions, wasn't it? The Company could support a whole portfolio of clandestine ops with that kind of money. And with Boyle dead and all evidence under their control, the CIA had Spears exactly where they wanted her. Basically, if she had nuts, they'd be in a vise.

"Did you have anything to do with putting Butler and me together on that mission to Phunal?"

He shook his head. "Can't take credit for that, I'm afraid, though I wish I could. Just a bit of good luck."

Chalmers turned to the FBI types. He said, "Let's wrap it up here."

Spears was on her feet and still bewildered, only now she was moving toward the front door as the filling in an FBI sandwich. There were no handcuffs.

"Before you go, Chalmers...that leg of yours. How'd you break it?"

"Leaving now, Cooper," he said without looking over his shoulder.

"Al Cooke was a big man—past his prime but still powerful. Did he put up more of a struggle than you expected? Is that when you slipped on the *Natusima*'s deck, on all those cigarette butts he'd been tossing?"

"Fuck you, Cooper," said Chalmers, calling on his stock answer to questions he didn't like. He leaned on his cane as he limped toward the door.

I was left alone in the room and even though everyone had gone, it still felt crowded. A movement caught my eye. It was the old doorman, still hovering outside in the hallway. I hoped he wasn't expecting another tip. I called out, "I'll lock up when I leave."

He nodded, tipped a finger to his cap, and disappeared.

My fingers closed around the small metal box in my jacket pocket, the digital recorder, the one Anna had given me. I took it out and held it up where I could see it, to make sure its beautiful red LED recording light was flashing. I clicked the off switch, picked up my glass of Glen Keith, and took a sip. The ice had melted. Watered-down Scotch reminded me of a bar I used to frequent back in my drinking days. I put the glass down and walked out, closing the door behind me.

FIFTY-SIX

The newspaper sat on my desk. I supposed Arlen had put it there. The headlines on the front page said something about the President drumming up support in the UN for trade sanctions against Pakistan. Translation: He'd stopped sucking his thumb. Pakistan was making noises about backing away from resuming its nuclear tests. The press still hadn't quite worked out what it was all about, the Pakistani connection to the Transamerica/Four Winds nightmare having so far evaded them, but they were getting closer with every edition.

More important, I noted the Redskins had managed to win five out of six and, in a miracle of no small proportion, scraped through into the playoffs. I gave a hoot and an air punch in support. I flicked through the rest of the paper, killing time, which, as far as I knew, still hadn't been made a crime.

A piece about the CIA getting into hot water with the GAO caught my attention. The story went that one of the CIA's operatives, unnamed for national security reasons, was double- and triple-dipping on his expenses. The GAO had launched a thorough investigation into the expenses of CIA personnel. The investigation so far had revealed the worst offender to be one Willard F. Norman, who'd been fiddling his accounts for years. The article said the guy was finished, washed up. I blinked. With Norman removed, would sharing the conversations recorded in Freddie Spears's apartment where Chalmers admitted to the CIA's involvement in—at the very least—evidence tampering, serve any useful purpose? The answer was yes. Without Chalmers's admissions, Spears would walk and Tanaka's spirit would keep visiting my dreams.

I gave some more thought to that wallet. I didn't think CIA had anything to do with the bombings of the Transamerica building and the Four Winds apartments. I did, however, believe that they'd put two and two together and come up with the right answer before anyone else had. They knew pretty much from the start that Boyle had been spirited away and that the bombings orchestrated by Pakistan had been used to cover his disappearance. This wasn't a stretch—CIA had more and better intelligence than anyone else, didn't they? CIA just wanted the rest of us to reach the conclusion the Pakistanis wanted us to arrive at because it suited CIA's—or maybe it was just Willard F. Norman's—plans, whatever they were. Why had analysis of Boyle's so-called wallet by independent forensics been denied? Because analysis would instantly have exposed the wallet as a fake, of course.

Unfortunately for CIA, Captain Eugene Metzler and Detective Sergeant Ed Rudenko had gone and made things difficult. Against orders they'd shown me the wallet and the body it was found under. They weren't supposed to have done that. CIA had ordered the SFPD to notify the CIA, and the CIA only, when the wallet CIA itself had planted turned up. The most I was supposed to have obtained was a report with all the blanks filled in. Instead, I'd seen a corpse and the wallet. I'd also seen the way Chalmers arrived to spirit the important evidence away, and instead of answers all I'd been left with were questions. But now every one of those questions was answered.

I turned the page and read a letter to the editor from a guy who'd admitted to spending a small fortune on a shrink to help him get over the reasons for his broken marriage. His ex-wife thought he was oversexed because he wanted it three times a week. Twenty thousand dollars' worth of therapy later, he still wanted it three times a week. The letter reminded me of the joke about the guy who goes to a shrink: "What do you think of when you see this?" the psychologist says, holding up an inkblot.

"Sex," says the guy. "Two people going for it doggy-style."

"How about this one?" says the shrink, showing him another inkblot.

"Oral sex," says the guy.

After seeing thirty inkblots and getting answers that range from "Three people having sex," to "A door-to-door insurance salesman getting blown by a customer in the kitchen," the shrink says, "Do you see sex in everything?"

The guy answers, kind of indignant, "Don't blame

me, Doc. You're the one who keeps showing me these goddamn lewd pictures."

An oldie, but a goodie.

I thought about Haiko Rossi. I wondered how she was getting along. I'd heard she'd been discharged from the hospital the previous week. I'd have visited, only I didn't know which hospital—the Company wasn't keen on giving out that information. I folded the newspaper and dropped it in the trash.

My door suddenly flew open. It was Bradley Chalmers, the aforementioned unnamed double-dipping CIA agent, leaning on his cane, his face the color of a coronary. He yelled, "I don't know how you did it, Cooper, but I came here to tell you that somehow, somewhere, I'm going to fucking get you. I'm going to make it my personal business; you hear me?"

He hobbled out and slammed the door behind him, leaving before I could get in a reply. Just as well. I'd probably only have made it worse. Or better, depending on whose view you took. You can't be buddies with everyone and I was sure on that point we both agreed.

The door opened again. I expected to see Chalmers back for an encore, but it was Arlen. "Who was that guy?" he wanted to know.

"An admirer," I said.

"Isn't everyone?" he replied. "Um, you got a minute, Cooper? The boss wants to see you."

"Do you know what about?"

"Yep," he said, looking sheepish.

"You want to let me in on it?"

"Nope."

Brigadier General James Wynngate was in a good mood, if the smile on his face was any indication. Last time I saw Wynngate, he'd had a bad cold, but now he was chuckling, sharing a joke with someone hidden by the wall. He glanced up and saw me. "Cooper, come in," he said, beckoning with a wave of his hand. The smile remained on his face when I walked in. That was unusual. In my experience with senior officers, more often than not the happiness seemed to evaporate when I turned up.

"Major," said Wynngate as I approached his desk. "You look awful. How you making out?"

"Fine, sir," I said.

"Good," he replied, moving right along. "The Office of the Inspector General believes we need to give our ranks a little extra manpower. So . . . I believe you know the major." He gestured at the someone I could sense behind my shoulder. "Major Masters has been telling me she's been angling for a transfer to Andrews for six months."

"Hello, Vin," said Anna, getting up off the sofa.

I knew the general was saying something, but I wasn't hearing it, the rush of emotions and questions causing serious pileups in half a dozen sections of my brain. "Major," I managed to say. "Good to see you." It was. And it also wasn't. Making the decision complicated was her lawyer boyfriend, and my time with Lieutenant Colonel Selwyn and the contents of her fridge.

There was a ringing in my ears. No, it was the

phone on Wynngate's desk. He bent forward to check the number. "Oh, I have to take this, people. Can you both give me a moment?"

"So..." said Anna as we left his office. "You look pretty good, considering. Arlen gave me a rundown."

"You've been trying to get a transfer for six months?"

"I put in for one twice and got nowhere. I gave up, pretty much thinking it was a lost cause. And then, a couple of days ago, it came through. Took me by surprise."

"What about Germany?"

"I'm a cop, Vin—just like you. There are just as many deadbeats here."

"What about your JAG lawyer? Is he making the jump too? Or are you going to have a Steinway relationship with him like the one we had?"

"Steinbeck," said Anna with a reluctant smile. "Um...we're engaged."

That took a moment to sink in. Even then, I needed to hear it a second time, just to make sure. "You're what?"

Wynngate came out of his office. "Am I interrupting something?"

"No, sir," said Anna.

"You're engaged?" I repeated.

I didn't get an answer. The general was gesturing at us to come back into his office. He ushered us onto the sofa, closed the door, and sat on the edge of his desk. "Major," he said, addressing Anna. "I was looking at your record. You worked a case with Cooper."

"Yes, sir," said Anna.

"Something's come up and I need a team on it." He leaned way back, counterbalancing with his feet stretched out in front of him, opened a drawer, and pulled out a sheaf of color photos. He separated the pile and handed a couple each to Anna and me. It took me a moment to make out the subject matter of one of the photos on account of the blood, which was everywhere, and because I had trouble concentrating. *She was engaged?*

I glanced at Anna and saw the color drain out of her face as she stared at the prints. Her skin took on the color of boiled chicken. "I-is that what I think it is?" She breathed hard, steeling herself, holding one of the photos up close and then away from her face to get a better, or different, perspective.

"Depends what you think *it* is," said Wynngate. "Cooper?"

I was still brooding about Anna's intended nuptials. *How long had she known this guy?* I glanced at Wynngate. He was wearing a frown, expecting an answer. I scanned the second photo beneath the first. This one clearly showed a man who had been jointed. Was I seeing this right? Jesus, even the digits of his fingers and toes had been separated. The pieces had then been carefully laid out on the carpet like he was spare parts. I was reminded of one of those plastic kits kids glue together. I kept it simple. "Looks like murder, sir."

"Yeah," said the general. "Meet our Air Attaché to Turkey. I want you both on a plane to Istanbul by oh-eight-hundred tomorrow."

About the Author

It was a slow day at the office sometime late in August 1999, and Australia was on the eve of its invasion of East Timor. That's how this writing game started for me. I wrote the synopsis for my first book in the afternoon and started tapping away at the manuscript that night. I had a completed manuscript six months later. This author game sort of snowballed from there. Perhaps after twenty years as an advertising copywriter, I had a few pent-up words.

I live in Sydney with my wife, three kids, and a spoodle. And most of the time, I'm working on the next book, *Hard Rain*.

—David Rollins

HARD
RAIN

A Thriller

DAVID ROLLINS

If you enjoyed David Rollins's
A KNIFE EDGE, you won't want
to miss any of his internationally
bestselling thrillers featuring Special
Agent Vin Cooper. Look for them
at your favorite bookseller.

And don't miss
the next Vin Cooper thriller,

HARD
RAIN

coming in hardcover from Bantam
in Spring 2010.